*Everyman, I will go with thee,*
*and be thy guide*

Charles Dickens

# MASTER HUMPHREY'S CLOCK
## AND OTHER STORIES

*Edited by*
PETER MUDFORD
*University of London*

*Series Editor*
MICHAEL SLATER
*University of London*

*with illustrations by*
GEORGE CRUIKSHANK
GEORGE CATTERMOLE
*and* H. K. BROWNE ('PHIZ')

EVERYMAN
J. M. DENT · LONDON
CHARLES E. TUTTLE
VERMONT

Introduction and other critical apparatus
© J. M. Dent 1997

'The Lamplighter's Story' and
'To be Read at Dusk' first published in Everyman
in 1921

This text first published in Everyman in 1997

Reprinted 1999

J. M. Dent
Orion Publishing Group
Orion House, 5 Upper St Martin's Lane, London WC2H 9EA
and
Charles E. Tuttle Co. Inc.
28 South Main Street, Rutland,
Vermont 05701, USA

Typeset in Sabon by Set Systems Ltd, Saffron Walden, Essex
Printed in Great Britain by
The Guernsey Press Co. Ltd., Guernsey, C.I.

British Library Cataloguing-in-Publication Data
is available upon request.

ISBN 0 460 87654 6

# CONTENTS

# NOTE ON THE AUTHOR, EDITOR
## AND SERIES EDITOR

CHARLES DICKENS was born at Portsea, Portsmouth, on 7 February 1812. In 1817 the Dickens family settled in Chatham. These years, 1817–22, were the happiest of Dickens's early life. They came to an end when his father, John Dickens, was recalled to London and the family began its slow slide towards bankruptcy. In February 1824, John Dickens was imprisoned for debt in the Marshalsea and the twelve-year-old Charles was sent to work in a run-down warehouse off the Strand, labelling and packaging bottles of boot blacking. His sense of humiliation and thwarted ambition was acute, and the experience (which may have lasted a year) proved traumatic. His father was discharged from prison later in 1824, under the Insolvent Debtors' Act, and some months later Charles was removed from the warehouse and sent to school. In 1827 he was articled as a solicitor's clerk in Gray's Inn. He learned shorthand, became a reporter at Doctors' Commons and later a skilled reporter of Parliamentary debates. In the years from 1833 to 1836 he wrote a number of short stories and sketches which were published in various journals and collected in *Sketches by Boz* (1836), accompanied by illustrations by George Cruikshank. In April of the same year he married Catherine Hogarth, daughter of a newspaper editor. *Pickwick Papers*, begun in that year as a monthly instalment publication, soon became a great popular success. It was followed by *Oliver Twist* in 1837, *Nicholas Nickleby* in 1838–9 and (in his weekly periodical *Master Humphrey's Clock*) *The Old Curiosity Shop* and *Barnaby Rudge*, 1841. He made a triumphant tour of the United States in 1842 and in the same year published a critical account of his experience there in *American Notes*.

*A Christmas Carol* was published in 1843 and inaugurated the highly successful series of Christmas Books in the 1840s. *Martin Chuzzlewit* appeared in 1843–4 and *Dombey and Son* in 1846–8. *David Copperfield* was completed in 1850, the year in which he founded his own weekly magazine *Household Words*, a characteristically vivacious and imaginative family miscellany, which carried the serialised *Hard Times* in 1854. In that novel, as in its predecessor *Bleak House* (1852–3) and its successor *Little Dorrit* (1855–7), Dickens anatomised and satirised the social and political condition of England. In 1858 he and his wife formally separated and he moved to his new home at Gad's Hill in Kent. In the same year he began his career as a professional public reader of his work, a strenuous enterprise that proved highly lucrative as well as seriously harmful to his health. *A Tale of Two Cities* appeared in 1859 and *Great Expectations* in 1860–1, both serialised in Dickens's successor to *Household Words*, *All the Year Round*. His last novel to be completed in the old twenty-number monthly format was *Our Mutual Friend* (1864–5). In the winter of 1867–8 he toured the United States with his readings. In 1870 he began *The Mystery of Edwin Drood*, but had completed only half of it when he suffered a stroke at Gad's Hill and died on 9 June.

PETER MUDFORD is Reader in Modern English Literature at Birkbeck College, University of London. His publications include editions of Samuel Butler's *Erewhon* (Penguin) and George Eliot's *Silas Marner*, *Brother Jacob* and *The Lifted Veil* (Everyman); *Birds of a Different Plumage: A Study of British Indian Relations*; *The Art of Celebration in Late Nineteenth- and Early Twentieth-century Literature*; *Memory and Desire: Representations of Passion in the Novella*, and *Graham Greene*.

MICHAEL SLATER is Professor of Victorian Literature at Birkbeck College, University of London, and a former Editor of *The Dickensian*. He is the author of *Dickens and Women* (1983) and has published a number of other books and articles relating to Dickens, as well as editions of *The Christmas Books* and *Nicholas Nickleby*. He is also Editor of the *Dent Uniform Edition of Dickens' Journalism*, of which three volumes have been published: *Sketches by Boz and Other Early Papers 1833–9* (1994), *'The Amusements of the People' and Other Papers: Reports, Essays and Reviews 1834–51* (1996), and *'Gone Astray' and Other Papers from Household Words 1851–59*.

# CHRONOLOGY OF DICKENS'S LIFE

# CHRONOLOGY OF HIS TIMES

| Year | Literary Context | Historical Events |
|------|------------------|-------------------|
| 1812 | Byron, *Childe Harold* I & II | 1811–20 Regency of George, Prince of Wales<br>1812–14 War with America |
| 1813 | Austen, *Pride and Prejudice*<br>Southey becomes Poet Laureate | |
| 1814 | Austen, *Mansfield Park*<br>Scott, *Waverley*<br>Wordsworth, *The Excursion* | |
| 1815 | | Battle of Waterloo |
| 1816 | Austen, *Emma* | Spa Fields Riots |
| 1817 | Keats, *Poems*<br>Austen dies | |
| 1818 | Mary Shelley, *Frankenstein* | |
| 1819 | Byron, *Don Juan* I & II<br>George Eliot born<br>Whitman born | Peterloo Massacre<br>The Six Acts |
| 1820 | Keats, *Lamia . . . and other Poems*<br>Flaubert born | Accession of George IV<br>Cato Street Conspiracy |
| 1821 | Keats dies<br>De Quincey, *Confessions . . . Opium Eater* | Greek War of Liberation<br>Napoleon dies |
| 1822 | Byron, *Vision of Judgement*<br>Shelley dies | Suicide of Castlereagh |
| 1823 | Grimm Brothers, *German Popular Stories* (illus. G. Cruikshank) | Agricultural unrest |
| 1824 | Byron dies | |
| 1825 | Hazlitt, *Spirit of the Age* | Stockton–Darlington railway opens |

| Year | Age | Life |
|------|-----|------|
| 1827 | 15 | Becomes junior clerk in solicitor's office |
| 1829 | 17 | Becomes a freelance reporter at Doctors' Commons |
| 1830 | 18 | Acquires British Museum Reader's Card |
| 1831 | 19 | Falls in love with Maria Beadnell. Appointed Parliamentary reporter |
| 1833 | 21 | First story written and published, 'A Dinner at Poplar Walk' |
| 1834 | 22 | Joins reporting staff of the *Morning Chronicle* |
| 1835 | 23 | Engaged to Catherine Hogarth |
| 1836 | 24 | *Sketches by Boz* published. Marries Catherine. *Pickwick Papers* begun. Resigns from the *Morning Chronicle* |
| 1837 | 25 | *Pickwick Papers* completed. Mary Hogarth (sister-in-law) dies. Becomes editor of *Bentley's Miscellany* |
| 1838 | 26 | *Oliver Twist* [dates given for publication of the novels refer to completion of their serialisation] |
| 1839 | 27 | *Nicholas Nickleby* |
| 1840 | 28 | Dickens begins *Master Humphrey's Clock* |
| 1841 | 29 | *The Old Curiosity Shop; Barnaby Rudge* |
| 1842 | 30 | Visits America (Jan.–June). *American Notes* |
| 1843 | 31 | *A Christmas Carol* |
| 1844 | 32 | Dickens and family stay in Genoa. *Martin Chuzzlewit; The Chimes* |

| Year | Literary Context | Historical Events |
|---|---|---|
| 1826 | Disraeli, *Vivian Gray* | |
| 1827 | Blake dies | University of London founded |
| 1828 | Meredith born<br>D. G. Rossetti born | |
| 1829 | Jerrold, *Black-ey'd Susan* | Catholic Emancipation Act |
| 1830 | Tennyson, *Poems Chiefly Lyrical* | Accession of William IV<br>July Revolution in France<br>Wellington's ministry falls |
| 1831 | | First cholera epidemic |
| 1832 | Lewis Carroll born<br>Walter Scott dies | First Reform Bill |
| 1833 | Carlyle, *Sartor Resartus*<br>Newman, *Tracts for the Times* | Abolition of slavery throughout British Empire<br>State funding of schools begins |
| 1834 | Bulwer-Lytton, *Last Days of Pompeii*<br>Coleridge and Lamb die | Tolpuddle Martyrs<br>New Poor Law |
| 1837 | Carlyle, *The French Revolution*<br>Lockhart, *Life of Scott* | Accession of Victoria |
| 1838 | | Anti-Corn Law League<br>Chartist petitions published<br>London–Birmingham railway opens |
| 1839 | Carlyle, *Chartism* | First Factory Inspectors' Report |
| 1840 | Hardy born | Penny postage introduced |
| 1841 | Carlyle, *Heroes and Hero-Worship* | Peel becomes Prime Minister |
| 1842 | Tennyson, *Poems*<br>Browning, *Dramatic Lyrics*<br>Macaulay, *Lays of Ancient Rome* | Chartist riots<br>Report on Sanitary Conditions of Labouring Population |
| 1843 | Carlyle, *Past and Present*<br>Ruskin, *Modern Painters* I<br>Wordsworth made Poet Laureate | |
| 1844 | Disraeli, *Coningsby*<br>Elizabeth Barrett, *Poems* | Rochdale Pioneers found Co-operative Store |

| Year | Literary Context | Historical Events |
|---|---|---|
| 1845 | Disraeli, *Sybil* | Railway speculation<br>Newman joins Catholic Church |
| 1846 | | Repeal of Corn Laws |
| 1847 | Emily Brontë, *Wuthering Heights*<br>Charlotte Brontë, *Jane Eyre*<br>Tennyson, *The Princess* | |
| 1848 | Emily Brontë dies<br>Thackeray, *Vanity Fair* | European Revolutions<br>Chartist movement collapses after mass meeting in London<br>Cholera epidemic<br>Pre-Raphaelite Brotherhood founded |
| 1849 | Thackeray, *Pendennis*<br>Ruskin, *Seven Lamps of Architecture* | |
| 1850 | Tennyson, *In Memoriam*<br>Wordsworth dies<br>Wordsworth, *The Prelude*<br>Kingsley, *Alton Locke* | Pope appoints Catholic bishops to England |
| 1851 | Ruskin, *The Stones of Venice*<br>Melville, *Moby-Dick* | Great Exhibition<br>Gold discovered in New South Wales<br>J. M. W. Turner dies |
| 1852 | Stowe, *Uncle Tom's Cabin*<br>Thackeray, *Henry Esmond* | Napoleon III becomes Emperor of France<br>Duke of Wellington dies |
| 1853 | Charlotte Brontë, *Villette* | Indian Civil Service open to competition |
| 1854 | Thoreau, *Walden* | Crimean War begins<br>Newspaper Stamp Duty abolished<br>Palmerston's premiership begins |
| 1855 | Browning, *Men and Women*<br>Gaskell, *North and South*<br>Kingsley, *Westward Ho!*<br>Charlotte Brontë dies | |
| 1856 | Elizabeth Barrett Browning, *Aurora Leigh*<br>Wilde and Shaw born | End of Crimean War |

| Year | Age | Life |
|------|-----|------|
| 1857 | 45 | *Little Dorrit*. Meets Ellen Ternan during performances of Wilkie Collins's play *The Frozen Deep* |
| 1858 | 46 | Separates from his wife. Begins professional public readings |
| 1859 | 47 | *A Tale of Two Cities*. *Household Words* incorporated into new weekly magazine, *All the Year Round* |
| 1861 | 49 | *Great Expectations* |
| 1865 | 53 | *Our Mutual Friend*. Staplehurst railway accident |
| 1867 | 55 | Public readings tour of America (Nov.–May 1868) |
| 1868 | 56 | Begins Farewell Reading Tour |
| 1870 | 58 | Final Farewell Reading in London (March). Begins *The Mystery of Edwin Drood*. Dies 9 June |

| Year | Literary Context | Historical Events |
|------|------------------|-------------------|
| 1857 | Trollope, *Barchester Towers*<br>Flaubert, *Madame Bovary* | Indian Mutiny |
| 1858 | Eliot, *Scenes of Clerical Life* | Indian Viceroyalty established |
| 1859 | Tennyson, *Idylls of the King*<br>Darwin, *Origin of Species*<br>Mill, *On Liberty*<br>Smiles, *Self-Help* | Rise of Fenianism in Ireland |
| 1860 | Collins, *The Woman in White*<br>Eliot, *The Mill on the Floss* | |
| 1861 | Reade, *The Cloister and the Hearth* | Death of Prince Consort<br>American Civil War begins |
| 1862 | Mill, *Utilitarianism* | |
| 1863 | Kingsley, *Water Babies*<br>Eliot, *Romola*<br>Thackeray dies | Gettysburg Address<br>Slavery abolished in USA |
| 1864 | Newman, *Apologia Pro Vita Sua* | |
| 1865 | Carroll, *Alice's Adventures in Wonderland*<br>Arnold, *Essays in Criticism* | President Lincoln assassinated<br>Palmerston dies<br>American Civil War ends |
| 1866 | Swinburne, *Poems and Ballads*<br>Dostoyevsky, *Crime and Punishment* | First Barnardo Home<br>Atlantic Cable laid |
| 1867 | Marx, *Das Kapital* | Disraeli's Reform Bill |
| 1868 | Browning, *The Ring and the Book*<br>Collins, *The Moonstone* | Gladstone becomes Prime Minister |
| 1869 | Arnold, *Culture and Anarchy*<br>Blackmore, *Lorna Doone* | Suez Canal opens<br>Mill advocates emancipation of women |
| 1870 | D. G. Rossetti, *Poems* | Education Act: free public education in Board Schools<br>Franco-Prussian War<br>Fall of Napoleon III |

# SERIES EDITOR'S PREFACE

The Everyman Dickens is intended to be the most complete edition of Dickens's works so far published. It is the first paperback edition to provide thorough and coherent coverage of all his shorter fiction as well as so much of his extensive non-fictional writings. In addition to the fifteen novels and the five *Christmas Books*, the Everyman Dickens includes all the Christmas stories from *Household Words* and *All the Year Round*, all other short fiction, the two travel books and all Dickens's writings for children. Four volumes of his journalistic writing, from *Sketches by Boz* to *The Uncommercial Traveller*, are published as *The Dent Uniform Edition of Dickens's Journalism*, which is linked with the Everyman Dickens. Each volume contains all the earliest illustrations to the work or works featured in it, kindly supplied by The Dickens House, and all Dickens's Prefaces.

Every volume is edited by a specialist in Victorian literature who has a particular interest in the work he or she is dealing with. Where appropriate, explanatory notes are supplemented by a historical appendix giving more general background information on the text in question.

Throughout the series references to Dickens's published letters are given as either 'Pilgrim' or 'Nonesuch'. 'Pilgrim' means *The Pilgrim Edition of the Letters of Charles Dickens*, eds M. House, G. Storey, K. Tillotson *et al* (1965—in progress), and 'Nonesuch' means *The Letters of Charles Dickens*, ed. W. Dexter, 3 vols (1938), part of the Nonesuch Press Edition of Dickens's Works.

MICHAEL SLATER

# INTRODUCTION

Of all the sparks which constantly flew from the anvil of Dickens's creative imagination – which he called his fancy – some expanded into constellations, others became single stars. This volume is concerned with the second. But the two processes are not separable and occurred from pressures, whether towards expansion or extinction, to which Dickens responded, but could not control. He wanted to write short stories, but these turned into novels of comprehensive vision; he thought of writing chronicles, and these became a buoyant episode in the life of a character not heard of again.

'Public Life of Mr Tulrumble' appeared in January 1837 in the first number of *Bentley's Miscellany*, the new monthly edited by Dickens. The following number contained the first two chapters of what was clearly intended to be a serialised story, also set in the riverside town of Mudfog. Its title was *Oliver Twist*. 'The Chronicles of Mudfog', proposed at the end of 'Mr Tulrumble', were not written, but the 'capital notion' of the little boy in the workhouse who asked for more grew into a tale of society's lack of true charity, and of a goodness which survives in spite of the forces of darkness opposed to it.[1]

Two years later, Dickens suggested to his publishers his idea for a weekly periodical. It would include sketches (of the kind which Dickens, under his pen-name of 'Boz', had made well known), letters from 'imaginary correspondents', satirical essays and articles on ancient London. There would also be stories, in the manner of *The Pickwick Papers*, told by a club of characters, meeting informally by Master Humphrey's fireside in a room where the ticking of the clock aroused memories of things past. But the friendly congeniality of these surroundings, and the miscellany of pieces which the periodical might have included, gave way before darker imaginings, inspired by Dickens's own night walks around London, and his 'Gothic' view of the city's history. The first episode of *The Old Curiosity Shop* appeared in the fourth number of 25 April 1840, the second in the seventh, and then continued without interruption until it was completed on 6 February 1841. *Barnaby Rudge* began the following week; and when that novel was finished, the clock fell silent. Something of the original plan and characters had survived, but they had been overtaken by a coach and four driving furiously to its journey's end.

A selection of Dickens's shorter fiction of the kind included here gives an insight into the way his creative imagination worked, fired by many different kinds of story-telling. It illustrates too Dickens's increasing stylistic control from the publication of 'Mr Tulrumble', when he was twenty-five, to his last completed fiction, 'George Silverman's Explanation', when he was fifty-six. Judged by the standard of his major fictions, some of these stories are slight; but even when they seem like quickly fading coals, they reveal the fieriness with which he thought and felt, and the quickening of his pulse at the knowledge of his power to entertain. When George Silverman walks down to the sea at the climax of his 'Explanation', he writes of the dawn: 'the ineffable splendour that then burst forth ... attuned my mind afresh after the discords of the night' (p. 225). Read as a metaphor, this phrase sums up the nature of the life-long relationship between Dickens's imagined worlds and the deep discordances within him which made them possible.

'Public Life of Mr Tulrumble', in its exuberant inventiveness and delight in the comedy of human character, might have been included in *The Pickwick Papers*, which Dickens was still publishing in monthly parts. Here was a young author so assured of his style that he could do with it as he pleased. The recollection of judges 'with very strong symptoms of dinner under their wigs' is slipped into the main narrative, and at once thrown out: 'However that's neither here nor there' (p. 11). And 'other matters which might be dilated upon to great advantage' (p. 13) come under the narrator's red pencil before they are born. The taut and complex control of 'George Silverman's Explanation' is still a long way off. Here, all is joyful revelation as Mr Tulrumble learns the advantages of not standing upon his dignity in order to heighten it.

Mudfog was based on Chatham, which Dickens had left at the age of twelve. He had observed the puffed-up conceits of provincial dignitaries, and used his experience to retell an old nursery tale about how pride takes a fall, even if, as here, it has a soft landing. As always with Dickens, whether in dark or festive mood, he sees things in terms of scenes. Mr Tulrumble, Mudfog's newly elected Mayor, puts on his own show to rival the Lord Mayor's in London. The appearance of the drunken Twigger in a medieval suit of armour, 'like a body in a brass coffin', appals the Mayor and delights the crowd whom the reader has joined. Undeterred by the misadventures of his show, Mr Tulrumble remains intent on imposing his authority, denying the Jolly Boatmen a licence for beer and music, and making himself hated, shunned even by friends. Morality, though always important, must not trespass upon what is naturally enjoyable. The spirit of life is celebratory, communal, good-hearted; and Mr Tulrumble, in his reforming zeal, offends against all of these and must acquire the humanity to re-enter the dance, where Ned Twigger will 'balance chairs on his chin and straws on his nose' (p. 21).

The trappings of office, put on here and finally discarded, were, in the less carnivalesque world of *Oliver Twist*, and in the character of the Beadle, never put off. Performance, as Dickens already knew, was at the heart of comic fun; and was also the stuff of which poseurs and hypocrites were made.[2]

Dickens first wrote 'The Lamplighter', as it was then called, in 1838. That year saw six dramatisations of *Oliver Twist*; and Dickens was drawn to writing his own plays. He read his farce to his friend William Macready, for many years established as one of the great actors of his time. Macready was impressed by the dialogue, and by Dickens's ability to read as well as an experienced actor, but was unconvinced by the meagreness of the plot.[3] Dickens did not pursue his career as a playwright, but was always loath to waste what he had written. Three years later, he turned his farce into a short story for publication in *The Pic-Nic Papers*.[4] As with many of his stories, he set the little play in a frame – a device he had absorbed in his rapturous childhood reading of *The Arabian Nights*. The lamplighters meet in a tavern to swap tales about their calling, which they regard with veneration: 'It is an article of their creed that the first glimmering of true civilisation shone in the first street-light maintained at the public expense'[5] (p. 149). And it is this brief portrait of a club of working men, who feel their calling to be on the edge of extinction as a result of the introduction of

gaslight (an unjustified fear as it turned out), which gives the
story its interest, for the farce itself, as Macready observed, is
slight. Dickens, more than any other writer, noted the qualities
of ordinary English people in their streets, their homes and their
jobs, and created from them the heart of his fiction.[6] Through
Tom Grig, the lamplighter, he shows here how character is
changed when expectations are altered: his farce contained a
seed of one of his greatest visions when twenty years later he
came to create Pip in *Great Expectations*.

As in 'The Lamplighter's Story', the frame for 'Master Humphrey's Clock' remains as interesting as the stories it includes.
The gentle spirits who form Master Humphrey's circle have a
complex and enigmatic origin. Master Humphrey, a 'mis-
shapen, deformed, old' man, who lives in a 'venerable suburb',
has as his companions men of equally secluded habits, one of
whom is deaf and whose name he does not even know. This
circle of ageing men, preferring the world of memory and dream
to the 'harsh realities' of the world outside, seems a curious
projection for the endlessly energetic, mobile and socially thrusting young author. But the quietism of this circle represents a
coming together of many feelings present in Dickens at this time.
Dickens had suffered almost unbearable grief on the death of
his young sister-in-law, Mary Hogarth, the previous year; and
he was exhausted by the prolonged labour of finishing *Nicholas
Nickleby*. The tone of 'Master Humphrey's Clock' is elegiac,
reflective and not a little melancholy.[7] Even the reintroduction
of Mr Pickwick and the Wellers, who become members of the
circle, only lightens the tone a little. Mr Pickwick has lost his
genius and become the narrator of an uninspired tale, though
the Wellers retain something of their original wild humour.
Unlike Thackeray and Trollope, Dickens never again brought
back from the shades the characters of his previous fictions.

In the tales drawn from the clock-case, the past of London
and England in the seventeenth century provided perhaps a
temporary alleviation for Dickens from the 'harsh realities' of
his private life and the sustained pressures of writing an extensive fiction. In the 'Giant Chronicles' (pp. 36–55) (itself a larger
project which peters out) and 'A Confession found in a prison
in the time of Charles the Second' (pp. 67–73), Dickens uses the
historical setting as a backcloth for tales about the psychopath-
ology of emotion. In the second of these, admired by Edgar

Allan Poe as 'a paper of remarkable power',[8] Dickens uses the narrative device of the confession, which was to remain important for him – for example, Miss Wade's confession in *Little Dorrit* – as a means of revealing the texture of the solitary and suffering mind.

Dickens's story is prescient too in a quite different way. Like other short fictions it retells an old cautionary tale: in this case that 'murder will out'. But the originality of Dickens's relation derives from an obsession with eyes. The mother of the boy who will be murdered fixes his killer with a look, before she dies, in which the crime seems to be foretold:

> It seems to me now, as if some strange and terrible foreshadowing of what has happened since, must have hung over us then. I was afraid of her, she haunted me, her fixed and steady look comes back now like the memory of a dark dream and makes my blood run cold.

The boy has inherited his mother's bright eyes, and after her death, they will follow and haunt the narrator, until by slow degrees the obsession with killing the little boy grows. At the moment of his murder, the mother's ghost looks from the child's eyes at his killer. This shared psychological understanding, which works below the level of the articulate and cannot avert disaster, belongs to neither the Gothic nor the supernatural, but to those states of mind of heightened and horrified awareness which Dickens had already portrayed after Sikes's murder of Nancy in *Oliver Twist*,[9] and which Dostoevsky, a passionate admirer of Dickens, was to explore more profoundly in *Crime and Punishment* (1866).

In 'To be Read at Dusk', written ten years later for publication in an annual, *The Keepsake*, Dickens returned to the theme of dreams and psychic possession, but now more vividly, using this particular tale for particular effects, as in performance art. The uncanny which grips the reader by making the invisible visible (or half so) appealed to Dickens's sense of the theatrical, the melodramatic and the revelatory. He knew the pleasure which was to be derived from being entertained and chilled. The title itself declared the intention of playing upon, and with, the uncertainty, anxiety and indistinctness of the twilit hour. Once again, Dickens starts from a frame, a conversation overheard, when the sun stains the snows of the Swiss Alps red.[10]

The 'Story of the English Bride', mainly set in one of the gloomy palazzi near Genoa which Dickens had visited, tells of a beautiful and happy young girl who three nights before her marriage in England becomes haunted by the dream of a stranger's face. In the palazzo, the face becomes reality when Signor Dellombra comes to visit. The bride's husband insists that she can only overcome the terror of her dream by receiving the Signor like an ordinary guest. But Dellombra continues to exercise some malign influence over her, looking at her 'fixedly out of the darkness'. When we last see her, she is crouched in the corner of Signor Dellombra's carriage, as 'she vanished into infamous oblivion, with the dreaded face beside her that she had seen in her dream' (p. 175).[11]

As often in Dickens, the impression left on the mind comes through repetition and contrast: the happy, beautiful, laughing girl, on the one hand; and the gloomy palazzo with its shadowy visitor (not just in name, though that too) on the other. Dickens, the journalist, draws his atmosphere out of a place, like a vapour; and he chooses a moment when psychic phenomena were beginning to be the subject of serious investigation in England. (The brief concluding narrative concerns telepathy.) But Dickens's story owes more than a little to the myth of Persephone, who in the fair field of Enna was carried off to the underworld by gloomy Dis. Only in this truncated version of the myth, Persephone does not return six months later, but is lost for ever on the spot where she disappears, reflecting that darker view of human character and fate which shaped Dickens's later fiction, as we shall see in 'George Silverman's Explanation'.

In 1838 or 1839, Dickens visited Newgate[12] Prison and met the poisoner, Thomas Wainewright, who became one source for the character of Julius Slinkton in his melodramatic tale of revenge, 'Hunted Down' (1859).[13] Dickens was always absorbed by how a tale should be told, and the recognition that this determined its effect. Here, a deliberate opacity in the narration – not giving too much away until the denouement – sustains the reader's curiosity and sense of suspense, reserving the *coup de théâtre* for the end; but this indirectness is also part of a more fundamental and unifying interest.

Images, as much as methods, signal Dickens's originality. The thick plate-glass window which separates the Manager's Office ('I could see through it what passed in the outer office without hearing a word'[p. 180]) is increasingly intruded upon by the poisoner, Mr Julius Slinkton ('I noticed that he came straight to the door in the glass partition and did not pause a single moment outside' [p. 186]). The parting in the middle of his hair suggests to the Manager a gravel path which must not be strayed from. 'Straight up here, if you please. Off the grass!' (p. 181). The liberty taken by Julius Slinkton is not a liberty he offers to others; and the parting of his hair provokes a feeling of 'very great aversion'.[14]

Throughout this tale there exists a subtle questioning of territory and space, an awareness of boundaries which should not be crossed, and remain unrecognised at peril. Slinkton's victims let him intrude and control their lives without questioning his kindness or suspecting their danger. The narrator remarks at the start: 'I confess, for my part, that I have been taken in, over and over again ... Believe me, my first impression of those people, founded on face and manner alone, was invariably true. My mistake was, in suffering them to come nearer to me, and explain themselves away' (p. 180). Proximity lowers the guard; only the parting straight up the middle continues to warn. Dickens's sense of the physicality of life was never less than 'intensely' real.

Space, or the lack of space, also causes the biter to be bit. Installing another potential victim in rooms opposite his own in the Middle Temple, Slinkton plies him, as he believes, with opium and drink, and in 'letting him in the door' gives him the chance to find the proof of his suspected villainy. Throughout this story of a lover determined to hunt down and kill the man who has ruined his life, Dickens's imagination conjures up images with the way in which the determination of space organises and controls relationships. The title, 'Hunted Down', invokes the quarry who has been finally cornered, and is suggestive too of the theme of revenge by which a man, in Francis Bacon's words, 'keeps his own wounds green'.

In all these previous short fictions, Dickens can be seen to be drawing upon his knowledge of fables and tales, and inventing his own variations on them. Only in the last does the telling of a tale itself become the subject of his ironic eye.

'Upon myself', Dickens wrote of 'George Silverman's Explanation', 'it has made the strongest impression of reality and originality! And I feel as if I had read something (by somebody

else) which I should never get out of my head!'[15] In attempting
to get his explanation out of his head, George Silverman makes
two false starts, which in a slighter fiction might have been
edited out. Instead they underline Dickens's complete assurance
as a master of style, and establish Silverman's diffidence as a
narrator. His 'explanation' attempts to explain to himself – as
he looks out at the graveyard – how he has come to be as he is,
and live as he has lived. But self-explanation is never simple,
whether for Silverman, the obscure unmarried clergyman, or
Dickens, the world-famous author not far from the end of his
life, because it depends on editing, evasion, distortions of
memory and a version of the self which by its very nature must
be incomplete. George Silverman's hesitancy – and final inad-
equacy – in explaining himself stems from a failure of consciousness, thought and language to represent how it is, and how it
was.

Silverman does not know this, though his creator does. And
so his narrative proceeds with an apparent simplicity, a linear
straight-forwardness. He has only a cloudy awareness ('Not as
yet directly aiming at how it came to pass, I will come upon it
by degrees' [p. 202]) of the problems his self-narration presents,
and even if he had the inclination to 'decode' himself, he would
be doomed to fail because, like Bottom's dream, his tale would
have no bottom.

'George Silverman's Explanation' reads with such compelling
ease because it depends on simplification, as we all simplify
when we attempt to explain our acts, our relationships, our
selves; and yet Dickens's artistry lies in the simplification, a
cohesive and plausible account which, as readers, we simul-
taneously accept and reject.

George Silverman first sees the light of day in a cellar; and in
this place of darkness, without love, food or warmth, he is
taught to perceive himself in his mother's words as a 'worldly
little devil'. A devil, driven by desire to compensate for the
poverty and want he has known in his childhood, might be
expected to emerge from this underworld. But his life – at least
in his explanation of himself – becomes the mirror-image of
his mother's 'curse': a need, as often repeated as it is unfulfilled
(how could it be?) to prove that he is not a worldly little devil.
The invitation to join in the dance of life must always be rejected
to prove an impossible innocence. And yet Silverman does not

altogether fail. He overcomes the dismal vapour which hangs about him from his life in the cellar, learns to perceive beauty, feels love for his Mother and Father, acquires education which he shares, and falls in love with a girl whom he might have married if that had not been a worldly thing to do. In Silverman, the man who overcomes the burden of his upbringing, Dickens portrays once more his belief in the survival of goodness (and its opposite, the instability of evil), which characterised *Oliver Twist* and lay close to the heart of his creative inspiration.

But in Silverman's case, the repeating process of self-denial involves an inability to defend himself against what is wrong. Cheated out of his inheritance from his grandfather by the hypocritical, avaricious and criminal activities of his guardian, Verity Hawkyard, Silverman not only foregoes any claim upon it, but thanks Hawkyard for his generosity to him, to confirm his own idea of himself as 'ungrasping'. Silverman, though, does not write of the hysterical self-righteousness of the non-conformist sect to which Brothers Hawkyard and Gimblet belong without revealing the hideous materialism of their behaviour, and Dickens's dislike of sectarian cant.

Silverman's need to deny his own desires culminates in the sacrifice of the girl he loves to a rival, and the loss of his livelihood. Silver-haired, deprived of silver, Silverman[16] retires to write his explanation of how he has come to be as he is. The horror of himself, once cruelly mirrored by the crowd who interposed a vessel of smoking disinfectant between themselves and the little boy who had just emerged from the cellar where his parents had died, has mellowed, but not been wiped out, as it had not been for Dickens. The prison-house (or blacking factory) in George Silverman's soul is never worked through because memory has embedded it deeply. Had Dickens been writing like E. M. Forster, forty years later, he would have stepped forward and commented on George Silverman's spiritual ruin; but every word in this tale belongs to George Silverman's consciousness only, and the limitations of his capacity, shared by us all, for seeing how things are. This restraint on Dickens's part, found also in the late fiction of Kipling, creates a style which is implosive, bursting inwards, so that the reader from the first false start is aware of the untold stories which lie beneath the narrative offered with quiet assurance.

Dickens's powers of observation, which had been noted in

him since the start of his career as a journalist, have become absorbed into a style which means more than it says. By taking the 'Private Way to the Counting House' and presenting Brother Hawkyard with a letter, vindicating his behaviour against the possibility of any 'dark scandal', George Silverman observes Brother Gimblet's reactions, which remind him of his facial expression when 'expounding' in the chapel: 'I call to mind a delighted snarl with which he used to detail from the platform the torments reserved for the wicked (meaning all human creation except the Brotherhood), as being remarkably hideous' (p. 215). Brother Gimblet's face assumes the looks of a medieval devil, or one possessed by the vices he claims to abhor. George Silverman's awareness of the physical – of things, of rooms, of looks (one as real as the other) – has been formed in him by his life in the cellar:

> I recollect the sound of Father's Lancashire clogs on the street pavement above, as being different in my young hearing from the sound of all other clogs; and I recollect that when Mother came down the cellar-steps, I used tremblingly to speculate on her feet having a good or an ill-tempered look . . .

This intense physicality in which seeing becomes a way of seeing through was among the unique gifts of his creator.

In this final tale where memory shapes experience, we may see reflections of Dickens's own life: Sylvia and Maria Beadnell, Adelina and Ellen Ternan, the cellar and the blacking factory. But they are only reflections, ghosts and spirits, which, as the sage women of the neighbourhood said, David Copperfield would be privileged to see, and which Dickens himself used in the service of his 'fabulous' art. The conclusion is sombre. The change in Mr Tulrumble becomes a reunion with life; the change in George Silverman a descent towards death, and back to the life underground from which he has never escaped.

PETER MUDFORD

## Notes

1. For an excellent discussion of the mythic in the novel, see Steven Connor's 'Introduction' to the Everyman Dickens, *Oliver Twist* (1994).

2. For a discussion of 'Personality as Performance in Dickens', see R. Garis, *The Dickens Theatre* (Oxford, 1965), pp. 63–86.

3. I am indebted here to Peter Ackroyd, *Dickens* (1990), p. 277. Dickens's talents as a reader and performer were to play a very large part in his later life, eventually exhausting him and contributing to his death at the age of fifty-eight.

4. For a full discussion of the changes which Dickens made in turning his farce into a story, see Joel J. Brattin, 'From Drama into Fiction: *The Lamplighter* and "The Lamplighter's Story"', *The Dickensian* 85, Autumn 1989, pp. 131–9. The illustration is the last known collaboration between Dickens and Cruikshank. Also Dickens's introduction of the frame for the story is of special interest.

5. For a discussion of street-lighting, see 'The Lamplighter's Story', p. 240, n. 1.

6. G. K. Chesterton, *Dickens* (edited with an introduction by Michael Slater, 1992), writes memorably about this, as about many other aspects of Dickens's art.

7. For an interesting discussion of the tendency to 'retreat' in this period of Dickens's life, see Malcolm Andrews, 'Introducing Master Humphrey', *The Dickensian* 67, 1971, pp. 70–86.

8. Quoted in Charles Dickens, *Selected Shorter Fiction* (edited by Deborah A. Thomas, 1976), p. 17.

9. Sikes is also haunted by the recollection of Nancy's eyes; see *Oliver Twist*, Chapter 48.

10. See Michael Slater, *Dickens and Women* (1983), pp. 124–5. When Dickens and his wife were travelling in Italy with the de la Rues, Dickens exercised his powers as an amateur mesmerist over Madame de la Rue, who suffered from terrifying fantasies. Catherine Dickens was disturbed by her husband's powers because she was no doubt aware of their potential erotic overtones. Dickens has used and refashioned this episode in 'To be Read at Dusk'.

11. In *The Lady from the Sea* (1888), Henrik Ibsen dramatised a similar idea of the power which an image can come to have over the mind, creating a neurosis. In Ibsen's play, the confrontation between Ellida and the Stranger, freely chosen by her, frees her from his power.

12. Dickens's horrifying and pathetic account of 'A Visit to Newgate' is to be found in *Sketches by Boz* and reprinted in *Selected Short Fiction, op. cit.*, pp. 112–25.

13. Philip Collins in *Dickens and Crime* (1962) has argued that

Slinkton was also based on Palmer of Rugeley, who was sentenced in 1856 for the murder of people he had insured.

14. Slinkton is not the only villain in Dickens portrayed with 'sleek black hair'. John Jasper in *The Mystery of Edwin Drood*, which Dickens left unfinished at the time of his death, is described as 'a dark man of some six-and-twenty, with thick, lustrous, well-arranged black hair and whiskers' (Chapter 2).

15. See Harry Stone, *George Silverman's Explanation* (edited with an introduction and notes, California State University Press, 1984), p. ix.

16. Harry Stone's excellent introduction in *ibid.*, discusses the names in this tale, and many other aspects of its artistry.

# NOTE ON THE TEXTS
# AND ILLUSTRATIONS

The texts used here have been reprinted from the original publications in England:

'Public Life of Mr Tulrumble': *Bentley's Miscellany*, January 1837.
*Master Humphrey's Clock*, 1840–41.
'The Lamplighter's Story': *The Pic-Nic Papers*, 1841.
'To be Read at Dusk': *The Keepsake*, 1852.
'Hunted Down': *All the Year Round*, 4 and 11 April 1860.
'George Silverman's Explanation': *All the Year Round*, 1, 15 and 29 February 1868.

The illustrations to 'Mr Tulrumble' (p. 14) and 'The Lamplighter' (p. 163) are by George Cruikshank. To illustrate *Master Humphrey's Clock* Dickens asked his friend the painter, George Cattermole, famous for his antiquarian scenes, to join his regular illustrator, Hablot K. Browne ('Phiz'), and was delighted when he agreed to do so. Cattermole's illustrations appear on pp. 22, 24, 27, 48, 54, 73, 78, 86, 99, 128, 147, Browne's on pp. 30, 35, 42, 57, 63, 91, 104, 111, 116, 117, 138.

*In affectionate memory of*
*J. I. M. Stewart*
*Student and Tutor of Christ Church, Oxford*

# MASTER HUMPHREY'S CLOCK
# AND OTHER STORIES

# PUBLIC LIFE OF MR TULRUMBLE,
## ONCE MAYOR OF MUDFOG

Mudfog is a pleasant town – a remarkably pleasant town – situated in a charming hollow by the side of a river, from which river, Mudfog derives an agreeable scent of pitch, tar, coals, and rope-yarn, a roving population in oil-skin hats, a pretty steady influx of drunken bargemen, and a great many other maritime advantages. There is a good deal of water about Mudfog, and yet it is not exactly the sort of town for a watering-place,[1] either. Water is a perverse sort of element at the best of times, and in Mudfog it is particularly so. In winter, it comes oozing down the streets and tumbling over the fields, – nay, rushes into the very cellars and kitchens of the houses, with a lavish prodigality that might well be dispensed with; but in the hot summer weather it *will* dry up, and turn green: and, although green is a very good colour in its way, especially in grass, still it certainly is not becoming to water; and it cannot be denied that the beauty of Mudfog is rather impaired, even by this trifling circumstance. Mudfog is a healthy place – very healthy; – damp, perhaps, but none the worse for that. It's quite a mistake to suppose that damp is unwholesome: plants thrive best in damp situations, and why shouldn't men? The inhabitants of Mudfog are unanimous in asserting that there exists not a finer race of people on the face of the earth; here we have an indisputable and veracious contradiction of the vulgar error at once. So, admitting Mudfog to be damp, we distinctly state that it is salubrious.

The town of Mudfog is extremely picturesque. Limehouse[2] and Ratcliffe Highway[3] are both something like it, but they give you a very faint idea of Mudfog. There are a great many more public-houses in Mudfog, – more than in Ratcliffe Highway and Limehouse put together. The public buildings, too, are very imposing. We consider the Town-hall one of the finest specimens of shed architecture, extant: it is a combination of the pig-sty and tea-garden-box, orders; and the simplicity of its design is of surpassing beauty. The idea of placing a large window on one side of the door, and a small one on the other, is particularly happy. There is a fine bold Doric[4] beauty, too, about the padlock and scraper, which is strictly in keeping with the general effect.

In this room do the mayor and corporation of Mudfog assemble together in solemn council for the public weal. Seated on the massive wooden benches, which, with the table in the centre, form the only furniture of the whitewashed apartment, the sage men of Mudfog spend hour after hour in grave deliberation. Here they settle at what hour of the night the public-houses shall be closed, at what hour of the morning they shall be permitted to open, how soon it shall be lawful for people to eat their dinner on church-days,[5] and other great political questions; and sometimes, long after silence has fallen on the town, and the distant lights from the shops and houses have ceased to twinkle, like far-off stars, to the sight of the boatmen on the river, the illumination in the two unequal-sized windows of the town-hall, warns the inhabitants of Mudfog that its little body of legislators, like a larger and better-known body of the same genus,[6] a great deal more noisy, and not a whit more profound, are patriotically dozing away in company, far into the night, for their country's good.

Among this knot of sage and learned men, no one was so eminently distinguished, during many years, for the quiet modesty of his appearance and demeanour, as Nicholas Tulrumble, the well-known coal-dealer. However exciting the subject of discussion, however animated the tone of the debate, or however warm the personalities exchanged, (and even in Mudfog we get personal sometimes,) Nicholas Tulrumble was always the same. To say truth, Nicholas, being an industrious man, and always up betimes,[7] was apt to fall asleep when a debate began, and to remain asleep till it was over, when he would wake up very much refreshed, and give his vote with the greatest complacency. The fact was, that Nicholas Tulrumble, knowing that everybody there had made up his mind beforehand, considered the talking as just a long botheration about nothing at all; and to the present hour it remains a question, whether, on this point at all events, Nicholas Tulrumble was not pretty near right.

Time, which strews[8] a man's head with silver, sometimes fills his pockets with gold. As he gradually performed one good office for Nicholas Tulrumble, he was obliging enough not to omit the other. Nicholas began life in a wooden tenement of four feet square, with a capital[9] of two and ninepence, and a stock in trade of three bushels[10] and a-half of coals, exclusive of the large lump which hung, by way of sign-board,[11] outside. Then he enlarged the shed, and kept a truck;[12] then he left the shed, and the truck too, and started a donkey[13] and a Mrs Tulrumble; then he moved again and set up a cart; the cart was soon afterwards exchanged for a waggon;[14] and so he went on, like his great predecessor Whittington[15] – only without a cat for a partner – increasing in wealth and fame, until at last he gave up business altogether, and retired with Mrs Tulrumble and family to Mudfog Hall, which he had himself erected, on something which he endeavoured to delude himself into the belief was a hill, about a quarter of a mile distant from the town of Mudfog.

About this time, it began to be murmured in Mudfog, that Nicholas Tulrumble was growing vain and haughty; that prosperity and success had corrupted the simplicity of his manners, and tainted the natural goodness of his heart; in short, that he was setting up for a public character, and a great gentleman, and affected to look down upon his old companions with compassion and contempt. Whether these reports were at the time well-founded, or not, certain it is that Mrs Tulrumble very shortly afterwards started a four-wheel chaise, driven by a tall postilion[16] in a yellow cap, – that Mr Tulrumble junior took to smoking cigars, and calling the footman a 'feller' – and that Mr Tulrumble from that time forth, was no more seen in his old seat in the chimney-corner of the Lighterman's Arms[17] at night. This looked bad; but, more than this, it began to be observed that Mr Nicholas Tulrumble attended the corporation meetings more frequently than heretofore; that he no longer went to sleep as he had done for so many years, but propped his eyelids open with his two fore-fingers; that he read the newspapers by himself at home; and that he was in the habit of indulging abroad in distant and mysterious allusions to 'masses of people,' and 'the property of the country,' and 'productive power,' and 'the monied interest:' all of which denoted and proved that Nicholas Tulrumble was either mad, or worse; and it puzzled the good people of Mudfog amazingly.

At length, about the middle of the month of October, Mr Tulrumble and family went up to London; the middle of

October being, as Mrs Tulrumble informed her acquaintance in Mudfog, the very height of the fashionable season.

Somehow or other, just about this time, despite the health-preserving air of Mudfog, the Mayor died. It was a most extraordinary circumstance; he had lived in Mudfog for eighty-five years. The corporation didn't understand it at all; indeed it was with great difficulty that one old gentleman, who was a great stickler for forms, was dissuaded from proposing a vote of censure on such unaccountable conduct. Strange as it was, however, die he did, without taking the slightest notice of the corporation; and the corporation were imperatively called upon to elect his successor. So, they met for the purpose; and being very full of Nicholas Tulrumble just then, and Nicholas Tulrumble being a very important man, they elected him, and wrote off to London by the very next post to acquaint Nicholas Tulrumble with his new elevation.

Now, it being November time, and Mr Nicholas Tulrumble being in the capital, it fell out that he was present at the Lord Mayor's show[18] and dinner, at sight of the glory and splendour whereof, he, Mr Tulrumble, was greatly mortified, inasmuch as the reflection would force itself on his mind, that, had he been born in London instead of in Mudfog, he might have been a Lord Mayor too, and have patronised the judges, and been affable to the Lord Chancellor, and friendly with the Premier, and coldly condescending to the Secretary to the Treasury, and have dined with a flag behind his back, and done a great many other acts and deeds which unto Lord Mayors of London peculiarly appertain. The more he thought of the Lord Mayor, the more enviable a personage he seemed. To be a King was all very well; but what was the King to the Lord Mayor! When the King made a speech, everybody knew it was somebody else's writing; whereas here was the Lord Mayor, talking away for half an hour – all out of his own head – amidst the enthusiastic applause of the whole company, while it was notorious that the King might talk to his parliament till he was black in the face without getting so much as a single cheer. As all these reflections passed through the mind of Mr Nicholas Tulrumble, the Lord Mayor of London appeared to him the greatest sovereign on the face of the earth, beating the Emperor of Russia all to nothing, and leaving the Great Mogul[19] immeasurably behind.

Mr Nicholas Tulrumble was pondering over these things, and

inwardly cursing the fate which had pitched his coal-shed in Mudfog, when the letter of the corporation was put into his hand. A crimson flush mantled over his face as he read it, for visions of brightness were already dancing before his imagination.

'My dear,' said Mr Tulrumble to his wife, 'they have elected me, Mayor of Mudfog.'

'Lor-a-mussy!'[20] said Mrs Tulrumble: 'why, what's become of old Sniggs?'

'The late Mr Sniggs, Mrs Tulrumble,' said Mr Tulrumble sharply, for he by no means approved of the notion of unceremoniously designating a gentleman who had filled the high office of Mayor, as 'old Sniggs,' – 'the late Mr Sniggs, Mrs Tulrumble, is dead.'

The communication was very unexpected; but Mrs Tulrumble only ejaculated 'Lor-a-mussy!' once again, as if a Mayor were a mere ordinary Christian, at which Mr Tulrumble frowned gloomily.

'What a pity 'tan't in London, ain't it?' said Mrs Tulrumble, after a short pause; 'what a pity 'tan't in London, where you might have had a show.'

'I *might* have a show in Mudfog, if I thought proper, I apprehend,' said Mr Tulrumble mysteriously.

'Lor! so you might, I declare,' replied Mrs Tulrumble.

'And a good one, too,' said Mr Tulrumble.

'Delightful!' exclaimed Mrs Tulrumble.

'One which would rather astonish the ignorant people down there,' said Mr Tulrumble.

'It would kill them with envy,' said Mrs Tulrumble.

So it was agreed that his Majesty's lieges[21] in Mudfog should be astonished with splendour, and slaughtered with envy, and that such a show should take place as had never been seen in that town, or in any other town before, – no, not even in London itself.

On the very next day after the receipt of the letter, down came the tall postilion in a post-chaise, – not upon one of the horses, but inside – actually inside the chaise, – and, driving up to the very door of the town-hall, where the corporation were assembled, delivered a letter, written by the Lord knows who, and signed by Nicholas Tulrumble, in which Nicholas said, all through four sides of closely-written, gilt-edged, hot-pressed,

Bath post letter-paper,[22] that he responded to the call of his fellow townsmen with feelings of heartfelt delight; that he accepted the arduous office which their confidence had imposed upon him; that they would never find him shrinking from the discharge of his duty; that he would endeavour to execute his functions with all that dignity which their magnitude and importance demanded; and a great deal more to the same effect. But even this was not all. The tall postilion produced from his right-hand top-boot,[23] a damp copy of that afternoon's number of the county paper; and there, in large type, running the whole length of the very first column, was a long address from Nicholas Tulrumble to the inhabitants of Mudfog, in which he said that he cheerfully complied with their requisition, and, in short, as if to prevent any mistake about the matter, told them over again what a grand fellow he meant to be, in very much the same terms as those in which he had already told them all about the matter in his letter.

The corporation stared at one another very hard at all this, and then looked as if for explanation to the tall postilion, but as the tall postilion was intently contemplating the gold tassel on the top of his yellow cap, and could have afforded no explanation whatever, even if his thoughts had been entirely disengaged, they contented themselves with coughing very dubiously, and looking very grave. The tall postilion then delivered another letter, in which Nicholas Tulrumble informed the corporation, that he intended repairing to the town-hall, in grand state and gorgeous procession, on the Monday afternoon then next ensuing. At this, the corporation looked still more solemn; but, as the epistle wound up with a formal invitation to the whole body to dine with the Mayor on that day, at Mudfog Hall, Mudfog Hill, Mudfog, they began to see the fun of the thing directly, and sent back their compliments, and they'd be sure to come.

Now there happened to be in Mudfog, as somehow or other there does happen to be, in almost every town in the British dominions, and perhaps in foreign dominions too – we think it very likely, but, being no great traveller, cannot distinctly say – there happened to be in Mudfog a merry-tempered, pleasant-faced, good-for-nothing sort of vagabond, with an invincible dislike to manual labour, and an unconquerable attachment to strong beer and spirits, whom everybody knew, and nobody, except his wife, took the trouble to quarrel with, who inherited from his ancestors the appellation of Edward Twigger, and rejoiced in the *sobriquet*[24] of Bottle-nosed Ned. He was drunk upon the average once a day, and penitent upon an equally fair calculation once a month; and when he was penitent, he was invariably in the very last stage of maudlin intoxication. He was a ragged, roving, roaring kind of fellow, with a burly form, a sharp wit, and a ready head, and could turn his hand to anything when he chose to do it. He was by no means opposed to hard labour on principle, for he would work away at a cricket-match by the day together, – running, and catching, and batting, and bowling, and revelling in toil which would exhaust a galley-slave. He would have been invaluable to a fire-office; never was a man with such a natural taste for pumping engines, running up ladders, and throwing furniture out of two-pair-of-stairs' windows: nor was this the only element in which he was at home; he was a humane society in himself, a portable drag,[25] an animated life-preserver, and had saved more people, in his time, from drowning, than the Plymouth life-boat, or Captain Manby's apparatus.[26] With all these qualifications, notwithstanding his dissipation, Bottle-nosed Ned was a general favourite; and the authorities of Mudfog, remembering his numerous services to the population, allowed him in return to get drunk in his own way, without the fear of stocks,[27] fine, or imprisonment. He had a general licence, and he showed his sense of the compliment by making the most of it.

We have been thus particular in describing the character and avocations of Bottle-nosed Ned, because it enables us to introduce a fact politely, without hauling it into the reader's presence with indecent haste by the head and shoulders, and brings us very naturally to relate, that on the very same evening on which Mr Nicholas Tulrumble and family returned to Mudfog, Mr Tulrumble's new secretary, just imported from London, with a pale face and light whiskers, thrust his head down to the very bottom of his neckcloth-tie, in at the tap-room door of the Lighterman's Arms, and enquiring whether one Ned Twigger was luxuriating within, announced himself as the bearer of a message from Nicholas Tulrumble, Esquire, requiring Mr Twigger's immediate attendance at the hall, on private and particular business. It being by no means Mr Twigger's interest to affront the Mayor, he rose from the fire-place with a slight sigh, and followed the light-whiskered secretary through the dirt and wet of Mudfog streets, up to Mudfog Hall, without further ado.

Mr Nicholas Tulrumble was seated in a small cavern with a skylight, which he called his library, sketching out a plan of the procession on a large sheet of paper; and into the cavern the secretary ushered Ned Twigger.

'Well, Twigger!' said Nicholas Tulrumble, condescendingly.

There was a time when Twigger would have replied, 'Well, Nick!' but that was in the days of the truck, and a couple of years before the donkey; so, he only bowed.

'I want you to go into training, Twigger,' said Mr Tulrumble.

'What for, sir?' enquired Ned, with a stare.

'Hush, hush, Twigger!' said the Mayor. 'Shut the door, Mr Jennings. Look here, Twigger.'

As the Mayor said this, he unlocked a high closet, and disclosed a complete suit of brass armour, of gigantic dimensions.

'I want you to wear this, next Monday, Twigger,' said the Mayor.

'Bless your heart and soul, sir!' replied Ned, 'you might as well ask me to wear a seventy-four pounder,[28] or a cast-iron boiler.'

'Nonsense, Twigger! nonsense!' said the Mayor.

'I couldn't stand under it, sir,' said Twigger; 'it would make mashed potatoes of me, if I attempted it.'

'Pooh, pooh, Twigger!' returned the Mayor. 'I tell you I have seen it done with my own eyes, in London, and the man wasn't half such a man as you are, either.'

'I should as soon have thought of a man's wearing the case of an eight-day clock[29] to save his linen,' said Twigger, casting a look of apprehension at the brass suit.

'It's the easiest thing in the world,' rejoined the Mayor.

'It's nothing,' said Mr Jennings.

'When you're used to it,' added Ned.

'You do it by degrees,' said the Mayor. 'You would begin with one piece tomorrow, and two the next day, and so on, till you had got it all on. Mr Jennings, give Twigger a glass of rum. Just try the breast-plate, Twigger. Stay; take another glass of rum first. Help me to lift it, Mr Jennings. Stand firm, Twigger! There! – it isn't half as heavy as it looks, is it?'

Twigger was a good strong, stout fellow; so, after a great deal of staggering, he managed to keep himself up, under the breast-plate, and even contrived, with the aid of another glass of rum, to walk about in it, and the gauntlets[30] into the bargain. He made a trial of the helmet, but was not equally successful, inasmuch as he tipped over instantly: – an accident which Mr Tulrumble clearly demonstrated to be occasioned by his not having a counteracting weight of brass on his legs.

'Now, wear that with grace and propriety on Monday next,' said Tulrumble, 'and I'll make your fortune.'

'I'll try what I can do, sir,' said Twigger.

'It must be kept a profound secret,' said Tulrumble.

'Of course, sir,' replied Twigger.

'And you must be sober,' said Tulrumble; 'perfectly sober.'

Mr Twigger at once solemnly pledged himself to be as sober as a judge, and Nicholas Tulrumble was satisfied, although, had we been Nicholas, we should certainly have exacted some promise of a more specific nature; inasmuch as, having attended the Mudfog assizes[31] in the evening more than once, we can solemnly testify to having seen judges with very strong symptoms of dinner under their wigs. However, that's neither here nor there.

The next day, and the day following, and the day after that, Ned Twigger was securely locked up in the small cavern with the skylight, hard at work at the armour. With every additional piece he could manage to stand upright in, he had an additional glass of rum; and at last, after many partial suffocations, he contrived to get on the whole suit, and to stagger up and down the room in it, like an intoxicated effigy from Westminster Abbey.

Never was man so delighted as Nicholas Tulrumble; never was woman so charmed as Nicholas Tulrumble's wife. Here was a sight for the common people of Mudfog! A live man in brass armour! Why, they would go wild with wonder!

The day – *the* Monday – arrived.

If the morning had been made to order, it couldn't have been better adapted to the purpose. They never showed a better fog in London on Lord Mayor's day, than enwrapped the town of Mudfog on that eventful occasion. It had risen slowly and surely from the green and stagnant water with the first light of morning, until it reached a little above the lamp-post tops; and there it had stopped, with a sleepy, sluggish obstinacy, which bade defiance to the sun, who had got up very blood-shot about the eyes, as if he had been at a drinking party over night, and was doing his day's work with the worst possible grace. The thick damp mist hung over the town like a huge gauze curtain. All was dim and dismal. The church-steeples had bidden a temporary adieu to the world below; and every object of lesser importance – houses, barns, hedges, trees, and barges – had all taken the veil.[32]

The church-clock struck one. A cracked trumpet from the front-garden of Mudfog Hall produced a feeble flourish, as if some asthmatic person had coughed into it accidentally; the gate flew open, and out came a gentleman, on a moist-sugar coloured charger, intended to represent a herald, but bearing a much stronger resemblance to a court-card[33] on horseback. This was one of the circus people, who always came down to Mudfog at that time of the year, and who had been engaged by Nicholas Tulrumble expressly for the occasion. There was the horse, whisking his tail about, balancing himself on his hind-legs, and flourishing away with his fore-feet, in a manner which would have gone to the hearts and souls of any reasonable crowd. But a Mudfog crowd never was a reasonable one, and in all probability never will be. Instead of scattering the very fog with their shouts, as they ought most indubitably to have done, and were fully intended to do, by Nicholas Tulrumble, they no sooner recognised the herald, than they began to growl forth the most unqualified disapprobation at the bare notion of his riding like any other man. If he had come out on his head indeed, or jumping through a hoop, or flying through a red-hot drum, or even standing on one leg with his other foot in his mouth, they might have had something to say to him;[34] but for a professional gentleman to sit astride in the saddle, with his feet in the stirrups, was rather too good a joke. So, the herald was a decided failure, and the crowd hooted with great energy, as he pranced ingloriously away.

On the procession came. We are afraid to say how many supernumeraries there were, in striped shirts and black velvet caps, to imitate the London watermen,[35] or how many base imitations of running-footmen,[36] or how many banners, which, owing to the heaviness of the atmosphere, could by no means be prevailed on to display their inscriptions: still less do we feel disposed to relate how the men who played the wind instruments, looking up into the sky (we mean the fog) with musical fervour, walked through pools of water and hillocks of mud, till they covered the powdered heads of the running footmen aforesaid with splashes, that looked curious, but not ornamental; or how the barrel-organ performer put on the wrong stop, and played one tune while the band played another; or how the horses, being used to the arena, and not to the streets, would stand still and dance, instead of going on and prancing; – all of which are matters which might be dilated upon to great advantage, but which we have not the least intention of dilating upon, notwithstanding.

Oh! it was a grand and beautiful sight to behold the corporation in glass coaches, provided at the sole cost and charge of Nicholas Tulrumble, coming rolling along, like a funeral out of mourning, and to watch the attempts the corporation made to look great and solemn, when Nicholas Tulrumble himself, in the four-wheel chaise, with the tall postilion, rolled out after them, with Mr Jennings on one side to look like the chaplain, and a supernumerary on the other, with an old life-guardsman's sabre, to imitate the sword-bearer;[37] and to see the tears rolling down the faces of the mob as they screamed with merriment. This was beautiful! and so was the appearance of Mrs Tulrumble and son, as they bowed with grave dignity out of their coach-window to all the dirty faces that were laughing around them: but it is not even with this that we have to do, but with the sudden stopping of the procession at another blast of the trumpet, whereat, and whereupon, a profound silence ensued, and all eyes were turned towards Mudfog Hall, in the confident anticipation of some new wonder.

'They won't laugh now, Mr Jennings,' said Nicholas Tulrumble.

'I think not, sir,' said Mr Jennings.

'See how eager they look,' said Nicholas Tulrumble. 'Aha! the laugh will be on our side now; eh, Mr Jennings?'

'No doubt of that, sir,' replied Mr Jennings; and Nicholas Tulrumble, in a state of pleasurable excitement, stood up in the four-wheel chaise, and telegraphed gratification to the Mayoress behind.

While all this was going forward, Ned Twigger had descended into the kitchen of Mudfog Hall for the purpose of indulging the servants with a private view of the curiosity that was to

George Cruikshank

**Ned Twigger in the kitchen of Mudfog house**

burst upon the town; and, somehow or other, the footman was so companionable, and the housemaid so kind, and the cook so friendly, that he could not resist the offer of the first-mentioned to sit down and take something – just to drink success to master in.

So, down Ned Twigger sat himself in his brass livery on the top of the kitchen-table; and in a mug of something strong, paid for by the unconscious Nicholas Tulrumble, and provided by the companionable footman, drank success to the Mayor and his procession; and, as Ned laid by his helmet to imbibe the something strong, the companionable footman put it on his own head, to the immeasurable and unrecordable delight of the cook and housemaid. The companionable footman was very facetious to Ned, and Ned was very gallant to the cook and housemaid by turns. They were all very cosy and comfortable; and the something strong went briskly round.

At last Ned Twigger was loudly called for, by the procession people: and, having had his helmet fixed on, in a very complicated manner, by the companionable footman, and the kind housemaid, and the friendly cook, he walked gravely forth, and appeared before the multitude.

The crowd roared – it was not with wonder, it was not with surprise; it was most decidedly and unquestionably with laughter.

'What!' said Mr Tulrumble, starting up in the four-wheel chaise. 'Laughing? If they laugh at a man in real brass armour, they'd laugh when their own fathers were dying. Why doesn't he go into his place, Mr Jennings? What's he rolling down towards us for? – he has no business here!'

'I am afraid, sir—' faltered Mr Jennings.

'Afraid of what, sir?' said Nicholas Tulrumble, looking up into the secretary's face.

'I am afraid he's drunk, sir;' replied Mr Jennings.

Nicholas Tulrumble took one look at the extraordinary figure that was bearing down upon them; and then, clasping his secretary by the arm, uttered an audible groan in anguish of spirit.

It is a melancholy fact that Mr Twigger having full licence to demand a single glass of rum on the putting on of every piece of the armour, got, by some means or other, rather out in his calculation in the hurry and confusion of preparation, and drank about four glasses to a piece instead of one, not to mention the something strong which went on the top of it. Whether the brass armour checked the natural flow of perspiration, and thus prevented the spirit from evaporating, we are not scientific enough to know; but, whatever the cause was, Mr Twigger no sooner found himself outside the gate of Mudfog Hall, than he also found himself in a very considerable state of intoxication; and hence his extraordinary style of progressing. This was bad enough, but, as if fate and fortune had conspired against Nicholas Tulrumble, Mr Twigger, not having been penitent for a good calendar month, took it into his head to be most especially and particularly sentimental, just when his repentance could have been most conveniently disposed with. Immense tears were rolling down his cheeks, and he was vainly endeavouring to conceal his grief by applying to his eyes a blue cotton pocket-handkerchief with white spots, – an article not strictly in keeping with a suit of armour some three hundred years old, or thereabouts.

'Twigger, you villain!' said Nicholas Tulrumble, quite forgetting his dignity, 'go back!'

'Never,' said Ned. 'I'm a miserable wretch. I'll never leave you.'

The by-standers of course received this declaration with acclamations of 'That's right, Ned; don't!'

'I don't intend it,' said Ned, with all the obstinacy of a very tipsy man. 'I'm very unhappy. I'm the wretched father of an unfortunate family; but I am very faithful, sir. I'll never leave you.' Having reiterated this obliging promise, Ned proceeded in broken words to harangue the crowd upon the number of years he had lived in Mudfog, the excessive respectability of his character, and other topics of the like nature.

'Here! will anybody lead him away?' said Nicholas: 'if they'll call on me afterwards, I'll reward them well.'

Two or three men stepped forward, with the view of bearing Ned off, when the secretary interposed.

'Take care! take care!' said Mr Jennings. 'I beg your pardon, sir; but they'd better not go too near him, because, if he falls over, he'll certainly crush somebody.'

At this hint the crowd retired on all sides to a very respectful distance, and left Ned, like the Duke of Devonshire, in a little circle of his own.[38]

'But, Mr Jennings,' said Nicholas Tulrumble, 'he'll be suffocated.'

'I'm very sorry for it, sir,' replied Mr Jennings; 'but nobody can get that armour off, without his own assistance. I'm quite certain of it, from the way he put it on.'

Here Ned wept dolefully, and shook his helmeted head, in a manner that might have touched a heart of stone; but the crowd had not hearts of stone, and they laughed heartily.

'Dear me, Mr Jennings,' said Nicholas, turning pale at the possibility of Ned's being smothered in his antique costume – 'Dear me, Mr Jennings, can nothing be done with him?'

'Nothing at all,' replied Ned, 'nothing at all. Gentlemen, I'm an unhappy wretch. I'm a body, gentlemen, in a brass coffin.' At this poetical idea of his own conjuring up, Ned cried so much that the people began to get sympathetic, and to ask what Nicholas Tulrumble meant by putting a man into such a machine as that; and one individual in a hairy waistcoat like the top of a trunk,[39] who had previously expressed his opinion that if Ned hadn't been a poor man, Nicholas wouldn't have dared to do it, hinted at the propriety of breaking the four-wheel chaise, or Nicholas's head, or both, which last compound proposition the crowd seemed to consider a very good notion.

It was not acted upon, however, for it had hardly been broached, when Ned Twigger's wife made her appearance abruptly in the little circle before noticed, and Ned no sooner caught a glimpse of her face and form, than from the mere force of habit he set off towards his home just as fast as his legs would carry him; and that was not very quick in the present instance either, for, however ready they might have been to carry *him*, they couldn't get on very well under the brass armour. So, Mrs Twigger had plenty of time to denounce Nicholas Tulrumble to his face: to express her opinion that he was a decided monster; and to intimate that, if her ill-used husband sustained any personal damage from the brass armour, she would have the law of Nicholas Tulrumble for manslaughter. When she had said all this with due vehemence, she posted after Ned, who was dragging himself along as best he could, and deploring his unhappiness in most dismal tones.

What a wailing and screaming Ned's children raised when he got home at last! Mrs Twigger tried to undo the armour, first in one place, and then in another, but she couldn't manage it; so she tumbled Ned into bed, helmet, armour, gauntlets, and all. Such a creaking as the bedstead made, under Ned's weight in his new suit! It didn't break down though; and there Ned lay, like the anonymous vessel in the Bay of Biscay,[40] till next day, drinking barley-water, and looking miserable: and every time he groaned, his good lady said it served him right, which was all the consolation Ned Twigger got.

Nicholas Tulrumble and the gorgeous procession went on together to the town-hall, amid the hisses and groans of all the spectators, who had suddenly taken it into their heads to consider poor Ned a martyr. Nicholas was formally installed in his new office, in acknowledgement of which ceremony he delivered himself of a speech, composed by the secretary, which was very long, and no doubt very good, only the noise of the people outside prevented anybody from hearing it, but Nicholas Tulrumble himself. After which, the procession got back to Mudfog Hall any how it could; and Nicholas and the corporation sat down to dinner.

But the dinner was flat, and Nicholas was disappointed. They were such dull sleepy old fellows, that corporation. Nicholas made quite as long speeches as the Lord Mayor of London had done, nay, he said the very same things that the Lord Mayor of London had said, and the deuce a cheer[41] the corporation gave him. There was only one man in the party who was thoroughly awake; and he was insolent, and called him Nick, Nick! What would be the consequence, thought Nicholas, of anybody presuming to call the Lord Mayor of London 'Nick'! He should like to know what the sword-bearer would say to that; or the recorder,[42] or the toast-master, or any other of the great officers of the city. They'd nick[43] him.

But these were not the worst of Nicholas Tulrumble's doings: if they had been, he might have remained a Mayor to this day, and have talked till he lost his voice. He contracted a relish for statistics, and got philosophical;[44] and the statistics and the philosophy together, led him into an act which increased his unpopularity and hastened his downfall.

At the very end of the Mudfog High-street, and abutting on the river-side, stands the Jolly Boatmen, an old-fashioned, low-roofed, bay-windowed house, with a bar, kitchen, and tap-room[45] all in one, and a large fire-place with a kettle to correspond, round which the working men have congregated

time out of mind on a winter's night, refreshed by draughts of
good strong beer, and cheered by the sounds of a fiddle and
tambourine: the Jolly Boatmen having been duly licensed by the
Mayor and corporation, to scrape the fiddle and thumb the
tambourine from time, whereof the memory of the oldest
inhabitants goeth not to the contrary.[46] Now Nicholas Tulrumble had been reading pamphlets on crime, and parliamentary
reports, – or had made the secretary read them to him, which is
the same thing in effect, – and he at once perceived that this
fiddle and tambourine must have done more to demoralize
Mudfog, than any other operating causes that ingenuity could
imagine. So he read up for the subject, and determined to come
out on the corporation with a burst, the very next time the
licence was applied for.

The licensing day came, and the red-faced landlord of the
Jolly Boatmen walked into the town-hall, looking as jolly as
need be, having actually put on an extra fiddle for that night, to
commemorate the anniversary of the Jolly Boatmen's music
licence. It was applied for in due form, and was just about to be
granted as a matter of course, when up rose Nicholas Tulrumble,
and drowned the astonished corporation in a torrent of elo-
quence. He descanted in glowing terms upon the increasing
depravity of his native town of Mudfog, and the excesses
committed by its population. Then, he related how shocked he
had been, to see barrels of beer sliding down into the cellar of
the Jolly Boatmen week after week; and how he had sat at a
window opposite the Jolly Boatmen for two days together, to
count the people who went in for beer between the hours of
twelve and one o'clock alone – which, by-the-bye, was the time
at which the great majority of the Mudfog people dined. Then,
he went on to state, how the number of people who came out
with beer-jugs, averaged twenty-one in five minutes, which,
being multiplied by twelve, gave two hundred and fifty-two
people with beer-jugs in an hour, and multiplied again by fifteen
(the number of hours during which the house was open daily)
yielded three thousand seven hundred and eighty people with
beer-jugs per day, or twenty-six thousand four hundred and
sixty people with beer-jugs per week. Then he proceeded to
show that a tambourine and moral degradation were synony-
mous terms, and a fiddle and vicious propensities wholly inseparable. All these arguments he strengthened and demonstrated

by frequent references to a large book with a blue cover,[47] and sundry quotations from the Middlesex magistrates;[48] and in the end, the corporation, who were posed with the figures, and sleepy with the speech, and sadly in want of dinner into the bargain, yielded the palm[49] to Nicholas Tulrumble, and refused the music licence to the Jolly Boatmen.

But although Nicholas triumphed, his triumph was short. He carried on the war against beer-jugs and fiddles, forgetting the time when he was glad to drink out of the one, and to dance to the other, till the people hated, and his old friends shunned him. He grew tired of the lonely magnificence of Mudfog Hall, and his heart yearned towards the Lighterman's Arms. He wished he had never set up as a public man, and sighed for the good old times of the coal-shop, and the chimney-corner.

At length old Nicholas, being thoroughly miserable, took heart of grace,[50] paid the secretary a quarter's wages in advance, and packed him off to London by the next coach. Having taken this step, he put his hat on his head, and his pride in his pocket, and walked down to the old room at the Lighterman's Arms. There were only two of the old fellows there, and they looked coldly on Nicholas as he proffered his hand.

'Are you going to put down pipes, Mr Tulrumble?' said one.

'Or trace the progress of crime to 'baccer?' growled the other.

'Neither,' replied Nicholas Tulrumble, shaking hands with them both, whether they would or not. 'I've come down to say that I'm very sorry for having made a fool of myself, and that I hope you'll give me up the old chair again.'

The old fellows opened their eyes, and three or four more old fellows opened the door, to whom Nicholas, with tears in his eyes, thrust out his hand too, and told the same story. They raised a shout of joy, that made the bells in the ancient church-tower vibrate again, and wheeling the old chair into the warm corner, thrust old Nicholas down into it, and ordered in the very largest-sized bowl of hot punch, with an unlimited number of pipes, directly.

The next day the Jolly Boatmen got the licence, and the next night, old Nicholas and Ned Twigger's wife led off a dance to the music of the fiddle and tambourine, the tone of which seemed mightily improved by a little rest, for they never had played so merrily before. Ned Twigger was in the very height of his glory, and he danced hornpipes, and balanced chairs on his chin, and straws on his nose, till the whole company, including the corporation, were in raptures of admiration at the brilliancy of his acquirements.

Mr Tulrumble, junior, couldn't make up his mind to be anything but magnificent, so he went up to London and drew bills on his father; and when he had overdrawn, and got into debt, he grew penitent and came home again.

As to old Nicholas, he kept his word, and having had six weeks of public life, never tried it any more. He went to sleep in the town-hall at the very next meeting; and, in full proof of his sincerity, has requested us to write this faithful narrative. We wish it could have the effect of reminding the Tulrumbles of another sphere, that puffed-up conceit is not dignity, and that snarling at the little pleasures they were once glad to enjoy, because they would rather forget the times when they were of lower station, renders them objects of contempt and ridicule.

This is the first time we have published any of our gleanings from this particular source. Perhaps, at some future period, we may venture to open the chronicles of Mudfog.

BOZ.

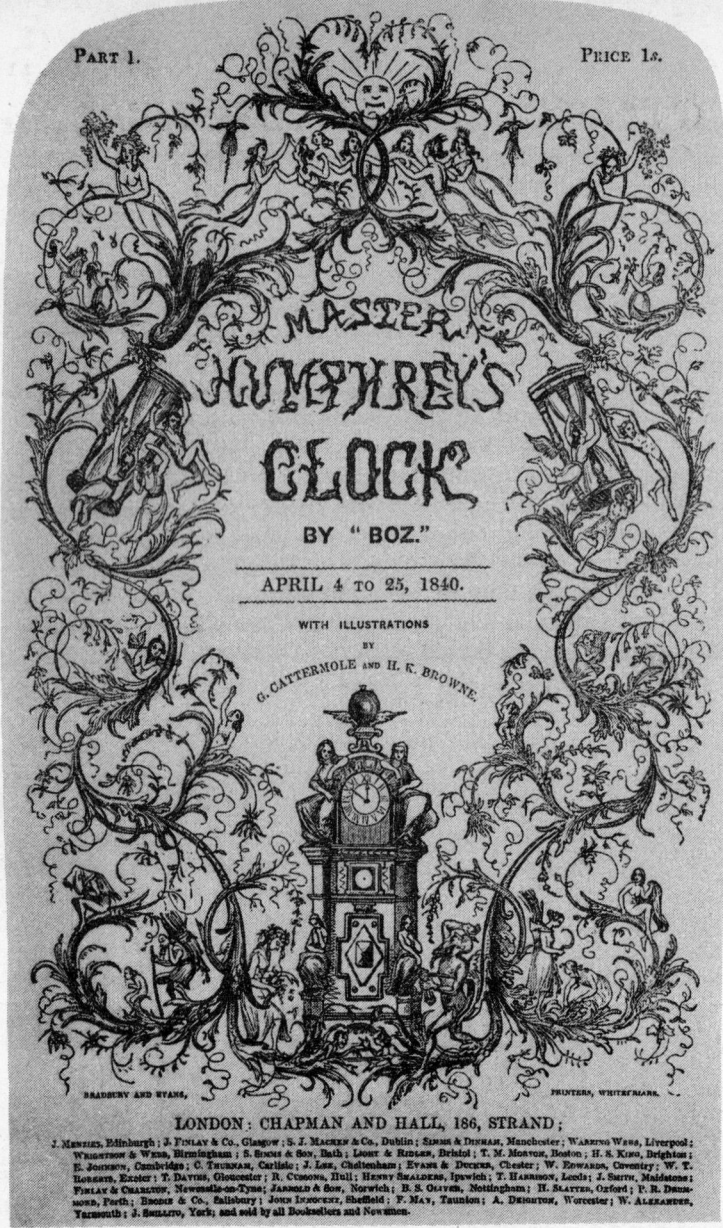

PART 1.                                                           PRICE 1s.

MASTER
HUMPHREY'S
CLOCK

BY "BOZ."

APRIL 4 TO 25, 1840.

WITH ILLUSTRATIONS
BY
G. CATTERMOLE AND H. K. BROWNE.

BRADBURY AND EVANS,                                    PRINTERS, WHITEFRIARS.

LONDON: CHAPMAN AND HALL, 186, STRAND;

J. MENZIES, Edinburgh; J. FINLAY & Co., Glasgow; S. J. MACHEN & Co., Dublin; SIMMS & DINHAM, Manchester; WARRING WEBB, Liverpool;
WRIGHTSON & WEBB, Birmingham; S. SIMMS & Son, Bath; LIGHT & RIDLER, Bristol; T. M. MORTON, Boston; H. S. KING, Brighton;
E. JOHNSON, Cambridge; C. THURNAM, Carlisle; J. LEE, Cheltenham; EVANS & DUCKER, Chester; W. EDWARDS, Coventry; W. T.
ROBERTS, Exeter; T. DAVIES, Gloucester; R. CUSSONS, Hull; HENRY SMALDEN, Ipswich; T. HARRISON, Leeds; J. SMITH, Maidstone;
FINLAY & CHARLTON, Newcastle-on-Tyne; JARROLD & SON, Norwich; B. S. OLIVER, Nottingham; H. SLATTER, Oxford; P. R. DRUM-
MOND, Perth; BROODIE & Co., Salisbury; JOHN INNOCENT, Sheffield; F. MAY, Taunton; A. DEIGHTON, Worcester; W. ALEXANDER,
Yarmouth; J. SHILLITO, York; and sold by all Booksellers and Newsmen.

Wrapper Design for Weekly Parts, 4 April 1840

# MASTER[1] HUMPHREY'S CLOCK

## PREFACE TO FIRST VOLUME

When the author commenced this Work, he proposed to himself three objects.

First. To establish a periodical, which should enable him to present, under one general head, and not as separate and distinct publications, certain fictions which he had it in contemplation to write.

Secondly. To produce these Tales in weekly numbers;[2] hoping that to shorten the intervals of communication between himself and his readers, would be to knit more closely the pleasant relations they had held, for Forty Months.

Thirdly. In the execution of this weekly task, to have as much regard as its exigencies would permit, to each story as a whole, and to the possibility of its publication at some distant day, apart from the machinery in which it had its origin.

The characters of Master Humphrey and his three friends, and the little fancy of the clock, were the result of these considerations. When he sought to interest his readers in those who talked, and read, and listened, he revived Mr Pickwick and his humble friends; not with any intention of reopening an exhausted and abandoned mine, but to connect them in the thoughts of those whose favourites they had been, with the tranquil enjoyments of Master Humphrey.

It was never the author's intention to make the Members of Master Humphrey's Clock, active agents in the stories they are supposed to relate. Having brought himself in the commencement of his undertaking to feel an interest in these quiet creatures, and to imagine them in their old chamber of meeting, eager listeners to all he had to tell, the author hoped – as authors will – to succeed in awakening some of his own emotions in the bosoms of his readers. Imagining Master Humphrey in his chimney-corner, resuming night after night, the narrative, – say, of the Old Curiosity Shop – picturing to himself the various

Frontispiece to Volume 1 of *Master Humphrey's Clock*, 1840

sensations of his hearers – thinking how Jack Redburn might incline to poor Kit, and perhaps lean too favourably even towards the lighter vices of Mr Richard Swiveller[3] – how the deaf gentleman would have his favourite, and Mr Miles his – and how all these gentle spirits would trace some faint reflection of their past lives in the varying current of the tale – he has insensibly fallen into the belief that they are present to his readers as they are to him, and has forgotten that like one whose vision is disordered he may be conjuring up bright figures where there is nothing but empty space.

The short papers which are to be found at the beginning of this volume were indispensable to the form of publication and the limited extent of each number, as no story of lengthened interest could be begun until 'The Clock' was wound up and fairly going.

The author would fain hope that there are not many who would disturb Master Humphrey and his friends in their seclusion; who would have them forego their present enjoyments, to exchange those confidences with each other, the absence of which is the foundation of their mutual trust. For when their occupation is gone,[4] when their tales are ended and but their personal histories remain, the chimney-corner will be growing cold, and the clock will be about to stop for ever.

One other word in his own person, and he returns to the more grateful task of speaking for those imaginary people whose little world lies within these pages.

It may be some consolation to the well-disposed ladies or gentlemen who, in the interval between the conclusion of his last work and the commencement of this, originated a report that he had gone raving mad,[5] to know that it spread as rapidly as could be desired, and was made the subject of considerable dispute; not as regarded the fact, for that was as thoroughly established as the duel between Sir Peter Teazle and Charles Surface in the School for Scandal;[6] but with reference to the unfortunate lunatic's place of confinement: one party insisting positively on Bedlam, another inclining favourably towards Saint Luke's, and a third swearing strongly by the asylum at Hanwell;[7] while each backed its case by circumstantial evidence of the same excellent nature as that brought to bear by Sir Benjamin Backbite[8] on the pistol shot, which struck against the little bronze bust of Shakespeare over the fireplace, grazed out of the window at a right angle, and wounded the postman, who was coming to the door with a double letter[9] from Northamptonshire.

It will be a great affliction to these ladies and gentlemen to learn – and he is so unwilling to give pain, that he would not whisper the circumstance on any account, did he not feel in a manner bound to do so, in gratitude to those among his friends who were at the trouble of being angry with the absurdity – that their invention made the author's home unusually merry, and gave rise to an extraordinary number of jests, of which he will only add, in the words of the good Vicar of Wakefield,[10] 'I cannot say whether we had more wit among us than usual; but I am sure we had more laughing.'

*Devonshire Terrace, York Gate,*
*September 1840.*

## MASTER HUMPHREY, FROM HIS CLOCK-SIDE
### IN THE CHIMNEY-CORNER

The reader must not expect to know where I live. At present, it is true, my abode may be a question of little or no import to anybody, but if I should carry my readers with me, as I hope to do, and there should spring up, between them and me, feelings of homely affection and regard attaching something of interest to matters ever so slightly connected with my fortunes or my speculations, even my place of residence might one day have a kind of charm for them. Bearing this possible contingency in mind, I wish them to understand in the outset, that they must never expect to know it.

I am not a churlish old man. Friendless I can never be, for all mankind are of my kindred, and I am on ill terms with no one member of my great family. But for many years I have led a lonely, solitary life; – what wound I sought to heal, what sorrow to forget, originally, matters not now; it is sufficient that retirement has become a habit with me, and that I am unwilling to break the spell which for so long a time has shed its quiet influence upon my home and heart.

I live in a venerable suburb of London, in an old house, which in bygone days was a famous resort for merry roysterers and peerless ladies, long since departed. It is a silent shady place, with a paved court-yard so full of echoes, that sometimes I am tempted to believe that faint responses to the noises of old times linger there yet, and that these ghosts of sound haunt my footsteps as I pace it up and down. I am the more confirmed in this belief, because, of late years, the echoes that attend my walks have been less loud and marked than they were wont to be; and it is pleasanter to imagine in them the rustling of silk brocade, and the light step of some lovely girl, than to recognise in their altered note the failing tread of an old man.

Those who like to read of brilliant rooms and gorgeous furniture, would derive but little pleasure from a minute description of my simple dwelling. It is dear to me for the same reason that they would hold it in slight regard. Its worm-eaten doors, and low ceilings crossed by clumsy beams; its walls of wainscot, dark stairs, and gaping closets; its small chambers, communicating with each other by winding passages or narrow steps; its many nooks, scarce larger than its corner-cupboards; its very dust and dullness, all are dear to me. The moth and spider are my constant tenants, for in my house the one basks in his long sleep, and the other plies his busy loom, secure and undisturbed. I have a pleasure in thinking on a summer's day, how many butterflies have sprung for the first time into light and sunshine from some dark corner of these old walls.

When I first came to live here, which was many years ago, the neighbours were curious to know who I was, and whence I came, and why I lived so much alone. As time went on, and they still remained unsatisfied on these points, I became the centre of a popular ferment, extending for half a mile around, and in one direction for a full mile. Various rumours were circulated to my prejudice. I was a spy, an infidel, a conjuror, a kidnapper of children, a refugee, a priest, a monster. Mothers caught up their infants and ran into their houses as I passed; men eyed me spitefully, and muttered threats and curses. I was the object of suspicion and distrust: ay, of downright hatred, too.

But when in course of time they found I did no harm, but, on the contrary, inclined towards them despite their unjust usage, they began to relent. I found my footsteps no longer dogged, as they had often been before, and observed that the women and children no longer retreated, but would stand and gaze at me as I passed their doors. I took this for a good omen, and waited patiently for better times. By degrees I began to make friends among these humble folks, and though they were yet shy of speaking, would give them 'good day', and so pass on. In a little time, those whom I had thus accosted, would make a point of coming to their doors and windows at the usual hour, and nod or curtsey to me; children, too, came timidly within my reach, and ran away quite scared when I patted their heads and bade them be good at school. These little people soon grew more familiar. From exchanging mere words of course with my older neighbours, I gradually became their friend and adviser, the depository of their cares and sorrows, and sometimes, it may be, the reliever, in my small way, of their distresses. And now I never walk abroad, but pleasant recognitions and smiling faces wait on Master Humphrey.

It was a whim of mine, perhaps as a whet[11] to the curiosity of my neighbours, and a kind of retaliation upon them for their suspicions, – it was, I say, a whim of mine, when I first took up my abode in this place, to acknowledge no other name than Humphrey. With my detractors, I was Ugly Humphrey. When I began to convert them into friends, I was Mr Humphrey, and Old Mr Humphrey. At length I settled down into plain Master Humphrey, which was understood to be the title most pleasant to my ear; and so completely a matter of course has it become, that sometimes when I am taking my morning walk in my little court-yard, I overhear my barber – who has a profound respect for me, and would not, I am sure, abridge my honours for the world – holding forth on the other side of the wall, touching the state of 'Master Humphrey's' health, and communicating to some friend the substance of the conversation that he and Master Humphrey have had together in the course of the shaving which he has just concluded.

That I may not make acquaintance with my readers under false pretences, or give them cause to complain hereafter that I have withheld any matter which it was essential for them to have learnt at first, I wish them to know – and I smile

see p. 27

see p. 43

see p. 57

see p. 76

see p. 108

see p. 117

Initial letter illustrations for beginnings of chapters

sorrowfully to think that the time has been when the confession would have given me pain – that I am a mis-shapen, deformed, old man.

I have never been made a misanthrope by this cause. I have never been stung by any insult, nor wounded by any jest upon my crooked figure. As a child I was melancholy and timid, but that was because the gentle consideration paid to my misfortune sunk deep into my spirit and made me sad, even in those early days. I was but a very young creature when my poor mother died, and yet I remember that often when I hung around her neck, and oftener still when I played about the room before her, she would catch me to her bosom, and bursting into tears, soothe me with every term of fondness and affection. God knows I was a happy child at those times – happy to nestle in her breast – happy to weep when she did – happy in not knowing why.

These occasions are so strongly impressed upon my memory, that they seem to have occupied whole years. I had numbered very very few when they ceased for ever, but before then their meaning had been revealed to me.

I do not know whether all children are imbued with a quick perception of childish grace and beauty and a strong love for it, but I was. I had no thought that I remember, either that I possessed it myself or that I lacked it, but I admired it with an intensity I cannot describe. A little knot of playmates – they must have been beautiful, for I see them now – were clustered one day round my mother's knee in eager admiration of some picture representing a group of infant angels, which she held in her hand. Whose the picture was, whether it was familiar to me or otherwise, or how all the children came to be there, I forget: I have some dim thought it was my birthday, but the beginning of my recollection is that we were all together in a garden, and it was summer weather – I am sure of that, for one of the little girls had roses in her sash. There were many lovely angels in this picture, and I remember the fancy coming upon me to point out which of them represented each child there, and that when I had gone through all my companions, I stopped and hesitated, wondering which was most like me. I remember the children looking at each other, and my turning red and hot, and their crowding round to kiss me, saying that they loved me all the same; and then, and when the old sorrow came into my dear mother's mild and tender look, the truth broke upon me for the first time, and I knew, while watching my awkward and ungainly sports, how keenly she had felt for her poor crippled boy.

I used frequently to dream of it afterwards, and now my heart aches for that child as if I had never been he, when I think how often he awoke from some fairy change to his own old form, and sobbed himself to sleep again.

Well, well – all these sorrows are past. My glancing at them may not be without its use, for it may help in some measure to explain why I have all my life been attached to the inanimate objects that people my chamber, and how I have come to look upon them rather in the light of old and constant friends, than as mere chairs and tables which a little money could replace at will.

Chief and first among all these is my Clock – my old cheerful companionable Clock. How can I ever convey to others an idea of the comfort and consolation that this old clock has been for years to me!

It is associated with my earliest recollections. It stood upon the staircase at home (I call it home still, mechanically) nigh sixty years ago. I like it for that, but it is not on that account, nor because it is a quaint old thing in a huge oaken case curiously and richly carved, that I prize it as I do. I incline to it as if it were alive, and could understand and give me back the love I bear it.

And what other thing that has not life could cheer me as it does; what other thing that has not life (I will not say how few things that have) could have proved the same patient, true, untiring friend! How often have I sat in the long winter evenings feeling such society in its cricket-voice,[12] that raising my eyes from my book and looking gratefully towards it, the face reddened by the glow of the shining fire has seemed to relax from its staid expression and to regard me kindly; how often in the summer twilight, when my thoughts have wandered back to a melancholy past, have its regular whisperings recalled them to the calm and peaceful present; how often in the dead tranquillity of night has its bell broken the oppressive silence, and seemed to give me assurance that the old clock was still a faithful watcher at my chamber door! My easy-chair, my desk, my ancient furniture, my very books, I can scarcely bring myself to love even these last, like my old clock!

It stands in a snug corner, midway between the fireside and a low arched door leading to my bedroom. Its fame is diffused so extensively throughout the neighbourhood, that I have often the satisfaction of hearing the publican or the baker, and sometimes even the parish-clerk, petitioning my housekeeper (of whom I shall have much to say bye and bye,) to inform him the exact time by Master Humphrey's Clock. My barber, to whom I have already referred, would sooner believe it than the sun. Nor are these its only distinctions. It has acquired, I am happy to say, another, inseparably connecting it not only with my enjoyments and reflections, but with those of other men; as I shall now relate.

I lived alone here for a long time without any friend or acquaintance. In the course of my wanderings by night and day, at all hours and seasons, in city streets and quiet country parts, I came to be familiar with certain faces, and to take it to heart as quite a heavy disappointment if they failed to present themselves each at its accustomed spot. But these were the only friends I knew, and beyond them I had none.

It happened, however, when I had gone on thus for a long time, that I formed an acquaintance with a deaf gentleman, which ripened into intimacy and close companionship. To this hour, I am ignorant of his name. It is his humour to conceal it, or he has a reason and purpose for so doing. In either case I feel that he has a right to require a return of the trust he has reposed, and as he has never sought to discover my secret, I have never sought to penetrate his. There may have been something in this tacit confidence in each other, flattering and pleasant to us both, and it may have imparted in the beginning an additional zest, perhaps, to our friendship. Be this as it may, we have grown to be like brothers, and still I only know him as the deaf gentleman.

I have said that retirement has become a habit with me. When I add that the deaf gentleman and I have two friends, I communicate nothing which is inconsistent with that declaration. I spend many hours of every day in solitude and study, have no friends or change of friends but these, only see them at stated periods, and am supposed to be of a retired spirit by the very nature and object of our association.

We are men of secluded habits with something of a cloud upon our early fortunes, whose enthusiasm nevertheless has not cooled with age, whose spirit of romance is not yet quenched, who are content to ramble through the world in a pleasant dream, rather than ever waken again to its harsh realities. We are alchemists[13] who would extract the essence of perpetual youth from dust and ashes, tempt coy Truth in many light and airy forms from the bottom of her well, and discover one crumb of comfort or one grain of good in the commonest and least regarded matter that passes through our crucible. Spirits of past times, creatures of imagination, and people of today, are alike the objects of our seeking, and, unlike the objects of search with most philosophers, we can ensure their coming at our command.

The deaf gentleman and I first began to beguile our days with these fancies, and our nights in communicating them to each other. We are now four. But in my room there are six old chairs, and we have decided that the two empty seats shall always be placed at our table when we meet, to remind us that we may yet increase our company by that number, if we should find two men to our mind. When one among us dies, his chair will always be set in its usual place, but never occupied again; and I have caused my will to be so drawn out, that when we are all dead, the house shall be shut up, and the vacant chairs still left in their accustomed places. It is pleasant to think that even then, our shades may, perhaps, assemble together as of yore[14] we did, and join in ghostly converse.

One night in every week, as the clock strikes ten, we meet. At the second stroke of two, I am alone.

And now shall I tell how that my old servant, besides giving us note of time, and ticking cheerful encouragement of our proceedings, lends its name to our society, which for its punctuality and my love, is christened 'Master Humphrey's Clock?' Now shall I tell, how that in the bottom of the old dark closet where the steady pendulum throbs and beats with healthy action, though the pulse of him who made it stood still long ago and never moved again, there are piles of dusty papers constantly placed there by our hands, that we may link our enjoyments with my old friend, and draw means to beguile time from the heart of time itself? Shall I, or can I, tell with what a secret pride I open this repository when we meet at night, and still find new store of pleasure in my dear old Clock?

Friend and companion of my solitude! mine is not a selfish

love; I would not keep your merits to myself, but disperse something of pleasant association with your image through the whole wide world; I would have men couple with your name cheerful and healthy thoughts; I would have them believe that you keep true and honest time; and how would it gladden me to know that they recognised some hearty English work in Master Humphrey's Clock!

THE CLOCK-CASE

It is my intention constantly to address my readers from the chimney-corner, and I would fain hope that such accounts as I shall give them of our histories and proceedings, our quiet speculations or more busy adventures, will never be unwelcome. Lest, however, I should grow prolix in the outset by lingering too long upon our little association, confounding the enthusiasm with which I regard this chief happiness of my life with that minor degree of interest which those to whom I address myself may be supposed to feel for it, I have deemed it expedient to break off as they have seen.

But, still clinging to my old friend and naturally desirous that all its merits should be known, I am tempted to open (somewhat irregularly and against our laws, I must admit) the clock-case. The first roll of paper on which I lay my hand is in the writing of the deaf gentleman. I shall have to speak of him in my next paper, and how can I better approach that welcome task than by prefacing it with a production of his own pen, consigned to the safe keeping of my honest clock by his own hands?

The manuscript runs thus:

### Introduction to the Giant Chronicles

Once upon a time, that is to say, in this our time, – the exact year, month, and day, are of no matter, – there dwelt in the city of London a substantial citizen, who united in his single person the dignities of wholesale fruiterer, alderman,[15] common-councilman,[16] and member of the worshipful company of Patten-makers:[17] who had superadded to these extraordinary distinctions the important post and title of Sheriff,[18] and who at length, and to crown all, stood next in rotation for the high and honourable office of Lord Mayor.

He was a very substantial citizen indeed. His face was like the full moon in a fog, with two little holes punched out for his eyes, a very ripe pear stuck on for his nose, and a wide gash to serve for a mouth. The girth of his waistcoat was hung up and lettered in his tailor's shop as an extraordinary curiosity. He breathed like a heavy snorer, and his voice in speaking came thickly forth, as if it were oppressed and stifled by feather-beds. He trod the ground like an elephant, and eat and drank like – like nothing but an alderman, as he was.

This worthy citizen had risen to his great eminence from small beginnings. He had once been a very lean, weazen[19] little boy, never dreaming of carrying such a weight of flesh upon his bones or of money in his pockets, and glad enough to take his dinner at a baker's door, and his tea at a pump. But he had long ago forgotten all this, as it was proper that a wholesale fruiterer, alderman, common-councilman, member of the worshipful company of Patten-makers, past sheriff, and above all, a Lord Mayor that was to be, should; and he never forgot it more completely in all his life than on the eighth of November in the year of his election to the great golden civic chair, which was the day before his grand dinner at the Guildhall.

It happened that as he sat that evening all alone in his counting-house, looking over the bill of fare for next day, and checking off the fat capons in fifties and the turtle-soup by the hundred quarts for his private amusement, – it happened that as he sat alone occupied in these pleasant calculations, a strange man came in and asked him how he did: adding, 'If I am half as much changed as you, sir, you have no recollection of me, I am sure.'

The strange man was not over and above well dressed, and was very far from being fat or rich-looking in any sense of the word, yet he spoke with a kind of modest confidence, and assumed an easy, gentlemanly sort of air, to which nobody but a rich man can lawfully presume. Besides this, he interrupted the good citizen just as he had reckoned three hundred and seventy-two fat capons and was carrying them over to the next column, and as if that were not aggravation enough, the learned recorder for the city of London had only ten minutes previously gone out at that very same door, and had turned round and said, 'Good night, my lord.' Yes, he had said, 'my lord'; – he, a man of birth and education, of the Honourable Society of the Middle Temple,[20] Barrister at Law – he who had an uncle in the House of Commons, and an aunt almost but not quite in the House of Lords (for she had married a feeble peer, and made him vote as she liked) – he, this man, this learned recorder,[21] had said, 'my lord'. 'I'll not wait till tomorrow to give you your title, my Lord Mayor,' says he, with a bow and a smile; 'you are Lord Mayor *de facto*, if not *de jure*.[22] Good night, my lord!'

The Lord Mayor elect thought of this, and turning to the stranger, and sternly bidding him 'go out of this private counting-house,' brought forward the three hundred and seventy-two fat capons, and went on with the account.

'Do you remember,' said the other, stepping forward, – 'Do you remember little Joe Toddyhigh?'

The port-wine fled for a moment from the fruiterer's nose as he muttered 'Joe Toddyhigh! What about Joe Toddyhigh?'

'*I* am Joe Toddyhigh,' cried the visitor. 'Look at me, look hard at me; – harder, harder. You know me now? you know little Joe again? What a happiness to us both, to meet the very night before your grandeur! Oh! give me your hand, Jack – both hands – both, for the sake of old times.'

'You pinch me, sir. You're a hurting of me,' said the Lord Mayor elect pettishly: 'don't – suppose anybody should come – Mr Toddyhigh, sir.'

'Mr Toddyhigh!' repeated the other ruefully.

'Oh! don't bother,' said the Lord Mayor elect, scratching his head. 'Dear me! Why, I thought you was dead. What a fellow you are!'

Indeed, it was a pretty state of things, and worthy the tone of vexation and disappointment in which the Lord Mayor spoke. Joe Toddyhigh had been a poor boy with him at Hull, and had oftentimes divided his last penny and parted his last crust to relieve his wants, for though Joe was a destitute child in those times, he was as faithful and affectionate in his friendship as ever man of might could be. They parted one day to seek their fortunes in different directions. Joe went to sea, and the now wealthy citizen begged his way to London. They separated with many tears like foolish fellows as they were, and agreed to remain fast friends, and if they lived, soon to communicate again.

When he was an errand-boy, and even in the early days of his apprenticeship, the citizen had many a time trudged to the Post-office to ask if there were any letter from poor little Joe, and had gone home again with tears in his eyes, when he found no news of his only friend. The world is a wide place, and it was a long time before the letter came; when it did, the writer was forgotten. It turned from white to yellow from lying in the Post-office with nobody to claim it, and in the course of time was torn up with five hundred others, and sold for waste paper. And now at last, and when it might least have been expected, here was this Joe Toddyhigh turning up and claiming acquaintance with a great public character, who on the morrow would be cracking jokes with the Prime Minister of England, and who had only, at any time during the next twelve months, to say the word, and he could shut up Temple Bar,[23] and make it no thoroughfare for the king himself!

'I am sure I don't know what to say, Mr Toddyhigh,' said the Lord Mayor elect; 'I really don't. It's very inconvenient. I'd sooner have given twenty pound – it's very inconvenient, really.'

A thought had struggled into his mind, that perhaps his old

friend might say something passionate which would give him an excuse for being angry himself. No such thing. Joe looked at him steadily, but very mildly, and did not open his lips.

'Of course I shall pay you what I owe you,' said the Lord Mayor elect, fidgetting in his chair. 'You lent me – I think it was a shilling or some small coin – when we parted company, and that of course I shall pay, with good interest. I can pay my way with any man, and always have done. If you look into the Mansion House the day after tomorrow – some time after dusk – and ask for my private clerk, you'll find he has a draft for you. I haven't got time to say anything more just now, unless – ' he hesitated, for, coupled with a strong desire to glitter for once in all his glory in the eyes of his former companion, was a distrust of his appearance which might be more shabby than he could tell by that feeble light – 'unless you'd like to come to the dinner tomorrow. I don't mind your having this ticket, if you like to take it. A great many people would give their ears for it, I can tell you.'

His old friend took the card without speaking a word, and instantly departed. His sunburnt face and grey hair were present to the citizen's mind for a moment; but by the time he reached three hundred and eighty-one fat capons, he had quite forgotten him.

Joe Toddyhigh had never been in the capital of Europe before, and he wandered up and down the streets that night, amazed at the number of churches and other public buildings, the splendour of the shops, the riches that were heaped up on every side, the glare of light in which they were displayed, and the concourse of people who hurried to and fro, indifferent apparently to all the wonders that surrounded them. But in all the long streets and broad squares, there were none but strangers; it was quite a relief to turn down a byway and hear his own footsteps on the pavement. He went home to his inn; thought that London was a dreary, desolate place, and felt disposed to doubt the existence of one true-hearted man in the whole worshipful company of Patten-makers. Finally, he went to bed, and dreamed that he and the Lord Mayor elect were boys again.

He went next day to the dinner, and when, in a burst of light and music, and in the midst of splendid decorations and surrounded by brilliant company, his former friend appeared at the head of the Hall, and was hailed with shouts and cheering, he cheered and shouted with the best, and for the moment could have cried. The next moment he cursed his weakness in behalf of a man so changed and selfish, and quite hated a jolly-looking old gentleman opposite for declaring himself, in the pride of his heart, a Patten-maker.

As the banquet proceeded, he took more and more to heart the rich citizen's unkindness, – and that, not from any envy, but because he felt that a man of his state and fortune could all the better afford to recognise an old friend, even if he were poor and obscure. The more he thought of this, the more lonely and sad he felt. When the company dispersed and adjourned to the ball-room, he paced the hall and passages alone, ruminating in a very melancholy condition upon the disappointment he had experienced.

It chanced, while he was lounging about in this moody state, that he stumbled upon a flight of stairs, dark, steep, and narrow, which he ascended without any thought about the matter, and so came into a little music-gallery, empty and deserted. From this elevated post, which commanded the whole hall, he amused himself in looking down upon the attendants, who were clearing away the fragments of the feast very lazily, and drinking out of all the bottles and glasses with most commendable perseverance.

His attention gradually relaxed, and he fell fast asleep.

When he awoke, he thought there must be something the matter with his eyes; but, rubbing them a little, he soon found that the moonlight was really streaming through the east window, that the lamps were all extinguished, and that he was alone. He listened, but no distant murmur in the echoing passages, not even the shutting of a door, broke the deep silence; he groped his way down the stairs, and found that the door at the bottom was locked on the other side. He began now to comprehend that he must have slept a long time, that he had been overlooked, and was shut up there for the night.

His first sensation, perhaps, was not altogether a comfortable one, for it was a dark, chilly, earthy-smelling place, and some-thing too large for a man so situated, to feel at home in. However, when the momentary consternation of his surprise was over, he made light of the accident, and resolved to feel his way up the stairs again, and make himself as comfortable as he could in the gallery until morning. As he turned to execute this purpose, he heard the clocks strike three.

Any such invasion of a dead stillness as the striking of distant clocks, causes it to appear the more intense and insupportable when the sound has ceased. He listened with strained attention in the hope that some clock, lagging behind its fellows, had yet to strike – looking all the time into the profound darkness before him until it seemed to weave itself into a black tissue, patterned with a hundred reflections of his own eyes. But the bells had all pealed out their warning for that once, and the gust of wind that moaned through the place seemed cold and heavy with their iron breath.

The time and circumstances were favourable to reflection. He tried to keep his thoughts to the current, unpleasant though it was, in which they had moved all day, and to think with what a romantic feeling he had looked forward to shaking his old friend by the hand before he died, and what a wide and cruel difference there was between the meeting they had had, and that which he had so often and so long anticipated. Still he was disordered by waking to such sudden loneliness, and could not prevent his mind from running upon odd tales of people of undoubted courage, who, being shut up by night in vaults or churches, or other dismal places, had scaled great heights to get out, and fled from silence as they had never done from danger. This brought to his mind the moonlight through the window, and bethinking himself of it, he groped his way back up the crooked stairs – but very stealthily, as though he were fearful of being overheard.

He was very much astonished when he approached the gallery again, to see a light in the building: still more so, on advancing hastily and looking round, to observe no visible source from which it could proceed. But how much greater yet was his astonishment at the spectacle which this light revealed!

The statues of the two giants, Gog and Magog,[24] each above fourteen feet in height, those which succeeded to still older and more barbarous figures after the Great Fire of London, and which stand in the Guildhall to this day, were endowed with life and motion. These guardian genii of the City had quitted their pedestals, and reclined in easy attitudes in the great stained glass window. Between them was an ancient cask, which seemed to be full of wine; for the younger Giant, clapping his huge hand upon it, and throwing up his mighty leg, burst into an exulting laugh, which reverberated through the hall like thunder.

Joe Toddyhigh instinctively stooped down, and, more dead

than alive, felt his hair stand on end, his knees knock together, and a cold damp break out upon his forehead. But even at that minute curiosity prevailed over every other feeling, and somewhat reassured by the good-humour of the Giants and their apparent unconsciousness of his presence, he crouched in a corner of the gallery, in as small a space as he could, and peeping between the rails, observed them closely.

It was then that the elder Giant, who had a flowing grey beard, raised his thoughtful eyes to his companion's face, and in a grave and solemn voice addressed him thus:

## First Night of the Giant Chronicles

Turning towards his companion, the elder Giant uttered these words in a grave majestic tone:

'Magog, does boisterous mirth beseem[25] the Giant Warder of this ancient city? Is this becoming demeanour for a watchful spirit over whose bodiless head so many years have rolled, so many changes swept like empty air – in whose impalpable nostrils the scent of blood and crime, pestilence cruelty and horror, has been familiar as breath to mortals – in whose sight Time has gathered in the harvest of centuries, and garnered so many crops of human pride, affections, hopes, and sorrows? Bethink you of our compact. The night wanes; feasting revelry and music have encroached upon our usual hours of solitude, and morning will be here apace. Ere we are stricken mute again, bethink you of our compact.'

Pronouncing these latter words with more of impatience than quite accorded with his apparent age and gravity the Giant raised a long pole (which he still bears in his hand) and tapped his brother Giant rather smartly on the head; indeed the blow was so smartly administered, that the latter quickly withdrew his lips from the cask to which they had been applied, and catching up his shield and halbert[26] assumed an attitude of defence. His irritation was but momentary, for he laid these weapons aside as hastily as he had assumed them, and said as he did so:

'You know, Gog, old friend, that when we animate these shapes which the Londoners of old assigned (and not unworthily) to the guardian genii of their city, we are susceptible of some of the sensations which belong to human kind. Thus when I taste wine, I feel blows; when I relish the one, I disrelish the other. Therefore, Gog, the more especially as your arm is none of the lightest, keep your good staff by your side, else we may chance to differ. Peace be between us.'

'Amen!' said the other, leaning his staff in the window-corner; 'Why did you laugh just now?'

'To think,' replied the Giant Magog, laying his hand upon the cask, 'of him who owned this wine, and kept it in a cellar hoarded from the light of day, for thirty years, – "till it should be fit to drink," quoth he. He was two score and ten years old when he buried it beneath his house, and yet never thought that he might be scarcely "fit to drink" when the wine became so. I wonder it never occurred to him to make himself unfit to be eaten. There is very little of him left by this time.'

'The night is waning,' said Gog mournfully.

'I know it,' replied his companion, 'and I see you are impatient. But look. Through the eastern window – placed opposite to us, that the first beams of the rising sun may every morning gild our giant faces – the moon-rays fall upon the pavement in a stream of light that to my fancy sinks through the cold stone and gushes into the old crypt below. The night is scarcely past its noon, and our great charge is sleeping heavily.'

They ceased to speak, and looked upward at the moon. The sight of their large black rolling eyes filled Joe Toddyhigh with such horror that he could scarcely draw his breath. Still they took no note of him, and appeared to believe themselves quite alone.

'Our compact,' said Magog after a pause, 'is, if I understand it, that, instead of watching here in silence through the dreary nights, we entertain each other with stories of our past experience; with tales of the past, the present, and the future; with legends of London and her sturdy citizens from the old simple times. That every night at midnight when Saint Paul's bell tolls out one and we may move and speak, we thus discourse, nor leave such themes till the first grey gleam of day shall strike us dumb. Is that our bargain, brother?'

'Yes,' said the Giant Gog, 'that is the league between us who guard this city, by day in spirit, and by night in body also; and never on ancient holidays have its conduits run wine[27] more merrily than we will pour forth our legendary lore. We are old chroniclers from this time hence. The crumbled walls encircle us once more, the postern-gates[28] are closed, the drawbridge is up, and pent in its narrow den beneath, the water foams and struggles with the sunken starlings.[29] Jerkins[30] and quarter-staves[31] are in the streets again, the nightly watch set, the rebel, sad and lonely in his Tower dungeon tries to sleep and weeps for home and children. Aloft upon the gates and walls are noble heads[32] glaring fiercely down upon the dreaming city, and vexing the hungry dogs that scent them in the air and tear the ground beneath with dismal howlings. The axe, the block, the rack,[33] in their dark chambers give signs of recent use. The Thames floating past long lines of cheerful windows whence comes a burst of music and a stream of light, bears sullenly to the Palace wall the last red stain brought on the tide from Traitor's-gate.[34] But your pardon, brother. The night wears, and I am talking idly.'

The other Giant appeared to be entirely of this opinion, for during the foregoing rhapsody of his fellow-centinel he had been scratching his head with an air of comical uneasiness, or rather with an air that would have been very comical if he had been a dwarf or an ordinary-sized man. He winked too, and though it could not be doubted for a moment that he winked to himself, still he certainly cocked his enormous eye towards the gallery where the listener was concealed. Nor was this all, for he gaped; and when he gaped, Joe was horribly reminded of the popular prejudice on the subject of giants, and of their fabled power of smelling out Englishmen,[35] however closely concealed.

His alarm was such that he nearly swooned and it was some little time before his power of sight or hearing was restored. When he recovered he found that the elder Giant was pressing the younger to commence the Chronicles, and that the latter was endeavouring to excuse himself, on the ground that the night was far spent and it would be better to wait until the next. Well assured by this, that he was certainly about to begin directly, the listener collected his faculties by a great effort, and distinctly heard Magog express himself to the following effect:

In the sixteenth century and in the reign of Queen Elizabeth of glorious memory (albeit her golden days are sadly rusted with blood) there lived in the city of London a bold young 'prentice who loved his master's daughter. There were no doubt within the walls a great many young 'prentices in this condition, but I speak of only one, and his name was Hugh Graham.

This Hugh was apprenticed to an honest Bowyer[36] who dwelt in the ward of Cheype[37] and was rumoured to possess great wealth. Rumour was quite as infallible in those days as at the present time but it happened then as now, to be sometimes right by accident. It stumbled upon the truth when it gave the old Bowyer a mint of money. His trade had been a profitable one in the time of King Henry the Eighth, who encouraged English archery to the utmost, and he had been prudent and discreet.

Thus it came to pass that Mistress Alice his only daughter was the richest heiress in all his wealthy ward. Young Hugh had often maintained with staff and cudgel that she was the handsomest. To do him justice, I believe she was.

If he could have gained the heart of pretty Mistress Alice by knocking this conviction into stubborn people's heads, Hugh would have had no cause to fear. But though the Bowyer's daughter smiled in secret to hear of his doughty deeds for her sake, and though her little waiting-woman reported all her smiles (and many more) to Hugh, and though he was at a vast expense in kisses and small coin to recompense her fidelity, he made no progress in his love. He durst not whisper it to Mistress Alice save on sure encouragement, and that she never gave him. A glance of her dark eye as she sat at the door on a summer's evening after prayer time, while he and the neighbouring 'prentices exercised themselves in the street with blunted sword and buckler[38] would fire Hugh's blood so that none could stand before him; but then she glanced at others quite as kindly as on him, and where was the use of cracking crowns if Mistress Alice smiled upon the cracked as well as on the cracker?

Still Hugh went on, and loved her more and more. He thought of her all day, and dreamed of her all night long. He treasured up her every word and gesture, and had a palpitation of the heart whenever he heard her footstep on the stairs or her voice in an adjoining room. To him, the old Bowyer's house was haunted by an angel; there was enchantment in the air and space in which she moved. It would have been no miracle to Hugh if flowers had sprung from the rush-strewn floors beneath the tread of lovely Mistress Alice.

Never did 'prentice long to distinguish himself in the eyes of his lady-love so ardently as Hugh. Sometimes he pictured to himself the house taking fire by night, and he, when all drew back in fear, rushing through flame and smoke and bearing her from the ruins in his arms. At other times he thought of a rising of fierce rebels, an attack upon the city, a strong assault upon the Bowyer's house in particular, and he falling on the threshold pierced with numberless wounds in defence of Mistress Alice. If he could only enact some prodigy of valour, do some wonderful deed and let her know that she had inspired it, he thought he could die contented.

Sometimes the Bowyer and his daughter would go out to

supper with a worthy citizen at the fashionable hour of six o'clock, and on such occasions Hugh wearing his blue 'prentice cloak as gallantly as 'prentice might, would attend with a lantern and his trusty club to escort them home. These were the brightest moments of his life. To hold the light while Mistress Alice picked her steps, to touch her hand as he helped her over broken ways, to have her leaning on his arm – it sometimes even came to that – this was happiness indeed!

When the nights were fair, Hugh followed in the rear, his eyes riveted on the graceful figure of the Bowyer's daughter as she and the old man moved on before him. So they threaded the narrow winding streets of the city, now passing beneath the overhanging gables of old wooden houses whence creaking signs projected into the street, and now emerging from some dark and frowning gateway into the clear moonlight. At such times, or when the shouts of straggling brawlers met her ear, the Bowyer's daughter would look timidly back at Hugh beseeching him to draw nearer; and then how he grasped his club and longed to do battle with a dozen rufflers,[39] for the love of Mistress Alice!

The old Bowyer was in the habit of lending money on interest to the gallants of the Court, and thus it happened that many a richly-dressed gentleman dismounted at his door. More waving plumes and gallant steeds, indeed, were seen at the Bowyer's house, and more embroidered silks and velvets sparkled in his dark shop and darker private closet than at any merchant's in the city. In those times no less than in the present it would seem that the richest-looking cavaliers often wanted money the most.

Of these glittering clients there was one who always came alone. He was always nobly mounted, and having no attendant gave his horse in charge to Hugh while he and the Bowyer were closeted within. Once as he sprung into the saddle Mistress Alice was seated at an upper window, and before she could withdraw he had doffed his jewelled cap and kissed his hand. Hugh watched him caracoling[40] down the street, and burnt with indignation. But how much deeper was the glow that reddened in his cheeks when raising his eyes to the casement he saw that Alice watched the stranger too!

He came again and often, each time arrayed more gaily than before, and still the little casement showed him Mistress Alice. At length one heavy day, she fled from home. It had cost her a

hard struggle, for all her old father's gifts were strewn about her chamber as if she had parted from them one by one and knew that the time must come when these tokens of his love would wring her heart – yet she was gone.

She left a letter commending her poor father to the care of Hugh, and wishing he might be happier than he could ever have been with her, for he deserved the love of a better and a purer heart than she had to bestow. The old man's forgiveness (she said) she had no power to ask, but she prayed God to bless him – and so ended with a blot upon the paper where her tears had fallen.

At first the old man's wrath was kindled, and he carried his wrong to the Queen's throne itself; but there was no redress he learnt at Court, for his daughter had been conveyed abroad. This afterwards appeared to be the truth, as there came from France, after an interval of several years, a letter in her hand. It was written in trembling characters, and almost illegible. Little could be made out save that she often thought of home and her old dear pleasant room – and that she had dreamt her father was dead and had not blessed her – and that her heart was breaking.

The poor old Bowyer lingered on, never suffering Hugh to quit his sight, for he knew now that he had loved his daughter and that was the only link that bound him to earth. It broke at length and he died, bequeathing his old 'prentice his trade and all his wealth, and solemnly charging him with his last breath to revenge his child if ever he who had worked her misery crossed his path in life again.

From the time of Alice's flight, the tilting-ground,[41] the fields, the fencing school, the summer evening sports, knew Hugh no more. His spirit was dead within him. He rose to great eminence and repute among the citizens, but was seldom seen to smile and never mingled in their revelries or rejoicing. Brave, humane, and generous, he was loved by all. He was pitied too by those who knew his story, and these were so many that when he walked along the streets alone at dusk, even the rude common people doffed their caps and mingled a rough air of sympathy with their respect.

One night in May – it was her birth-night and twenty years since she had left her home – Hugh Graham sat in the room she had hallowed in his boyish days. He was now a grey-haired man though still in the prime of life. Old thoughts had borne him company for many hours and the chamber had gradually grown quite dark, when he was roused by a low knocking at the outer door.

He hastened down, and opening it, saw by the light of a lamp which he had seized upon the way, a female figure crouching in the portal. It hurried swiftly past him and glided up the stairs. He looked out for pursuers. There were none in sight. No, not one.

He was inclined to think it a vision of his own brain when suddenly a vague suspicion of the truth flashed upon his mind. He barred the door and hastened wildly back. Yes, there she was – there, in the chamber he had quitted, – there in her old innocent happy home, so changed that none but he could trace one gleam of what she had been – there upon her knees – with her hands clasped in agony and shame before her burning face.

'My God, my God!' she cried, 'now strike me dead! Though I have brought death and shame and sorrow on this roof, oh, let me die at home in mercy!'

There was no tear upon her face then, but she trembled and glanced around the chamber. Everything was in its old place. Her bed looked as if she had risen from it but that morning. The sight of these familiar objects marking the dear remembrance in which she had been held, and the blight she had brought upon herself was more than the woman's better nature that had carried her there, could bear. She wept and fell upon the ground.

A rumour was spread about, in a few days' time, that the Bowyer's cruel daughter had come home, and that Master Graham had given her lodging in his house. It was rumoured too that he had resigned her fortune, in order that she might bestow it in acts of charity, and that he had vowed to guard her in her solitude, but that they were never to see each other more. These rumours greatly incensed all virtuous wives and daughters in the ward, especially when they appeared to receive some corroboration from the circumstance of Master Graham taking up his abode in another tenement hard by. The estimation in which he was held, however, forbade any questioning on the subject, and as the Bowyer's house was close shut up, and nobody came forth when public shows and festivities were in progress, or to flaunt in the public walks, or to buy new fashions at the mercers'[42] booths, all the well-conducted females agreed among themselves that there could be no woman there.

These reports had scarcely died away when the wonder of every good citizen, male and female, was utterly absorbed and swallowed up by a Royal Proclamation, in which her Majesty, strongly censuring the practice of wearing long Spanish rapiers of preposterous length (as being a bullying and swaggering custom, tending to bloodshed and public disorder) commanded that on a particular day therein named, certain grave citizens should repair to the city gates, and there, in public, break all rapiers worn or carried by persons claiming admission, that exceeded, though it were only by a quarter of an inch, three standard feet in length.

Royal Proclamations usually take their course, let the public wonder never so much. On the appointed day two citizens of high repute took up their stations at each of the gates, attended by a party of the city guard: the main body to enforce the Queen's will, and take custody of all such rebels (if any) as might have the temerity to dispute it: and a few to bear the standard measures and instruments for reducing all unlawful sword-blades to the prescribed dimensions. In pursuance of these arrangements, Master Graham and another were posted at Lud Gate,[43] on the hill before Saint Paul's.

A pretty numerous company were gathered together at this spot, for, besides the officers in attendance to enforce the proclamation, there was a motley crowd of lookers-on of various degrees, who raised from time to time such shouts and cries as the circumstances called forth. A spruce young courtier was the first who approached; he unsheathed a weapon of burnished steel that shone and glistened in the sun, and handed it with the newest air to the officer, who, finding it exactly three feet long, returned it with a bow. Thereupon the gallant raised his hat and crying, 'God save the Queen,' passed on amidst the plaudits of the mob. Then came another – a better courtier still – who wore a blade but two feet long, whereat the people laughed, much to the disparagement of his honour's dignity. Then came a third, a sturdy old officer of the army, girded with a rapier at least a foot and a half beyond her Majesty's pleasure; at him they raised a great shout and most of the spectators (but especially those who were armourers or cutlers) laughed very heartily at the breakage which would ensue. But they were disappointed, for the old campaigner, coolly unbuckling his sword and bidding his servant carry it home again, passed through unarmed, to the great indignation of all the beholders. They relieved themselves in some degree by hooting a tall blustering fellow with a prodigious weapon, who stopped short on coming in sight of the preparations, and after a little consideration turned back again; but all this time no rapier had been broken although it was high noon, and all cavaliers of any quality or appearance were taking their way towards Saint Paul's churchyard.

During these proceedings Master Graham had stood apart, strictly confining himself to the duty imposed upon him, and taking little heed of anything beyond. He stepped forward now as a richly dressed gentleman on foot, followed by a single attendant, was seen advancing up the hill.

As this person drew nearer, the crowd stopped their clamour and bent forward with eager looks. Master Graham standing alone in the gateway, and the stranger coming slowly towards him, they seemed, as it were, set face to face. The nobleman (for he looked one) had a haughty and disdainful air, which bespoke the slight estimation in which he held the citizen. The citizen on the other hand preserved the resolute bearing of one who was not to be frowned down or daunted, and who cared very little for any nobility but that of worth and manhood. It was perhaps some consciousness on the part of each, of these feelings in the other, that infused a more stern expression into their regards as they came closer together.

'Your rapier worthy Sir!'

At the instant that he pronounced these words Graham started, and falling back some paces, laid his hand upon the dagger in his belt.

'You are the man whose horse I used to hold before the Bowyer's door? You are that man? Speak!'

'Out, you 'prentice hound!' said the other.

'You are he! I know you well now!' cried Graham. 'Let no man step between us two, or I shall be his murderer.' With that he drew his dagger and rushed in upon him.

The stranger had drawn his weapon from the scabbard ready for the scrutiny, before a word was spoken. He made a thrust at his assailant, but the dagger which Graham clutched in his left hand being the dirk[44] in use at that time for parrying such blows promptly turned the point aside. They closed. The dagger fell rattling upon the ground, and Graham wresting his adversary's sword from his grasp, plunged it through his heart. As he drew it out it snapped in two, leaving a fragment in the dead man's body.

All this passed so swiftly that the by-standers looked on without an effort to interfere; but the man was no sooner down than an uproar broke forth which rent the air. The attendant rushing through the gate proclaimed that his master, a nobleman, had been set upon and slain by a citizen; the word quickly spread from mouth to mouth; Saint Paul's cathedral and every bookshop[45] ordinary[46] and smoking house in the churchyard poured out its stream of cavaliers and their followers, who, mingling together in a dense tumultuous body, struggled, sword in hand, towards the spot.

With equal impetuosity and stimulating each other by loud cries and shouts the citizens and common people took up the quarrel on their side and encircling Master Graham a hundred deep, forced him from the gate. In vain he waved the broken sword above his head, crying that he would die on London's threshold for their sacred homes. They bore him on, and ever keeping him in the midst so that no man could attack him, fought their way into the city.

The clash of swords and roar of voices, the dust and heat and pressure, the trampling under foot of men, the distracted looks and shrieks of women at the windows above as they recognised their relatives or lovers in the crowd, the rapid tolling of alarm bells, the furious rage and passion of the scene were fearful. Those who being on the outskirts of each crowd could use their weapons with effect fought desperately, while those behind maddened with baffled rage struck at each other over the heads of those before them, and crushed their own fellows. Wherever the broken sword was seen above the people's heads, towards that spot the cavaliers made a new rush. Every one of these charges was marked by sudden gaps in the throng where men were trodden down, but as fast as they were made, the tide swept over them and still the multitude pressed on again, a confused mass of swords clubs staves broken plumes fragments of rich cloaks and doublets[47] and angry bleeding faces, all mixed up together in inextricable disorder.

The design of the people was to force Master Graham to take refuge in his dwelling, and to defend it until the authorities could interfere or they could gain time for parley. But either from ignorance or in the confusion of the moment they stopped at his old house which was closely shut. Some time was lost in beating the doors open and passing him to the front. About a score of the boldest of the other party threw themselves into the torrent while this was being done, and reaching the door at the same moment with himself cut him off from his defenders.

'I never will turn in such a righteous cause so help me Heaven!' cried Graham in a voice that at last made itself heard, and confronting them as he spoke. 'Least of all will I turn upon this threshold which owes its desolation to such men as ye. I give no quarter, and I will have none! Strike!'

For a moment they stood at bay. At that moment a shot from an unseen hand, apparently fired by some person who had gained access to one of the opposite houses, struck Graham in the brain and he fell dead. A low wail was heard in the air — many people in the concourse cried that they had seen a spirit glide across the little casement window of the Bowyer's house—

A dead silence succeeded. After a short time some of the flushed and heated throng lay down their arms and softly carried the body within doors. Others fell off or slunk away in knots of two or three, others whispered together in groups, and before a numerous guard which then rode up could muster in the street it was nearly empty.

Those who carried Master Graham to the bed upstairs were shocked to see a woman lying beneath the window with her hands clasped together. After trying to recover her in vain, they laid her near the citizen who still retained, tightly grasped in his right hand, the first and last sword that was broken that day at Lud Gate.

The Giant uttered these concluding words with sudden precipitation, and on the instant the strange light which had filled the hall, faded away. Joe Toddyhigh glanced involuntarily at the eastern window and saw the first pale gleam of morning. He turned his head again towards the other window in which the

Giants had been seated. It was empty. The cask of wine was gone, and he could dimly make out that the two great figures stood mute and motionless upon their pedestals.

After rubbing his eyes and wondering for full half an hour, during which time he observed morning come creeping on apace, he yielded to the drowsiness which overpowered him and fell into a refreshing slumber. When he awoke it was broad day; the building was open, and workmen were busily engaged in removing the vestiges of last night's feast.

Stealing gently down the little stairs and assuming the air of some early lounger who had dropped in from the street, he walked up to the foot of each pedestal in turn, and attentively examined the figure it supported. There could be no doubt about the features of either; he recollected the exact expression they had worn at different passages of their conversation, and recognized in every line and lineament the Giants of the night. Assured that it was no vision but that he had heard and seen with his own proper senses, he walked forth, determining at all hazards to conceal himself in the Guildhall again that evening. He further resolved to sleep all day, so that he might be very wakeful and vigilant, and above all that he might take notice of the figures at the precise moment of their becoming animated and subsiding into their old state, which he greatly reproached himself for not having done already.

## CORRESPONDENCE

### To Master Humphrey

'Sir,

'Before you proceed any further in your account of your friends and what you say and do when you meet together, excuse me if I proffer my claim to be elected to one of the vacant chairs in that old room of yours. Don't reject me without full consideration for if you do you'll be sorry for it afterwards – you will upon my life.

'I inclose my card, sir, in this letter. I never was ashamed of my name, and I never shall be. I am considered a devilish gentlemanly fellow, and I act up to the character. If you want a reference, ask any of the men at our club. Ask any fellow who goes there to write his letters, what sort of conversation mine is. Ask him if he thinks I have the sort of voice that will suit your deaf friend and make him hear if he can hear anything at all. Ask the servants what they think of me. There's not a rascal among 'em sir, but will tremble to hear my name. That reminds me – don't you say too much about that housekeeper of yours; it's a low subject, damned low.

'I tell you what sir. If you vote me into one of those empty chairs, you'll have among you a man with a fund of gentlemanly information that'll rather astonish you. I can let you into a few anecdotes about some fine women of title, that are quite high life sir – the tip-top sort of thing. I know the name of every man who has been out on an affair of honour within the last five-and-twenty years; I know the private particulars of every cross and squabble that has taken place upon the turf, at the gaming-table or elsewhere, during the whole of that time. I have been called the gentlemanly chronicle. You may consider yourself a lucky dog; upon my soul you may congratulate yourself, though I say so.

'It's an uncommon good notion that of yours, not letting anybody know where you live. I have tried it, but there has always been an anxiety respecting me which has found me out. Your deaf friend is a cunning fellow to keep his name so close. I have tried that too, but have always failed. I shall be proud to make his acquaintance – tell him so, with my compliments.

'You must have been a queer fellow when you were a child, confounded queer. It's odd all that about the picture in your first paper, – prosy, but told in a devilish gentlemanly sort of way. In places like that, I could come in with great effect with a touch of life – Don't you feel that?

'I am anxiously waiting for your next paper to know whether your friends live upon the premises, and at your expense, which I take it for granted is the case. If I am right in this impression I know a charming fellow (an excellent companion and most delightful company) who will be proud to join you. Some years ago he seconded a great many prize-fighters and once fought an amateur match himself; since then, he has driven several mails, broken at different periods all the lamps on the right-hand side of Oxford-street, and six times carried away every bell-handle[48] in Bloomsbury-square, besides turning off the gas in various thoroughfares. In point of gentlemanliness he is unrivalled, and I should say that next to myself he is of all men the best suited to your purpose.

'Expecting your reply,

'I am,

'&c. &c.'

---

Master Humphrey informs this gentleman that his application, both as it concerns himself and his friend, is rejected.

*No. 3 (18 April 1840)*

## MASTER HUMPHREY FROM HIS CLOCK-SIDE IN THE CHIMNEY-CORNER

My old companion tells me it is midnight. The fire glows brightly, crackling with a sharp and cheerful sound as if it loved to burn. The merry cricket on the hearth (my constant visitor) this ruddy blaze, my clock, and I, seem to share the world among us, and to be the only things awake. The wind, high and boisterous but now, has died away and hoarsely mutters in its sleep. I love all times and seasons each in its turn, and am apt perhaps to think the present one the best, but past or coming I always love this peaceful time of night, when long buried thoughts favoured by the gloom and silence steal from their graves and haunt the scenes of faded happiness and hope.

The popular faith in ghosts has a remarkable affinity with the whole current of our thoughts at such an hour as this, and seems to be their necessary and natural consequence. For who can wonder that man should feel a vague belief in tales of disembodied spirits wandering through those places which they once dearly affected, when he himself, scarcely less separated from his old world than they, is for ever lingering upon past emotions and by-gone times, and hovering, the ghost of his former self, about the places and people that warmed his heart of old? It is thus that at this quiet hour I haunt the house where I was born, the rooms I used to tread, the scenes of my infancy, my boyhood and my youth; it is thus that I prowl around my buried treasure (though not of gold or silver) and mourn my loss; it is thus that I revisit the ashes of extinguished fires, and take my silent stand at old bedsides. If my spirit should ever glide back to this chamber when my body is mingled with the dust, it will but follow the course it often took in the old man's lifetime and add but one more change to the subjects of its contemplation.

In all my idle speculations I am greatly assisted by various legends connected with my venerable house, which are current in the neighbourhood, and are so numerous that there is scarce a cupboard or corner that has not some dismal story of its own. When I first entertained thoughts of becoming its tenant I was assured that it was haunted from roof to cellar, and I believe the bad opinion in which my neighbours once held me had its rise in my not being torn to pieces or at least distracted with terror on the night I took possession: in either of which cases I should doubtless have arrived by a short cut at the very summit of popularity.

But traditions and rumours all taken into account, who so abets me in every fancy and chimes with my every thought, as my dear deaf friend; and how often have I cause to bless the day that brought us two together! Of all days in the year I rejoice to think that it should have been Christmas Day, with which from childhood we associate something friendly, hearty, and sincere.

I had walked out to cheer myself with the happiness of others, and in the little tokens of festivity and rejoicing of which the streets and houses present so many upon that day, had lost some hours. Now I stopped to look at a merry party hurrying through the snow on foot to their place of meeting, and now turned back to see a whole coachful of children safely deposited at the welcome house. At one time, I admired how carefully the working-man carried the baby in its gaudy hat and feathers, and how his wife, trudging patiently on behind, forgot even her care of her gay clothes, in exchanging greetings with the child as it crowed and laughed over the father's shoulder; at another, I pleased myself with some passing scene of gallantry or courtship, and was glad to believe that for a season half the world of poverty was gay.

As the day closed in, I still rambled through the streets, feeling a companionship in the bright fires that cast their warm reflection on the windows as I passed, and losing all sense of my own loneliness in imagining the sociality and kind-fellowship that everywhere prevailed. At length I happened to stop before a Tavern and encountering a Bill of Fare in the window, it all at once brought it into my head to wonder what kind of people dined alone in Taverns upon Christmas Day.

Solitary men are accustomed, I suppose, unconsciously to look upon solitude as their own peculiar property. I had sat alone in my room on many, many, anniversaries of this great holiday, and had never regarded it but as one of universal assemblage and rejoicing. I had expected, and with an aching heart, a crowd of prisoners and beggars, but *these* were not the men for whom the Tavern doors were open. Had they any customers, or was it a mere form? a form no doubt.

Trying to feel quite sure of this I walked away, but before I had gone many paces, I stopped and looked back. There was a provoking air of business in the lamp above the door, which I could not overcome. I began to be afraid there might be many customers – young men perhaps struggling with the world, utter strangers in this great place, whose friends lived at a long distance off, and whose means were too slender to enable them to make the journey. The supposition gave rise to so many distressing little pictures that in preference to carrying them home with me, I determined to encounter the realities. So I turned, and walked in.

I was at once glad and sorry to find that there was only one person in the dining-room; glad to know that there were not more, and sorry to think that he should be there by himself. He did not look so old as I, but like me he was advanced in life, and his hair was nearly white. Though I made more noise in entering and seating myself than was quite necessary, with the view of attracting his attention and saluting him in the good old form of that time of year, he did not raise his head but sat with it resting on his hand, musing over his half-finished meal.

I called for something which would give me an excuse for remaining in the room (I had dined early as my housekeeper was engaged at night to partake of some friend's good cheer) and sat where I could observe without intruding on him. After a time he looked up. He was aware that somebody had entered, but could see very little of me as I sat in the shade and he in the light. He was sad and thoughtful, and I forbore to trouble him by speaking.

Let me believe that it was something better than curiosity which riveted my attention and impelled me strongly towards this gentleman. I never saw so patient and kind a face. He should have been surrounded by friends, and yet here he sat dejected and alone when all men had their friends about them. As often as he roused himself from his reverie he would fall into it again, and it was plain that whatever were the subject of his thoughts they were of a melancholy kind, and would not be controlled.

He was not used to solitude. I was sure of that, for I know by myself that if he had been, his manner would have been different and he would have taken some slight interest in the arrival of another. I could not fail to mark that he had no appetite – that he tried to eat in vain – that time after time the plate was pushed away, and he relapsed into his former posture.

His mind was wandering among old Christmas Days, I thought. Many of them sprung up together, not with a long gap between each but in unbroken succession like days of the week. It was a great change to find himself for the first time (I quite settled that it *was* the first) in an empty silent room with no soul to care for. I could not help following him in imagination through crowds of pleasant faces, and then coming back to that dull place with its bough of mistletoe sickening in the gas, and sprigs of holly parched up already by a Simoom[49] of roast and boiled. The very waiter had gone home, and his representative, a poor lean hungry man, was keeping Christmas in his jacket.

I grew still more interested in my friend. His dinner done, a decanter of wine was placed before him. It remained untouched for a long time, but at length with a quivering hand he filled a glass and raised it to his lips. Some tender wish to which he had been accustomed to give utterance on that day, or some beloved name that he had been used to pledge, trembled upon them at the moment. He put it down very hastily – took it up once more – again put it down – pressed his hand upon his face – yes – and tears stole down his cheeks, I am certain.

Without pausing to consider whether I did right or wrong, I stepped across the room, and sitting down beside him laid my hand gently on his arm.

'My friend,' I said, 'forgive me if I beseech you to take comfort and consolation from the lips of an old man. I will not preach to you what I have not practised, indeed. Whatever be your grief, be of a good heart – be of a good heart, pray!'

'I see that you speak earnestly,' he replied, 'and kindly I am very sure, but—'

I nodded my head to show that I understood what he would say, for I had already gathered from a certain fixed expression in his face and from the attention with which he watched me while I spoke, that his sense of hearing was destroyed. 'There should be a freemasonry[50] between us,' said I, pointing from himself to me to explain my meaning – 'if not in our gray hairs, at least in our misfortunes. You see that I am but a poor cripple.'

I have never felt so happy under my affliction since the trying moment of my first becoming conscious of it, as when he took my hand in his with a smile that has lighted my path in life from that day, and we sat down side by side.

This was the beginning of my friendship with the deaf gentleman, and when was ever the slight and easy service of a kind word in season, repaid by such attachment and devotion as he has shown to me!

He produced a little set of tablets and a pencil to facilitate our conversation, on that our first acquaintance, and I well remember how awkward and constrained I was in writing down my

share of the dialogue, and how easily he guessed my meaning
before I had written half of what I had to say. He told me in a
faltering voice that he had not been accustomed to be alone on
that day – that it had always been a little festival with him – and
seeing that I glanced at his dress in the expectation that he wore
mourning, he added hastily that it was not that; if it had been,
he thought he could have borne it better. From that time to the
present we have never touched upon this theme. Upon every
return of the same day we have been together, and although we
make it our annual custom to drink to each other hand in hand
after dinner, and to recall with affectionate garrulity every
circumstance of our first meeting, we always avoid this one as if
by mutual consent.

Meantime we have gone on strengthening in our friendship
and regard and forming an attachment which, I trust and
believe, will only be interrupted by death, to be renewed in
another existence. I scarcely know how we communicate as we
do, but he has long since ceased to be deaf to me. He is
frequently the companion of my walks, and even in crowded
streets replies to my slightest look or gesture as though he could
read my thoughts. From the vast number of objects which pass
in rapid succession before our eyes, we frequently select the
same for some particular notice or remark, and when one of
these little coincidences occurs I cannot describe the pleasure
that animates my friend, or the beaming countenance he will
preserve for half an hour afterwards at least.

He is a great thinker from living so much within himself, and
having a lively imagination has a facility of conceiving and
enlarging upon odd ideas which renders him invaluable to our
little body, and greatly astonishes our two friends. His powers
in this respect, are much assisted by a large pipe which he
assures us once belonged to a German Student.[51] Be this as it
may, it has undoubtedly a very ancient and mysterious appearance, and is of such capacity that it takes three hours and a half
to smoke it out. I have reason to believe that my barber who is
the chief authority of a knot of gossips who congregate every
evening at a small tobacconist's hard by, has related anecdotes
of this pipe and the grim figures that are carved upon its bowl
at which all the smokers in the neighbourhood have stood
aghast, and I know that my housekeeper while she holds it in
high veneration, has a superstitious feeling connected with it

which would render her exceedingly unwilling to be left alone in its company after dark.

Whatever sorrow my deaf friend has known, and whatever grief may linger in some secret corner of his heart, he is now a cheerful, placid, happy creature. Misfortune can never have fallen upon such a man but for some good purpose, and when I see its traces in his gentle nature and his earnest feeling, I am the less disposed to murmur at such trials as I may have undergone myself. With regard to the pipe, I have a theory of my own; I cannot help thinking that it is in some manner connected with the event that brought us together, for I remember that it was a long time before he even talked about it; that when he did, he grew reserved and melancholy; and that it was a long time yet before he brought it forth. I have no curiosity, however, upon this subject, for I know that it promotes his tranquillity and

comfort, and I need no other inducement to regard it with my utmost favour.

Such is the deaf gentleman. I can call up his figure now, clad in sober grey, and seated in the chimney corner. As he puffs out the smoke from his favourite pipe he casts a look on me brimful of cordiality and friendship, and says all manner of kind and genial things in a cheerful smile; then he raises his eyes to my clock which is just about to strike, and glancing from it to me and back again, seems to divide his heart between us. For myself, it is not too much to say that I would gladly part with one of my poor limbs, could he but hear the old clock's voice.

Of our two friends, the first has been all his life one of that easy wayward truant class whom the world is accustomed to designate as nobody's enemies but their own. Bred to a profession for which he never qualified himself, and reared in the expectation of a fortune he has never inherited, he has undergone every vicissitude of which such an existence is capable. He and his younger brother, both orphans from their childhood, were educated by a wealthy relative who taught them to expect an equal division of his property: but too indolent to court, and too honest to flatter, the elder gradually lost ground in the affections of a capricious old man, and the younger, who did not fail to improve his opportunity, now triumphs in the possession of enormous wealth. His triumph is to hoard it in solitary wretchedness, and probably to feel with the expenditure of every shilling a greater pang than the loss of his whole inheritance ever cost his brother.

Jack Redburn – he was Jack Redburn at the first little school he went to where every other child was mastered and surnamed, and he has been Jack Redburn all his life or he would perhaps have been a richer man by this time – has been an inmate of my house these eight years past. He is my librarian, secretary, steward, and first minister: director of all my affairs and inspector-general of my household. He is something of a musician, something of an author, something of an actor, something of a painter, very much of a carpenter, and an extraordinary gardener: having had all his life a wonderful aptitude for learning everything that was of no use to him. He is remarkably fond of children and is the best and kindest nurse in sickness that ever drew the breath of life. He has mixed with every grade of society and known the utmost distress, but there never was a less selfish, a more tender-hearted a more enthusiastic or a more guileless man, and I dare say if few have done less good fewer still have done less harm in the world than he. By what chance Nature forms such whimsical jumbles I don't know, but I do know that she sends them among us very often and that the king of the whole race is Jack Redburn.

I should be puzzled to say how old he is. His health is none of the best, and he wears a quantity of iron-grey hair which shades his face and gives it rather a worn appearance; but we consider him quite a young fellow notwithstanding, and if a youthful spirit surviving the roughest contact with the world confers upon its possessor any title to be considered young, then he is a mere child. The only interruptions to his careless cheerfulness are on a wet Sunday when he is apt to be unusually religious and solemn, and sometimes of an evening when he has been blowing a very slow tune on the flute. On these last-named occasions he is apt to incline towards the mysterious or the terrible. As a specimen of his powers in this mood, I refer my readers to the extract from the clock-case which follows this paper; he brought it to me not long ago at midnight and informed me that the main incident had been suggested by a dream of the night before.

His apartments are two cheerful rooms looking towards the garden, and one of his great delights is to arrange and re-arrange the furniture in these chambers and put it in every possible variety of position. During the whole time he has been here, I do not think he has slept for two nights running with the head of his bed in the same place, and every time he moves it, is to be the last. My housekeeper was at first well nigh distracted by these frequent changes but she has become quite reconciled to them by degrees and has so fallen in with his humour that they often consult together with great gravity upon the next final alteration. Whatever his arrangements are, however, they are always a pattern of neatness, and every one of the manifold articles connected with his manifold occupations, is to be found in its own particular place. Until within the last two or three years he was subject to an occasional fit (which usually came upon him in very fine weather) under the influence of which he would dress himself with peculiar care, and going out under pretence of taking a walk, disappear for several days together.

At length after the interval between each outbreak of this disorder had gradually grown longer and longer, it wholly disappeared, and now he seldom stirs abroad except to stroll out a little way on a summer's evening. Whether he yet mistrusts his own constancy in this respect and is therefore afraid to wear a coat I know not, but we seldom see him in any other upper garment than an old spectral-looking dressing gown with very disproportionate pockets, full of a miscellaneous collection of odd matters which he picks up wherever he can lay his hands upon them.

Everything that is a favourite with our friend is a favourite with us, and thus it happens that the fourth among us is Mr Owen Miles, a most worthy gentleman who had treated Jack with great kindness before my deaf friend and I encountered him by an accident to which I may refer on some future occasion. Mr Miles was once a very rich merchant, but receiving a severe shock in the death of his wife, he retired from business and devoted himself to a quite unostentatious life. He is an excellent man of thoroughly sterling character: not of quick apprehension, and not without some amusing prejudices, which I shall leave to their own development. He holds us all in profound veneration, but Jack Redburn he esteems as a kind of pleasant wonder, that he may venture to approach familiarly. He believes, not only that no man ever lived who could do so many things as Jack, but that no man ever lived who could do anything so well, and he never calls my attention to any of his ingenious proceedings but he whispers in my ear, nudging me at the same time with his elbow – 'If he had only made it his trade sir – if he had only made it his trade!' –

They are inseparable companions; one would almost suppose that although Mr Miles never by any chance does anything in the way of assistance, Jack could do nothing without him. Whether he is reading, writing, painting, carpentering, gardening, flute-playing, or what not, there is Mr Miles beside him, buttoned up to the chin in his blue coat, and looking on with a face of incredulous delight as though he could not credit the testimony of his own senses and had a misgiving that no man could be so clever but in a dream.

These are my friends; I have now introduced myself and them.

# THE CLOCK-CASE

## A Confession Found in a Prison in the Time of
## Charles the Second

I held a lieutenant's commission in His Majesty's army and served abroad in the campaigns of 1677 and 1678. The treaty of Nimeguen[52] being concluded, I returned home, and retiring from the service withdrew to a small estate lying a few miles east of London, which I had recently acquired in right of my wife.

This is the last night I have to live, and I will set down the naked truth without disguise. I was never a brave man, and had always been from my childhood of a secret sullen distrustful nature. I speak of myself as if I had passed from the world, for while I write this my grave is digging and my name is written in the black book of death.

Soon after my return to England, my only brother was seized with mortal illness. This circumstance gave me slight or no pain, for since we had been men we had associated but very little together. He was open-hearted and generous, handsomer than I, more accomplished, and generally beloved. Those who sought my acquaintance abroad or at home because they were friends of his, seldom attached themselves to me long, and would usually say in our first conversation that they were surprised to find two brothers so unlike in their manners and appearance. It was my habit to lead them on to this avowal, for I knew what comparisons they must draw between us, and having a rankling envy in my heart, I sought to justify it to myself.

We had married two sisters. This additional tie between us, as it may appear to some, only estranged us the more. His wife knew me well. I never struggled with any secret jealousy or gall when she was present but that woman knew it as well as I did. I never raised my eyes at such times but I found hers fixed upon me; I never bent them on the ground or looked another way, but I felt that she overlooked me always. It was an inexpressible relief to me when we quarrelled, and a greater relief still when I heard abroad that she was dead. It seems to me now as if some strange and terrible foreshadowing of what has happened since, must have hung over us then. I was afraid of her, she haunted me, her fixed and steady look comes back upon me now like the memory of a dark dream and makes my blood run cold.

She died shortly after giving birth to a child – a boy. When my brother knew that all hope of his own recovery was past, he called my wife to his bedside and confided this orphan, a child of four years old, to her protection. He bequeathed to him all the property he had, and willed that in case of the child's death it should pass to my wife as the only acknowledgement he could make her for her care and love. He exchanged a few brotherly words with me deploring our long separation, and being exhausted, fell into a slumber from which he never awoke.

We had no children, and as there had been a strong affection between the sisters, and my wife had almost supplied the place of a mother to this boy, she loved him as if he had been her own. The child was ardently attached to her; but he was his mother's image in face and spirit and always mistrusted me.

I can scarcely fix the date when the feeling first came upon me, but I soon began to be uneasy when this child was by. I never roused myself from some moody train of thought but I marked him looking at me: not with mere childish wonder, but with something of the purpose and meaning that I had so often noted in his mother. It was no effort of my fancy, founded on close resemblance of feature and expression. I never could look the boy down.[53] He feared me, but seemed by some instinct to despise me while he did so; and even when he drew back beneath my gaze – as he would when we were alone, to get nearer to the door – he would keep his bright eyes upon me still.

Perhaps I hide the truth from myself, but I do not think that when this began, I meditated to do him any wrong. I may have thought how serviceable his inheritance would be to us, and may have wished him dead, but I believe I had no thought of compassing his death. Neither did the idea come upon me at once, but by very slow degrees, presenting itself at first in dim shapes at a very great distance, as men may think of an earthquake or the last day – then drawing nearer and nearer and losing something of its horror and improbability – then coming to be part and parcel, nay nearly the whole sum and substance of my daily thoughts, and resolving itself into a question of means and safety; not of doing or abstaining from the deed.

While this was going on within me, I never could bear that

the child should see me looking at him, and yet I was under a fascination which made it a kind of business with me to contemplate his slight and fragile figure and think how easily it might be done. Sometimes I would steal up stairs and watch him as he slept, but usually I hovered in the garden near the window of the room in which he learnt his little tasks, and there as he sat upon a low seat beside my wife, I would peer at him for hours together from behind a tree: starting like the guilty wretch I was at every rustling of a leaf, and still gliding back to look and start again.

Hard by our cottage, but quite out of sight, and (if there were any wind astir) of hearing too, was a deep sheet of water. I spent days in shaping with my pocket-knife a rough model of a boat, which I finished at last and dropped in the child's way. Then I withdrew to a secret place which he must pass if he stole away alone to swim this bauble, and lurked there for his coming. He came neither that day nor the next, though I waited from noon till nightfall. I was sure that I had him in my net, for I had heard him prattling of the toy, and knew that in his infant pleasure he kept it by his side in bed. I felt no weariness or fatigue, but waited patiently, and on the third day he passed me, running joyously along, with his silken hair streaming in the wind and he singing – God have mercy upon me! – singing a merry ballad – who could hardly lisp the words.

I stole down after him, creeping under certain shrubs which grow in that place, and none but devils know with what terror I, a strong full-grown man, tracked the footsteps of that baby as he approached the water's brink. I was close upon him, had sunk upon my knee and raised my hand to thrust him in, when he saw my shadow in the stream and turned him round.

His mother's ghost was looking from his eyes. The sun burst forth from behind a cloud: it shone in the bright sky, the glistening earth, the clear water, the sparkling drops of rain upon the leaves. There were eyes in everything. The whole great universe of light was there to see the murder done. I know not what he said; he came of bold and manly blood, and child as he was, he did not crouch or fawn upon me. I heard him cry that he would try to love me – not that he did – and then I saw him running back towards the house. The next I saw was my own sword naked in my hand and he lying at my feet stark dead – dabbled here and there with blood but otherwise no different from what I had seen him in his sleep – in the same attitude too, with his cheek resting upon his little hand.

I took him in my arms and laid him – very gently now that he was dead – in a thicket. My wife was from home that day and would not return until the next. Our bedroom window, the only sleeping room on that side of the house, was but a few feet from the ground, and I resolved to descend from it at night and bury him in the garden. I had no thought that I had failed in my design, no thought that the water would be dragged and nothing found, that the money must now lie waste since I must encourage the idea that the child was lost or stolen. All my thoughts were bound up and knotted together, in the one absorbing necessity of hiding what I had done.

How I felt when they came to tell me that the child was missing, when I ordered scouts in all directions, when I gasped and trembled at every one's approach, no tongue can tell or mind of man conceive. I buried him that night. When I parted the boughs and looked into the dark thicket, there was a glow-worm shining like the visible spirit of God upon the murdered child. I glanced down into his grave when I had placed him there and still it gleamed upon his breast: an eye of fire looking up to Heaven in supplication to the stars that watched me at my work.

I had to meet my wife, and break the news, and give her hope that the child would soon be found. All this I did – with some appearance, I suppose, of being sincere, for I was the object of no suspicion. This done, I sat at the bedroom window all day long and watched the spot where the dreadful secret lay.

It was in a piece of ground which had been dug up to be newly turfed, and which I had chosen on that account as the traces of my spade were less likely to attract attention. The men who laid down the grass must have thought me mad. I called to them continually to expedite their work, ran out and worked beside them, trod down the turf with my feet, and hurried them with frantic eagerness. They had finished their task before night, and then I thought myself comparatively safe.

I slept – not as men do who wake refreshed and cheerful, but I did sleep, passing from vague and shadowy dreams of being hunted down, to visions of the plot of grass, through which now a hand and now a foot and now the head itself was starting out. At this point I always woke and stole to the window to make sure that it was not really so. That done I crept to bed again, and thus I spent the night in fits and starts, getting up and lying down full twenty times and dreaming the same dream over and over again – which was far worse than lying awake, for every dream had a whole night's suffering of its own. Once I thought the child was alive and that I had never tried to kill him. To wake from that dream was the most dreadful agony of all.

The next day I sat at the window again, never once taking my eyes from the place, which, although it was covered by the grass, was as plain to me – its shape, its size, its depth, its jagged sides, and all – as if it had been open to the light of day. When a servant walked across it, I felt as if he must sink in; when he had passed I looked to see that his feet had not worn the edges. If a bird lighted there, I was in terror lest by some tremendous interposition it should be instrumental in the discovery; if a breath of air sighed across it, to me it whispered murder. There was not a sight or sound how ordinary mean or unimportant soever, but was fraught with fear. And in this state of ceaseless watching I spent three days.

On the fourth, there came to the gate one who had served with me abroad, accompanied by a brother officer of his whom I had never seen. I felt that I could not bear to be out of sight of the place. It was a summer evening, and I bade my people take a table and a flask of wine into the garden. Then I sat down *with my chair upon the grave*, and being assured that nobody could disturb it now, without my knowledge, tried to drink and talk.

They hoped that my wife was well – that she was not obliged to keep her chamber – that they had not frightened her away. What could I do but tell them with a faltering tongue about the child? The officer whom I did not know was a down-looking man and kept his eyes upon the ground while I was speaking. Even that terrified me! I could not divest myself of the idea that he saw something there which caused him to suspect the truth. I asked him hurriedly if he supposed that – and stopped. 'That the child has been murdered?' said he, looking mildly at me. 'Oh, no! what could a man gain by murdering a poor child?' *I* could have told him what a man gained by such a deed, no one better, but I held my peace and shivered as with an ague.

Mistaking my emotion they were endeavouring to cheer me

with the hope that the boy would certainly be found – great cheer that was for me – when we heard a low deep howl, and presently there sprung over the wall two great dogs, who bounding into the garden repeated the baying sound we had heard before.

'Blood-hounds!' cried my visitors.

What need to tell me that! I had never seen one of that kind in all my life, but I knew what they were and for what purpose they had come. I grasped the elbows of my chair, and neither spoke nor moved.

'They are of the genuine breed,' said the man whom I had known abroad, 'and being out for exercise have no doubt escaped from their keeper.'

Both he and his friend turned to look at the dogs, who with their noses to the ground moved restlessly about, running to and fro, and up and down, and across, and round in circles, careering about like wild things, and all this time taking no notice of us, but ever and again lifting their heads and repeating the yell we had heard already, then dropping their noses to the ground again and tracking earnestly here and there. They now began to snuff the earth more eagerly than they had done yet, and although they were still very restless, no longer beat about in such wide circuits, but kept near to one spot, and constantly diminished the distance between themselves and me.

At last they came up close to the great chair on which I sat, and raising their frightful howl once more, tried to tear away the wooden rails that kept them from the ground beneath. I saw how I looked, in the faces of the two who were with me.

'They scent some prey,' said they, both together.

'They scent no prey!' cried I.

'In Heaven's name move,' said the one I knew, very earnestly, 'or you will be torn to pieces.'

'Let them tear me limb from limb, I'll never leave this place!' cried I. 'Are dogs to hurry men to shameful deaths? Hew them down, cut them in pieces.'

'There is some foul mystery here!' said the officer whom I did not know, drawing his sword. 'In King Charles's name assist me to secure this man.'

They both set upon me and forced me away, though I fought and bit and caught at them like a madman. After a struggle they got me quietly between them, and then, my God! I saw the

angry dogs tearing at the earth and throwing it up into the air like water.

What more have I to tell? That I fell upon my knees and with chattering teeth confessed the truth and prayed to be forgiven. That I have since denied and now confess to it again. That I have been tried for the crime, found guilty, and sentenced. That I have not the courage to anticipate my doom or to bear up manfully against it. That I have no compassion, no consolation, no hope, no friend. That my wife has happily lost for the time those faculties which would enable her to know my misery or hers. That I am alone in this stone dungeon with my evil spirit, and that I die tomorrow!

## CORRESPONDENCE

Master Humphrey has been favoured with the following letter, written on strongly-scented paper, and sealed in light blue wax with the representation of two very plump doves, interchanging beaks. It does not commence with any of the usual forms of address, but begins as is here set forth.

Bath, Wednesday Night.

Heavens! into what an indiscretion do I suffer myself to be betrayed! To address these faltering lines to a total stranger, and that stranger one of a conflicting sex! – and yet I am precipitated into the abyss, and have no power of self snatchation (forgive me if I coin that phrase) from the yawning gulf before me.

Yes, I am writing to a man, but let me not think of that, for madness is in the thought. You will understand my feelings? Oh yes! I am sure you will! and you will respect them too, and not despise them – will you?

Let me be calm. That portrait – smiling as once he smiled on me – that cane dangling as I have seen it dangle from his hand I know not how oft – those legs that have glided through my nightly dreams and never stopped to speak – the perfectly gentlemanly though false original – can I be mistaken? oh no no.

Let me be calmer yet; I would be calm as coffins. You have published a letter from one whose likeness is engraved, but whose name (and wherefore?) is suppressed. Shall *I* breathe that name! Is it – but why ask when my heart tells me too truly that it is!

I would not upbraid him with his treachery, I would not remind him of those times when he plighted the most eloquent of vows, and procured from me a small pecuniary accommodation – and yet I would see him – see him did I say – *him* – alas! such is woman's nature. For as the poet beautifully says – but you will already have anticipated the sentiment. Is it not sweet? oh yes!

It was in this city (hallowed by the recollection) that I met him first, and assuredly if mortal happiness be recorded anywhere, then those rubbers with their three-and-sixpenny points are scored on tablets of celestial brass. He always held an honour – generally two. On that eventful night, we stood at eight.[54] He raised his eyes (luminous in their seductive sweetness) to my agitated face. '*Can* you?' said he, with peculiar meaning. I felt the gentle pressure of his foot on mine; our corns throbbed in unison. '*Can* you?' he said again, and every lineament of his expressive countenance added the words 'resist me?' I murmured 'No,' and fainted.

They said when I recovered, it was the weather. *I* said it was the nutmeg in the negus. How little did they suspect the truth! How little did they guess the deep mysterious meaning of that inquiry! He called next morning on his knees – I do not mean to say that he actually came in that position to the house door, but that he went down upon those joints directly the servant had retired. He brought some verses in his hat which he said were original, but which I have since found were Milton's. Likewise a little bottle labelled laudanum: also a pistol and a swordstick. He drew the latter, uncocked the former, and clicked the trigger of the pocket fire-arm. He had come, he said, to conquer or to die. He did not die. He wrested from me an avowal of my love, and let off the pistol out of a back window previous to partaking of a slight repast.

Faithless, inconstant man! How many ages seem to have elapsed since his unaccountable and perfidious disappearance! Could I still forgive him both that and the borrowed lucre that he promised to pay next week! Could I spurn him from my feet if he approached in penitence, and with a matrimonial object! Would the blandishing enchanter still weave his spells around me, or should I burst them all and turn away in coldness! I dare not trust my weakness with the thought.

My brain is in a whirl again. You know his address, his occupations, his mode of life, are acquainted perhaps with his inmost thoughts. You are a humane and philanthropic character – reveal all you know – all; but especially the street and number of his lodgings. The post is departing, the bellman rings – pray Heaven it be not the knell of love and hope to

BELINDA

P.S. Pardon the wanderings of a bad pen and a distracted mind. Address to the Post-office. The bellman rendered impatient by delay is ringing dreadfully in the passage.

P.P.S. I open this to say that the bellman is gone and that you must not expect it till the next post, so don't be surprised when you don't get it.

————

Master Humphrey does not feel himself at liberty to furnish his fair correspondent with the address of the gentleman in question, but he publishes her letter as a public appeal to his faith and gallantry.

## No. 5 (2 May 1840)

## MASTER HUMPHREY'S VISITOR

When I am in a thoughtful mood, I often succeed in diverting the current of some mournful reflections, by conjuring up a number of fanciful associations with the objects that surround me, and dwelling upon the scenes and characters they suggest.

I have been led by this habit to assign to every room in my house and every old staring portrait on its walls, a separate interest of its own. Thus, I am persuaded that a stately dame, terrible to behold in her rigid modesty, who hangs above the chimney-piece of my bedroom, is the former lady of the mansion. In the court-yard below, is a stone face of surpassing ugliness, which I have somehow – in a kind of jealousy, I am afraid – associated with her husband. Above my study, is a little room with ivy peeping through the lattice, from which I bring their daughter, a lovely girl of eighteen or nineteen years of age and dutiful in all respects save one, that one being her devoted attachment to a young gentleman on the stairs, whose grand-mother (degraded to a disused laundry in the garden) piques herself upon an old family quarrel and is the implacable enemy of their love. With such materials as these, I work out many a little drama, whose chief merit is, that I can bring it to a happy end at will; I have so many of them on hand, that if on my return home one of these evenings I were to find some bluff old wight[55] of two centuries ago comfortably seated in my easy chair, and a love-lorn damsel vainly appealing to his obdurate heart and leaning her white arm upon my clock itself, I verily believe I should only express my surprise that they had kept me waiting so long, and never honoured me with a call before.

I was, in such a mood as this, sitting in my garden yesterday morning under the shade of a favourite tree, revelling in all the bloom and brightness about me, and feeling every sense of hope and enjoyment quickened by this most beautiful season of Spring, when my meditations were interrupted by the unexpected appearance of my barber at the end of the walk, who I immediately saw was coming towards me with a hasty step that betokened something remarkable.

My barber is at all times a very brisk, bustling, active little man – for he is, as it were, chubby all over, without being stout or unwieldy – but yesterday his alacrity was so very uncommon that it quite took me by surprise. Nor could I fail to observe when he came up to me, that his grey eyes were twinkling in a most extraordinary manner, that his little red nose was in an unusual glow, that every line in his round bright face was twisted and curved into an expression of pleased surprise, and that his whole countenance was radiant with glee. I was still more surprised to see my housekeeper, who usually preserves a very staid air and stands somewhat upon her dignity, peeping round the hedge at the bottom of the walk, and exchanging nods and smiles with the barber who twice or thrice looked over his shoulder for that purpose. I could conceive no announcement to which these appearances could be the prelude, unless it were that they had married each other that morning.

I was, consequently, a little disappointed when it only came out that there was a gentleman in the house who wished to speak with me.

'And who is it?' said I.

The barber with his face screwed up still tighter than before, replied that the gentleman would not send his name, but wished to see me. I pondered for a moment, wondering who this visitor might be, and I remarked that he embraced the opportunity of exchanging another nod with the housekeeper who still lingered in the distance.

'Well!' said I, 'bid the gentleman come here.'

This seemed to be the consummation of the barber's hopes, for he turned sharp round, and actually ran away.

Now, my sight is not very good at a distance, and therefore

when the gentleman first appeared in the walk, I was not quite clear whether he was a stranger to me or otherwise. He was an elderly gentleman, but came tripping along in the pleasantest manner conceivable, avoiding the garden-roller and the borders of the beds with inimitable dexterity, picking his way among the flower-pots, and smiling with unspeakable good-humour. Before he was half way up the walk he began to salute me; then I thought I knew him; but when he came towards me with his hat in his hand, the sun shining on his bald head, his bland face, his bright spectacles, his fawn-coloured tights and his black gaiters – then, my heart warmed towards him and I felt quite certain that it was Mr Pickwick.[56]

'My dear sir' – said that gentleman as I rose to receive him, 'pray be seated. Pray sit down. Now, do not stand on my account. I must insist upon it, really.' With these words Mr Pickwick gently pressed me down into my seat, and taking my hand in his, shook it again and again with a warmth of manner perfectly irresistible. I endeavoured to express in my welcome, something of that heartiness and pleasure which the sight of him awakened and made him sit down beside me. All this time he kept alternately releasing my hand, and grasping it again, and surveying me through his spectacles with such a beaming countenance as I never beheld.

'You knew me directly!' said Mr Pickwick. 'What a pleasure it is to think that you knew me directly!'

I remarked that I had read his adventures very often, and that his features were quite familiar to me from the published portraits. As I thought it a good opportunity of adverting to the circumstance, I condoled with him upon the various libels on his character which had found their way into print.[57] Mr Pickwick shook his head and for a moment looked very indignant, but smiling again directly, added that no doubt I was acquainted with Cervantes' introduction to the second part of Don Quixote,[58] and that it fully expressed his sentiments on the subject.

'But now' said Mr Pickwick, 'don't you wonder how I found you out?'

'I will never wonder, and with your good leave, never know,' said I, smiling in my turn. 'It is enough for me that you give me this gratification. I have not the least desire that you should tell me by what means I have obtained it.'

'You are very kind,' returned Mr Pickwick, shaking me by the hand again, 'you are so exactly what I expected! But for what particular purpose do you think I have sought you out my dear sir? Now, what *do* you think I have come for?'

Mr Pickwick put this question as though he were persuaded that it was morally impossible that I could by any means divine the deep purpose of his visit, and that it must be hidden from all human ken. Therefore, although I was rejoiced to think that I anticipated his drift, I feigned to be quite ignorant of it, and after a brief consideration shook my head despairingly.

'What should you say,' said Mr Pickwick, laying the forefinger of his left hand upon my coat-sleeve, and looking at me with his head thrown back, and a little on one side, 'what should you say if I confessed that after reading your account of yourself and your little society, I had come here, a humble candidate for one of those empty chairs?'

'I should say,' I returned, 'that I know of only one circumstance which could still further endear that little society to me, and that would be the associating with it my old friend – for you must let me call you so – my old friend Mr Pickwick.'

As I made him this answer, every feature of Mr Pickwick's face fused itself into one all-pervading expression of delight. After shaking me heartily by both hands at once, he patted me gently on the back, and then – I well understood why – coloured up to the eyes, and hoped with great earnestness of manner that he had not hurt me.

If he had, I would have been content that he should have repeated the offence a hundred times rather than suppose so, but as he had not, I had no difficulty in changing the subject by making an enquiry which had been upon my lips twenty times already.

'You have not told me,' said I, 'anything about Sam Weller.'

'Oh! Sam,' replied Mr Pickwick, 'is the same as ever. The same true faithful fellow that he ever was. What should I tell you about Sam, my dear Sir, except that he is more indispensable to my happiness and comfort every day of my life?'

'And Mr Weller senior?' said I.

'Old Mr Weller,' returned Mr Pickwick, 'is in no respect more altered than Sam, unless it be that he is a little more opinionated than he was formerly, and perhaps at times more talkative. He spends a good deal of his time now in our neighbourhood, and has so constituted himself a part of my body-guard, that when I ask permission for Sam to have a seat in your kitchen on clock nights (supposing your three friends think me worthy to fill one of the chairs) I am afraid I must often include Mr Weller too.'

I very readily pledged myself to give both Sam and his father a free admission to my house at all hours and seasons, and this point settled, we fell into a lengthy conversation which was carried on with as little reserve on both sides as if we had been intimate friends from our youth, and which conveyed to me the comfortable assurance that Mr Pickwick's buoyancy of spirit, and indeed all his old cheerful characteristics, were wholly unimpaired. As he had spoken of the consent of my friends as being yet in abeyance, I repeatedly assured him that his proposal was certain to receive their most joyful sanction, and several times entreated that he would give me leave to introduce him to Jack Redburn and Mr Miles (who were near at hand) without further ceremony.

To this proposal, however, Mr Pickwick's delicacy would by no means allow him to accede, for he urged that his eligibility must be formally discussed, and that until this had been done, he could not think of obtruding himself further. The utmost I could obtain from him was, a promise that he would attend upon our next night of meeting, that I might have the pleasure of presenting him immediately on his election.

Mr Pickwick having with many blushes placed in my hands a small roll of paper, which he termed his 'qualification', put a great many questions to me touching my friends and particularly Jack Redburn, whom he repeatedly termed 'a fine fellow,' and in whose favour I could see he was strongly predisposed. When I had satisfied him on these points, I took him up into my room that he might make acquaintance with the old chamber which is our place of meeting.

'And this,' said Mr Pickwick stopping short, 'is the clock! Dear me! And this is really the old clock!'

I thought he would never have come away from it. After advancing towards it softly, and laying his hand upon it with as much respect and as many smiling looks as if it were alive, he set himself to consider it in every possible direction, now mounting on a chair to look at the top, now going down upon his knees to examine the bottom, now surveying the sides with his spectacles almost touching the case, and now trying to peep between it and the wall to get a slight view of the back. Then, he would retire a pace or two and look up at the dial to see it go, and then draw near again and stand with his head on one side to hear it tick: never failing to glance towards me at intervals of a few seconds each, and nod his head with such complacent gratification as I am quite unable to describe. His admiration was not confined to the clock either, but extended itself to every article in the room, and really when he had gone through them every one, and at last sat himself down in all the six chairs one after another to try how they felt, I never saw such a picture of good-humour and happiness as he presented, from the top of his shining head down to the very last button of his gaiters.

I should have been well pleased, and should have had the utmost enjoyment of his company, if he had remained with me all day, but my favourite, striking the hour, reminded him that he must take his leave. I could not forbear telling him once more how glad he had made me, and we shook hands all the way down stairs.

We had no sooner arrived in the Hall, than my housekeeper

gliding out of her little room (she had changed her gown and cap I observed) greeted Mr Pickwick with her best smile and curtsey, and the barber feigning to be accidentally passing on his way out, made him a vast number of bows. When the housekeeper curtseyed, Mr Pickwick bowed with the utmost politeness, and when he bowed the housekeeper curtseyed again; between the housekeeper and the barber, I should say that Mr Pickwick faced about and bowed with undiminished affability, fifty times at least.

I saw him to the door; an omnibus was at the moment passing the corner of the lane, which Mr Pickwick hailed and ran after with extraordinary nimbleness. When he had got about half way he turned his head, and seeing that I was still looking after him and that I waved my hand, stopped, evidently irresolute whether to come back and shake hands again, or to go on. The man behind the omnibus[59] shouted, and Mr Pickwick ran a little way towards him: then he looked round at me, and ran a little way back again. Then there was another shout and he turned round once more and ran the other way. After several of these vibrations, the man settled the question by taking Mr Pickwick by the arm and putting him into the carriage, but his last action was to let down the window and wave his hat to me as it drove off.

I lost no time in opening the parcel he had left with me. The following were its contents:

## MR PICKWICK'S TALE

A good many years have passed away since old John Podgers lived in the town of Windsor, where he was born, and where in course of time he came to be comfortably and snugly buried. You may be sure that in the time of King James the First, Windsor was a very quaint old town, and you may take it upon my authority that John Podgers was a very quaint queer old fellow; consequently he and Windsor fitted each other to a nicety, and seldom parted company even for half a day.

John Podgers was broad, sturdy, Dutch-built, short, and a very hard eater, as men of his figure often are. Being a hard sleeper likewise, he divided his time pretty equally between these two recreations, always falling asleep when he had done eating and always taking another turn at the trencher[60] when he had done sleeping, by which means he grew more corpulent and more drowsy every day of his life. Indeed it used to be currently reported that when he sauntered up and down the sunny side of the street before dinner (as he never failed to do in fair weather) he enjoyed his soundest nap, but many people held this to be a fiction as he had several times been seen to look after fat oxen on market days, and had even been heard by persons of good credit and reputation to chuckle at the sight, and say to himself with great glee 'Live beef, live beef!' It was upon this evidence that the wisest people in Windsor (beginning with the local authorities of course) held that John Podgers was a man of strong sound sense – not what is called smart, perhaps, and it might be of a rather lazy and apoplectic turn, but still a man of solid parts and one who meant much more than he cared to show. This impression was confirmed by a very dignified way he had of shaking his head and imparting at the same time a pendulous motion to his double chin; in short he passed for one of those people who being plunged into the Thames would make no vain efforts to set it afire,[61] but would straightaway flop down to the bottom with a deal of gravity to be highly respected in consequence by all good men.

Being well to do in the world, and a peaceful widower – having a great appetite, which, as he could afford to gratify it, was a luxury and no inconvenience, and a power of going to sleep which as he had no occasion to keep awake was a most enviable faculty – you will readily suppose that John Podgers was a happy man. But appearances are often deceptive and when they least seem so, and the truth is that notwithstanding his extreme sleekness he was rendered uneasy in his mind and exceedingly uncomfortable by a constant apprehension that beset him night and day.

You know very well that in those times there flourished divers evil old women who under the name of Witches[62] spread great disorder through the land, and inflicted various dismal tortures upon Christian men: sticking pins and needles into them when they least expected it, and causing them to walk in the air with their feet upwards to the great terror of their wives and families, who were naturally very much disconcerted when the master of the house unexpectedly came home, knocking at the door with his heels and combing his hair on the scraper.[63] These were their commonest pranks, but they every day played a hundred others, of which none were less objectionable and many were much more so, being improper besides; the result was that vengeance was denounced against all old women, with whom even the king himself had no sympathy (as he certainly ought to have had) for with his own most Gracious hand he penned a most Gracious consignment of them to everlasting wrath,[64] and devised most Gracious means for their confusion and slaughter, in virtue whereof scarcely a day passed but one witch at the least was most graciously hanged, drowned or roasted in some part of his dominions. Still the press teemed with strange and terrible news from the North or the South or the East or the West relative to witches and their unhappy victims in some corner of the country, and the Public's hair stood on end to that degree that it lifted its hat off its head, and made its face pale with terror.

You may believe that the little town of Windsor did not escape the general contagion. The inhabitants boiled a witch on the King's birthday and sent a bottle of the broth to court, with a dutiful address expressive of their loyalty. The King being rather frightened by the present, piously bestowed it upon the Archbishop of Canterbury, and returned an answer to the address wherein he gave them golden rules for discovering witches and laid great stress upon certain protecting charms, and especially horse shoes.[65] Immediately the townspeople went to work nailing up horse-shoes over every door, and so many anxious parents apprenticed their children to farriers,[66] to keep them out of harm's way, that it became quite a genteel trade and flourished exceedingly.

In the midst of all this bustle John Podgers ate and slept as usual but shook his head a great deal oftener than was his custom, and was observed to look at the oxen less, and at the old women more. He had a little shelf put up in his sitting room, whereon was displayed in a row which grew longer every week all the witchcraft literature of the time; he grew learned in charms and exorcisms, hinted at certain questionable females on broomsticks whom he had seen from his chamber window riding in the air at night, and was in constant terror of being bewitched. At length from perpetually dwelling upon this one idea which being alone in his head had it all its own way, the fear of witches became the single passion of his life. He, who up to that time had never known what it was to dream, began to have visions of witches whenever he fell asleep; waking, they were incessantly present to his imagination likewise; and sleeping or waking he had not a moment's peace. He began to set witch-traps in the highway, and was often seen lying in wait round the corner for hours together, to watch their effect. These engines were of simple construction, usually, consisting of two straws disposed in the form of a cross, or a piece of a bible-cover with a pinch of salt upon it, but they were infallible, and if an old woman chanced to stumble over them (as not unfrequently happened, the chosen spot being a broken and stony place) John started from a doze, pounced out upon her, and hung round her neck till assistance arrived, when she was immediately carried away and drowned. By dint of constantly inveigling old ladies and disposing of them in this summary manner, he acquired the reputation of a great public character, and as he received no harm in these pursuits beyond a scratched face or so, he came in course of time to be considered witch-proof.

There was but one person who entertained the least doubt of John Podgers's gifts, and that person was his own nephew, a wild roving young fellow of twenty who had been brought up in his uncle's house and lived there still – that is to say when he was at home, which was not as often as it might have been. As he was an apt scholar it was he who read aloud every fresh piece of strange and terrible intelligence that John Podgers bought; and this he always did of an evening in the little porch in front of the house, round which the neighbours would flock in crowds to hear the direful news – for people like to be frightened, and when they can be frightened for nothing and at another man's expense, they like it all the better.

One fine midsummer evening, a group of persons were gathered in this place listening intently to Will Marks (that was the nephew's name) as with his cap very much on one side, his arm coiled slyly round the waist of a pretty girl who sat beside him, and his face screwed into a comical expression intended to represent extreme gravity, he read – with Heaven knows how many embellishments of his own – a dismal account of a gentleman down in Northamptonshire under the influence of

witchcraft and taken forcible possession of by the Devil, who
was playing his very self with him. John Podgers in a high sugar-
loaf hat and short cloak filled the opposite seat and surveyed the
auditory with a look of mingled pride and horror very edifying
to see, while the hearers with their heads thrust forward and
their mouths open, listened and trembled, and hoped there was
a great deal more to come. Sometimes Will stopped for an
instant to look round upon his eager audience, and then with a
more comical expression of face than before and a settling of
himself comfortably which included a squeeze of the young lady
before mentioned, he launched into some new wonder surpassing all the others.

The setting sun shed his last golden rays upon this little party
who, absorbed in their present occupation, took no heed of the
approach of night or the glory in which the day went down,
when the sound of a horse approaching at a good round trot,
invading the silence of the hour, caused the reader to make a
sudden stop and the listeners to raise their heads in wonder. Nor

was their wonder diminished when a horseman dashed up to the porch, and abruptly checking his steed, inquired where one John Podgers dwelt.

'Here!' cried a dozen voices, while a dozen hands pointed out sturdy John, still basking in the terrors of the pamphlet.

The rider giving his bridle to one of those who surrounded him, dismounted, and approached John hat in hand, but with great haste.

'Whence come ye?' said John.

'From Kingston, Master.'

'And wherefore?'

'On most pressing business.'

'Of what nature?'

'Witchcraft.'

Witchcraft! Everybody looked aghast at the breathless messenger, and the breathless messenger looked equally aghast at everybody – except Will Marks, who finding himself unobserved, not only squeezed the lady again, but kissed her twice. Surely he must have been bewitched himself, or he never could have done it – and the young lady too, or she never would have let him.

'Witchcraft!' cried Will, drowning the sound of his last kiss which was rather a loud one.

The messenger turned towards him, and with a frown repeated the word more solemnly than before, then told his errand, which was, in brief, that the people of Kingston had been greatly terrified for some nights past by hideous revels, held by witches beneath the gibbet[67] within a mile of the town, and related and deposed to by chance wayfarers who had passed within ear-shot of the spot – that the sound of their voices in their wild orgies had been plainly heard by many persons – that three old women laboured under strong suspicion, and that precedents had been consulted and solemn council had, and it was found that to identify the hags some single person must watch upon the spot alone – that no single person had the courage to perform the task – and that he had been despatched express to solicit John Podgers to undertake it that very night, as being a man of great renown, who bore a charmed life, and was proof against unholy spells.

John received this communication with much composure, and said in few words, that it would have afforded him inexpressible pleasure to do the Kingston people so slight a service, if it were not for his unfortunate propensity to fall asleep, which no man regretted more than himself upon the present occasion, but which quite settled the question. Nevertheless, he said, there *was* a gentleman present (and here he looked very hard at a tall farrier) who having been engaged all his life in the manufacture of horse-shoes must be quite invulnerable to the power of witches, and who, he had no doubt, from his known reputation for bravery and good nature, would readily accept the commission. The farrier politely thanked him for his good opinion, which it would always be his study to deserve, but added that with regard to the present little matter he couldn't think of it on any account, as his departing on such an errand would certainly occasion the instant death of his wife, to whom as they all knew he was tenderly attached. Now, so far from this circumstance being notorious, everybody had suspected the reverse, as the farrier was in the habit of beating his lady rather more than tender husbands usually do; all the married men present, however, applauded his resolution with great vehemence, and one and all declared that they would stop at home and die if needful (which happily it was not) in defence of their lawful partners.

This burst of enthusiasm over, they began to look as by one consent toward Will Marks, who with his cap more on one side than ever, sat watching the proceedings with extraordinary unconcern. He had never been heard openly to express his disbelief in witches, but had often cut such jokes at their expense as left it to be inferred, publicly stating on several occasions that he considered a broomstick an inconvenient charger and one especially unsuited to the dignity of the female character, and indulging in other free remarks of the same tendency to the great amusement of his wild companions.

As they looked at Will, they began to whisper and murmur among themselves, and at length one man cried, 'Why don't you ask Will Marks?'

As this was what everybody had been thinking of, they all took up the word, and cried in concert, 'Ah! why don't you ask Will?'

'*He* don't care,' said the farrier.

'Not he,' added another voice in the crowd.

'He don't believe in it you know,' sneered a little man with a

yellow face and a taunting nose and chin, which he thrust out
from under the arm of a long man before him.

'Besides,' said a red-faced gentleman with a gruff voice, 'he's
a single man.'

'That's the point!' said the farrier; and all the married men
murmured, ah! that was it, and they only wished they were
single themselves; they would show him what spirit was, very
soon.

The messenger looked towards Will Marks beseechingly.

'It will be a wet night friend, and my grey nag is tired after
yesterday's work – '

Here there was a general titter.

'But,' resumed Will looking about him with a smile, 'if nobody
else puts in a better claim to go for the credit of the town, I am
your man, and I would be if I had to go afoot. In five minutes I
shall be in the saddle, unless I am depriving any worthy
gentleman here, of the honour of the adventure, which I
wouldn't do for the world.'

But here arose a double difficulty, for not only did John
Podgers combat the resolution with all the words he had,
which were not many, but the young lady combatted it too
with all the tears she had, which were very many indeed.
Will, however, being inflexible, parried his uncle's objections
with a joke, and coaxed the young lady into a smile in three
short whispers. As it was plain that he would go and set
his mind upon it, John Podgers offered him a few first-rate
charms out of his own pocket which he dutifully declined to
accept, and the young lady gave him a kiss which he also
returned.

'You see what a rare thing it is to be married,' said Will, 'and
how careful and considerate all these husbands are. There's not
a man among them but his heart is leaping to forestal me in this
adventure and yet a strong sense of duty keeps him back. The
husbands in this one little town are a pattern to the world, and
so must the wives be too, for that matter, or they could never
boast half the influence they have!'

Waiting for no reply to this sarcasm, he snapped his fingers
and withdrew into the house, and thence into the stable, while
some busied themselves in refreshing the messenger, and others
in baiting his steed. In less than the specified time, he returned
by another way, with a good cloak hanging over his arm, a

good sword girded by his side, and leading his good horse caparisoned for the journey.

'Now,' said Will leaping into the saddle at a bound, 'up and away. Upon your mettle friend and push on. Good night!'

He kissed his hand to the girl, nodded to his drowsy uncle, waved his cap to the rest – and off they flew pell-mell as if all the witches in England were in their horses' legs. They were out of sight in a minute.

The men who were left behind, shook their heads doubtfully, stroked their chins, and shook their heads again. The farrier said that certainly Will Marks was a good horseman, nobody should ever say he denied that, but he was rash, very rash, and there was no telling what the end of it might be – what did he go for, that was what he wanted to know? He wished the young fellow no harm, but why did he go? Everybody echoed these words, and shook their heads again, having done which they wished John Podgers good night, and straggled home to bed.

The Kingston people were in their first sleep, when Will Marks and his conductor rode through the town and up to the door of a house where sundry grave functionaries were assembled, anxiously expecting the arrival of the renowned Podgers. They were a little disappointed to find a gay young man in his place, but they put the best face upon the matter and gave him full instructions how he was to conceal himself behind the gibbet, and watch and listen to the witches, and how at a certain time he was to burst forth and cut and slash among them vigorously, so that the suspected parties might be found bleeding in their beds next day, and thoroughly confounded. They gave him a great quantity of wholesome advice besides, and – which was more to the purpose with Will – a good supper. All these things being done, and midnight nearly come, they sallied forth to show him the spot where he was to keep his dreary vigil.

The night was by this time dark and threatening. There was a rumbling of distant thunder, and a low sighing of wind among the trees, which was very dismal. The potentates of the town kept so uncommonly close to Will that they trod upon his toes, or stumbled against his ankles, or nearly tripped up his heels at every step he took, and besides these annoyances their teeth chattered so with fear that he seemed to be accompanied by a dirge of castanets.[68]

At last they made a halt at the opening of a lonely desolate space, and pointing to a black object at some distance, asked Will if he saw that, yonder.

'Yes,' he replied. 'What then?'

Informing him abruptly that it was the gibbet where he was to watch, they wished him good night in an extremely friendly manner, and ran back as fast as their feet would carry them.

Will walked boldly to the gibbet and glancing upward when he came under it saw – certainly with satisfaction – that it was empty, and that nothing dangled from the top but some iron chains which swung mournfully to and fro as they were moved by the breeze. After a careful survey of every quarter, he determined to take his station with his face towards the town; both because that would place him with his back to the wind, and because if any trick or surprise were attempted it would probably come from that direction in the first instance. Having taken these precautions, he wrapped his cloak about him so that it left the handle of his sword, free, and ready to his hand, and leaning against the gallows-tree, with his cap not quite so much on one side as it had been before, took up his position for the night.

SECOND CHAPTER OF MR PICKWICK'S TALE

We left Will Marks leaning under the gibbet with his face towards the town, scanning the distance with a keen eye which sought to pierce the darkness and catch the earliest glimpse of any person or persons that might approach towards him. But all was quiet, and, save the howling of the wind as it swept across the heath in gusts, and the creaking of the chains that dangled above his head, there was no sound to break the sullen stillness of the night. After half an hour or so, this monotony became more disconcerting to Will than the most furious uproar would have been, and he heartily wished for some one antagonist with whom he might have a fair stand-up fight if it were only to warm himself.

Truth to tell, it was a bitter wind and seemed to blow to the very heart of a man whose blood, heated but now with rapid riding, was the more sensitive to the chilling blast. Will was a daring fellow and cared not a jot for hard knocks or sharp blades, but he could not persuade himself to move or walk about, having just that vague expectation of a sudden assault which made it a comfortable thing to have something at his back, even though that something were a gallows tree. He had no great faith in the superstitions of the age, still such of them as occurred to him did not serve to lighten the time or to render his situation the more endurable. He remembered how witches were said to repair at that ghostly hour to churchyards and gibbets and such like dismal spots, to pluck the bleeding mandrake[69] or scrape the flesh from dead men's bones as choice ingredients for their spells; how, stealing by night to lonely places, they dug graves with their finger-nails or anointed themselves before riding in the air, with a delicate pomatum[70] made of the fat of infants newly boiled. These, and many other fabled practices of a no less agreeable nature, and all having some reference to the circumstances in which he was placed, passed and repassed in quick succession through the mind of Will Marks, and adding a shadowy dread to that distrust and watchfulness which his situation inspired, rendered it upon the whole sufficiently uncomfortable. As he had foreseen too, the rain began to descend heavily, and driving before the wind in a thick mist obscured even those few objects which the darkness of the night had before imperfectly revealed.

'Look!' shrieked a voice, 'Great Heaven it has fallen down and stands erect as if it lived!'

The speaker was close behind him – the voice was almost at his ear. Will threw off his cloak, drew his sword, and darting swiftly round, seized a woman by the wrist, who recoiling from him with a dreadful shriek, fell struggling upon her knees. Another woman clad like her whom he had grasped, in mourning garments, stood rooted to the spot on which they were, gazing upon his face with mild and glaring eyes that quite appalled him.

'Say,' cried Will, when they had confronted each other thus, for some time, 'What are ye?'

'Say what are *you*,' returned the woman, 'who trouble even this obscene resting-place of the dead, and strip the gibbet of its honoured burden! Where is the body?'

He looked in wonder and affright from the woman who questioned him, to the other whose arm he clutched.

'Where is the body?' repeated his questioner more firmly than before; 'You wear no livery which marks you for the hireling of the government. You are no friend to us, or I should recognise you, for the friends of such as we are few in number. What are you then, and wherefore are you here?'

'I am no foe to the distressed and helpless,' said Will. 'Are ye among that number? ye should be by your looks.'

'We are!' was the answer.

'It is ye who have been wailing and weeping here, under cover of the night?' said Will.

'It is,' replied the woman sternly, and pointing, as she spoke, towards her companion, 'she mourns a husband and I a brother. Even the bloody law that wreaks its vengeance on the dead does not make that a crime, and if it did 'twould be alike to us who are past its fear or favour.'

Will glanced at the two females, and could barely discern that the one whom he addressed was much the elder, and that the other was young and of a slight figure. Both were deadly pale, their garments wet and worn, their hair dishevelled and streaming in the wind, themselves bowed down with grief and misery;

their whole appearance most dejected, wretched, and forlorn. A sight so different from any he had expected to encounter touched him to the quick, and all idea of anything but their pitiable condition, vanished before it.

'I am a rough, blunt yeoman,'[71] said Will; 'why I came here is told in a word; you have been overheard at a distance in the silence of the night, and I have undertaken a watch for hags or spirits. I came here expecting an adventure and prepared to go through with any. If there be aught that I can do to help or aid you, name it, and on the faith of a man who can be secret and trusty I will stand by you to the death.'

'How comes this gibbet to be empty?' asked the elder female.

'I swear to you,' replied Will, 'that I know as little as yourself. But this I know, that when I came here an hour ago or so, it was as it is now; and if, as I gather from your question, it was not so last night, sure I am that it has been secretly disturbed without the knowledge of the folks in yonder town. Bethink you, therefore, whether you have no friends in league with you or with him on whom the law has done its worst, by whom these sad remains have been removed for burial.'

The women spoke together, and Will retired a pace or two while they conversed apart. He could hear them sob and moan, and saw that they wrung their hands in fruitless agony. He could make out little that they said, but between whiles he gathered enough to assure him that his suggestion was not very wide of the mark, and that they not only suspected by whom the body had been removed, but also whither it had been conveyed. When they had been in conversation a long time, they turned towards him once more. This time the younger female spoke.

'You have offered us your help?'

'I have.'

'And given a pledge that you are still willing to redeem?'

'Yes. So far as I may, keeping all plots and conspiracies at arm's length.'

'Follow us, friend.'

Will, whose self-possession was now quite restored, needed no second bidding, but with his drawn sword in his hand, and his cloak so muffled over his left arm as to serve for a kind of shield without offering any impediment to its free action, suffered them to lead the way. Through mud and mire and wind and rain, they walked in silence a full mile. At length they turned into a dark lane, where, suddenly starting out from beneath some trees where he had taken shelter, a man appeared having in his charge three saddled horses. One of these (his own apparently) in obedience to a whisper from the women, he consigned to Will, who seeing that they mounted, mounted also. Then without a word spoken they rode on together, leaving the attendant behind.

They made no halt nor slackened their pace until they arrived near Putney.[72] At a large wooden house which stood apart from any other, they alighted, and giving their horses to one who was already waiting, passed in by a side door, and so up some narrow creaking stairs into a small panelled chamber, where Will was left alone. He had not been here very long, when the door was softly opened, and there entered to him a cavalier whose face was concealed beneath a black mask.

Will stood upon his guard, and scrutinised this figure from head to foot. The form was that of a man pretty far advanced in life, but of a firm and stately carriage. His dress was of a rich and costly kind, but so soiled and disordered that it was scarcely to be recognised for one of those gorgeous suits which the expensive taste and fashion of the time prescribed for men of any rank or station. He was booted and spurred, and bore about him even as many tokens of the state of the roads as Will himself. All this he noted while the eyes behind the mask regarded him with equal attention. This survey over, the cavalier broke silence.

'Thou'rt young and bold, and wouldst be richer than thou art?'

'The two first I am,' returned Will. 'The last I have scarcely thought of. But be it so. Say that I would be richer than I am; what then?'

'The way lies before thee now,' replied the Mask.

'Show it me.'

'First let me inform thee, that thou wert brought here to-night lest thou shouldst too soon have told thy tale to those who placed thee on the watch.'

'I thought as much when I followed,' said Will. 'But I am no blab, not I.'

'Good,' returned the Mask. 'Now listen. He who was to have executed the enterprise of burying that body which as thou hast suspected was taken down to-night, has left us in our need.'

Will nodded, and thought within himself that if the Mask were to attempt to play any tricks, the first eyelet-hole on the left-hand side of his doublet, counting from the buttons up the front, would be a very good place in which to pink[73] him neatly.

'Thou art here, and the emergency is desperate. I propose his task to thee. Convey the body (now coffined in this house) by means that I shall show, to the church of Saint Dunstan[74] in London tomorrow night, and thy service shall be richly paid. Thou'rt about to ask whose corpse it is. Seek not to know. I warn thee, seek not to know. Felons hang in chains on every moor and heath. Believe, as others do, that this was one, and ask no further. The murders of state policy, its victims or avengers, had best remain unknown to such as thee.'

'The mystery of this service,' said Will, 'bespeaks its danger. What is the reward?'

'One hundred golden unities,'[75] replied the cavalier. 'The danger to one who cannot be recognised as the friend of a fallen cause is not great, but there is some hazard to be run. Decide between that and the reward.'

'What if I refuse?' said Will.

'Depart in peace, in God's name,' returned the Mask in a melancholy tone 'and keep our secret: remembering that those who brought thee here were crushed and stricken women, and that those who bade thee go free could have had thy life with one word, and no man the wiser.'

Men were readier to undertake desperate adventures in those times, than they are now. In this case the temptation was great and the punishment even in case of detection was not likely to be very severe, as Will came of a loyal stock, and his uncle was in good repute, and a passable tale to account for his possession of the body and his ignorance of the identity, might be easily devised. The cavalier explained that a covered cart had been prepared for the purpose; that the time of departure could be arranged so that he should reach London Bridge at dusk and proceed through the City after the day had closed in; that people would be ready at his journey's end to place the coffin in a vault without a minute's delay; that officious enquirers in the streets would be easily repelled by the tale that he was carrying for interment the corpse of one who had died of the plague;[76] and in short showed him every reason why he should succeed and none why he should fail. After a time they were joined by another gentleman, masked like the first, who added new arguments to those which had been already urged; the wretched wife too added her tears and prayers to their calmer representations; and in the end Will, moved by compassion and good nature, by a love of the marvellous, by a mischievous anticipation of the terrors of the Kingston people when he should be missing next day, and finally by the prospect of gain, took upon himself the task, and devoted all his energies to its successful execution.

The following night when it was quite dark, the hollow echoes of old London Bridge[77] responded to the rumbling of the cart which contained the ghastly load, the object of Will Marks's care. Sufficiently disguised to attract no attention by his garb, Will walked at the horse's head, as unconcerned as a man could be who was sensible that he had now arrived at the most dangerous part of his undertaking, but full of boldness and confidence.

It was now eight o'clock. After nine, none could walk the streets without danger of their lives, and even at this hour, robberies and murder were of no uncommon occurrence. The shops upon the bridge were all closed; the low wooden arches thrown across the way were like so many black pits, in every one of which ill-favored fellows lurked in knots of three or four, some standing upright against the wall lying in wait, others skulking in gateways and thrusting out their uncombed heads and scowling eyes, others crossing and re-crossing and constantly jostling both horse and man to provoke a quarrel, others stealing away and summoning their companions in a low whistle. Once, even in that short passage, there was the noise of scuffling and the clash of swords behind him, but Will, who knew the city and its ways, kept straight on and scarcely turned his head.

The streets being unpaved, the rain of the night before had converted them into a perfect quagmire, which the splashing water spouts from the gables, and the filth and offal cast from the different houses, swelled in no small degree. These odious matters being left to putrify in the close and heavy air, emitted an insupportable stench, to which every court and passage poured forth a contribution of its own. Many parts even of the main streets, with their projecting stories tottering overhead and nearly shutting out the sky, were more like huge chimneys than open ways. At the corners of some of these, great bonfires were burning to prevent infection from the plague, of which it was rumoured that some citizens had lately died; and few, who availing themselves of the light thus afforded paused for a moment to look around them, would have been disposed to doubt the existence of the disease or wonder at its dreadful visitations.

But it was not in such scenes as these, or even in the deep and miry road, that Will Marks found the chief obstacles to his progress. There were kites and ravens feeding in the streets (the only scavengers the City kept) who scenting what he carried, followed the cart or fluttered on its top and croaked their knowledge of its burden and their ravenous appetite for prey. There were distant fires where the poor wood and plaster tenements wasted fiercely, and whither crowds made their way clamouring eagerly for plunder, beating down all who came within their reach, and yelling like devils let loose. There were single-handed men flying from bands of ruffians, who pursued them with naked weapons, and hunted them savagely; there were drunken desperate robbers issuing from their dens and staggering through the open streets where no man dared molest them; there were vagabond servitors returning from the Bear Garden,[78] where had been good sport that day, dragging after them their torn and bleeding dogs or leaving them to die and rot upon the road. Nothing was abroad but cruelty, violence and disorder.

Many were the interruptions which Will Marks encountered from these stragglers, and many the narrow escapes he made. Now some stout bully would take his seat upon the cart insisting to be driven to his own home, and now two or three men would come down upon him together and demand that on peril of his life he showed them what he had inside. Then a party of the City watch upon their round would draw across the road, and not satisfied with his tale, question him closely and revenge themselves by a little cuffing and hustling for maltreatment sustained at other hands that night. All these assailants had to be rebutted, some by fair words, some by foul, and some by blows. But Will Marks was not the man to be stopped or turned back now he had penetrated so far, and though he got on slowly, still he made his way down Fleet-street and reached the church at last.

As he had been forewarned, all was in readiness. Directly he stopped, the coffin was removed by four men who appeared so suddenly that they seemed to have started from the earth. A fifth mounted the cart, and scarcely allowing Will time to snatch from it a little bundle containing such of his own clothes as he had thrown off on assuming his disguise, drove briskly away. Will never saw cart or man again.

He followed the body into the church, and it was well he lost no time in doing so, for the door was immediately closed. There was no light in the building save that which came from a couple of torches borne by two men in cloaks who stood upon the brink of a vault. Each supported a female figure, and all observed a profound silence.

By this dim and solemn glare, which made Will feel as though light itself were dead, and its tomb the dreary arches that frowned above, they placed the coffin in the vault, with uncovered heads, and closed it up. One of the torch-bearers then turned to Will and stretched forth his hand in which was a purse of gold. Something told him directly that those were the same eyes which he had seen beneath the mask.

'Take it,' said the cavalier in a low voice, 'and be happy. Though these have been hasty obsequies, and no priest has blessed the work, there will not be the less peace with thee hereafter, for having laid his bones beside those of his little children. Keep thy own counsel, for thy sake no less than ours, and God be with thee!'

'The blessing of a widowed mother on thy head, good friend!' cried the younger lady through her tears; 'the blessing of one who has now no hope or rest but in this grave!'

Will stood with the purse in his hand, and involuntarily made a gesture as though he would return it, for though a thoughtless fellow he was of a frank and generous nature. But the two gentlemen extinguishing their torches cautioned him to be gone, as their common safety would be endangered by a longer delay; and at the same time their retreating footsteps sounded through the church. He turned, therefore, towards the point at which he had entered, and seeing by a faint gleam in the distance that the door was again partially open, groped his way towards it and so passed into the street.

Meantime the local authorities of Kingston had kept watch and ward all the previous night, fancying every now and then that dismal shrieks were borne towards them on the wind, and frequently winking to each other and drawing closer to the fire as they drank the health of the lonely sentinel, upon whom a clerical gentleman present was especially severe by reason of his levity and youthful folly. Two or three of the gravest in company who were of a theological turn, propounded to him the question whether such a character was not but poorly armed for single combat with the devil, and whether he himself would not have been a stronger opponent; but the clerical gentleman, sharply reproving them for their presumption in discussing such questions, clearly showed that a fitter champion than Will could scarcely have been selected, not only for that being a child of Satan he was the less likely to be alarmed by the appearance of his own father, but because Satan himself would be at his ease in such company, and would not scruple to kick up his heels to an extent which it was quite certain he would never venture before clerical eyes, under whose influence (as was notorious) he became quite a tame and milk-and-water character.

But when next morning arrived and with it no Will Marks, and when a strong party repairing to the spot, as a strong party ventured to do in broad day, found Will gone and the gibbet empty, matters grew serious indeed. The day passing away and no news arriving, and the night going on also without any intelligence, the thing grew more tremendous still; in short the neighbourhood worked itself up to such a comfortable pitch of mystery and horror that it is a great question whether the general feeling was not one of excessive disappointment when, on the second morning, Will Marks returned.

However this may be, back Will came in a very cool and collected state, and appearing not to trouble himself much about anybody except old John Podgers, who having been sent for, was sitting in the Town Hall crying slowly and dozing between whiles. Having embraced his uncle and assured him of his safety, Will mounted on a table and told his story to the crowd.

And surely they would have been the most unreasonable crowd that ever assembled together, if they had been in the least respect disappointed with the tale he told them, for besides describing the Witches' Dance to the minutest motion of their legs, and performing it in character on the table, with the assistance of a broomstick, he related how they had carried off the body in a copper cauldron and so bewitched him that he lost his senses until he found himself lying under a hedge at least ten miles off, whence he had straightway returned as they then beheld. The story gained such universal applause that it soon afterwards brought down express from London the great witch-finder of the age, the Heaven-born Hopkins,[79] who having examined Will closely on several points, pronounced it the most extraordinary and the best accredited witch story ever known, under which title it was published at the Three-Bibles on London Bridge, in small quarto, with a view of the cauldron from an original drawing, and a portrait of the clerical gentleman as he sat by the fire.

On one point, Will was particularly careful; and that was to describe for the witches he had seen, three impossible old females whose likenesses never were or will be. Thus he saved the lives of the suspected parties, and of all other old women who were dragged before him to be identified.

This circumstance occasioned John Podgers much grief and sorrow, until happening one day to cast his eye upon his housekeeper, and observing her to be plainly afflicted with rheumatism, he procured her to be burnt as an undoubted witch. For this service to the state, he was immediately knighted, and became from that time Sir John Podgers.

Will Marks never gained any clue to the mystery in which he had been an actor, nor did any inscription in the church which he often visited afterwards, nor any of the limited inquiries that he dared to make, yield him the least assistance. As he kept his own secret, he was compelled to spend the gold discreetly and sparingly. In course of time he married the young lady of whom I have already told you, whose maiden name is not recorded, with whom he led a prosperous and happy life. Years and years after this adventure, it was his wont to tell her upon a stormy night that it was a great comfort to him to think that those bones, to whomsoever they might have once belonged, were not bleaching in the troubled air, but were mouldering away with the dust of their own kith and kindred in a quiet grave.

### FURTHER PARTICULARS OF
### MASTER HUMPHREY'S VISITOR

Being very full of Mr Pickwick's application and highly pleased with the compliment he had paid me, it will be readily supposed that long before our next night of meeting I communicated it to my three friends, who unanimously voted his admission into our body. We all looked forward with some impatience to the occasion which would enrol him among us, but I am greatly mistaken if Jack Redburn and myself were not by many degrees the most impatient of the party.

At length the night came, and a few minutes after ten Mr Pickwick's knock was heard at the street-door. He was shown into a lower room, and I directly took my crooked stick and went to accompany him up stairs, in order that he might be presented with all honour and formality.

'Mr Pickwick,' said I on entering the room, 'I am rejoiced to see you – rejoiced to believe that this is but the opening of a long series of visits to this house, and but the beginning of a close and lasting friendship.'

That gentleman made a suitable reply with a cordiality and frankness peculiarly his own, and glanced with a smile towards two persons behind the door, whom I had not at first observed, and whom I immediately recognised as Mr Samuel Weller and his father.

It was a warm evening, but the elder Mr Weller was attired notwithstanding in a most capacious great coat, and had his chin enveloped in a large speckled shawl, such as is usually worn by stage coachmen on active service. He looked very rosy and very stout, especially about the legs, which appeared to have been compressed into his top-boots[80] with some difficulty. His broad-brimmed hat he held under his left arm, and with the fore-finger of his right hand he touched his forehead a great many times, in acknowledgment of my presence.

'I am very glad to see you in such good health, Mr Weller,' said I.

'Why, thankee sir' returned Mr Weller, 'the axle an't broke yet. We keeps up a steady pace – not too severe but with a moderate degree o' friction – and the consekens is that ve're still a runnin' and comes in to the time, reg'lar. – My son Samivel sir, as you may have read on in history' added Mr Weller, introducing his first-born.

I received Sam very graciously, but before he could say a word, his father struck in again.

'Samivel Veller, sir,' said the old gentleman, 'has conferred upon me the ancient title o' grandfather vich had long laid dormouse, and wos s'posed to be nearly hextinct, in our family. Sammy, relate a anecdote o' vun o' them boys – that 'ere little anecdote about young Tony sayin' as he *vould* smoke a pipe unbeknown to his mother.'

'Be quiet, can't you?' said Sam, 'I never see such a old magpie – never.'

'That 'ere Tony is the blessedest boy' – said Mr Weller, heedless of this rebuff, 'the blessedest boy as ever *I* see in *my* days! of all the charmin'est infants as ever I heerd tell on, includin' them as wos kivered over by the robin redbreasts arter they'd committed sooicide with blackberries,[81] there never wos any like that 'ere little Tony. He's alvays a playin' vith a quart pot that boy is! To see him a settin' down on the door step pretending to drink out of it, and fetching a long breath artervards, and smoking a bit of fire-vood and sayin' "Now I'm grandfather" – to see him a doin' that at two year old is better than any play as wos ever wrote. "Now I'm grandfather!" He wouldn't take a pint pot if you wos to make him a present on it, but he gets his quart and then he says, "Now I'm grandfather!"'

Mr Weller was so overpowered by this picture that he straightaway fell into a most alarming fit of coughing, which must certainly have been attended with some fatal result but for the dexterity and promptitude of Sam, who taking a firm grasp of the shawl just under his father's chin shook him to and fro with great violence, at the same time administering some smart blows between his shoulders. By this curious mode of treatment Mr Weller was finally recovered, but with a very crimson face and in a state of great exhaustion.

'He'll do now, Sam,' said Mr Pickwick who had been in some alarm himself.

'He'll do sir!' cried Sam looking reproachfully at his parent, 'Yes, he *will* do one o' these days – he'll do for his-self and then he'll wish he hadn't. Did anybody ever see sich a inconsiderate old file,[82] – laughing into conwulsions afore company, and stamping on the floor as if he'd brought his own carpet vith him and wos under a wager to punch the pattern out in a given time? He'll begin again in a minute. There – he's a goin' off – I said he would!'

In fact, Mr Weller, whose mind was still running upon his precocious grandson, was seen to shake his head from side to side, while a laugh, working like an earthquake, below the surface, produced various extraordinary appearances in his face, chest, and shoulders, the more alarming because unaccompanied by any noise whatever. These emotions, however, gradually subsided and after three or four short relapses he wiped his eyes with the cuff of his coat, and looked about him with tolerable composure.

'Afore the governor vithdraws' said Mr Weller, 'there is a pint, respecting vich Sammy has a qvestion to ask. Vile that qvestion is a perwadin this here conwersation, p'raps the genl'men vill permit me to retire.'

'Wot are you goin' away for?' demanded Sam, seizing his father by the coat tail.

'I never see such a undootiful boy as you Samivel' returned Mr Weller. 'Didn't you make a solemn promise amountin' almost to a speeches o' wow,[83] that you'd put that ere qvestion on my account?'

'Well, I'm agreeable to do it,' said Sam, 'but not if you go cuttin' away like that, as the bull turned round and mildly observed to the drover ven they wos a goadin' him into the butcher's door. The fact is, sir,' said Sam addressing me, 'that he wants to know somethin' respectin' that ere lady as is housekeeper here.'

'Aye. What is that?'

'Vy sir,' said Sam grinning still more, 'he wishes to know vether she—'

'In short,' interposed old Mr Weller, decisively, a perspiration breaking out upon his forehead, 'vether that 'ere old creetur is or is not a widder.'

Mr Pickwick laughed heartily and so did I, as I replied decisively that 'my housekeeper was a spinster.'

'There!' cried Sam, 'now you're satisfied. You hear she's a spinster.'

'A wot?' said his father with deep scorn.

'A spinster,' replied Sam.

Mr Weller looked very hard at his son for a minute or two, and then said,

'Never mind vether she makes jokes or not, that's no matter. Wot I say is, is that ere female a widder, or is she not?'

'Wot do you mean by her making jokes?' demanded Sam, quite aghast at the obscurity of his parent's speech.

'Never you mind Samivel,' returned Mr Weller gravely, 'puns may be wery good things or they may be wery bad 'uns, and a female may be none the better or she may be none the vurse for making of 'em; that's got nothing to do with widders.'

'Wy now,' said Sam looking round, 'would anybody believe as a man at his time o' life could be a running his head agin spinsters and punsters being the same thing?'

'There an't a straw's difference between 'em,' said Mr Weller. 'Your father didn't drive a coach for so many years, not to be ekal to his own langvidge as far as *that* goes Sammy.'

Avoiding the question of etymology, upon which the old gentleman's mind was quite made up, he was several times assured that the housekeeper had never been married. He expressed great satisfaction on hearing this, and apologised for the question, remarking that he had been greatly terrified by a widow not long before and that his natural timidity was increased in consequence.

'It wos on the rail,' said Mr Weller with strong emphasis; 'I wos a goin' down to Birmingham by the rail, and I wos locked up in a close carriage vith a living widder. Alone we wos; the widder and me wos alone; and I believe it wos only because we *wos* alone and there wos no clergyman in the conwayance, that that 'ere widder didn't marry me afore ve reached the halfway station. Ven I think how she began a screaming as we wos a goin' under them tunnels in the dark – how she kept on a faintin' and ketchin' hold o' me – and how I tried to bust open the door as was tight-locked and perwented all escape – Ah! It was a awful thing, most awful!'

Mr Weller was so very much overcome by this retrospect that

he was unable, until he had wiped his brow several times, to return any reply to the question whether he approved of railway communication, notwithstanding that it would appear from the answer which he ultimately gave, that he entertained strong opinions on the subject.

'I con-sider' said Mr Weller, 'that the rail is unconstitootional and an inwaser o' priwileges, and I should wery much like to know what that 'ere old Carter[84] as once stood up for our liberties and wun 'em too – I should like to know wot he vould say if he wos alive now, to Englishmen being locked up with widders, or with anybody, again their wills. Wot a old Carter would have said, a old Coachman may say, and I assert that in that pint o' view alone, the rail is an inwaser. As to the comfort, vere's the comfort o' sittin' in a harm cheer lookin' at brick walls or heaps o' mud, never comin' to a public house, never seein' a glass o' ale, never goin' through a pike,[85] never meetin' a change o' no kind (horses or othervise), but always comin' to a place, ven you come to one at all, the wery picter o' the last, vith the same p'leesemen standing about, the same blessed old bell a ringin', the same unfort'nate people standing behind the bars, a waitin' to be let in; and everythin' the same except the name, vich is wrote up in the same sized letters as the last name and vith the same colors. As to the *h*onour and dignity o' travellin', vere can that be vithout a coachman; and wot's the rail to sich coachmen and guards as is sometimes forced to go by it, but a outrage and a insult? As to the pace, wot sort o' pace do you think I, Tony Veller, could have kept a coach goin' at, for five hundred thousand pound a mile, paid in adwance afore the coach was on the road? And as to the ingein – a nasty wheezin', creaking, gasping, puffin, bustin' monster, alvays out o' breath, vith a shiny green and gold back, like a unpleasant beetle in that 'ere gas magnifier[86] – as to the ingein as is alvays a pourin' out red hot coals at night, and black smoke in the day, the sensiblest thing it does in my opinion, is, ven there's somethin' in the vay and it sets up that 'ere frightful scream vich seems to say "Now here's two hundred and forty passengers in the wery greatest extremity o' danger, and here's their two hundred and forty screams in vun!" '

By this time I began to fear that my friends would be rendered impatient by my protracted absence. I therefore begged Mr Pickwick to accompany me up stairs, and left the two Mr

Wellers in the care of the housekeeper; laying strict injunctions upon her to treat them with all possible hospitality.

*No. 7 (16 May 1840)*

### THE CLOCK

As we were going up stairs, Mr Pickwick put on his spectacles which he had held in his hand hitherto; arranged his neckerchief, smoothed down his waistcoat, and made many other little preparations of that kind which men are accustomed to be mindful of, when they are going among strangers for the first time and are anxious to impress them pleasantly. Seeing that I smiled, he smiled too, and said that if it had occurred to him before he left home, he would certainly have presented himself in pumps[87] and silk stockings.

'I would indeed, my dear sir,' he said very seriously, 'I would have shown my respect for the society, by laying aside my gaiters.'

'You may rest assured,' said I, 'that they would have regretted your doing so, very much, for they are quite attached to them.'

'No, really!' cried Mr Pickwick with manifest pleasure. 'Do you think they care about my gaiters? Do you seriously think that they identify me at all with my gaiters?'[88]

'I am sure they do,' I replied.

'Well now,' said Mr Pickwick, 'that is one of the most charming and agreeable circumstances that could possibly have occurred to me!'

I should not have written down this short conversation, but that it developed a slight point in Mr Pickwick's character, with which I was not previously acquainted. He has a secret pride in his legs. The manner in which he spoke, and the accompanying glance he bestowed upon his tights, convince me that Mr Pickwick regards his legs with much innocent vanity.

'But here are our friends,' said I, opening the door and taking his arm in mine; 'let them speak for themselves. Gentlemen, I present to you Mr Pickwick.'

Mr Pickwick and I must have been a good contrast just then. I leaning quietly on my crutch-stick with something of a careworn, patient, air; he having hold of my arm, and bowing in every direction with the most elastic politeness, and an expression of face whose sprightly cheerfulness and good-humour knew no bounds. The difference between us must have been more striking yet as we advanced towards the table, and the amiable gentleman, adapting his jocund step to my poor tread, had his attention divided between treating my infirmities with the utmost consideration, and affecting to be wholly unconscious that I required any.

I made him personally known to each of my friends in turn. First, to the deaf gentleman, whom he regarded with much interest, and accosted with great frankness and cordiality. He had evidently some vague idea, at the moment, that my friend being deaf must be dumb also; for when the latter opened his lips to express the pleasure it afforded him to know a gentleman of whom he had heard so much, Mr Pickwick was so extremely disconcerted that I was obliged to step in to his relief.

His meeting with Jack Redburn was quite a treat to see. Mr Pickwick smiled, and shook hands, and looked at him through his spectacles, and under them, and over them, and nodded his head approvingly, and then nodded to me, as much as to say, 'this is just the man; you were quite right,' and then turned to Jack and said a few hearty words, and then did and said everything over again with unimpaired vivacity. As to Jack himself, he was quite as much delighted with Mr Pickwick, as Mr Pickwick could possibly be with him. Two people never can have met together since the world began, who exchanged a warmer or more enthusiastic greeting.

It was amusing to observe the difference between this encounter, and that which succeeded, between Mr Pickwick and Mr Miles. It was clear that the latter gentleman viewed our new member as a kind of rival in the affections of Jack Redburn, and besides this, he had more than once hinted to me, in secret, that although he had no doubt Mr Pickwick was a very worthy man, still he did consider that some of his exploits were unbecoming a gentleman of his years and gravity. Over and above these grounds of distrust, it is one of his fixed opinions that the law never can by possibility do anything wrong; he therefore looks upon Mr Pickwick as one who has justly suffered in purse and peace for a breach of his plighted faith to an unprotected female,[89] and holds that he is called upon to regard him with some suspicion on that account. These causes led to a rather cold and formal reception; which Mr Pickwick acknowledged with the same stateliness and intense politeness as was displayed on the other side. Indeed he assumed an air of such majestic defiance that I was fearful he might break out into some solemn protest or declaration, and therefore inducted him into his chair without a moment's delay.

This piece of generalship was perfectly successful. The instant he took his seat, Mr Pickwick surveyed us all with a most benevolent aspect, and was taken with a fit of smiling, full five minutes long. His interest in our ceremonies was immense. They are not very numerous or complicated, and a description of them may be comprised in very few words. As our transactions have already been, and must necessarily continue to be, more or less anticipated by being presented in these pages at different times and under various forms, they do not require a detailed account.

Our first proceeding when we are assembled, is, to shake hands all round, and greet each other with cheerful and pleasant looks. Remembering that we assemble, not only for the promotion of our own happiness, but with the view of adding something to the common stock, an air of languor or indifference in any member of our body would be regarded by the others as a kind of treason. We have never had an offender in this respect; but if we had, there is no doubt that he would be taken to task, pretty severely.

Our salutation over, the venerable piece of antiquity from which we take our name is wound up in silence. This ceremony is always performed by Master Humphrey himself, (in treating of the club, I may be permitted to assume the historical style, and speak of myself in the third person), who mounts upon a chair for the purpose, armed with a large key. While it is in progress, Jack Redburn is required to keep at the further end of the room under the guardianship of Mr Miles, for he is known to entertain certain aspiring and unhallowed thoughts connected with the clock, and has even gone so far as to state that if he might take the works out for a day or two, he thinks he could improve them. We pardon him his presumption in consideration of his good intentions, and his keeping this respectful distance, which last penalty is insisted on, lest by secretly wounding the object of our regard in some tender part, in the ardour of his zeal for its improvement, he should fill us all with dismay and consternation.

This regulation afforded Mr Pickwick the highest delight, and seemed, if possible, to exalt Jack in his good opinion.

The next ceremony is the opening of the clock-case (of which Master Humphrey has likewise the key), the taking from it as many papers as will furnish forth our evening's entertainment, and arranging in the recess such new contributions as have been provided since our last meeting. This is always done with peculiar solemnity. The deaf gentleman then fills and lights his

pipe, and we once more take our seats round the table before-mentioned, Master Humphrey acting as president – if we can be said to have any president, where all are on the same social footing – and our friend Jack as secretary. Our preliminaries being now concluded, we fall into any train of conversation that happens to suggest itself, or proceed immediately to one of our readings. In the latter case, the paper selected is consigned to Master Humphrey, who flattens it carefully on the table and makes dog's ears in the corner of every page, ready for turning over easily; Jack Redburn trims the lamp with a small machine of his own invention which usually puts it out; Mr Miles looks on with great approval notwithstanding; the deaf gentleman draws in his chair, so that he can follow the words on the paper or on Master Humphrey's lips, as he pleases; and Master Humphrey himself, looking round with mighty gratification and glancing up at his old clock, begins to read aloud.

Mr Pickwick's face while his tale was being read would have attracted the attention of the dullest man alive. The complacent motion of his head and forefinger as he gently beat time and corrected the air with imaginary punctuation, the smile that mantled on his features at every jocose[90] passage and the sly look he stole around to observe its effect, the calm manner in which he shut his eyes and listened when there was some little piece of description, the changing expression with which he acted the dialogue to himself, his agony that the deaf gentleman should know what it was all about, and his extraordinary anxiety to correct the reader when he hesitated at a word in the manuscript or substituted a wrong one, were alike worthy of remark. And when at last, after endeavouring to communicate with the deaf gentleman by means of the finger alphabet, with which he constructed such words as are unknown in any civilised or savage language, he took up a slate and wrote in large text, one word in a line, the question, 'How – do – you – like – it?' – when he did this, and handing it over the table awaited the reply, with a countenance only brightened and improved by his great excitement, even Mr Miles relaxed, and could not forbear looking at him for the moment with interest and favour.

'It has occurred to me,' said the deaf gentleman, who had watched Mr Pickwick and everybody else with silent satisfaction, 'it has occurred to me,' said the deaf gentleman, taking his pipe from his lips, 'that now is our time for filling our only empty chair.'

As our conversation had naturally turned upon the vacant seat, we lent a willing ear to this remark, and looked at our friend inquiringly.

'I feel sure,' said he, 'that Mr Pickwick must be acquainted with somebody who would be an acquisition to us; that he must know the man we want. Pray let us not lose any time, but set this question at rest. Is it so, Mr Pickwick?'

The gentleman addressed was about to return a verbal reply, but remembering our friend's infirmity he substituted for this kind of answer some fifty nods. Then taking up the slate and printing on it a gigantic 'Yes,' he handed it across the table, and rubbing his hands as he looked round upon our faces, protested that he and the deaf gentleman quite understood each other, already.

'The person I have in my mind,' said Mr Pickwick, 'and whom I should not have presumed to mention to you until some time hence, but for the opportunity you have given me, is a very strange old man. His name is Bamber.'

'Bamber!'[91] said Jack, 'I have certainly heard the name before.'

'I have no doubt then,' returned Mr Pickwick, 'that you remember him in those adventures of mine (the Posthumous Papers of our old club, I mean) although he is only incidentally mentioned; and, if I remember right, appears but once.'

'That's it,' said Jack. 'Let me see. He is the person who had a grave interest in old mouldy chambers and the Inns of court, and who relates some anecdotes having reference to his favourite theme – and an odd ghost-story – is that the man?'

'The very same. Now,' said Mr Pickwick, lowering his voice to a mysterious and confidential tone, 'he is a very extraordinary and remarkable person; living, and talking, and looking, like some strange spirit, whose delight is to haunt old buildings; and absorbed in that one subject which you have just mentioned, to an extent which is quite wonderful. When I retired into private life, I sought him out, and I do assure you that the more I see of him, the more strongly I am impressed with the strange and dreamy character of his mind.'

'Where does he live?' I inquired.

'He lives,' said Mr Pickwick, 'in one of those dull lonely old places with which his thoughts and stories are all connected; quite alone, and often shut up close, for several weeks together. In the dusty solitude, he broods upon the fancies he has so long indulged, and when he goes into the world, or anybody from the world without goes to see him, they are still present to his mind and still his favourite topic. I may say, I believe, that he has brought himself to entertain a regard for me, and an interest in my visits; feelings which I am certain he would extend to Master Humphrey's Clock if he were once tempted to join us. All I wish you to understand, is, that he is a strange secluded visionary, in the world but not of it; and as unlike anybody here as he is unlike anybody elsewhere, that ever I have met, or known.'

Mr Miles received this account of our proposed companion with rather a wry face, and after murmuring that perhaps he was a little mad, inquired if he were rich.

'I never asked him,' said Mr Pickwick.

'You might know, Sir, for all that,' retorted Mr Miles, sharply.

'Perhaps so, Sir,' said Mr Pickwick, no less sharply than the other, 'but I do not. Indeed,' he added, relapsing into his usual mildness, 'I have no means of judging. He lives poorly, but that would seem to be in keeping with his character. I never heard him allude to his circumstances, and never fell into the society of any man who had the slightest acquaintance with them. I really have told you all I know about him, and it rests with you to say whether you wish to know more, or know quite enough already.'

We were unanimously of opinion that we would seek to know more; and as a sort of compromise with Mr Miles (who, although he said 'yes – oh certainly – he should like to know more about the gentleman – he had no right to put himself in opposition to the general wish' – and so forth, shook his head doubtfully and hemmed several times with peculiar gravity), it was arranged that Mr Pickwick should carry me with him on an evening visit to the subject of our discussion, for which purpose an early appointment between that gentleman and myself was immediately agreed upon; it being understood that I was to act upon my own responsibility, and invite him to join us, or not, as I might think proper. This solemn question determined, we returned to the clock-case, (where we have been forestalled by the reader,) and between its contents, and the conversation they occasioned, the remainder of our time passed very quickly.

When we broke up, Mr Pickwick took me aside, to tell me that he had spent a most charming and delightful evening. Having made this communication with an air of the strictest secrecy, he took Jack Redburn into another corner to tell him the same, and then retired into another corner with the deaf gentleman and the slate, to repeat the assurance. It was amusing to observe the contest in his mind, whether he should extend this confidence to Mr Miles, or treat him with dignified reserve. Half-a-dozen times he stepped up behind him with a friendly air, and as often stepped back again without saying a word; at last, when he was close at that gentleman's ear and upon the very point of whispering something conciliating and agreeable, Mr Miles happened suddenly to turn his head, upon which Mr Pickwick skipped away, and said with some fierceness, 'Good night, Sir – I was about to say good night, Sir – nothing more;' and so made a bow and left him.

'Now, Sam,' said Mr Pickwick, when he got down stairs.

'All right, Sir,' replied Mr Weller. 'Hold hard, Sir. Right arm fust – now the left – now one strong conwulsion, and the great-coat's on, Sir.'

Mr Pickwick acted upon these directions, and being further assisted by Sam who pulled at one side of the collar, and the elder Mr Weller who pulled hard at the other, was speedily enrobed. Mr Weller senior then produced a full-sized stable lantern, which he had carefully deposited in a remote corner, on his arrival, and inquired whether Mr Pickwick would have 'the lamps alight'.

'I think not to-night,' said Mr Pickwick.

'Then if this here lady vill per-mit,' rejoined Mr Weller, 'we'll leave it here, ready for next journey. This here lantern, mum,' said Mr Weller, handing it to the housekeeper, 'vunce belonged to the celebrated Bill Blinder as is now at grass, as all on us vill be in our turns. Bill, mum, wos the hostler as had charge o' them two vell known piebald leaders that run in the Bristol fast coach, and vould never go to no other tune but a sutherly vind and a cloudy sky,[92] which wos consekvently played incessant, by the guard, venever they wos on duty. He wos took wery bad one arternoon, arter having been off his feed, and wery shaky on his legs for some veeks; and he says to his mate, "Matey," he says, "I think I'm a-goin' the wrong side o' the post, and that my foot's wery near the bucket. Don't say I a'nt," he says, "for I know I am, and don't let me be interrupted," he says, "for I've saved a little money, and I'm a-goin' into the stable to make my last vill and testymint." "I'll take care as nobody interrupts," says his mate, "but you on'y hold up your head, and shake your ears a bit, and you're good for twenty year to come." Bill Blinder makes him no answer, but he goes away into the stable, and there he soon artervards lays himself down a'tween the two piebalds, and dies, – previously a-writin' outside the corn-chest, "This is the last vill and testymint of Villiam Blinder." They wos nat'rally wery much amazed at this, and arter looking among the litter, and up in the loft, and vere not, they opens the corn-chest, and finds that he'd been and chalked his vill inside the lid; so the lid wos obligated to be took off the hinges, and sent up to Doctor Commons[93] to be proved, and under that ere wery instrument this here lantern was passed to 'Tony Veller, vich circumstarnce, mum, gives it a wally in my eyes, and makes me rek-vest if you vill be so kind, as to take partickler care on it.'

The housekeeper graciously promised to keep the object of Mr Weller's regard in the safest possible custody, and Mr Pickwick, with a laughing face, took his leave. The bodyguard followed, side by side: old Mr Weller buttoned and wrapped up from his boots to his chin; and Sam with his hands in his pockets and his hat half off his head, remonstrating with his father, as he went, on his extreme loquacity.

I was not a little surprised, on turning to go up stairs, to encounter the barber in the passage at that late hour; for his attendance is usually confined to some half-hour in the morning. But Jack Redburn, who finds out (by instinct, I think) everything that happens in the house, informed me with great glee, that a society in imitation of our own had been that night formed in the kitchen, under the title of 'Mr Weller's Watch,' of which the barber was a member; and that he could pledge himself to find means of making me acquainted with the whole of its future proceedings, which I begged him, both on my own account and that of my readers, by no means to neglect doing.

*No. 9 (30 May 1840)*

MR WELLER'S WATCH

It seems that the housekeeper and the two Mr Wellers were no sooner left together on the occasion of their first becoming acquainted, than the housekeeper called to her assistance Mr Slithers the barber, who had been lurking in the kitchen in

expectation of her summons; and with many smiles and much sweetness introduced him as one who would assist her in the responsible office of entertaining her distinguished visitors. 'Indeed,' said she, 'without Mr Slithers, I should have been placed in quite an awkward situation.'

'There is no call for any hock'erdness, mum' said Mr Weller with the utmost politeness; 'no call wotsumever. A lady' added the old gentleman, looking about him with the air of one who establishes an incontrovertible position, 'a lady can't be hock'erd. Natur has otherwise purwided.'

The housekeeper inclined her head and smiled yet more sweetly. The barber, who had been fluttering about Mr Weller and Sam in a state of great anxiety to improve their acquaintance, rubbed his hands and cried 'Hear! hear! Very true sir;' whereupon Sam turned about and steadily regarded him for some seconds in silence.'

'I never knew' said Sam, fixing his eyes in a ruminative manner upon the blushing barber, 'I never knew but vun o'your trade, but *he* wos worth a dozen and wos indeed dewoted to his callin'!'

'Was he in the easy shaving way sir,' inquired Mr Slithers; 'or in the cutting and curling line?'

'Both' replied Sam; 'easy shavin' was his natur, and cuttin' and curlin' was his pride and glory. His whole delight wos in his trade. He spent all his money in bears,[94] and run in debt for 'em besides, and there they wos a growling avay down in the front cellar all day long, and ineffectooally gnashing their teeth, vile the grease o' their relations and friends wos being re-tailed in gallipots[95] in the shop above, and the first-floor winder wos ornamented vith their heads; not to speak o' the dreadful aggrawation it must have been to 'em to see a man alvays a walkin' up and down the pavement outside, vith the portrait of a bear in his last agonies, and underneath in large letters "Another fine animal wos slaughtered yesterday at Jinkinson's!" Hows'ever, there they wos, and there Jinkinson wos, till he wos took wery ill with some inn'ard disorder, lost the use of his legs, and wos confined to his bed vere he laid a wery long time, but sich wos his pride in his profession even then, that wenever he wos worse than usual the doctor used to go down stairs and say "Jinkinson's wery low this mornin'; we must give the bears a stir;" and as sure as ever they stirred 'em up a bit and made 'em roar, Jinkinson opens his eyes if he wos ever so bad, calls out "There's the bears!" and rewives agin.'

'Astonishing!' cried the barber.

'Not a bit,' said Sam, 'human natur neat as imported. Vun day the doctor happenin' to say "I shall look in as usual tomorrow mornin', Jinkinson catches hold of his hand and says "Doctor" he says, "will you grant me one favor?" "I will Jinkinson" says the doctor; "then doctor" says Jinkinson "vill you come unshaved, and let me shave you?" "I will" says the doctor. "God bless you" says Jinkinson. Next day the doctor came, and arter he'd been shaved all skilful and reg'lar, he says "Jinkinson," he says "it's wery plain this does you good. Now" he says "I've got a coachman as has got a beard that it 'ud warm your heart to work on, and though the footman" he says "hasn't got much of a beard, still he's a trying it on vith a pair o' viskers to that extent that razors is christian charity. If they take it in turns to mind the carriage wen it's a waitin' below" he says "wot's to hinder you from operatin' on both of 'em ev'ry day as well as upon me? you've got six children" he says, "wot's to hinder you from shavin' all their heads and keepin' 'em shaved? you've got two assistants in the shop down stairs, wot's to hinder you from cuttin' and curlin' them as often as you like? Do this" he says "and you're a man agin." Jinkinson squeedged the doctor's hand and begun that wery day; he kept his tools upon the bed, and wenever he felt his-self gettin' worse, he turned to at vun o' the children who wos a runnin' about the house vith heads like clean Dutch cheeses, and shaved him agin. Vun day the lawyer come to make his vill; all the time he wos a takin' it down, Jinkinson was secretly a clippin' away at his hair with a large pair of scissors. "Wot's that 'ere snippin' noise?" says the lawyer every now and then, "it's like a man havin' his hair cut." "It *is* wery like a man havin' his hair cut" says poor Jinkinson hidin' the scissors and lookin' quite innocent. By the time the lawyer found it out, he was wery nearly bald. Jinkinson was kept alive in this vay for a long time, but at last vun day he has in all the children vun arter another, shaves each on 'em wery clean, and gives him vun kiss on the crown of his head; then he has in the two assistants and arter cuttin' and curlin' of 'em in the first style of elegance, says he should like to hear the woice o' the greasiest bear, vich rekvest is immedetly complied with; then he says that he feels wery happy in his mind and vishes to be left alone; and then he dies, prevously cuttin' his own hair and makin' one flat curl in the wery middle of his forehead.'

This anecdote produced an extraordinary effect, not only upon Mr Slithers but upon the housekeeper also, who evinced so much anxiety to please and to be pleased, that Mr Weller, with a manner betokening some alarm, conveyed a whispered inquiry to his son whether he had gone 'too fur.'

'Wot do you mean by too fur?' demanded Sam.

'In that 'ere little compliment respectin' the want of hock'erdness in ladies Sammy' replied his father.

'You don't think she's fallen in love with you in consekens o' that, do you!' said Sam.

'More unlikelier things have come to pass my boy,' replied Mr Weller in a hoarse whisper; 'I'm always afeerd of inadwertent captiwation Sammy. If I know'd how to make myself ugly or unpleasant I'd do it, Samivel, rayther than live in this here state of perpetival terror!'

Mr Weller had, at that time, no further opportunity of dwelling upon the apprehensions which beset his mind, for the immediate occasion of his fears proceeded to lead the way down stairs, apologising as they went for conducting him into the kitchen, which apartment, however, she was induced to proffer for his accommodation in preference to her own little room, the rather as it afforded greater facilities for smoking, and was immediately adjoining the ale-cellar. The preparations which were already made sufficiently proved that these were not mere words of course, for on the deal table were a sturdy ale jug and glasses, flanked with clean pipes and a plentiful supply of tobacco for the old gentleman and his son, while on a dresser hard by was goodly store of cold meat and other eatables. At sight of these arrangements Mr Weller was at first distracted between his love of joviality and his doubts whether they were not to be considered as so many evidences of captivation having already taken place; but he soon yielded to his natural impulse, and took his seat at the table with a very jolly countenance.

'As to imbibin' any o' this here flagrant veed, mum, in the presence of a lady,' said Mr Weller, taking up a pipe and laying it down again, 'it couldn't be. Samivel, total abstinence, if *you* please.'

'But I like it of all things,' said the housekeeper.

'No,' rejoined Mr Weller, shaking his head. 'No.'

'Upon my word I do,' said the housekeeper. 'Mr Slithers knows I do.'

Mr Weller coughed, and notwithstanding the barber's confirmation of the statement, said No again, but more feebly than before. The housekeeper lighted a piece of paper and insisted on applying it to the bowl of the pipe with her own fair hands; Mr Weller resisted; the housekeeper cried that her fingers would be burnt; Mr Weller gave way. The pipe was ignited, Mr Weller drew a long puff of smoke, and detecting himself in the very act of smiling on the housekeeper, put a sudden constraint upon his countenance and looked sternly at the candle, with a determination not to captivate, himself, or encourage thoughts of captivation in others. From this iron frame of mind he was roused by the voice of his son.

'I don't think,' said Sam who was smoking with great composure and enjoyment, 'that if the lady wos agreeable, it 'ud be wery far out o' the vay for us four to make up a club of our own like the governors does up stairs, and let him,' Sam pointed with the stem of his pipe towards his parent, 'be the president.'

The housekeeper affably declared that it was the very thing she had been thinking of. The barber said the same. Mr Weller said nothing, but he laid down his pipe as if in a fit of inspiration, and performed the following manœuvres.

Unbuttoning the three lower buttons of his waistcoat, and pausing for a moment to enjoy the easy flow of breath consequent upon this process, he laid violent hands upon his watch-chain and slowly and with extreme difficulty drew from his fob[96] an immense double-cased silver watch, which brought the lining of the pocket with it and was not to be disentangled but by great exertions and an amazing redness of face. Having fairly got it out at last, he detached the outer case, and wound it up with a key of corresponding magnitude, then put the case on again, and having applied the watch to his ear to ascertain that it was still going, gave it some half-dozen hard knocks on the table to improve its performance.

'That,' said Mr Weller, laying it on the table with its face upwards, 'is the title and emblem o' this here society. Sammy, reach them two stools this vay for the wacant cheers. Ladies and gen'lmen, Mr Weller's watch is vound up and now a goin'. Order!'

By way of enforcing this proclamation, Mr Weller, using the watch after the manner of a president's hammer, and remarking with great pride that nothing hurt it and that falls and concussions of all kinds materially enhanced the excellence of the works and assisted the regulator, knocked the table a great many times and declared the association formally constituted.

'And don't let's have no grinnin' at the cheer Samivel,' said Mr Weller to his son, 'or I shall be committin' you to the cellar, and then p'raps we may get into wot the 'Merrikins call a fix, and the English a qvestion o' privileges.'[97]

Having uttered this friendly caution, the president settled himself in his chair with great dignity, and requested that Mr Samuel would relate an anecdote.

'I've told one,' said Sam.

'Wery good sir; tell another,' returned the chair.

'We wos a talking jist now sir,' said Sam turning to Slithers, 'about barbers. Pursuing that 'ere fruitful theme sir, I'll tell you in a wery few words a romantic little story about another barber, as pr'aps you may never have heerd.'

'Samivel!' said Mr Weller, again bringing his watch and the table into smart collision, 'address your observations to the cheer, sir, and not to priwate indiwiduals!'

'And if I might rise to order,' said the barber in a soft voice, and looking round him with a conciliatory smile as he leant over the table with the knuckles of his left hand resting upon it, 'if I *might* rise to order, I would suggest that "barbers" is not exactly the kind of language which is agreeable and soothing to our feelings. You, sir, will correct me if I'm wrong, but I believe there *is* such a word in the dictionary as hair-dressers.'

'Well, but suppose he wasn't a hair-dresser,' suggested Sam.

'Wy then sir, be parliamentary, and call him vun[98] all the more,' returned his father. 'In the same vay as ev'ry gen'lman in another place is a *h*onorable, ev'ry barber in this place is a hair-dresser. Ven you read the speeches in the papers, and see as vun gen'lman says of another, "the *h*onorable member if he vill allow me to call him so," you vill understand sir that that means, "if he vill allow me to keep up that 'ere pleasant and uniwersal fiction?"'

It is a common remark, confirmed by history and experience, that great men rise with the circumstances in which they are placed. Mr Weller came out so strong in his capacity of chairman, that Sam was for some time prevented from speaking by a grin of surprise, which held his faculties enchained and at last subsided in a long whistle of a single note. Nay, the old gentleman appeared even to have astonished himself, and that to no small extent, as was demonstrated by the vast amount of chuckling in which he indulged after the utterance of these lucid remarks.

'Here's the story,' said Sam. 'Vunce upon a time there wos a young hair-dresser as opened a wery smart little shop with four wax dummies in the winder, two gen'lmen and two ladies – the gen'lmen with blue dots for their beards, wery large viskers, oudacious heads of hair, uncommon clear eyes, and nostrils of amazin' pinkness – the ladies vith their heads o' one side, their right forefingers on their lips, and their forms deweloped beautiful, in vich last respect they had the adwantage over the gen'lmen, as wasn't allowed but wery little shoulder and terminated rayther abrupt, in fancy drapery. He had also a many hairbrushes and toothbrushes bottled up in the winder, neat glass-cases on the counter, a floor-clothed cuttin' room up-stairs, and a weighin' macheen in the shop, right opposite the door; but the great attraction and ornament wos the dummies, which this here young hairdresser wos constantly a runnin' out in the road to look at, and constantly a runnin' in agin to touch up and polish; in short he was so proud on 'em that ven Sunday come, he wos always wretched and mis'rable to think they wos behind the shutters, and looked anxiously for Monday on that account. Vun o' these dummies wos a fav'rite vith him beyond the others, and ven any of his acquaintance asked him wy he didn't get married – as the young ladies he know'd, in partickler, often did – he used to say, "Never! I never vill enter into the bonds of vedlock," he says, "until I meet with a young 'ooman as realizes my idea o' that ere fairest dummy vith the light hair. Then and not till then," he says, "I vill approach the altar!' All the young ladies he know'd as had got dark hair told him this wos wery sinful and that he wos wurshippin' a idle, but them as wos at all near the same shade as the dummy coloured up wery much, and wos observed to think him a wery nice young man.'

'Samivel,' said Mr Weller gravely; 'a member o' this assosiashun bein' one o' that 'ere tender sex which is now immedetly referred to, I have to rekvest that you vill make no reflexions.'

'I ain't a makin' any, am I?' inquired Sam.

'Order sir!' rejoined Mr Weller with severe dignity; then sinking the chairman in the father, he added in his usual tone of voice, 'Samivel, drive on!'

Sam interchanged a smile with the housekeeper, and proceeded:

'The young hair-dresser hadn't been in the habit o' makin' this awowal above six months, ven he encountered a young lady as wos the wery picter o' the fairest dummy. "Now," he says, "it's all up. I am a slave!" The young lady wos not only the picter o' the fairest dummy, but she wos wery romantic as the young hair-dresser wos too, and he says "Oh!" he says "here's a community o' feelin', here's a flow o' soul!" he says, "here's a interchange o' sentiment!" The young lady didn't say much o' course, but she expressed herself agreeable, and shortly artervards vent to see him vith a mutual friend. The hair-dresser rushes out to meet her, but d'rectly she sees the dummies she changes colour and falls a tremblin' wiolently. "Look up my love" says the hair-dresser, "behold your imige in my winder, but not correcter than in my art!" "My imige!" she says. "Your'n!" replies the hair-dresser. "But whose imige is *that!*" she says, a pinting at vun o' the gen'lmen. "No vun's my love" he says "it is but a idea." "A idea!" she cries, "it is a portrait, I feel it is a portrait, and that 'ere noble face must be in the milingtary!" "Wot do I hear!" says he a crumplin' his curls. "Villiam Gibbs" she says quite firm, "never renoo the subject. I respect you as a friend" she says "but my affections is set upon that manly brow." "This" says the hairdresser "is a reg'lar blight, and in it I perceive the hand of Fate. Farevell!" Vith these vords he rushes into the shop, breaks the dummy's nose vith a blow of his curlin' irons, melts him down at the parlour fire, and never smiles artervards.'

'The young lady, Mr Weller?' said the housekeeper.

'Why ma'am' said Sam, 'finding that Fate had a spite agin her and everybody she come into contact vith, she never smiled neither, but read a deal o' poetry and pined avay – by rayther slow degrees, for she an't dead yet. It took a deal o' poetry to kill the hair-dresser, and some people say arter all that it was more the gin and water as caused him to be run over; p'raps it wos a little o' both, and came o' mixing the two.'

The barber declared that Mr Weller had related one of the most interesting stories that had ever come within his knowledge, in which opinion the housekeeper entirely concurred.

'Are you a married man sir?' inquired Sam.

The barber replied that he had not that honour.

'I s'pose you mean to be?' said Sam.

'Well,' replied the barber rubbing his hands smirkingly, 'I don't know, I don't think it's very likely.'

'That's a bad sign' said Sam, 'if you'd said you meant to be vun o' these days, I should ha' looked upon you as bein' safe. You're in a wery precarious state.'

'I am not conscious of any danger, at all events,' returned the barber.

'No more wos I sir,' said the elder Mr Weller, interposing, 'those vere my symptoms exactly. I've been took that vay twice. Keep your vether eye open my friend, or you're gone.'

There was something so very solemn about this admonition, both in its matter and manner, and also in the way in which Mr Weller still kept his eye fixed upon the unsuspecting victim, that nobody cared to speak for some little time, and might not have cared to do so for some time longer, if the housekeeper had not happened to sigh, which called off the old gentleman's attention and gave rise to a gallant inquiry whether, 'there wos anythin' wery piercin' in that 'ere little heart.'

'Dear me, Mr Weller!' said the housekeeper, laughing.

'No, but is there anythin' as agitates it?' pursued the old gentleman. 'Has it always been obderrate, always opposed to the happiness o' human creeturs? Eh? Has it?'

At this critical juncture for her blushes and confusion, the housekeeper discovered that more ale was wanted, and hastily withdrew into the cellar to draw the same, followed by the barber who insisted on carrying the candle. Having looked after her with a very complacent expression of face, and after him with some disdain, Mr Weller caused his glance to travel slowly round the kitchen until at length it rested on his son.

'Sammy,' said Mr Weller, 'I mistrust that barber.'

'Wot for?' returned Sam, 'wot's he got to do with you? You're a nice man, you are, arter pretendin' all kinds o' terror, to go a payin' compliments and talkin' about hearts and piercers.'

The imputation of gallantry appeared to afford. Mr Weller the utmost delight, for he replied in a voice choked by suppressed laughter and with the tears in his eyes.

'Wos I a talkin' about hearts and piercers – was I though, Sammy, eh?'

'Wos you; of course you wos.'

'She don't know no better Sammy, there an't no harm in it – no danger Sammy; she's only a punster. She seemed pleased though, didn't she? O' course she wos pleased, it's nat'ral she should be, wery nat'ral.'

'He's wain of it!' exclaimed Sam, joining in his father's mirth. 'He's actually wain!'

'Hush!' replied Mr Weller, composing his features, 'they're a comin' back, the little heart's a comin' back. But mark these wurds o' mine once more, and remember 'em ven your father says he said 'em. Samivel, I mistrust that 'ere deceitful barber.'

*From No. 11 (13 June 1840)*

MASTER HUMPHREY FROM HIS CLOCK-SIDE
IN THE CHIMNEY-CORNER

Two or three evenings after the Institution of Mr Weller's Watch, I thought I heard as I walked in the garden the voice of Mr Weller himself at no great distance; and stopping once or twice to listen more attentively, I found that the sounds proceeded from my housekeeper's little sitting-room which is at the back of the house. I took no further notice of the circumstance at that time, but it formed the subject of a conversation between me and my friend Jack Redburn next morning, when I found that I had not been deceived in my impression. Jack furnished me with the following particulars, and as he appeared to take extraordinary pleasure in relating them, I have begged him in future to jot down any such domestic scenes or occurrences that may please his humour, in order that they may be told in his own way. I must confess that as Mr Pickwick and he are constantly together, I have been influenced, in making this request, by a secret desire to know something of their proceedings.

On the evening in question, the housekeeper's room was arranged with particular care, and the housekeeper herself was very smartly dressed. The preparations, however, were not confined to mere showy demonstrations, as tea was prepared for three persons, with a small display of preserves and jams and sweet cakes, which heralded some uncommon occasion. Miss Benton (my housekeeper bears that name) was in a state of great expectation too, frequently going to the front door and looking anxiously down the lane, and more than once observing to the servant girl that she expected company and hoped no accident had happened to delay them.

A modest ring at the bell at length allayed her fears, and Miss Benton hurrying into her own room and shutting herself up in order that she might preserve that appearance of being taken by surprise which is so essential to the polite reception of visitors, awaited their coming with a smiling countenance.

'Good ev'nin mum,' said the older Mr Weller looking in at the door after a prefatory tap, 'I'm afeerd we've come in, rayther arter the time mum, but the young colt being full o' wice has been a boltin' and shyin' and gettin' his leg over the traces to sich a ex-tent that if he an't wery soon broke in, he'll wex me into a broken heart, and then he'll never be brought out no more except to learn his letters from the writin' on his grandfather's tombstone.'

With these pathetic words, which were addressed to something outside the door about two feet six from the ground, Mr Weller introduced a very small boy firmly set upon a couple of very sturdy legs, who looked as if nothing could ever knock him down. Besides having a very round face strongly resembling Mr Weller's, and a stout little body of exactly his build, this young gentleman standing with his little legs very wide apart as if the top boots were familiar to them, actually winked upon the housekeeper with his infant eye, in imitation of his grandfather.

'There's a naughty boy mum,' said Mr Weller bursting with delight, 'there's a immoral Tony. Wos there ever a little chap o' four year and eight months old as vinked his eye at a strange lady, afore?'

As little affected by this observation as by the former appeal

to his feelings, Master Weller elevated in the air a small model of a coach whip which he carried in his hand, and addressing the housekeeper with a shrill 'ya – hip!' inquired if she was 'going down the road;' at which happy adaptation of a lesson he had been taught from infancy, Mr Weller could restrain his feelings no longer, but gave him twopence on the spot.

'It's in wain to deny it mum,' said Mr Weller, 'this here is a boy arter his grandfather's own heart, and beats out all the boys as ever wos or will be. Though at the same time mum,' added Mr Weller trying to look gravely down upon his favourite, 'it was wery wrong on him to want to over all the posts as we come along, and wery cruel on him to force poor grandfather to lift him cross-legged over every vun of 'em. He wouldn't pass vun single blessed post mum, and at the top o' the lane there's seven-and-forty on 'em all in a row and wery close together.'

Here Mr Weller, whose feelings were in a perpetual conflict between pride in his grandson's achievements, and a sense of his own responsibility and the importance of impressing him with moral truths, burst into a fit of laughter, and suddenly checking himself, remarked in a severe tone that little boys as made their grandfather put 'em over posts, never went to heaven at any price.

By this time the housekeeper had made tea, and little Tony placed on a chair beside her with his eyes nearly on a level with the top of the table, was provided with various delicacies which yielded him extreme contentment. The housekeeper (who seemed rather afraid of the child notwithstanding her caresses) then patted him on the head and declared that he was the finest boy she had ever seen.

'Wy, mum,' said Mr Weller, 'I don't think you'll see a many sich, and that's the truth. But if my son Samivel vould give me my vay, mum, and only dis-pense vith his – *might* I wenter to say the vurd?'

'What word Mr Weller?' said the housekeeper, blushing slightly.

'Petticuts, mum,' returned that gentleman, laying his hand upon the garments of his grandson. 'If my son Samivel, mum, vould only dis-pense vith these here, you'd see such a alteration in his appearance, as the imagination can't depicter.'

'But what would you have the child wear instead, Mr Weller?' said the housekeeper.

'I've offered my son Samivel, mum, agen and agen,' returned the old gentleman, 'to purwide him at my own cost vith a suit o' clothes as 'ud be the makin' on him, and form his mind in infancy for those pursuits as I hope the family o' the Vellers vill always dewote themselves to. Tony, my boy, tell the lady wot them clothes are, as grandfather says, father ought to let you vear.'

'A little white hat and a little sprig[99] weskut and little knee cords[100] and little top-boots and a little green coat with little bright buttons and a little welvet collar,' replied Tony with great readiness and no stops.

'That's the cos-toom, mum' said Mr Weller, looking proudly at the housekeeper. 'Once make sich a model on him as that, and you'd say he *wos* a angel!'

Perhaps the housekeeper thought that in such a guise young Tony would look more like the angel at Islington[101] than anything else of that name, or perhaps she was disconcerted to find her previously conceived ideas disturbed, as angels are not commonly represented in top-boots and sprig waistcoats. She coughed doubtfully, but said nothing.

'How many brothers and sisters have you my dear?' she asked after a short silence.

'One brother and no sisters at all,' replied Tony. 'Sam his name is, and so's my father's. Do you know my father?'

'Oh yes, I know him,' said the housekeeper, graciously.

'Is my father fond of you?' pursued Tony.

'I hope so,' rejoined the smiling housekeeper.

Tony considered a moment, and then said, 'Is my grandfather fond of you?'

This would seem a very easy question to answer, but instead of replying to it, the housekeeper smiled in great confusion, and said that really children did ask such extraordinary questions that it was the most difficult thing in the world to talk to them. Mr Weller took upon himself to reply that he was very fond of the lady; but the housekeeper entreating that he would not put such things into the child's head, Mr Weller shook his own while she looked another way, and seemed to be troubled with a misgiving that captivation was in progress. It was perhaps on this account that he changed the subject precipitately.

'It's wery wrong in little boys to make game o' their grandfathers, a'nt it mum?' said Mr Weller, shaking his head waggishly, until Tony looked at him, when he counterfeited the deepest dejection and sorrow.

'Oh very sad!' assented the housekeeper. 'But I hope no little boys do that?'

'There is vun young Turk, mum,' said Mr Weller, 'as havin' seen his grandfather a little overcome with drink on the occasion of a friend's birthday, goes a reelin' and staggerin' about the house, and makin' believe that he's the old gen'lm'n.'

'Oh quite shocking!' cried the housekeeper.

'Yes mum,' said Mr Weller, 'and prevously to so doin', this here young traitor that I'm a speakin' of, pinches his little nose to make it red, and then he gives a hiccup and says "Im all right" he says "give us another song!" Ha ha! "Give us another song" he says. Ha ha ha!'

In his excessive delight, Mr Weller was quite unmindful of his moral responsibility, until little Tony kicked up his legs and laughing immoderately cried 'That was me, that was:'

whereupon the grandfather by a great effort became extremely solemn.

'No Tony, not you,' said Mr Weller. 'I hope it warn't you Tony. It must ha' been that 'ere naughty little chap as comes sometimes out o' the empty watch-box[102] round the corner – that same little chap as wos found standing on the table afore the looking-glass, pretending to shave himself vith a oyster-knife.'

'He didn't hurt himself I hope?' observed the housekeeper.

'Not he mum,' said Mr Weller proudly, 'bless your heart you might trust that 'ere boy vith a steam engine a'most, he's such a knowin' young' – but suddenly recollecting himself and observing that Tony perfectly understood and appreciated the compliment, the old gentleman groaned and observed that 'it wos all wery shockin' – wery.'

'Oh he's a bad 'un,' said Mr Weller, 'is that 'ere watch-box boy, makin' such a noise and litter in the back-yard, he does, waterin' wooden horses and feedin' of 'em vith grass, and perpetivally spillin' his little brother out of a veel-barrow and frightenin' his mother out of her wits, at the wery moment wen she's expectin' to increase his stock of happiness vith another play-feller – oh he's a bad 'un! He's even gone so far as to put on a pair o' paper spectacles as he got his father to make for him, and walk up and down the garden vith his hands behind him in imitation of Mr Pickwick – but Tony don't do sich things, oh no!'

'Oh no!' echoed Tony.

'He knows better, he does,' said Mr Weller, 'he knows that if he wos to come sich games as these, nobody wouldn't love him, and that his grandfather in partickler couldn't abear the sight on him; for vich reasons Tony's always good.'

'Always good,' echoed Tony; and his grandfather immediately took him on his knee and kissed him, at the same time with many nods and winks slyly pointing at the child's head with his thumb, in order that the housekeeper, otherwise deceived by the admirable manner in which he (Mr Weller) had sustained his character, might not suppose that any other young gentleman was referred to, and might clearly understand that the boy of the watch-box was but an imaginary creation, and a fetch[103] of Tony himself, invented for his improvement and reformation.

Not confining himself to a mere verbal description of his

grandson's abilities, Mr Weller, when tea was finished, incited him by various gifts of pence and half-pence to smoke imaginary pipes, drink visionary beer from real pots, imitate his grandfather without reserve, and in particular to go through the drunken scene, which threw the old gentleman into ecstacies and filled the housekeeper with wonder. Nor was Mr Weller's pride satisfied with even this display, for when he took his leave he carried the child like some rare and astonishing curiosity, first to the barber's house and afterwards to the tobacconist's, at each of which places he repeated his performances with the utmost effect to applauding and delighted audiences. It was halfpast nine o'clock when Mr Weller was last seen carrying him home upon his shoulder, and it has been whispered abroad that at that time the infant Tony was rather intoxicated.

*From No. 45 (6 February 1841)*

## MASTER HUMPHREY FROM HIS CLOCK-SIDE IN THE CHIMNEY-CORNER

I was musing the other evening upon the characters and incidents with which I had been so long engaged; wondering how I could ever have looked forward with pleasure to the completion of my tale, and reproaching myself for having done so, as if it were a kind of cruelty to those companions of my solitude whom I had now dismissed, and could never again recall; when my clock struck ten. Punctual to the hour, my friends appeared.

On our last night of meeting, we had finished the story which the reader has just concluded. Our conversation took the same current as the meditations which the entrance of my friends had interrupted, and the Old Curiosity Shop was the staple of our discourse.

I may confide to the reader now, that in connexion with this little history I had something upon my mind – something to communicate which I had all along with difficulty repressed – something I had deemed it, during the progress of the story, necessary to its interest to disguise, and which, now that it was over, I wished, and was yet reluctant to disclose.

To conceal anything from those to whom I am attached, is not in my nature. I can never close my lips where I have opened my heart. This temper and the consciousness of having done some violence to it in my narrative, laid me under a restraint which I should have had great difficulty in overcoming, but for a timely remark from Mr Miles, who, as I hinted in a former paper, is a gentleman of business habits, and of great exactness and propriety in all his transactions.

'I could have wished,' my friend objected; 'that we had been made acquainted with the single gentleman's[104] name. I don't like his withholding his name. It made me look upon him at first with suspicion, and caused me to doubt his moral character, I assure you. I am fully satisfied by this time of his being a worthy creature, but in this respect he certainly would not appear to have acted at all like a man of business.'

'My friends,' said I, drawing to the table at which they were by this time seated in their usual chairs, 'do you remember that this story bore another title besides that one we have so often heard of late?'

Mr Miles had his pocket-book out in an instant, and referring to an entry therein, rejoined 'Certainly. Personal adventures of Master Humphrey. Here it is. I made a note of it at the time.'

I was about to resume what I had to tell them, when the same Mr Miles again interrupted me, observing that the narrative originated in a personal adventure of my own, and that was no doubt the reason for its being thus designated.

This led me to the point at once.

'You will one and all forgive me,' I returned, 'if, for the greater convenience of the story, and for its better introduction, that adventure was fictitious. I had my share indeed – no light or trivial one – in the pages we have read, but it was not the share I feigned to have at first. The younger brother, the single gentleman, the nameless actor in this little drama, stands before you now.'

It was easy to see they had not expected this disclosure.

'Yes,' I pursued. 'I can look back upon my part in it with a calm, half-smiling pity for myself as for some other man. But I am he indeed; and now the chief sorrows of my life are yours.'

I need not say what true gratification I derived from the sympathy and kindness with which this acknowledgment was received; nor how often it had risen to my lips before; nor how difficult I had found it – how impossible, when I came to those passages which touched me most, and most nearly concerned me – to sustain the character I had assumed. It is enough to say that I replaced in the clock-case the record of so many trials – sorrowfully, it is true, but with a softened sorrow which was almost pleasure; and felt that in living through the past again, and communicating to others the lesson it had helped to teach me, I had been a happier man.

We lingered so long over the leaves from which I had read, that as I consigned them to their former resting-place, the hand of my trusty clock pointed to twelve, and there came towards us upon the wind the voice of the deep and distant bell of St Paul's as it struck the hour of midnight.

'This,' said I, returning with a manuscript I had taken, at the moment, from the same repository, 'to be opened to such music, should be a tale where London's face by night is darkly seen, and where some deed of such a time as this is dimly shadowed out. Which of us here has seen the working of that great machine whose voice has just now ceased?'

Mr Pickwick had, of course, and so had Mr Miles. Jack and my deaf friend were in the minority.

I had seen it but a few days before, and could not help telling them of the fancy I had had about it.

I paid my fee of twopence upon entering, to one of the money-changers who sit within the Temple; and falling, after a few turns up and down, into the quiet train of thought which such a place awakens, paced the echoing stones like some old monk whose present world lay all within its walls. As I looked afar up into the lofty dome, I could not help wondering what were his reflections whose genius[105] reared that mighty pile, when, the last small wedge of timber fixed, the last nail driven into its home for many centuries, the clang of hammers, and the hum of busy voices, gone, and the Great Silence whole years of noise had helped to make, reigning undisturbed around, he mused as I did now, upon his work, and lost himself amid its vast extent. I could not quite determine whether the contemplation of it would impress him with a sense of greatness or of insignificance; but when I remembered how long a time it had taken to erect, in how short a space it might be traversed even to its remotest parts, for how brief a term he, or any of those who cared to bear his name, would live to see it, or know of its existence, I imagined him far more melancholy than proud, and looking with regret upon his labour done. With these thoughts in my mind, I began to ascend, almost unconsciously, the flight of steps leading to the several wonders of the building, and found myself before a barrier where another money-taker sat, who demanded which among them I would choose to see. There were the stone-gallery, he said, and the whispering gallery, the geometrical staircase, the room of models, the clock[106] – the clock being quite in my way, I stopped him there, and chose that sight from all the rest.

I groped my way into the Turret which it occupies, and saw before me, in a kind of loft, what seemed to be a great, old, oaken press with folding doors. These being thrown back by the attendant (who was sleeping when I came upon him, and looked a drowsy fellow, as though his close companionship with Time had made him quite indifferent to it) disclosed a complicated crowd of wheels and chains in iron and brass – great, sturdy, rattling engines – suggestive of breaking a finger put in here or there, and grinding the bone to powder – and these were the Clock! Its very pulse, if I may use the word, was like no other clock. It did not mark the flight of every moment with a gentle second stroke as though it would check old Time, and have him stay his pace in pity, but measured it with one sledge-hammer beat, as if its business were to crush the seconds as they came trooping on, and remorselessly to clear a path before the Day of Judgment.

I sat down opposite it, and hearing its regular and never-changing voice, that one deep constant note, uppermost amongst all the noise and clatter in the streets below – marking that, let that tumult rise or fall, go on or stop – let it be night or noon, tomorrow or today, this year or next – it still performed its functions with the same dull constancy, and regulated the progress of the life around, the fancy came upon me that this was London's Heart, and that when it should cease to beat, the City would be no more.

It is night. Calm and unmoved amidst the scenes that darkness favours, the great heart of London throbs in its Giant breast. Wealth and beggary, vice and virtue, guilt and innocence, repletion and the direst hunger, all treading on each other and crowding together, are gathered round it. Draw but a little circle above the clustering house-tops, and you shall have within its space, everything with its opposite extreme and contradiction, close beside. Where yonder feeble light is shining, a man is but this moment dead. The taper at a few yards' distance, is seen by eyes that have this instant opened on the world. There are two houses separated by but an inch or two of wall. In one, there are quiet minds at rest; in the other a waking conscience that one might think would trouble the very air. In that close corner where the roofs shrink down and cower together as if to hide their secrets from the handsome street hard by, there are such dark crimes, such miseries and horrors, as could be hardly told in whispers. In the handsome street, there are folks asleep who have dwelt there all their lives, and have no more knowledge of these things than if they had never been, or were transacted at the remotest limits of the world – who, if they were hinted at, would shake their heads, look wise, and frown, and say they were impossible, and out of Nature – as if all great towns were not. Does not this Heart of London, that nothing moves, nor stops, nor quickens – that goes on the same, let what will be done – does it not express the city's character well?

The day begins to break, and soon there is the hum and noise of life. Those who had spent the night on doorsteps and cold stones, crawl off to beg; they who have slept in beds, come forth to their occupation too, and business is astir. The fog of sleep rolls slowly off, and London shines awake. The streets are filled with carriages, and people gaily clad. The jails are full, too, to the throat, nor have the workhouses or hospitals much room to spare. The courts of law are crowded. Taverns have their regular frequenters by this time, and every mart[107] of traffic has its throng. Each of these places is a world, and has its own inhabitants; each is distinct from, and almost unconscious of the existence of any other. There are some few people well to do, who remember to have heard it said, that numbers of men and women – thousands they think it was – get up in London every day, unknowing where to lay their heads at night; and that there are quarters of the town where misery and famine always are. They don't believe it quite – there may be some truth in it, but it is exaggerated of course. So, each of these thousand worlds goes on, intent upon itself, until night comes again – first with its lights and pleasures, and its cheerful streets; then with its guilt and darkness.

Heart of London, there is a moral in thy every stroke! as I

look on at thy indomitable working, which neither death, nor press of life, nor grief, nor gladness out of doors will influence one jot, I seem to hear a voice within thee which sinks into my heart, bidding me, as I elbow my way among the crowd, have some thought for the meanest wretch that passes, and, being a man, to turn away with scorn and pride from none that bear the human shape.[108]

I am by no means sure that I might not have been tempted to enlarge upon this subject, had not the papers that lay before me on the table, been a silent reproach for even this digression. I took them up again when I had got thus far, and seriously prepared to read.

The handwriting was strange to me, for the manuscript had been fairly copied. As it is against our rules in such a case to inquire into the authorship until the reading is concluded, I could only glance at the different faces round me, in search of some expression which should betray the writer. Whoever he might be, he was prepared for this, and gave no sign for my enlightenment.

I had the papers in my hand, when my deaf friend interposed with a suggestion.

'It has occurred to me,' he said, 'bearing in mind your sequel to the tale we have finished, that if such of us as have anything to relate of our own lives, could interweave it with our contribution to the Clock, it would be well to do so. This need be no restraint upon us, either as to time, or place, or incident, since any real passage of this kind may be surrounded by fictitious circumstances, and represented by fictitious characters. What if we made this, an article of agreement among ourselves?'

The proposition was cordially received, but the difficulty appeared to be that here was a long story written before we had thought of it.

'Unless,' said I, 'it should have happened that the writer of this tale – which is not impossible, for men are apt to do so when they write – has actually mingled with it something of his own endurance and experience.'

Nobody spoke, but I thought I detected in one quarter that this was really the case.

'If I have no assurance to the contrary,' I added therefore, 'I shall take it for granted that he has done so, and that even these papers come within our new agreement. Everybody being mute, we hold that understanding if you please.'

And here I was about to begin again, when Jack informed us softly, that during the progress of our last narrative, Mr Weller's Watch had adjourned its sittings from the kitchen, and regularly met outside our door, where he had no doubt that august body would be found at the present moment. As this was for the convenience of listening to our stories, he submitted that they might be suffered to come in, and hear them more pleasantly.

To this we one and all yielded a ready assent, and the party being discovered as Jack had supposed, and invited to walk in, entered (though not without great confusion at having been detected) and were accommodated with chairs at a little distance.

Then, the lamp being trimmed, the fire well-stirred and burning brightly, the hearth clean swept, the curtains closely drawn, the clock wound up, we entered on our new story – BARNABY RUDGE.[109]

## MASTER HUMPHREY FROM HIS CLOCK-SIDE
## IN THE CHIMNEY-CORNER

It is again midnight. My fire burns cheerfully; the room is filled with my old friend's sober voice; and I am left to muse upon the story we have just now finished.

It makes me smile, at such a time as this, to think if there were any one to see me sitting in my easy chair, my grey head hanging down, my eyes bent thoughtfully upon the glowing embers, and my crutch – emblem of my helplessness – lying upon the hearth at my feet, how solitary I should seem. Yet though I am the sole tenant of this chimney corner, though I am childless and old, I have no sense of loneliness at this hour; but am the centre of a silent group whose company I love.

Thus, even age and weakness have their consolations. If I were a younger man; if I were more active; more strongly bound and tied to life; these visionary friends would shun me, or I should desire to fly from them. Being what I am, I can court their society; and delight in it; and pass whole hours in picturing to myself the shadows that perchance flock every night into this chamber, and in imagining with pleasure what kind of interest they have in the frail, feeble mortal, who is its sole inhabitant.

All the friends I have ever lost, I find again among these visitors. I love to fancy their spirits hovering about me, feeling still some earthly kindness for their old companion, and watching his decay. 'He is weaker, he declines apace, he draws nearer and nearer to us, and will soon be conscious of our existence.' What is there to alarm me in this! It is encouragement and hope.

These thoughts have never crowded on me half so fast as they have done tonight. Faces I had long forgotten, have become familiar to me once again; traits I had endeavoured to recal for years, have come before me in an instant; nothing is changed but me: and even I can be my former self at will.

Raising my eyes but now to the face of my old clock, I remember, quite involuntarily, the veneration, not unmixed with a sort of childish awe, with which I used to sit and watch it, as it ticked unheeded in a dark staircase corner. I recollect looking more grave and steady when I met its dusty face, as if, having that strange kind of life within it, and being free from all excess of vulgar appetite, and warning all the house by night and day, it were a sage. How often have I listened to it as it told the beads of time, and wondered at its constancy! How often watched it slowly pointing round the dial, and, while I panted for the eagerly expected hour to come, admired, despite myself, its steadiness of purpose, and lofty freedom from all human strife, impatience, and desire!

I thought it cruel once. It was very hard of heart, to my mind, I remember. It was an old servant, even then; and I felt as though it ought to show some sorrow; as though it wanted sympathy with us in our distress; and were a dull heartless, mercenary creature. Ah! how soon I learnt to know that in its ceaseless going on, and in its being checked or stayed by nothing, lay its greatest kindness, and the only balm for grief and wounded peace of mind!

To-night, to-night, when this tranquillity and calm are on my spirits, and memory presents so many shifting scenes before me, I take my quiet stand, at will, by many a fire that has been long extinguished, and mingle with the cheerful group that cluster round it. If I could be sorrowful in such a mood, I should grow sad to think what a poor blot I was upon their youth and beauty once, and now how few remain to put me to the blush; I should grow sad to think that such among them, as I sometimes meet with in my daily walks, are scarcely less infirm than I; that time has brought us to a level; and that all distinctions fade and vanish as we take our trembling steps towards the grave.

But memory was given us for better purposes than this: and mine is not a torment, but a source of pleasure. To muse upon the gaiety and youth I have known, suggests to me glad scenes of harmless mirth that may be passing now. From contemplating them apart, I soon become an actor in these little dramas; and humouring my fancy, lose myself among the beings it invokes.

When my fire is bright and high, and a warm blush mantles in the walls and ceiling of this ancient room; when my clock makes cheerful music, like one of those chirping insects who delight in the warm hearth, and are sometimes, by a good superstition, looked upon as the harbingers of fortune and plenty to that household in whose mercies they put their humble trust; when everything is in a ruddy genial glow, and there are voices in the crackling flame, and smiles in its flashing light; other smiles and other voices congregate around me,[110] invading with their pleasant harmony the silence of the time.

For then a knot of youthful creatures gather round my fireside, and the room re-echoes to their merry voices. My solitary chair no longer holds its ample place before the fire, but is wheeled into a smaller corner, to leave more room for the broad circle formed about the cheerful hearth. I have sons and daughters, and grandchildren; and we are assembled on some occasion of rejoicing common to us all. It is a birthday, perhaps, or perhaps it may be Christmas-time: but be it what it may, there is rare holyday among us, we are full of glee.

In the chimney-corner, opposite myself, sits one who has grown old beside me. She is changed, of course; much changed; and yet I recognise the girl, even in that grey hair and wrinkled brow. Glancing from the laughing child who half hides in her ample skirts, and half peeps out, – and from her to the little matron of twelve years old, who sits so womanly and so demure at no great distance from me, – and from her again to a fair girl in the full bloom of early womanhood: the centre of the group: who has glanced more than once towards the opening door, and by whom the children, whispering and tittering among themselves *will* leave a vacant chair, although she bids them not, – I see her image thrice repeated, and feel how long it is before one form and set of features wholly pass away, if ever, from among the living. While I am dwelling upon this, and tracing out the gradual change from infancy to youth; from youth to perfect growth; from that to age; and thinking, with an old man's pride, that she is comely yet; I feel a slight thin hand upon my arm, and, looking down, see seated at my feet a crippled boy – a gentle patient child – whose aspect I know well. He rests upon a little crutch – I know it, too – and leaning on it as he climbs my footstool, whispers in my ear, 'I am hardly one of these, dear grandfather, although I love them dearly. They are very kind to me, but you will be kinder still, I know.'

I have my hand upon his neck, and stoop to kiss him: when my clock strikes, my chair is in its old spot, and I am alone.

What if I be? What if this fireside be tenantless, save for the presence of one weak old man! From my house-top I can look upon a hundred homes, in every one of which these social companies are matters of reality. In my daily walks I pass a thousand men whose cares are all forgotten, whose labours are made light, whose dull routine of work from day to day is cheered and brightened, by their glimpses of domestic joy at home. Amid the struggles of this struggling town, what cheerful sacrifices are made; what toil endured with readiness; what patience shown, and fortitude displayed; for the mere sake of home and its affections! Let me thank Heaven that I can people my fireside with shadows such as these: with shadows of bright objects that exist in crowds about me: and let me say, 'I am alone no more.'

I never was less so, – I write it with a grateful heart, – than I am to-night. Recollections of the past and visions of the present, come to bear me company: the meanest man to whom I have ever given alms, appears to add his mite of peace and comfort to my stock: and whenever the fire within me shall grow cold, to light my path upon this earth no more, I pray that it may be at such an hour as this, and when I love the world as well as I do now.

### The Deaf Gentleman from his Own Apartment

Our dear friend laid down his pen at the end of the foregoing paragraph, to take it up no more. I little thought ever to employ mine upon so sorrowful a task as that which he has left me, and to which I now devote it.

As he did not appear among us at his usual hour next morning, we knocked gently at his door. No answer being given, it was softly opened; and then, to our surprise, we saw him seated before the ashes of his fire, with a little table I was accustomed to set at his elbow when I left him for the night, at a short distance from him; as though he had pushed it away with the idea of rising and retiring to his bed. His crutch and footstool lay at his feet as usual, and he was dressed in his chamber-gown, which he had put on before I left him. He was reclining in his chair, in his accustomed posture, with his face towards the fire, and seemed absorbed in meditation, – indeed, at first, we almost hoped he was.

Going up to him, we found him dead. I have often, very often, seen him sleeping, and always peacefully; but I never saw him look so calm and tranquil. His face wore a serene, benign expression, which had impressed me very strongly when we last shook hands: not that he had ever any other look, God knows: but there was something in this so very spiritual, so strangely and indefinably allied to youth, although his head was grey and venerable, that it was new even in him. It came upon me all at once, when on some slight pretence he called me back upon the previous night, to take me by the hand again, and once more say, 'God bless you.'

A bell-rope hung within his reach, but he had not moved towards it, nor had he stirred, we all agreed, except, as I have said, to push away his table, which he could have done, and no doubt did, with a very slight motion of his hand. He had relapsed for a moment into his late train of meditation, and with a thoughtful smile upon his face, had died.

I had long known it to be his wish, that whenever this event should come to pass, we might be all assembled in the house. I therefore lost no time in sending for Mr Pickwick and for Mr Miles: both of whom arrived before the messenger's return.

It is not my purpose to dilate upon the sorrow, and affectionate emotions, of which I was at once the witness and the sharer. But I may say, of the humbler mourners, that his faithful housekeeper was fairly heartbroken; that the poor barber would not be comforted; and that I shall respect the homely truth and warmth of heart of Mr Weller and his son, to the last moment of my life.

'And the sweet, old creetur, sir,' said the older Mr Weller to me in the afternoon, 'has bolted. Him as had no wice, and was so free from temper that a infant might ha' drove him, has been took at last with that 'ere unawoidable fit o' staggers as we all must come to, and gone off his feed for ever! I see him,' said the old gentleman, with a moisture in his eye which could not be mistaken, 'I see him gettin', every journey, more and more groggy; I says to Samivel, "My boy! the Grey's a going at the knees;" and now my predilictions is fatally werified; and him as I could never do enough to serve or shew my likin' for, is up the great uniwersal spout o' natur'.'[111]

I was not the less sensible of the old man's attachment, because he expressed it in his peculiar manner. Indeed, I can truly assert, of both him and his son, that notwithstanding the extraordinary dialogues they held together, and the strange commentaries and corrections with which each of them illustrated the other's speech, I do not think it possible to exceed the sincerity of their regret: and that I am sure their thoughtfulness and anxiety, in anticipating the discharge of many little offices of sympathy, would have done honour to the most delicate-minded persons.

Our friend had frequently told us that his will would be found in a box in the Clock-case; the key of which was in his writing-desk. As he had told us also that he desired it to be opened immediately after his death, whenever that should happen, we met together that night, for the fulfilment of his request.

We found it where he had told us; wrapped in a sealed paper: and with it, a codicil of recent date, in which he named Mr Miles and Mr Pickwick his executors – as having no need of any greater benefit from his estate, than a generous token (which he bequeathed to them) of his friendship and remembrance.

After pointing out the spot in which he wished his ashes to repose, he gave to 'his dear old friends,' Jack Redburn and myself, his house, his books, his furniture – in short, all that his house contained: and with this legacy, more ample means of maintaining it in its present state, than we, with our habits, and at our terms of life, can ever exhaust. Besides these gifts, he left to us, in trust, an annual sum of no insignificant amount, to be distributed in charity among his accustomed pensioners – they are a long list – and such other claimants on his bounty as might, from time to time, present themselves. And as true charity not only covers a multitude of sins, but includes a multitude of virtues; such as forgiveness, liberal construction, gentleness and mercy to the faults of others, and the remembrance of our own imperfections and advantages; he bade us not inquire too closely into the venial errors of the poor, but finding that they *were* poor, first to relieve, and then endeavour – at an advantage – to reclaim them.

To the housekeeper, he left an annuity; sufficient for her comfortable maintenance and support through life. For the barber, who has attended him many years, he made a similar provision. And I may make two remarks in this place: first, that I think this pair are very likely to club their means together and make a match of it; and secondly, that I think my friend had this result in his mind: for I have heard him say, more than once, that he could not concur with the generality of mankind, in censuring equal marriages made in later life, since there were many cases in which such unions could not fail to be a wise and rational source of happiness to both parties.

The elder Mr Weller is so far from viewing this prospect with any feelings of jealousy, that he appears to be very much relieved by its contemplation; and his son, if I am not mistaken, participates in this feeling. We are all of opinion, however, that the old gentleman's danger, even at its crisis, was very slight; and that he merely laboured under one of those transitory weaknesses, to which persons of his temperament are now and then liable, and which become less and less alarming at every return, until they wholly subside. I have no doubt he will remain a jolly old widower, for the rest of his life: as he has already inquired of me, with much gravity, whether a writ of habeas corpus[112] would enable him to settle his property upon Tony, beyond the possibility of recal; and has, in my presence, conjured his son with tears in his eyes, that in the event of his ever becoming amorous again, he will put him in a strait-waistcoat until the fit is passed, and distinctly inform the lady that his property is 'made over.'

Although I have very little doubt that Sam would dutifully comply with these injunctions in a case of extreme necessity, and that he would do so with perfect composure and coolness, I do not apprehend things will ever come to that pass: as the old gentleman seems perfectly happy in the society of his son, his pretty daughter-in-law, and his grandchildren; and has solemnly announced his determination to 'take arter the old un in all respects:' from which I infer that it is his intention to regulate his conduct by the model of Mr Pickwick, who will certainly set him the example of a single life.

I have diverged for a moment from the subject with which I set out, for I know that my friend was interested in these little matters, and I have a natural tendency to linger upon any topic that occupied his thoughts, or gave him pleasure and amusement. His remaining wishes are very briefly told. He desired that we would make him the frequent subject of our conversation; at the same time, that we would never speak of him with an air of gloom or restraint, but frankly, and as one whom we still loved, and hoped to meet again. He trusted that the old house would wear no aspect of mourning, but that it would be lively and cheerful; and that we would not remove or cover up his picture, which hangs in our dining-room, but make it our companion, as he had been. His own room, our place of meeting, remains, at his desire, in its accustomed state: our seats are placed about the table, as of old; his easy chair, his desk, his crutch, his footstool, hold their accustomed places; and the clock stands in its familiar corner. We go into the chamber at stated times, to see that all is as it should be; and to take care that the light, and air, are not shut out: for on that point, he expressed a strong solicitude. But it was his fancy, that the apartment should not be inhabited; that it should be religiously preserved in this condition; and that the voice of his old companion should be heard no more.

My own history may be summed up in very few words; and even those I should have spared the reader, but for my friend's allusion to me some time since. I have no deeper sorrow than the loss of a child – an only daughter, who is living, and who fled from her father's house but a few weeks before our friend and I first met. I had never spoken of this, even to him; because I have always loved her, and I could not bear to tell him of her error, until I could tell him also of her sorrow and regret. Happily I was enabled to do so some time ago. And it will not be long, with Heaven's good leave, before she is restored to me – before I find, in her and her husband, the support of my declining years.

For my pipe – it is an old relic of home, a thing of no great worth, a poor trifle: but sacred to me for her sake.

Thus, since the death of our venerable friend, Jack Redburn and I have been the sole tenants of the old house; and, day by day, have lounged together in his favourite walks. Mindful of his injunctions, we have long been able to speak of him with ease and cheerfulness; and to remember him as he would be remembered. From certain allusions which Jack has dropped, to his having been deserted and cast off in early life, I am inclined to believe that some passages of his youth may possibly be shadowed out in the history of Mr Chester[113] and his son: but seeing that he avoids the subject, I have not pursued it.

My task is done. The chamber in which we have whiled away so many hours, not I hope without some pleasure and some profit, is deserted: our happy hour of meeting strikes no more: the chimney corner has grown cold: and MASTER HUMPHREY'S CLOCK has stopped for ever.

# THE LAMPLIGHTER'S STORY[1]

'If you talk of Murphy and Francis Moore,[2] gentlemen,' said the
lamplighter who was in the chair, 'I mean to say that neither of
'em ever had any more to do with the stars than Tom Grig had.'

'And what had *he* to do with 'em?' asked the lamplighter who
officiated as vice.[3]

'Nothing at all,' replied the other; 'just exactly nothing at all.'

'Do you mean to say you don't believe in Murphy, then?'
demanded the lamplighter who had opened the discussion.

'I mean to say that I believe in Tom Grig,' replied the
chairman. 'Whether I believe in Murphy, or not, is a matter
between me and my conscience; and whether Murphy believes
in himself, or not, is a matter between him and *his* conscience.
Gentlemen, I drink your healths.'

The lamplighter who did the company this honour, was seated
in the chimney corner of a certain tavern, which has been, time
out of mind the Lamplighters' House of Call. He sat in the midst
of a circle of lamplighters, and was the cacique,[4] or chief of the
tribe.

If any of our readers have had the good fortune to behold a
lamplighter's funeral, they will not be surprised to learn that
lamplighters are a strange and primitive people; that they rigidly
adhere to old ceremonies and customs which have been handed
down among them from father to son since the first public lamp
was lighted out of doors; that they intermarry, and betroth their
children in infancy; that they enter into no plots or conspiracies
(for who ever heard of a traitorous lamplighter?); that they
commit no crimes against the laws of their country (there being
no instance of a murderous or burglarious lamplighter); that
they are, in short, notwithstanding their apparently volatile and
restless character, a highly moral and reflective people: having
among themselves as many traditional observances as the Jews,
and being, as a body, if not as old as the hills, at least as old as
the streets. It is an article of their creed that the first faint
glimmering of true civilization shone in the first street light
maintained at the public expense. They trace their existence and

high position in the public esteem, in a direct line to the heathen mythology; and hold that the history of Prometheus[5] himself is but a pleasant fable, whereof the true hero is a lamplighter.

'Gentlemen,' said the lamplighter in the chair, 'I drink your healths.'

'And perhaps, Sir,' said the vice, holding up his glass, and rising a little way off his seat and sitting down again, in token that he recognised and returned the compliment, 'perhaps you will add to that condescension by telling us who Tom Grig was, and how he came to be connected in your mind with Francis Moore, Physician.'

'Hear, hear, hear!' cried the lamplighters generally.

'Tom Grig, gentlemen,' said the chairman, 'was one of us; and it happened to him as it don't often happen to a public character in our line, that he had his what-you-may-call-it cast.'

'His head?' said the vice.

'No,' replied the chairman, 'not his head.'

'His face, perhaps?' said the vice. 'No, not his face.' 'His legs?' 'No, not his legs.' Nor yet his arms, nor his hands, nor his feet, nor his chest, all of which were severally suggested.

'His nativity, perhaps?'

'That's it,' said the chairman, awakening from his thoughtful attitude at the suggestion. 'His nativity. That's what Tom had cast,[6] gentlemen.'

'In plaister?' asked the vice.

'I don't rightly know how it's done,' returned the chairman, 'but I suppose it was.'

And there he stopped as if that were all he had to say; whereupon there arose a murmur among the company which at length resolved itself into a request, conveyed through the vice, that he would go on. This being exactly what the chairman wanted, he mused for a little time, performed that agreeable ceremony which is popularly termed wetting one's whistle,[7] and went on thus:

'Tom Grig, gentlemen, was, as I have said, one of us; and I may go further, and say he was an ornament to us, and such a one as only the good old times of oil and cotton[8] could have produced. Tom's family, gentlemen, were all lamplighters.'

'Not the ladies, I hope?' asked the vice.

'They had talent enough for it, Sir,' rejoined the chairman, 'and would have been, but for the prejudices of society. Let women have their rights, Sir, and the females of Tom's family would have been every one of 'em in office. But that emancipation hasn't come yet, and hadn't then, and consequently they confined themselves to the bosoms of their families, cooked the dinners, mended the clothes, minded the children, comforted their husbands, and attended to the house-keeping generally. It's a hard thing upon the women, gentlemen, that they are limited to such a sphere of action as this; very hard.

'I happen to know all about Tom, gentlemen, from the circumstance of his uncle by his mother's side, having been my particular friend. His (that's Tom's uncle's) fate was a melancholy one. Gas[9] was the death of him. When it was first talked of, he laughed. He wasn't angry; he laughed at the credulity of human nature. "They might as well talk," he says, "of laying on an everlasting succession of glow-worms;" and then he laughed again, partly at his joke, and partly at poor humanity.

'In course of time, however, the thing got ground, the experiment was made, and they lighted up Pall Mall.[10] Tom's uncle went to see it. I've heard that he fell off his ladder fourteen times that night from weakness, and that he would certainly have gone on falling till he killed himself, if his last tumble hadn't been into a wheelbarrow which was going his way, and humanely took him home. "I foresee in this," says Tom's uncle faintly, and taking to his bed as he spoke – "I foresee in this," he says, "the breaking up of our profession. There's no more going the rounds to trim by daylight, no more dribbling down of the oil on the hats and bonnets of ladies and gentlemen when one feels in spirits. Any low fellow can light a gas-lamp. And it's all up." In this state of mind, he petitioned the government for – I want a word again, gentlemen – what do you call that which they give to people when it's found out, at last, that they've never been of any use, and have been paid too much for doing nothing?'

'Compensation?' suggested the vice.

'That's it,' said the chairman. 'Compensation. They didn't give it him though, and then he got very fond of his country all at once, and went about saying that gas was a death-blow to his native land, and that it was a plot of the radicals to ruin the country and destroy the oil and cotton trade for ever, and that the whales would go and kill themselves privately, out of sheer spite and vexation at not being caught. At last he got right-down cracked; called his tobacco-pipe a gas-pipe; thought his tears were lamp-oil; and went on with all manner of nonsense of that sort, till one night he hung himself on a lamp-iron in Saint Martin's Lane,[11] and there was an end of *him*.

'Tom loved him, gentlemen, but he survived it. He shed a tear over his grave, got very drunk, spoke a funeral oration that night in the watch-house,[12] and was fined five shillings for it, in the morning. Some men are none the worse for this sort of thing. Tom was one of 'em. He went that very afternoon on a new beat: as clear in his head, and as free from fever as Father Mathew[13] himself.

'Tom's new beat, gentlemen, was – I can't exactly say where, for that he'd never tell; but I know it was in a quiet part of town, where there were some queer old houses. I have always had it in my head that it must have been somewhere near Canonbury Tower[14] in Islington, but that's a matter of opinion. Wherever it was, he went upon it, with a bran new[15] ladder, a white hat, a brown holland jacket and trousers, a blue neck-kerchief, and a sprig of full-blown double wall-flower in his button-hole. Tom was always genteel in his appearance, and I have heard from the best judges, that if he had left his ladder at home that afternoon, you might have took him for a lord.

'He was always merry, was Tom, and such a singer, that if there was any encouragement for native talent, he'd have been at the opera. He was on his ladder, lighting his first lamp, and singing to himself in a manner more easily to be conceived than described, when he hears the clock strike five, and suddenly sees an old gentleman with a telescope in his hand, throw up a window and look at him very hard.

'Tom didn't know what could be passing in his old gentleman's mind. He thought it likely enough that he might be saying within himself, "Here's a new lamplighter – a good-looking young fellow – shall I stand something to drink?" Thinking this possible, he keeps quite still, pretending to be very particular about the wick, and looks at the old gentleman sideways, seeming to take no notice of him.

'Gentlemen, he was one of the strangest and most mysterious-looking files[16] that ever Tom clapped his eyes on. He was dressed all slovenly and untidy, in a great gown of a kind of bed-furniture pattern, with a cap of the same on his head; and a long old flapped waistcoat; with no braces, no strings, very few buttons – in short, with hardly any of those artificial contrivances that hold society together. Tom knew by these signs, and by his not being shaved, and by his not being over-clean, and by a sort of wisdom not quite awake, in his face, that he was a scientific old gentleman. He often told me that if he could have conceived the possibility of the whole Royal Society[17] being boiled down into one man, he should have said the old gentleman's body was that Body.

'The old gentleman claps the telescope to his eye, looks all round, sees nobody else in sight, stares at Tom again, and cries out very loud:

'"Hal-loa!"

'"Holloa, Sir," says Tom from the ladder; "and holloa again, if you come to that."

'"Here's an extraordinary fulfilment," says the old gentleman, "of a prediction of the planets."

'"Is there?" says Tom, "I'm very glad to hear it."

'"Young man," says the old gentleman, "you don't know me."

'"Sir," says Tom, "I have not that honour; but I shall be happy to drink your health, notwithstanding."

'"I read," cries the old gentleman, without taking any notice of this politeness on Tom's part – "I read what's going to happen, in the stars."

'Tom thanked him for the information, and begged to know if any thing particular was going to happen in the stars, in the course of a week or so; but the old gentleman, correcting him, explained that he read in the stars what was going to happen on dry land, and that he was acquainted with all the celestial bodies.

'"I hope they're all well, Sir," says Tom, – "every body."

'"Hush!" cries the old gentleman. "I have consulted the book of Fate with rare and wonderful success. I am versed in the great sciences of astrology and astronomy. In my house here, I have every description of apparatus for observing the course and motion of the planets. Six months ago, I derived from this source, the knowledge that precisely as the clock struck five this afternoon, a stranger would present himself – the destined husband of my young and lovely niece – in reality of illustrious and high descent, but whose birth would be enveloped in uncertainty and mystery. Don't tell me yours isn't," says the old gentleman, who was in such a hurry to speak that he couldn't get the words out fast enough, "for I know better."

'Gentlemen, Tom was so astonished when he heard him say this, that he could hardly keep his footing on the ladder, and found it necessary to hold on by the lamp-post. There *was* a mystery about his birth. His mother had always admitted it. Tom had never known who was his father, and some people had gone so far as to say that even *she* was in doubt.

'While he was in this state of amazement, the old gentleman leaves the window, bursts out of the housedoor, shakes the ladder, and Tom, like a ripe pumpkin, comes sliding down into his arms.

'"Let me embrace you," he says, folding his arms about him, and nearly lighting up his old bed-furniture gown at Tom's link.[18] "You're a man of noble aspect. Every thing combines to prove the accuracy of my observations. You have had mysterious promptings within you," he says; "I know you have had whisperings of greatness, eh?" he says.

'"I think I have," says Tom – Tom was one of those who can persuade themselves to any thing they like – "I've often thought I wasn't the small beer[19] I was taken for."

'"You were right," cries the old gentleman, hugging him again. "Come in. My niece awaits us."

'"Is the young lady tolerable good-looking, Sir?" says Tom, hanging fire rather, as he thought of her playing the piano, and knowing French, and being up to all manner of accomplishments.

'"She's beautiful!" cries the old gentleman, who was in such a terrible bustle that he was all in a perspiration. "She has a graceful carriage, an exquisite shape, a sweet voice, a countenance beaming with animation and expression; and the eye," he says, rubbing his hands, "of a startled fawn."

'Tom supposed this might mean, what was called among his circle of acquaintance, "a game eye;"[20] and, with a view to this defect, inquired whether the young lady had any cash.

'"She has five thousand pounds," cries the old gentleman. "But what of that? what of that? A word in your ear. I'm in search of the philosopher's stone.[21] I have very nearly found it – not quite. It turns every thing to gold; that's its property."

'Tom naturally thought it must have a deal of property; and said that when the old gentleman did get it, he hoped he'd be careful to keep it in the family.

'"Certainly," he says, "of course. Five thousand pounds!

What's five thousand pounds to us? What's five million?" he says. "What's five thousand million? Money will be nothing to us. We shall never be able to spend it fast enough."

'"We'll try what we can do, Sir," says Tom.

'"We will," says the old gentleman. "Your name?"

'"Grig," says Tom.

'The old gentleman embraced him again, very tight; and without speaking another word, dragged him into the house in such an excited manner, that it was as much as Tom could do to take his link and ladder with him, and put them down in the passage.

'Gentlemen, if Tom hadn't been always remarkable for his love of truth, I think you would still have believed him when he said that all this was like a dream. There is no better way for a man to find out whether he really is asleep or awake, than calling for something to eat. If he's in a dream, gentlemen, he'll find something wanting in the flavour, depend upon it.

'Tom explained his doubts to the old gentleman, and said that if there was any cold meat in the house, it would ease his mind very much to test himself at once. The old gentleman ordered up a venison pie, a small ham, and a bottle of very old Madeira. At the first mouthful of pie, and the first glass of wine, Tom smacks his lips and cries out, "I'm awake – wide awake;" and to prove that he was so, gentlemen, he made an end of 'em both.

'When Tom had finished his meal (which he never spoke of afterwards without tears in his eyes), the old gentleman hugs him again, and says, "Noble stranger! let us visit my young and lovely niece." Tom, who was a little elevated with the wine, replies, "The noble stranger is agreeable!" At which words the old gentleman took him by the hand, and led him to the parlour; crying as he opened the door, "Here is Mr Grig, the favourite of the planets!"

'I will not attempt a description of female beauty, gentlemen, for every one of us has a model of his own that suits his own taste best. In his parlour that I'm speaking of, there were two young ladies; and if every gentleman present, will imagine two models of his own in their places, and will be kind enough to polish 'em up to the very highest pitch of perfection, he will then have a faint conception of their uncommon radiance.

'Besides these two young ladies, there was their waiting-woman, that under any other circumstances Tom would have looked upon as a Venus;[22] and besides her, there was a tall, thin, dismal-faced young gentleman, half man and half boy, dressed in a childish suit of clothes very much too short in the legs and arms; and looking, according to Tom's comparison, like one of the wax juveniles from a tailor's door, grown up and run to seed. Now, this youngster stamped his foot upon the ground and looked very fierce at Tom, and Tom looked fierce at him – for to tell the truth, gentlemen, Tom more than half suspected that when they entered the room he was kissing one of the young ladies; and for any thing Tom knew, you observe, it might be *his* young lady – which was not pleasant.

'"Sir," says Tom, "before we proceed any further, will you have the goodness to inform me who this young Salamander" – Tom called him that for aggravation, you perceive, gentlemen – "who this young Salamander[23] may be?"

'"That, Mr Grig," says the old gentleman, "is my little boy. He was christened Galileo Isaac Newton Flamstead. Don't mind him. He's a mere child."

'"A very fine child, too," says Tom – still aggravating, you'll observe – "of his age, and as good as fine, I have no doubt. How do you do, my man?" with which kind and patronising expressions, Tom reached up to pat him on the head, and quoted two lines about little boys, from Doctor Watts's[24] Hymns, which he had learnt at a Sunday School.

'It was very easy to see, gentlemen, by this youngster's frowning, and by the waiting-maid's tossing her head and turning up her nose, and by the young ladies turning their backs and talking together at the other end of the room, that nobody but the old gentleman took very kindly to the noble stranger. Indeed, Tom plainly heard the waiting-woman say of her master, that so far from being able to read the stars as he pretended, she didn't believe he knew his letters in 'em, or at best that he had got further than words in one syllable; but Tom, not minding this (for he was in spirits after the Madeira), looks with an agreeable air towards the young ladies, and, kissing his hand to both, says to the old gentleman, "Which is which?"

'"This," says the old gentleman, leading out the handsomest, if one of 'em could possibly be said to be handsomer than the other – "this is my niece, Miss Fanny Barker."

'"If you'll permit me, Miss," says Tom, "being a noble stranger and a favourite of the planets, I will conduct myself as

THE LAMPLIGHTER'S STORY 157

such." With these words, he kisses the young lady in a very affable way, turns to the old gentleman, slaps him on the back, and says, "When's it to come off, my buck?"[25]

'The young lady coloured so deep, and her lip trembled so much, gentlemen, that Tom really thought she was going to cry. But she kept her feelings down, and turning to the old gentleman, says, "Dear uncle, though you have the absolute disposal of my hand and fortune, and though you mean well in disposing of 'em thus, I ask you whether you don't think this is a mistake? Don't you think, dear uncle," she says, "that the stars must be in error? Is it not possible that the comet may have put 'em out?"

'"The stars," says the old gentleman, "couldn't make a mistake if they tried. Emma," he says to the other young lady.

'"Yes, papa," says she.

'"The same day that makes your cousin Mrs Grig, will unite you to the gifted Mooney. No remonstrance – no tears. Now, Mr Grig, let me conduct you to that hallowed ground, that philosophical retreat, where my friend and partner, the gifted Mooney of whom I have just now spoken, is even now pursuing those discoveries which shall enrich us with the precious metal, and make us masters of the world. Come, Mr Grig," he says.

'"With all my heart, Sir," replies Tom; "and luck to the gifted Mooney, say I – not so much on his account as for our worthy selves!" With this sentiment, Tom kissed his hand to the ladies again, and followed him out; having the gratification to perceive, as he looked back, that they were all hanging on by the arms and legs of Galileo Isaac Newton Flamstead, to prevent him from following the noble stranger, and tearing him to pieces.

'Gentlemen, Tom's father-in-law that was to be, took him by the hand, and having lighted a little lamp, led him across a paved court-yard at the back of the house, into a very large, dark, gloomy room: filled with all manner of bottles, globes, books, telescopes, crocodiles, alligators, and other scientific instruments of every kind. In the centre of this room was a stove or furnace, with what Tom called a pot, but which in my opinion was a crucible, in full boil. In one corner was a sort of ladder leading through the roof; and up this ladder the old gentleman pointed, as he said in a whisper:

'"The observatory. Mr Mooney is even now watching for the precise time at which we are to come into all the riches of the earth. It will be necessary for he and I, alone in that silent place, to cast your nativity before the hour arrives. Put the day and minute of your birth on this piece of paper, and leave the rest to me."

'"You don't mean to say," says Tom, doing as he was told and giving him back the paper, "that I'm to wait here long, do you? It's a precious dismal place."

'"Hush!" says the old gentleman, "it's hallowed ground. Farewell!"

'"Stop a minute," says Tom, "what a hurry you're in. What's in that large bottle yonder?"

'"It's a child with three heads," says the old gentleman; "and every thing else in proportion."

'"Why don't you throw him away?" says Tom. "What do you keep such unpleasant things here for?"

'"Throw him away!" cries the old gentleman. "We use him constantly in astrology. He's a charm."

'"I shouldn't have thought it," says Tom, "from his appearance. *Must* you go, I say?"

'The old gentleman makes him no answer, but climbs up the ladder in a greater bustle than ever. Tom looked after his legs till there was nothing of him left, and then sat down to wait; feeling, (so he used to say), as comfortable as if he was going to be made a freemason, and they were heating the pokers.

'Tom waited so long, gentlemen, that he began to think it must be getting on for midnight at least, and felt more dismal and lonely than ever he had done in all his life. He tried every means of wiling away the time, but it never had seemed to move so slow. First, he took a nearer view of the child with three heads, and thought what a comfort it must have been to his parents. Then he looked up a long telescope which was pointed out of the window, but saw nothing particular, in consequence of the stopper being on at the other end. Then he came to a skeleton in a glass case, labelled, "Skeleton of a Gentleman – prepared by Mr Mooney," – which made him hope that Mr Mooney might not be in the habit of preparing gentlemen that way without their own consent. A hundred times, at least, he looked into the pot where they were boiling the philosopher's stone down to the proper consistency, and wondered whether it was nearly done. "When it is," thinks Tom, "I'll send out for sixpenn'orth of sprats, and turn 'em into gold fish for a first experiment." Besides which, he made up his mind, gentlemen, to have a country-house and a park; and to plant a bit of it with a double row of gas lamps a mile long, and go out every night with a french-polished mahogany ladder, and two servants in livery behind him, to light 'em for his own pleasure.

'At length and at last, the old gentleman's legs appeared upon the steps leading through the roof, and he came slowly down: bringing along with him, the gifted Mooney. This Mooney, gentlemen, was even more scientific in appearance than his friend; and had, as Tom often declared upon his word and honour, the dirtiest face we can possibly know of, in this imperfect state of existence.

'Gentlemen, you are all aware that if a scientific man isn't absent in his mind, he's of no good at all. Mr Mooney was so absent, that when the old gentleman said to him, "shake hands with Mr Grig," he put out his leg. "Here's a mind, Mr Grig!" cries the old gentleman in a rapture. "Here's philosophy! Here's rumination! Don't disturb him," he says, "for this is amazing!"

'Tom had no wish to disturb him, having nothing particular to say; but he was so uncommonly amazing, that the old gentleman got impatient, and determined to give him an electric shock to bring him to – "for you must know, Mr Grig," he says, "that we always keep a strongly charged battery, ready for that purpose." These means being resorted to, gentlemen, the gifted Mooney revived with a loud roar, and he no sooner came to himself, than both he and the old gentleman looked at Tom with compassion, and shed tears abundantly.

'"My dear friend," says the old gentleman to the Gifted, "prepare him."

'"I say," cries Tom, falling back, "none of that, you know. No preparing by Mr Mooney, if you please."

'"Alas!" replies the old gentleman, "you don't understand us. My friend, inform him of his fate. – I can't."

'The Gifted mustered up his voice, after many efforts, and informed Tom that his nativity had been carefully cast, and he would expire at exactly thirty-five minutes, twenty-seven seconds, and five-sixths of a second, past nine o'clock, A.M., on that day two months.

'Gentlemen, I leave you to judge what were Tom's feelings at this announcement, on the eve of matrimony and endless riches. "I think," he says in a trembling way, "there must be a mistake in the working of that sum. Will you do me the favour to cast it up again?" – "There is no mistake," replies the old gentleman, "it is confirmed by Francis Moore, Physician. Here is the prediction for tomorrow two months." And he showed him the page, where sure enough were these words – "The decease of a great person may be looked for, about this time."

'"Which," says the old gentleman, "is clearly you, Mr Grig."

'"Too clearly," cries Tom, sinking into a chair, and giving one hand to the old gentleman, and one to the Gifted. "The orb of day has set on Thomas Grig for ever!"

'At this affecting remark, the Gifted shed tears again, and the other two mingled their tears with his, in a kind – if I may use the expression – of Mooney and Co.'s entire. But the old gentleman recovering first, observed that this was only a reason for hastening the marriage, in order that Tom's distinguished race might be transmitted to posterity; and requesting the Gifted to console Mr Grig during his temporary absence, he withdrew to settle the preliminaries with his niece immediately.

'And now, gentlemen, a very extraordinary and remarkable occurrence took place; for as Tom sat in a melancholy way in one chair, and the Gifted sat in a melancholy way in another, a couple of doors were thrown violently open, the two young ladies rushed in, and one knelt down in a loving attitude at Tom's feet, and the other at the Gifted's. So far, perhaps, as Tom was concerned – as he used to say – you will say there was nothing strange in this; but you will be of a different opinion when you understand that Tom's young lady was kneeling to the Gifted, and the Gifted's young lady was kneeling to Tom.

'"Halloa! stop a minute!" cries Tom; "here's a mistake. I need condoling with by sympathising woman, under my afflicting circumstances; but we're out in the figure. Change partners, Mooney."

'"Monster!" cries Tom's young lady, clinging to the Gifted.

'"Miss!" says Tom. "Is *that* your manners?"

'"I abjure thee!" cries Tom's young lady. "I renounce thee. I never will be thine. Thou," she says to the Gifted, "art the object of my first and all-engrossing passion. Wrapt in thy sublime visions, thou hast not perceived my love; but, driven to despair, I now shake off the woman and avow it. Oh, cruel, cruel man!" With which reproach she laid her head upon the Gifted's breast, and put her arms about him in the tenderest manner possible, gentlemen.

'"And I," says the other young lady, in a sort of ecstasy, that made Tom start – "I hereby abjure my chosen husband too. Hear me, Goblin!" – this was to the Gifted – "Hear me! I hold thee in the deepest detestation. The maddening interview of this one night has filled my soul with love – but not for thee. It is for thee, for thee, young man," she cries to Tom. "As Monk Lewis[26] finely observes, Thomas, Thomas, I am thine, Thomas, Thomas, thou art mine: thine for ever, mine for ever!" with which words, she became very tender likewise.

'Tom and the Gifted, gentlemen, as you may believe, looked at each other in a very awkward manner, and with thoughts not at all complimentary to the young ladies. As to the Gifted, I have heard Tom say often, that he was certain he was in a fit, and had it inwardly.

'"Speak to me! oh, speak to me!" cries Tom's young lady to the Gifted.

'"I don't want to speak to anybody," he says, finding his voice at last, and trying to push her away. "I think I had better go. I'm – I'm frightened," he says, looking about as if he had lost something.

'"Not one look of love!" she cries. "Hear me, while I declare—'

'"I don't know how to look a look of love," he says, all in a maze. "Don't declare any thing. I don't want to hear anybody."

'"That's right!" cries the old gentleman (who it seems had been listening). "That's right! Don't hear her. Emma shall marry you tomorrow, my friend, whether she likes it or not, and *she* shall marry Mr Grig."

'Gentlemen, these words were no sooner out of his mouth than Galileo Isaac Newton Flamstead (who it seems had been listening too) darts in, and spinning round and round, like a young giant's top, cries, "Let her. Let her. I'm fierce; I'm furious. I give her leave. I'll never marry anybody after this – never. It isn't safe. She is the falsest of the false," he cries, tearing his hair and gnashing his teeth; "and I'll live and die a bachelor!"

'"The little boy," observed the Gifted gravely, "albeit of tender years, has spoken wisdom. I have been led to the contemplation of woman-kind, and will not adventure on the troubled waters of matrimony."

'"What!" says the old gentleman, "not marry my daughter! Won't you, Mooney? Not if I make her? Won't you? Won't you?"

'"No," says Mooney, "I won't. And if anybody asks me any more, I'll run away, and never come back again."

'"Mr Grig," says the old gentleman, "the stars must be obeyed. You have not changed your mind because of a little girlish folly – eh, Mr Grig?"

'Tom, gentlemen, had had his eyes about him, and was pretty sure that all this was a device and trick of the waiting-maid, to put him off his inclination. He had seen her hiding and skipping about the two doors, and had observed that a very little whispering from her pacified the Salamander directly. "So," thinks Tom, "this is a plot – but it won't fit."

'"Eh, Mr Grig?" says the old gentleman.

'"Why, Sir," says Tom, pointing to the crucible, "if the soup's nearly ready—"

'"Another hour beholds the consummation of our labours," returned the old gentleman.

'"Very good," says Tom, with a mournful air. "It's only for two months, but I may as well be the richest man in the world even for that time. I'm not particular. I'll take her, Sir. I'll take her."

'The old gentleman was in a rapture to find Tom still in the same mind, and drawing the young lady towards him by little and little, was joining their hands by main force, when all of a sudden, gentlemen, the crucible blows up with a great crash; everybody screams; the room is filled with smoke; and Tom, not knowing what may happen next, throws himself into a Fancy attitude, and says, "Come on, if you're a man!" without addressing himself to anybody in particular.

'"The labours of fifteen years!" says the old gentleman, clasping his hands and looking down upon the Gifted, who was saving the pieces, "are destroyed in an instant!" – And I am told, gentlemen, by-the-bye, that this same philosopher's stone would have been discovered a hundred times at least, to speak within bounds, if it wasn't for the one unfortunate circumstance that the apparatus always blows up, when it's on the very point of succeeding.

'Tom turns pale when he hears the old gentleman expressing himself to this unpleasant effect, and stammers out that if it's

George Cruikshank fecit

The Philosopher's Stone

quite agreeable to all parties, he would like to know exactly what has happened, and what change has really taken place in the prospects of that company.

'"We have failed for the present, Mr Grig," says the old gentleman, wiping his forehead, "and I regret it the more, because I have in fact invested my niece's five thousand pounds in this glorious speculation. But don't be cast down," he says, anxiously – "in another fifteen years, Mr Grig—"

'"Oh!" cries Tom, letting the young lady's hand fall. "Were the stars very positive about this union, Sir?"

'"They were," says the old gentleman.

'"I'm sorry to hear it," Tom makes answer, "for it's no go, Sir."

'"No what!" cries the old gentleman.

'"Go, Sir," says Tom, fiercely, "I forbid the banns."[27] And with these words – which are the very words he used – he sat himself down in a chair, and, laying his head upon the table, thought with a secret grief of what was to come to pass on that day two months.

'Tom always said, gentlemen, that that waiting-maid was the artfullest minx he had ever seen; and he left it in writing in this country when he went to colonize abroad, that he was certain in his own mind she and the Salamander had blown up the philosopher's stone on purpose, and to cut him out of his property. I believe Tom was in the right, gentlemen; but whether or no, she comes forward at this point, and says, "May I speak, Sir?" and the old gentleman answering "Yes, you may," she goes on to say that "the stars are no doubt quite right in every respect, but Tom is not the man." And she says, "Don't you remember, Sir, that when the clock struck five this afternoon, you gave Master Galileo a rap on the head with your telescope, and told him to get out of the way?" "Yes, I do," says the old gentleman. "Then," says the waiting-maid, "I say he's the man, and the prophecy is fulfilled." The old gentleman staggers at this, as if somebody had hit him a blow on the chest, and cries, "He! why, he's a boy!" Upon that, gentlemen, the Salamander cries out that he'll be twenty-one next Lady-day;[28] and complains that his father has always been so busy with the sun round which the earth revolves, that he has never taken any notice of the son that revolves round him; and that he hasn't had a new suit of clothes since he was fourteen; and that he wasn't even taken out of nankeen[29] frocks and trowsers till he was quite unpleasant in 'em; and touches on a good many more family matters to the same purpose. To make short of a long story, gentlemen, they all talk together, and cry together, and remind the old gentleman that as to the noble family, his own grandfather would have been lord mayor if he hadn't died at a dinner the year before; and they show him by all kinds of arguments that if the cousins are married, the prediction comes true every way. At last, the old gentleman, being quite convinced, gives in; and joins their hands; and leaves his daughter to marry anybody she likes; and they are all well pleased; and the Gifted as well as any of them.

'In the middle of this little family party, gentlemen, sits Tom all the while, as miserable as you like. But, when every thing else is arranged, the old gentleman's daughter says, that their strange conduct was a little device of the waiting-maid's to disgust the lovers he had chosen for 'em, and will he forgive her? and if he will perhaps he might even find her a husband – and when she says that, she looks uncommon hard at Tom. Then the waiting-maid says that, oh dear! she couldn't abear Mr Grig should think she wanted him to marry her; and that she had even gone so far as to refuse the last lamplighter, who was now a literary character (having set up as a bill-sticker);[30] and that she hoped Mr Grig would not suppose she was on her last legs by any means, for the baker was very strong in his attentions at that moment, and as to the butcher, he was frantic. And I don't know how much more she might have said, gentlemen (for, as you know, this kind of young women are rare ones to talk), if the old gentleman hadn't cut in suddenly, and asked Tom if he'd have her, with ten pounds to recompense him for his loss of time and disappointment, and as a kind of bribe to keep the story secret.

' "It don't much matter, Sir," says Tom, "I an't for this world. Eight weeks of marriage, especially with this young woman, might reconcile me to my fate. I think," he says, "I could go off easy, after that." With which he embraces her with a very dismal face, and groans in a way that might move a heart of stone – even of philosopher's stone.

' "Egad," says the old gentleman, "that reminds me – this bustle put it out of my head – there was a figure wrong. He'll live to a green old age – eighty-seven at least!"

'"How much, Sir?" cries Tom.

'"Eighty-seven!" says the old gentleman.

'Without another word, Tom flings himself on the old gentleman's neck; throws up his hat; cuts a caper; defies the waiting-maid; and refers her to the butcher.

'"You won't marry her!" says the old gentleman, angrily.

'"And live after it!" says Tom. "I'd sooner marry a mermaid, with a small-tooth comb and looking-glass."

'"Then take the consequences," says the other.

'With those words – I beg your kind attention here, gentlemen, for it's worth your notice – the old gentleman wetted the forefinger of his right hand in some of the liquor from the crucible that was spilt on the floor, and drew a small triangle on Tom's forehead. The room swam before his eyes, and he found himself in the watch-house.'

'Found himself *where?*' cried the vice, on behalf of the company generally.

'In the watch-house,' said the chairman. 'It was late at night, and he found himself in the very watch-house from which he had been let out that morning.'

'Did he go home?' asked the vice.

'The watch-house people rather objected to that,' said the chairman; 'so he stopped there that night, and went before the magistrate in the morning. "Why, you're here again, are you?" says the magistrate, adding insult to injury; "we'll trouble you for five shillings more, if you can conveniently spare the money." Tom told him he had been enchanted, but it was of no use. He told the contractors the same, but they wouldn't believe him. It was very hard upon him, gentlemen, as he often said, for was it likely he'd go and invent such a tale? They shook their heads and told him he'd say any thing but his prayers – as indeed he would; there's no doubt about that. It was the only imputation on his moral character that ever *I* heard of.'

# TO BE READ AT DUSK

One, two, three, four, five. There were five of them.

Five couriers, sitting on a bench outside the convent on the summit of the Great St Bernard[1] in Switzerland, looking at the remote heights, stained by the setting sun, as if a mighty quantity of red wine had been broached[2] upon the mountain top, and had not yet had time to sink into the snow.

This is not my simile. It was made for the occasion by the stoutest courier, who was a German. None of the others took any more notice of it than they took of me, sitting on another bench on the other side of the convent door, smoking my cigar, like them, and – also like them – looking at the reddened snow, and at the lonely shed hard by, where the bodies of belated travellers, dug out of it, slowly wither away, knowing no corruption in that cold region.

The wine upon the mountain top soaked in as we looked; the mountain became white; the sky, a very dark blue; the wind rose; and the air turned piercing cold. The five couriers buttoned their rough coats. There being no safer man to imitate in all such proceedings than a courier, I buttoned mine.

The mountain in the sunset had stopped the five couriers in a conversation. It is a sublime sight, likely to stop conversation. The mountain being now out of the sunset, they resumed. Not that I had heard any part of their previous discourse; for, indeed, I had not then broken away from the American gentleman, in the travellers' parlour of the convent, who, sitting with his face to the fire, had undertaken to realise to me the whole progress of events which had led to the accumulation by the Honourable Ananias Dodger of one of the largest acquisitions of dollars ever made in our country.[3]

'My God!' said the Swiss courier, speaking in French, which I do not hold (as some authors appear to do) to be such an ill-sufficient excuse for a naughty word, that I have only to write it in that language to make it innocent; 'if you talk of ghosts—'

'But I *don't* talk of ghosts,' said the German.

'Of what then?' asked the Swiss.

'If I knew of what then,' said the German, 'I should probably know a great deal more.'

It was a good answer, I thought, and it made me curious. So, I moved my position to that corner of my bench which was nearest to them, and leaning my back against the convent-wall, heard perfectly, without appearing to attend.

'Thunder and lightning,' said the German, warming, 'when a certain man is coming to see you, unexpectedly; and, without his own knowledge, sends some invisible messenger, to put the idea of him in your head all day, what do you call that? When you walk along a crowded street – at Frankfort, Milan, London, Paris – and think that a passing stranger is like your friend Heinrich, and then that another passing stranger is like your friend Heinrich, and so begin to have a strange foreknowledge that presently you'll meet your friend Heinrich – which you do, though you believed him at Trieste – what do you call *that?*'

'It's not uncommon either,' murmured the Swiss and the other three.

'Uncommon!' said the German. 'It's as common as cherries in the Black Forest. It's as common as maccaroni at Naples. And Naples reminds me! When the old Marchesa Senzanima shrieks at a card party on the Chiaja[4] – as I heard and saw her, for it happened in a Bavarian family of mine, and I was overlooking the service[5] that evening – I say, when the old Marchesa starts up at the card-table, white through her rouge, and cries, "My sister in Spain is dead! I felt her cold touch on my back!" – and when that sister *is* dead at the moment – what do you call that?'

'Or when the blood of San Gennaro[6] liquefies at the request of the clergy, – as all the world knows that it does regularly once a-year, in my native city,' said the Neapolitan courier after a pause, with a comical look, 'what do you call that?'

'*That!*' cried the German. 'Well! I think I know a name for that.'

'Miracle?' said the Neapolitan, with the same sly face.

The German merely smoked and laughed; and they all smoked and laughed.

'Bah!' said the German, presently. 'I speak of things that really happen. When I want to see the conjurer, I pay to see a professed one, and have my money's worth. Very strange things do happen without ghosts. Ghosts! Giovanni Baptista, tell your story of the English bride. There's no ghost in that, but something full as strange. Will any man tell me what?'

As there was a silence among them, I glanced around. He whom I took to be Baptista was lighting a fresh cigar. He presently went on to speak. He was a Genoese, as I judged.

'The story of the English bride?' said he. 'Basta! one ought not to call so slight a thing a story. Well, it's all one. But it's true. Observe me well, gentlemen, it's true. That which glitters is not always gold; but what I am going to tell, is true.'

He repeated this more than once.

Ten years ago, I took my credentials to an English gentleman at Long's Hotel,[7] in Bond Street, London, who was about to travel – it might be for one year, it might be for two. He approved of them; likewise of me. He was pleased to make inquiry. The testimony that he received was favourable. He engaged me by the six months, and my entertainment was generous.

He was young, handsome, very happy. He was enamoured of a fair young English lady, with a sufficient fortune, and they were going to be married. It was the wedding trip, in short, that we were going to take. For three months' rest in the hot weather (it was early summer then) he had hired an old palace on the Riviera, at an easy distance from my city, Genoa, on the road to Nice. Did I know that place? Yes; I told him I knew it well. It was an old palace, with great gardens. It was a little bare, and it was a little dark and gloomy, being close surrounded by trees; but it was spacious, ancient, grand, and on the sea shore. He said it had been so described to him exactly, and he was well pleased that I knew it. For its being a little bare of furniture, all such places were. For its being a little gloomy, he had hired it principally for the gardens, and he and my mistress would pass the summer weather in their shade.

'So all goes well, Baptista?' said he.

'Indubitably, signor; very well.'

We had a travelling chariot for our journey, newly built for us, and in all respects complete. All we had was complete; we wanted for nothing. The marriage took place. They were happy. *I* was happy, seeing all so bright, being so well situated, going to my own city, teaching my language in the rumble[8] to the maid, la bella Carolina, whose heart was gay with laughter: who was young and rosy.

The time flew. But I observed – listen to this, I pray! (and here
the courier dropped his voice) – I observed my mistress sometimes brooding in a manner very strange; in a frightened manner;
in an unhappy manner; with a cloudy, uncertain alarm upon
her. I think that I began to notice this when I was walking up
hills by the carriage side, and master had gone on in front. At
any rate, I remember that it impressed itself upon my mind one
evening in the South of France, when she called to me to call
master back; and when he came back, and walked for a long
way, talking encouragingly and affectionately to her, with his
hand upon the open window, and hers in it. Now and then, he
laughed in a merry way, as if he were bantering her out of
something. By and by, she laughed, and then all went well again.

It was curious. I asked la bella Carolina, the pretty little one,
Was mistress unwell? – No. Out of spirits? – No. Fearful of bad
roads, or brigands? – No. And what made it more mysterious
was, the pretty little one would not look at me in giving answer,
but *would* look at the view.

But, one day she told me the secret.

'If you must know,' said Carolina, 'I find, from what I have
overheard, that mistress is haunted.'

'How haunted?'

'By a dream.'

'What dream?'

'By a dream of a face. For three nights before her marriage, she
saw a face in a dream – always the same face, and only One.'

'A terrible face?'

'No. The face of a dark, remarkable-looking man, in black,
with black hair and a grey moustache – a handsome man, except
for a reserved and secret air. Not a face she ever saw, or at all
like a face she ever saw. Doing nothing in the dream but looking
at her fixedly, out of darkness.'

'Does the dream come back?'

'Never. The recollection of it, is all her trouble.'

'And why does it trouble her?'

Carolina shook her head.

'That's master's question,' said la bella. 'She don't know. She
wonders why, herself. But I heard her tell him, only last night,
that if she was to find a picture of that face in our Italian house
(which she is afraid she will), she did not know how she could
ever bear it.'

Upon my word I was fearful after this (said the Genoese courier) of our coming to the old palazzo, lest some such ill-starred picture should happen to be there. I knew there were many there; and, as we got nearer and nearer to the place, I wished the whole gallery in the crater of Vesuvius. To mend the matter, it was a stormy dismal evening when we, at last, approached that part of the Riviera. It thundered; and the thunder of my city and its environs, rolling among the high hills, is very loud. The lizards ran in and out of the chinks in the broken stone wall of the garden, as if they were frightened; the frogs bubbled and croaked their loudest; the sea-wind moaned, and the wet trees dripped; and the lightning – body of San Lorenzo, how it lightened!

We all know what an old palazzo in or near Genoa is – how time and the sea air have blotted it – how the drapery painted on the outer walls has peeled off in great flakes of plaster – how the lower windows are darkened with rusty bars of iron – how the courtyard is overgrown with grass – how the outer buildings are dilapidated – how the whole pile seems devoted to ruin. Our palazzo was one of the true kind. It had been shut up close for months. Months? – years! It had an earthy smell, like a tomb. The scent of the orange-trees on the broad back terrace, and of the lemons ripening on the wall, and of some shrubs that grew around a broken fountain, had got into the house somehow, and had never been able to get out again. There it was, in every room, an aged smell, grown faint with confinement. It pined in all the cupboards and drawers. In the little rooms of communi-cation between great rooms, it was stifling. If you turned a picture – to come back to the pictures – there it still was, clinging to the wall behind the frame, like a sort of bat.

The lattice-blinds were close shut, all over the house. There were two ugly grey old women in the house, to take care of it; one of them with a spindle, who stood winding and mumbling in the doorway, and who would as soon have let in the devil as the air. Master, mistress, la bella Carolina and I, went all through the palazzo. I went first, though I have named myself last, opening the windows and the lattice-blinds, and shaking down on myself splashes of rain, and scraps of mortar, and now and then a dozing mosquito, or a monstrous, fat, blotchy, Genoese spider.

When I had let the evening light into a room, master, mistress, and la bella Carolina, entered. Then, we looked round at all the pictures, and I went forward again into another room. Mistress secretly had great fear of meeting with the likeness of that face – we all had; but there was no such thing. The Madonna and Bambino, San Francisco, San Sebastiano, Venus, Santa Caterina, Angels, Brigands, Friars, Temples at Sunset, Battles, White Horses, Forests, Apostles, Doges, all my old acquaintance many times repeated?[9] – yes. Dark handsome man in black, reserved and secret, with black hair and grey moustache, looking fixedly at mistress out of darkness? – no.

At last we got through all the rooms and all the pictures, and came out into the gardens. They were pretty well kept, being rented by a gardener, and were large and shady. In one place, there was a rustic theatre, open to the sky; the stage a green slope: the coulisses,[10] three entrances upon a side, sweet-smelling leafy screens. Mistress moved her bright eyes, even there, as if she looked to see the face come in upon the scene: but all was well.

'Now Clara,' master said, in a low voice, 'you see that it is nothing? You are happy.'

Mistress was much encouraged. She soon accustomed herself to that grim palazzo, and would sing, and play the harp, and copy the old pictures, and stroll with master under the green trees and vines, all day. She was beautiful. He was happy. He would laugh and say to me, mounting his horse for his morning ride before the heat:

'All goes well, Baptista!'

'Yes, signore, thank God; very well!'

We kept no company. I took la bella to the Duomo and Annunciata, to the Café, to the Opera, to the village Festa, to the Public Garden, to the Day Theatre, to the Marionetti.[11] The pretty little one was charmed with all she saw. She learnt Italian – heavens! miraculously! Was mistress quite forgetful of that dream? I asked Carolina sometimes. Nearly, said la bella – almost. It was wearing out.

One day master received a letter, and called me.

'Baptista!'

'Signore.'

'A gentleman who is presented to me will dine here today. He is called the Signor Dellombra. Let me dine like a prince.'

It was an odd name. I did not know that name. But, there had been many noblemen and gentlemen pursued by Austria on political suspicions,[12] lately, and some names had changed. Perhaps this was one. Altro![13] Dellombra was as good a name to me as another.

When the Signor Dellombra came to dinner (said the Genoese courier in the low voice, into which he had subsided once before), I showed him into the reception-room, the great sala of the old palazzo. Master received him with cordiality, and presented him to mistress. As she rose, her face changed, she gave a cry, and fell upon the marble floor.

Then, I turned my head to the Signor Dellombra, and saw that he was dressed in black, and had a reserved and secret air, and was a dark remarkable-looking man, with black hair and a grey moustache.

Master raised mistress in his arms, and carried her to her own room, where I sent la bella Carolina straight. La bella told me afterwards that mistress was nearly terrified to death, and that she wandered in her mind about her dream, all night.

Master was vexed and anxious – almost angry, and yet full of solicitude. The Signor Dellombra was a courtly gentleman, and spoke with great respect and sympathy of mistress's being so ill. The African wind had been blowing for some days, (they had told him at his hotel of the Maltese Cross), and he knew that it was often hurtful. He hoped the beautiful lady would recover soon. He begged permission to retire, and to renew his visit when he should have the happiness of hearing that she was better. Master would not allow of this, and they dined alone.

He withdrew early. Next day he called at the gate, on horseback, to inquire for mistress. He did so two or three times in that week.

What I observed myself, and what la bella Carolina told me, united to explain to me that master had now set his mind on curing mistress of her fanciful terror. He was all kindness, but he was sensible and firm. He reasoned with her, that to encourage such fancies was to invite melancholy, if not madness. That it rested with herself to be herself. That if she once resisted her strange weakness, so successfully as to receive the Signor Dellombra as an English lady would receive any other guest, it was for ever conquered. To make an end, the signor came again, and mistress received him without marked distress (though with constraint and apprehension still), and the evening passed serenely. Master was so delighted with this change, and so anxious to confirm it, that the Signor Dellombra became a constant guest. He was accomplished in pictures, books, and music; and his society, in any grim palazzo, would have been welcome.

I used to notice, many times, that mistress was not quite recovered. She would cast down her eyes and droop her head, before the Signor Dellombra, or would look at him with a terrified and fascinated glance, as if his presence had some evil influence or power upon her. Turning from her to him, I used to see him in the shaded gardens, or the large half-lighted sala, looking, as I might say, 'fixedly upon her out of darkness.' But, truly, I had not forgotten la bella Carolina's words describing the face in the dream.

After his second visit I heard master say:

'Now see, my dear Clara, it's over! Dellombra has come and gone, and your apprehension is broken like glass.'

'Will he – will he ever come again?' asked mistress.

'Again? Why, surely, over and over again! Are you cold?' (She shivered.)

'No, dear – but – he terrifies me: are you sure that he need come again?'

'The surer for the question, Clara!' replied master, cheerfully.

But, he was very hopeful of her complete recovery now, and grew more and more so every day. She was beautiful. He was happy.

'All goes well, Baptista?' he would say to me again.

'Yes, signore, thank God; very well.'

We were all (said the Genoese courier, constraining himself to speak a little louder), we were all at Rome for the Carnival.[14] I had been out, all day, with a Sicilian, a friend of mine and a courier, who was there with an English family. As I returned at night to our hotel, I met the little Carolina, who never stirred from home alone, running distractedly along the Corso.[15]

'Carolina! What's the matter?'

'O Baptista! Oh, for the Lord's sake! where is my mistress?'

'Mistress, Carolina?'

'Gone since morning – told me, when master went out on his day's journey, not to call her, for she was tired with not resting in the night (having been in pain), and would lie in bed until the evening; then get up refreshed. She is gone! – she is gone! Master has come back, broken down the door, and she is gone! My beautiful, my good, my innocent mistress!'

The pretty little one so cried, and raved, and tore herself, that I could not have held her, but for her swooning on my arm as if she had been shot. Master came up – in manner, face, or voice, no more the master that I knew, than I was he. He took me (I laid the little one upon her bed in the hôtel, and left her with the chamber-women), in a carriage, furiously through the darkness, across the desolate Campagna. When it was day, and we stopped at a miserable posthouse, all the horses had been hired twelve hours ago, and sent away in different directions. Mark me! – by the Signor Dellombra, who had passed there in a carriage, with a frightened English lady crouching in one corner.

I never heard (said the Genoese courier, drawing a long breath) that she was ever traced beyond that spot. All I know is, that she vanished into infamous oblivion, with the dreaded face beside her that she had seen in her dream.

'What do you call *that?*' said the German courier, triumphantly: 'Ghosts! There are no ghosts *there!* What do you call this, that I am going to tell you? Ghosts! There are no ghosts *here!*'

*I* took an engagement once (pursued the German courier) with an English gentleman, elderly and a bachelor, to travel through my country, my Fatherland. He was a merchant who traded with my country and knew the language, but who had never been there since he was a boy – as I judge, some sixty years before.

His name was James, and he had a twin-brother John, also a bachelor. Between these brothers there was a great affection. They were in business together, at Goodman's Fields[16] but they did not live together. Mr James dwelt in Poland Street, turning out of Oxford Street, London. Mr John resided by Epping Forest.

Mr James and I were to start for Germany in about a week. The exact day depended on business. Mr John came to Poland Street (where I was staying in the house), to pass that week with Mr James. But, he said to his brother on the second day, 'I don't feel very well, James. There's not much the matter with me; but I think I am a little gouty. I'll go home and put myself under the care of my old housekeeper, who understands my ways. If I get quite better, I'll come back and see you before you go. If I don't feel well enough to resume my visit where I leave it off, why *you* will come and see *me* before you go.' Mr James, of course, said he would, and they shook hands – both hands, as they always did – and Mr John ordered out his old-fashioned chariot and rumbled home.

It was on the second night after that – that is to say, the fourth in the week – when I was awoke out of my sound sleep by Mr James coming into my bedroom in his flannel-gown, with a lighted candle. He sat upon the side of my bed, and looking at me, said:

'Wilhelm, I have reason to think I have got some strange illness upon me.'

I then perceived that there was a very unusual expression in his face.

'Wilhelm,' said he, 'I am not afraid or ashamed to tell you, what I might be afraid or ashamed to tell another man. You come from a sensible country, where mysterious things are inquired into, and are not settled to have been weighed and measured – or to have been unweighable and unmeasurable – or in either case to have been completely disposed of, for all time – ever so many years ago. I have just now seen the phantom of my brother.'

I confess (said the German courier) that it gave me a little tingling of the blood to hear it.

'I have just now seen,' Mr James repeated, looking full at me, that I might see how collected he was, 'the phantom of my brother John. I was sitting up in bed, unable to sleep, when it came into my room, in a white dress, and, regarding me earnestly, passed up to the end of the room, glanced at some papers on my writing-desk, turned, and, still looking earnestly at me as it passed the bed, went out at the door. Now, I am not in the least mad, and am not in the least disposed to invest that phantom with any external existence out of myself. I think it is a warning to me that I am ill; and I think I had better be bled.'

I got out of bed directly (said the German courier) and began to get on my clothes, begging him not to be alarmed, and telling him that I would go myself to the doctor. I was just ready, when we heard a loud knocking and ringing at the street door. My room being an attic at the back, and Mr James's being the second-floor room in the front, we went down to his room, and put up the window, to see what was the matter.

'Is that Mr James?' said a man below, falling back to the opposite side of the way to look up.

'It is,' said Mr James, 'and you are my brother's man, Robert.'

'Yes, sir. I am sorry to say, sir, that Mr John is ill. He is very bad, sir. It is even feared that he may be lying at the point of death. He wants to see you, sir. I have a chaise here. Pray come to him. Pray lose no time.'

Mr James and I looked at one another. 'Wilhelm,' said he, 'this is strange. I wish you to come with me!' I helped him to dress, partly there and partly in the chaise; and no grass grew under the horses' iron shoes between Poland Street and the Forest.

Now, mind! (said the German courier.) I went with Mr James into his brother's room, and I saw and heard myself what follows.

His brother lay upon his bed, at the upper end of a long bed-chamber. His old housekeeper was there, and others were there: I think three others were there, if not four, and they had been with him since early in the afternoon. He was in white, like the figure – necessarily so, because he had his night-dress on. He looked like the figure – necessarily so, because he looked earnestly at his brother when he saw him come into the room.

But, when his brother reached the bedside, he slowly raised himself in bed, and looking full upon him, said these words:

'JAMES, YOU HAVE SEEN ME BEFORE, TO-NIGHT – AND YOU KNOW IT!'

And so died!

I waited, when the German courier ceased, to hear something said of this strange story. The silence was unbroken. I looked round, and the five couriers were gone: so noiselessly that the ghostly mountain might have absorbed them into its eternal snows. By this time, I was by no means in a mood to sit alone in that awful scene, with the chill air coming solemnly upon me – or, if I may tell the truth, to sit alone anywhere. So I went back into the convent-parlour, and, finding the American gentleman still disposed to relate the biography of the Honourable Ananias Dodger, heard it all out.

# HUNTED DOWN

## IN TWO PORTIONS. PORTION THE FIRST

### I

Most of us see some romances in life. In my capacity as Chief-Manager of a Life Assurance Office, I think I have, within the last thirty years, seen more romances than the generality of men, however unpromising the opportunity may at first sight seem.

As I have retired, and live at my ease, I possess the means that I used to want, of considering what I have seen, at leisure. My experiences have a more remarkable aspect, so reviewed, than they had when they were in progress. I have come home from the Play now, and can recal the scenes of the Drama upon which the curtain has fallen, free from the glare, bewilderment, and bustle, of the Theatre.

Let me recal one of these Romances of the real world.

There is nothing truer (I believe) than physiognomy, taken in connexion with manner. The art of reading that book of which Eternal Wisdom obliges every human creature to present his or her own page with the individual character written on it, is a difficult one, perhaps, and is little studied. It may require some natural aptitude, and it must require (for everything does) some patience and some pains. That, these are not usually given to it – that, numbers of people accept a few stock common-place expressions of face as the whole list of characteristics, and neither seek nor recognise the refinements that are truest – that You, for instance, give a great deal of time and attention to the reading of music, Greek, Latin, French, Italian, Hebrew, if you please, and do not qualify yourself to read the face of the master or mistress looking over your shoulder teaching it to you – I assume to be five hundred times more probable than improbable. Perhaps some little self-sufficiency may be at the bottom of this; facial expression requires no study from you, you think; it comes by nature to you to know enough about it, and you are not to be taken in.

I confess, for my part, that I have been taken in, over and over and over again. I have been taken in by acquaintances, and I have been taken in (of course) by friends; far oftener by friends than by any other class of persons. How came I to be so deceived? Had I quite misread their faces? No. Believe me, my first impression of those people, founded on face and manner alone, was invariably true. My mistake was, in suffering them to come nearer to me, and explain themselves away.

## II

The partition which separated my own office from our general outer office, in the City, was of thick plate-glass. I could see through it what passed in the outer office, without hearing a word. I had had it put up, in place of a wall that had been there for years – ever since the house was built. It is no matter whether I did or did not make the change, in order that I might derive my first impression of strangers who came to us on business, from their faces alone, without being influenced by anything they said. Enough to mention that I turned my glass partition to that account, and that a Life Assurance Office is at all times exposed to be practised upon by the most crafty and cruel of the human race.

It was through my glass partition that I first saw the gentleman whose story I am going to tell.

He had come in without my observing it, and had put his hat and umbrella on the broad counter, and was bending over it to take some papers from one of the clerks. He was about forty or so, dark, exceedingly well dressed in black – being in mourning – and the hand he extended with a polite air, had a particularly well-fitting black kid glove upon it. His hair, which was elaborately brushed and oiled, was parted straight up the middle; and he presented this parting to the clerk, exactly (to my thinking) as if he had said, in so many words: 'You must take me, if you please, my friend, just as I show myself. Come straight up here, follow the gravel path, keep off the grass, I allow no trespassing.'

I conceived a very great aversion to that man, the moment I thus saw him.

He had asked for some of our printed forms, and the clerk was giving them to him, and explaining them. An obliged and agreeable smile was on his face, and his eyes met those of the clerk with a sprightly look. (I have known a vast quantity of nonsense talked about bad men not looking you in the face. Don't trust that conventional idea. Dishonesty will stare honesty out of countenance, any day in the week, if there is anything to be got by it.)

I saw, in the corner of his eyelash, that he became aware of my looking at him. Immediately, he turned the parting in his hair towards the glass partition, as if he said to me with a sweet smile, 'Straight up here, if you please. Off the grass!'

In a few moments he had put on his hat and taken up his umbrella, and was gone.

I beckoned the clerk into my room, and asked, 'Who was that?'

He had the gentleman's card in his hand. 'Mr Julius Slinkton, Middle Temple.'

'A barrister, Mr Adams?'

'I think not, sir.'

'I should have thought him a clergyman, but for his having no Reverend here,' said I.

'Probably, from his appearance,' Mr Adams replied, 'he is reading for orders.'[1]

I should mention that he wore a dainty white cravat, and dainty linen altogether.

'What did he want, Mr Adams?'

'Merely a form of proposal, sir, and a form of reference.'

'Recommended here? Did he say?'

'Yes; he said he was recommended here by a friend of yours. He noticed you, but said that as he had not the pleasure of your personal acquaintance he would not trouble you.'

'Did he know my name?'

'Oh yes, sir! He said, "There *is* Mr Sampson, I see."'

'A well-spoken gentleman, apparently?'

'Remarkably so, sir.'

'Insinuating manners, apparently?'

'Very much so, indeed, sir.'

'Hah!' said I. 'I want nothing at present, Mr Adams.'

Within a fortnight of that day, I went to dine with a friend of mine – a merchant, a man of taste, who buys pictures and books; and the first person I saw among the company was Mr Julius Slinkton. There he was, standing before the fire, with good large eyes and an open expression of face; but still (I thought) requiring everybody to come at him by the prepared way he offered, and by no other.

I noticed him ask my friend to introduce him to Mr Sampson, and my friend did so. Mr Slinkton was very happy to see me. Not too happy; there was no overdoing of the matter; happy, in a thoroughly well-bred, perfectly unmeaning way.

'I thought you had met,' our host observed.

'No,' said Mr Slinkton. 'I did look in at Mr Sampson's office, on your recommendation; but I really did not feel justified in troubling Mr Sampson himself, on a point within the everyday routine of an ordinary clerk.'

I said I should have been glad to show him any attention on our friend's introduction.

'I am sure of that,' said he, 'and am much obliged. At another time, perhaps, I may be less delicate. Only, however, if I have real business; for I know, Mr Sampson, how precious business time is, and what a vast number of impertinent people there are in the world.'

I acknowledged his consideration with a slight bow. 'You were thinking,' said I, 'of effecting a policy on your life?'

'Oh dear, no! I am afraid I am not so prudent as you pay me the compliment of supposing me to be, Mr Sampson. I merely inquired for a friend. But you know what friends are, in such matters. Nothing may ever come of it. I have the greatest reluctance to trouble men of business with inquiries for friends, knowing the probabilities to be a thousand to one that the friends will never follow them up. People are so fickle, so selfish, so inconsiderate. Don't you, in your business, find them so every day, Mr Sampson?'

I was going to give a qualified answer; but, he turned his smooth, white parting on me, with its 'Straight up here, if you please!' and I answered, 'Yes.'

'I hear, Mr Sampson,' he resumed, presently, for our friend had a new cook, and dinner was not so punctual as usual, 'that your profession has recently suffered a great loss.'

'In money?' said I.

He laughed at my ready association of loss with money, and replied, 'No; in talent and vigour.'

Not at once following out his allusion, I considered for a moment. '*Has* it sustained a loss of that kind?' said I. 'I was not aware of it.'

'Understand me, Mr Sampson. I don't imagine that you have retired. It is not so bad as that. But Mr Meltham—'

'Oh, to be sure!' said I. 'Yes! Mr Meltham, the young actuary[2] of the "Inestimable"?'

'Just so,' he returned, in a consoling way.

'He is a great loss. He was at once the most profound, the most original, and the most energetic man, I have ever known connected with Life Assurance.'

I spoke strongly; for I had a high esteem and admiration for Meltham, and my gentleman had indefinitely conveyed to me some suspicion that he wanted to sneer at him. He recalled me to my guard, by presenting that trim pathway up his head, with its infernal, 'Not on the grass, if you please – the gravel.'

'You knew him, Mr Slinkton?'

'Only by reputation. To have known him as an acquaintance, or as a friend, is an honour I should have sought, if he had remained in society: though I might never have had the good fortune to attain it, being a man of far inferior mark. He was scarcely above thirty, I suppose.'

'About thirty.'

'Ah!' He sighed in his former consoling way. 'What creatures we are! To break up, Mr Sampson, and become incapable of business at that time of life! – Any reason assigned for the melancholy fact?'

('Humph!' thought I, as I looked at him. 'But I WON'T go up the track, and I WILL go on the grass.')

'What reason have you heard assigned, Mr Slinkton?' I asked, point blank.

'Most likely a false one. You know what Rumour is, Mr Sampson. I never repeat what I hear; it is the only way of paring the nails and shaving the head of Rumour. But, when you ask me what reason I have heard assigned for Mr Meltham's passing away from among men, it is another thing. I am not gratifying idle gossip then. I was told, Mr Sampson, that Mr Meltham had relinquished all his avocations and all his prospects, because he was, in fact, broken-hearted. A disappointed attachment, I heard – though it hardly seems probable, in the case of a man so distinguished and so attractive.'

'Attractions and distinctions are no armour against death,' said I.

'Oh! She died? pray, pardon me. I did not hear that. That,

indeed, makes it very very sad. Poor Mr Meltham! She died? Ah, dear me! Lamentable, lamentable!'

I still thought his pity not quite genuine, and I still suspected an unaccountable sneer under all this, until he said, as we were parted, like the other knots of talkers, by the announcement of dinner:

'Mr Sampson, you are surprised to see me so moved, on behalf of a man whom I have never known. I am not so disinterested as you may suppose. I myself have suffered, and recently too, from death. I have lost one of two charming nieces, who were my constant companions. She died young – barely three-and-twenty – and even her remaining sister is far from strong. The world is a grave!'

He said this with deep feeling, and I felt reproached for the coldness of my manner. Coldness and distrust had been engendered in me, I knew, by my bad experiences; they were not natural to me; and I often thought how much I had lost in life, losing trustfulness, and how little I had gained, gaining hard caution. This state of mind being habitual to me, I troubled myself more about this conversation than I might have troubled myself about a greater matter. I listened to his talk at dinner, and observed how readily other men responded to it, and with what a graceful instinct he adapted his subjects to the knowledge and habits of those he talked with. As, in talking with me, he had easily started the subject I might be supposed to understand best, and to be the most interested in, so, in talking with others, he guided himself by the same rule. The company was of a varied character; but, he was not at fault, that I could discover, with any member of it. He knew just as much of each man's pursuit as made him agreeable to that man in reference to it, and just as little as made it natural in him to seek modestly for information when the theme was broached.

As he talked and talked – but really not too much, for the rest of us seemed to force it upon him – I became quite angry with myself. I took his face to pieces in my mind, like a watch, and examined it in detail. I could not say much against any of his features separately; I could say even less against them when they were put together. 'Then is it not monstrous,' I asked myself, 'that because a man happens to part his hair straight up the middle of his head, I should permit myself to suspect, and even to detest, him?'

(I may stop to remark that this was no proof of my good sense. An observer of men who finds himself steadily repelled by some apparently trifling thing in a stranger, is right to give it great weight. It may be the clue to the whole mystery. A hair or two will show where a lion is hidden. A very little key will open a very heavy door.)

I took my part in the conversation with him after a time, and we got on remarkably well. In the drawing-room, I asked the host how long he had known Mr Slinkton? He answered, not many months; he had met him at the house of a celebrated painter then present, who had known him well when he was travelling with his nieces in Italy for their health. His plans in life being broken by the death of one of them, he was reading, with the intention of going back to college as a matter of form, taking his degree, and going into orders. I could not but argue with myself that here was the true explanation of his interest in poor Meltham, and that I had been almost brutal in my distrust on that simple head.

### III

On the very next day but one, I was sitting behind my glass partition as before, when he came into the outer office as before. The moment I saw him again without hearing him, I hated him worse than ever.

It was only for a moment that he gave me this opportunity; for, he waved his tight-fitting black glove the instant I looked at him, and came straight in.

'Mr Sampson, good day! I presume, you see, upon your kind permission to intrude upon you. I don't keep my word in being justified by business, for my business here – if I may so abuse the word – is of the slightest nature.'

I asked, was it anything I could assist him in?

'I thank you, no. I merely called to inquire outside, whether my dilatory friend has been so false to himself, as to be practical and sensible. But, of course, he has done nothing. I gave him your papers with my own hand, and he was hot upon the intention, but of course he has done nothing. Apart from the general human disinclination to do anything that ought to be done, I dare say there is a speciality about assuring one's life? You find it like will-making? People are so superstitious, and take it for granted they will die soon afterwards.'

– Up here, if you please. Straight up here, Mr Sampson. Neither to the right nor to the left! I almost fancied I could hear him breathe the words, as he sat smiling at me, with that intolerable parting exactly opposite the bridge of my nose.

'There is such a feeling sometimes, no doubt,' I replied; 'but I don't think it obtains to any great extent.'

'Well!' said he, with a shrug and a smile, 'I wish some good angel would influence my friend in the right direction. I rashly promised his mother and sister in Norfolk, to see it done, and he promised them that he would do it. But I suppose he never will.'

He spoke for a minute or two on indifferent topics, and went away.

I had scarcely unlocked the drawers of my writing-table next morning when he reappeared. I noticed that he came straight to the door in the glass partition, and did not pause a single moment outside.

'Can you spare me two minutes, my dear Mr Sampson?'

'By all means.'

'Much obliged,' laying his hat and umbrella on the table. 'I came early, not to interrupt you. The fact is, I am taken by surprise, in reference to this proposal my friend has made.'

'Has he made one?' said I.

'Ye-es,' he answered, deliberately looking at me; and then a bright idea seemed to strike him; – 'or he only tells me he has. Perhaps that may be a new way of evading the matter. By Jupiter, I never thought of that!'

Mr Adams was opening the morning's letters in the outer office. 'What is the name, Mr Slinkton?' I asked.

'Beckwith.'

'I looked out at the door and requested Mr Adams, if there were a proposal in that name, to bring it in. He had already laid it out of his hand on the counter. It was easily selected from the rest, and he gave it me. Alfred Beckwith. Proposal to effect a Policy with us for two thousand pounds. Dated yesterday.

'From the Middle Temple,[3] I see, Mr Slinkton.'

'Yes. He lives on the same staircase with me; his door is opposite mine. I never thought he would make me his reference, though.'

'It seems natural enough that he should.'

'Quite so, Mr Sampson; but I never thought of it. Let me see.'

He took the printed paper from his pocket. 'How am I to answer all these questions?'

'According to the truth, of course,' said I.

'Oh! Of course,' he answered, looking up from the paper with a smile: 'I meant, they were so many. But, you do right to be particular. It stands to reason that you must be particular. Will you allow me to use your pen and ink?'

'Certainly.'

'And your desk?'

'Certainly.'

He had been hovering about between his hat and his umbrella, for a place to write on. He now sat down in my chair, at my blotting paper and inkstand, with the long walk up his head in accurate perspective before me, as I stood with my back to the fire.

Before answering each question, he ran over it aloud, and discussed it. How long had he known Mr Alfred Beckwith? That he had to calculate by years, upon his fingers. What were his habits? No difficulty about *them*; temperate in the last degree, and took a little too much exercise, if anything. All the answers were satisfactory. When he had written them all, he looked them over, and finally signed them in a very pretty hand. He supposed he had now done with the business? I told him he was not likely to be troubled any further. Should he leave the papers here? If he pleased. Much obliged. Good morning!

I had had one other visitor before him; not at the office, but at my own house. That visitor had come to my bedside when it was not yet daylight, and had been seen by no one else but by my faithful confidential servant.

A second reference paper (for we always required two) was sent down into Norfolk, and was duly received back by post. This, likewise, was satisfactorily answered in every respect. Our forms were all complied with, we accepted the proposal, and the premium for one year was paid.

IN TWO PORTIONS. PORTION THE SECOND

IV

For six or seven months, I saw no more of Mr Slinkton. He called once at my house, but I was not at home; and he once asked me to dine with him in the Temple, but I was engaged. His friend's Assurance was effected in March. Late September or early in October, I was down at Scarborough[4] for a breath of sea air, where I met him on the beach. It was a hot evening; he came towards me with his hat in his hand; and there was the walk I had felt so strongly disinclined to take, in perfect order again, exactly in front of the bridge of my nose.

He was not alone; he had a young lady on his arm. She was dressed in mourning, and I looked at her with great interest. She had the appearance of being extremely delicate, and her face was remarkably pale and melancholy; but she was very pretty. He introduced her, as his niece, Miss Niner.

'Are you strolling, Mr Sampson? Is it possible you can be idle?'

It *was* possible, and I *was* strolling.

'Shall we stroll together?'

'With pleasure.'

The young lady walked between us, and we walked on the cool sea sand in the direction of Filey.

'There have been wheels here,' said Mr Slinkton. 'And now I look again, the wheels of a hand-carriage! Margaret, my love, your shadow, without doubt!'

'Miss Niner's shadow?' I repeated, looking down at it on the sand.

'Not that one,' Mr Slinkton returned, laughing. 'Margaret, my dear, tell Mr Sampson.'

'Indeed,' said the young lady, turning to me, 'there is nothing to tell – except that I constantly see the same invalid old gentleman, at all times, wherever I go. I have mentioned it to my uncle, and he calls the gentleman my shadow.'

'Does he live in Scarborough?' I asked.

'He is staying here.'

'Do you live in Scarborough?'

'No, I am staying here. My uncle has placed me with a family here, for my health.'

'And your shadow?' said I, smiling.

'My shadow,' she answered, smiling too, 'is – like myself – not very robust, I fear; for, I lose my shadow sometimes, as my shadow loses me at other times. We both seem liable to confinement to the house. I have not seen my shadow for days and days; but it does oddly happen, occasionally, that wherever I go, for many days together, this gentleman goes. We have come together in the most unfrequented nooks on this shore.'

'Is this he?' said I, pointing before us.

The wheels had swept down to the water's edge, and described a great loop on the sand in turning. Bringing the loop back towards us, and spinning it out as it came, was a hand-carriage drawn by a man.

'Yes,' said Miss Niner, 'this really is my shadow, uncle!'

As the carriage approached us and we approached the carriage, I saw within it an old man, whose head was sunk on his breast, and who was enveloped in a variety of wrappers. He was drawn by a very quiet but very keen-looking man, with iron-grey hair, who was slightly lame. They had passed us, when the carriage stopped, and the old gentleman within putting out his arm, called to me by my name. I went back, and was absent from Mr Slinkton and his niece for about five minutes.

When I rejoined them, Mr Slinkton was the first to speak. Indeed, he said to me in a raised voice before I came up with him: 'It is well you have not been longer, or my niece might have died of curiosity to know who her shadow is, Mr Sampson.'

'An old East India Director,'[5] said I. 'An intimate friend of our friend's at whose house I first had the pleasure of meeting you. A certain Major Banks. You have heard of him?'

'Never.'

'Very rich, Miss Niner; but very old, and very crippled. An amiable man – sensible – much interested in you. He has just been expatiating on the affection that he has observed to exist between you and your uncle.'

Mr Slinkton was holding his hat again, and he passed his hand up the straight walk, as if he himself went up it serenely, after me.

'Mr Sampson,' he said, tenderly pressing his niece's arm in his, 'our affection was always a strong one, for we have had but

few near ties. We have still fewer now. We have associations to
bring us together, that are not of this world, Margaret.'

'Dear uncle!' murmured the young lady, and turned her face
aside to hide her tears.

'My niece and I have such remembrances and regrets in
common, Mr Sampson,' he feelingly pursued, 'that it would be
strange indeed if the relations between us were cold or indifferent. If you remember a conversation you and I once had
together, you will understand the reference I make. Cheer up,
dear Margaret. Don't droop, don't droop. My Margaret! I
cannot bear to see you droop!'

The poor young lady was very much affected, but controlled
herself. His feelings, too, were very acute. In a word, he found
himself under such great need of a restorative, that he presently
went away, to take a bath of sea water; leaving the young lady
and me sitting on a point of rock, and probably presuming –
but, that, you will say, was a pardonable indulgence in a luxury
– that she would praise him with all her heart.

She did, poor thing. With all her confiding heart, she praised
him to me, for his care of her dead sister, and for his untiring
devotion in her last illness. The sister had wasted away very
slowly, and wild and terrible fantasies had come over her
towards the end; but he had never been impatient with her, or
at a loss; had always been gentle, watchful, and self-possessed.
The sister had known him, and she knew him, to be the best of
men, the kindest of men, and yet a man of such admirable
strength of character, as to be a very tower for the support of
their weak natures while their poor lives endured.

'I shall leave him, Mr Sampson, very soon,' said the young
lady; 'I know my life is drawing to an end; and when I am gone,
I hope he will marry and be happy. I am sure he has lived single
so long, only for my sake, and for my poor poor sister's.'

The little hand-carriage had made another great loop on the
damp sand, and was coming back again, gradually spinning out
a slim figure of eight, half a mile long.

'Young lady,' said I, looking around, laying my hand upon
her arm, and speaking in a low voice; 'time presses. You hear
the gentle murmur of that sea?'

She looked at me with the utmost wonder and alarm, saying,
'Yes!'

'And you know what a voice is in it when the storm comes?'

'Yes!'

'You see how quiet and peaceful it lies before us, and you know what an awful sight of power without pity it might be, this very night?'

'Yes!'

'But if you had never heard or seen it, or heard of it, in its cruelty, could you believe that it beats every inanimate thing in its way to pieces, without mercy, and destroys life without remorse?'

'You terrify me, sir, by these questions!'

'To save you, young lady, to save you! For God's sake, collect your strength and collect your firmness! If you were here alone and hemmed in by the rising tide on the flow to fifty feet above your head, you could not be in greater danger than the danger you are now to be saved from.'

The figure on the sand was spun out, and straggled off into a crooked little jerk that ended at the cliff very near us.

'As I am, before Heaven and the Judge of all mankind, your friend, and your dead sister's friend, I solemnly entreat you, Miss Niner, without one moment's loss of time, to come to this gentleman with me!'

If the little carriage had been less near to us, I doubt if I could have got her away; but, it was so near, that we were there, before she had recovered the hurry of being urged from the rock. I did not remain there with her, two minutes. Certainly within five, I had the inexpressible satisfaction of seeing her – from the point we had sat on, and to which I had returned – half supported and half carried up some rude steps notched in the cliff by the figure of an active man. With that figure beside her, I knew she was safe anywhere.

I sat alone on the rock, awaiting Mr Slinkton's return. The twilight was deepening and the shadows were heavy, when he came round the point, with his hat hanging at his buttonhole, smoothing his wet hair with one of his hands, and picking out the old path with the other and a pocket-comb.

'My niece not here, Mr Sampson?' he said, looking about.

'Miss Niner seemed to feel a chill in the air after the sun was down, and has gone home.'

He looked surprised, as though she was not accustomed to do anything without him: even to originate so slight a proceeding. 'I persuaded Miss Niner,' I explained.

'Ah!' said he. 'She is easily persuaded – for her good. Thank you, Mr Sampson; she is better within doors. The bathing-place was further than I thought, to say the truth.'

'Miss Niner is very delicate,' I observed.

He shook his head and drew a deep sigh. 'Very, very, very. You may recollect my saying so? The time that has since intervened, has not strengthened her. The gloomy shadow that fell upon her sister so early in life, seems, in my anxious eyes, to gather over her too, ever darker, ever darker. Dear Margaret, dear Margaret! But we must hope.'

The hand-carriage was spinning away before us, at a most indecorous pace for an invalid vehicle, and was making most irregular curves upon the sand. Mr Slinkton, noticing it after he had put his handkerchief to his eyes, said:

'If I may judge from appearances, your friend will be upset, Mr Sampson.'

'It looks probable, certainly,' said I.

'The servant must be drunk.'

'The servants of old gentlemen will get drunk sometimes,' said I.

'The major draws very light,' Mr Sampson.'

'The major does draw light,' said I.

By this time, the carriage, much to my relief, was lost in the darkness. We walked on for a little, side by side over the sand, in silence. After a short while he said, in a voice still affected by the emotion that his niece's state of health had awakened in him:

'Do you stay here long, Mr Sampson?'

'Why, no. I am going away tonight.'

'So soon? But, business always holds you in request. Men like Mr Sampson are too important to others, to be spared to their own need of relaxation and enjoyment.'

'I don't know about that,' said I. 'However, I am going back.'

'To London?

'To London.'

'I shall be there too, soon after you.'

I knew that, as well as he did. But, I did not tell him so. Any more than I told him what defensive weapon my right hand rested on in my pocket as I walked by his side. Any more than I told him why I did not walk on the sea-side of him, with the night closing in.

We left the beach, and our ways diverged. We exchanged Good night, and had parted indeed, when he said, returning:

'Mr Sampson, *may* I ask? Poor Meltham, whom we spoke of. – Dead yet?'

'Not when I last heard of him; but too broken a man to live long, and hopelessly lost to his old calling.'

'Dear, dear, dear!' said he, with great feeling. 'Sad, sad, sad! The world is a grave!' And so went his way.

It was not his fault if the world were not a grave; but, I did not call that observation after him, any more than I had mentioned those other things just now enumerated. He went his way, and I went mine with all expedition. This happened, as I have said, either at the end of September or beginning of October. The next time I saw him, and the last time, was late in November.

## V

I had a very particular engagement, to breakfast in the Temple. It was a bitter north-easterly morning, and the sleet and slush lay inches deep in the streets. I could get no conveyance, and was soon wet to the knees; but I should have been true to that appointment though I had had to wade to it, up to my neck in the same impediments.

The appointment took me to some chambers in the Temple. They were at the top of a lonely corner house overlooking the river. The name MR ALFRED BECKWITH was painted on the outer door. On the door opposite, on the same landing, the name MR JULIUS SLINKTON. The doors of both sets of chambers[7] stood open, so that anything said aloud in one set, could be heard in the other.

I had never been in those chambers before. They were dismal, close, unwholesome, and oppressive; the furniture, originally good, and not yet old, was faded and dirty; the rooms were in great disorder; there was a strong pervading smell of opium[8] brandy, and tobacco; the grate and fire-irons were splashed all over, with unsightly blotches of rust; and on a sofa by the fire, in the room where breakfast had been prepared, lay the host, Mr Beckwith: a man with all the appearances upon him of the worst kind of drunkard, very far advanced upon his shameful way to death.'

'Slinkton is not come yet,' said this creature, staggering up when I went in; 'I'll call him. Halloa! Julius Cæsar!⁹ Come and drink!' As he hoarsely roared this out, he beat the poker and tongs together in a mad way, as if that were his usual manner of summoning his associate.

The voice of Mr Slinkton was heard through the clatter, from the opposite side of the staircase, and he came in. He had not expected the pleasure of meeting me. I have seen several artful men brought to a stand, but I never saw a man so aghast as he was when his eyes rested on mine.

'Julius Cæsar,' cried Beckwith, staggering between us, 'Mist' Sampson! Mist' Sampson, Julius Cæsar! Julius, Mist' Sampson, is the friend of my soul. Julius keeps me plied with liquor, morning, noon, and night. Julius is a real benefactor. Julius threw the tea and coffee out of window when I used to have any. Julius empties all the water jugs of their contents, and fills 'em with spirits. Julius winds me up and keeps me going. Boil the brandy, Julius!'

There was a rusty and furred saucepan in the ashes – the ashes looked like the accumulation of weeks – and Beckwith, rolling and staggering between us as if he were going to plunge headlong into the fire, got the saucepan out, and tried to force it into Slinkton's hand.

'Boil the brandy, Julius Cæsar! Come! Do your usual office. Boil the brandy!'

He became so fierce in his gesticulations with the saucepan, that I expected to see him lay open Slinkton's head with it. He reeled back to the sofa, and sat there, panting, shaking, and red-eyed, in his rags of dressing-gown, looking at us both. I noticed then, that there was nothing to drink on the table but brandy, and nothing to eat but salted herrings, and a hot, sickly, highly-peppered stew.

'At all events, Mr Sampson,' said Slinkton, offering me the smooth gravel path for the last time, 'I thank you for interfering between me and this unfortunate man's violence. However you came here, Mr Sampson, or with whatever motive you came here, at least I thank you for that.'

'Boil the brandy!'¹⁰ muttered Beckwith.

Without gratifying his desire to know how I came there, I said quietly, 'How is your niece, Mr Slinkton?'

He looked hard at me, and I looked hard at him.

'I am sorry to say, Mr Sampson, that my niece has proved

treacherous and ungrateful to her best friend. She left me, without a word of notice or explanation. She was misled, no doubt, by some designing rascal. Perhaps you may have heard of it?'

'I did hear that she was misled by a designing rascal. In fact, I have proof of it.'

'Are you sure of it?' said he.

'Quite.'

'Boil the brandy!' muttered Beckwith. 'Company to breakfast, Julius Cæsar! Do your usual office – provide the usual breakfast, dinner, tea, and supper – boil the brandy!'

The eyes of Slinkton looked from him to me, and he said, after a moment's consideration:

'Mr Sampson, you are a man of the world, and so am I. I will be plain with you.'

'Oh, no, you won't,' said I, shaking my head.

'I tell you, sir, I will be plain with you.'

'And I tell you, you will not,' said I. 'I know all about you. *You* plain with any one? Nonsense, nonsense!'

'I plainly tell you, Mr Sampson,' he went on, with a manner almost composed, 'that I understand your object. You want to save your funds, and escape from your liabilities; these are old tricks of trade with you Office-gentlemen. But you will not do it, sir: you will not succeed. You have not an easy adversary to play against, when you play against me. We shall have to inquire, in due time, when and how Mr Beckwith fell into his present habits. With that remark, sir, I put this poor creature and his incoherent wanderings of speech, aside, and wish you a good morning and a better case next time.'

While he was saying this, Beckwith had filled a half-pint glass with brandy. At this moment he threw the brandy at his face, and threw the glass after it. Slinkton put his hands up, half blinded with the spirit, and cut with the glass across the forehead. At the sound of the breakage, a fourth person came into the room, closed the door, and stood at it. He was a very quiet but very keen looking man, with iron-grey hair, and slightly lame.

Slinkton pulled out his handkerchief, assuaged the pain in his smarting eyes, and dabbled the blood on his forehead. He was a long time about it, and I saw that, in the doing of it, a tremendous change came over him, occasioned by the change in

Beckwith – who ceased to pant and tremble, sat upright, and never took his eyes off him. I never in my life saw a face in which abhorrence and determination were so forcibly painted, as in Beckwith's then.

'Look at me, you villain,' said Beckwith, 'and see me as I really am. I took these rooms, to make them a trap for you. I came into them as a drunkard, to bait the trap for you. You fell into the trap, and you will never leave it alive. On the morning when you last went to Mr Sampson's office, I had seen him first. Your plot has been known to both of us, all along, and you have been counterplotted all along. What? Having been cajoled into putting that prize of two thousand pounds in your power, I was to be done to death with brandy, and, brandy not proving quick enough, with something quicker? Have I never seen you, when you thought my senses gone, pouring from your little bottle into my glass? Why, you Murderer and Forger, alone here with you in the dead of the night, as I have so often been, I have had my hand upon the trigger of a pistol, twenty times, to blow your brains out!'

This sudden starting up of the thing that he had supposed to be his imbecile victim, into a determined man, with a settled resolution to hunt him down and be the death of him mercilessly expressed from head to foot, was, in the first shock, too much for him. Without any figure of speech, he staggered under it. But, there is no greater mistake than to suppose, that a man who is a calculating criminal, is, in any phase of his guilt, otherwise than true to himself and perfectly consistent with his whole character. Such a man commits murder, and murder is the natural culmination of his course; such a man has to outface murder, and he will do it with hardihood and effrontery. It is a sort of fashion to express surprise that any notorious criminal, having such crime upon his conscience, can so brave it out. Do you think that if he had it on his conscience, or had a conscience to have it upon, he would ever have committed the crime?

Perfectly consistent with himself, as I believe all such monsters to be, this Slinkton recovered himself, and showed a defiance that was sufficiently cold and quiet. He was white, he was haggard, he was changed; but, only as a sharper[11] who had played for a great stake, and had been outwitted and had lost the game.

'Listen to me, you villain,' said Beckwith, 'and let every word you hear me say, be a stab in your wicked heart. When I took these rooms, to throw myself in your way and lead you on to the scheme which I knew my appearance and supposed character and habits would suggest to such a devil, how did I know that? Because you were no stranger to me. I knew you well. And I knew you to be the cruel wretch who, for so much money, had killed one innocent girl while she trusted him implicitly, and who was, by inches, killing another.'

Slinkton took out a snuff-box, took a pinch of snuff, and laughed.

'But, see here,' said Beckwith, never looking away, never raising his voice, never relaxing his face, never unclenching his hand. 'See what a dull wolf you have been, after all! The infatuated drunkard who never drank a fiftieth part of the liquor you plied him with, but poured it away, here, there, everywhere, almost before your eyes – who bought over the fellow you set to watch him and to ply him, by outbidding you in his bribe, before he had been at his work three days – with whom you have observed no caution, yet who was so bent on ridding the earth of you as a wild beast, that he would have defeated you if you had been ever so prudent – that drunkard whom you have many a time left on the floor of this room, and who has even let you go out of it, alive and undeceived, when you have turned him over with your foot – has, almost as often, on the same night, within an hour, within a few minutes, watched you awake, had his hand at your pillow when you were asleep, turned over your papers, taken samples from your bottles and packets of powder, changed their contents, rifled every secret of your life!'

He had had another pinch of snuff in his hand, but had gradually let it drop from between his fingers to the floor, where he now smoothed it out with his foot, looking down at it the while.

'That drunkard,' said Beckwith, 'who had free access to your rooms at all times, that he might drink the strong drinks you left in his way and be the sooner ended, holding no more terms with you than he would hold with a tiger, has had his master-key for all your locks, his test for all your poisons, his clue to your cipher writing.[12] He can tell you, as well as you can tell him, how long it took to complete that deed, what doses there were, what intervals, what signs of gradual decay upon mind and body, what distempered fancies were produced, what observable changes, what physical pain. He can tell you, as well as you can tell him, that all this was recorded day by day, as a lesson of experience for future service. He can tell you, better than you can tell him, where that journal is at this moment.'

Slinkton stopped the action of his foot, and looked at Beckwith.

'No,' said the latter, as if answering a question from him. 'Not in the drawer of the writing-desk that opens with the spring; it is not there, and it never will be there again.'

'Then you are a thief!' said Slinkton.

Without any change whatever in the inflexible purpose which it was quite terrific even to me to contemplate, and from the power of which I had all along felt convinced it was impossible for this wretch to escape, Beckwith returned:

'And I am your niece's shadow, too.'

With an imprecation, Slinkton put his hand to his head, tore out some hair, and flung it on the ground. It was the end of the smooth walk; he destroyed it in the action, and it will soon be seen that his use for it was past.

Beckwith went on: 'Whenever you left here, I left here. Although I understood that you found it necessary to pause in the completion of that purpose, to avert suspicion, still I watched you close, with the poor confiding girl. When I had your diary, and could read it word by word – it was only about the night before your last visit to Scarborough – you remember the night? you slept with a small flat phial tied to your wrist – I sent to Mr Sampson, who was kept out of view. This is Mr Sampson's trusty servant standing by the door. We three saved your niece among us.'

Slinkton looked at us all, took an uncertain step or two from the place where he had stood, returned to it, and glanced about him in a very curious way – as one of the meaner reptiles might, when looking for a hole to hide in. I noticed at the same time, that a singular change took place in the figure of the man – as if it collapsed within his clothes, and they consequently became ill-shapen and ill-fitting.

'You shall know,' said Beckwith, 'for I hope the knowledge will be bitter and terrible to you, why you have been pursued by one man, and why, when the whole interest that Mr Sampson represents, would have expended any money in hunting you down, you have been tracked to death at a single individual's charge. I hear you have had the name of Meltham on your lips sometimes?'

I saw, in addition to those other changes, a sudden stoppage come upon his breathing.

'When you sent the sweet girl whom you murdered (you know with what artfully-made-out surroundings and probabilities you sent her), to Meltham's office before taking her abroad, to originate the transaction that doomed her to the grave, it fell to Meltham's lot to see her and to speak with her. It did not fall to his lot to save her, though I know he would freely give his own life to have done it. He admired her; – I would say, he loved her deeply, if I thought it possible that you could understand the word. When she was sacrificed, he was thoroughly assured of your guilt. Having lost her, he had but one object left in life, and that was, to avenge her and destroy you.'

I saw the villain's nostrils rise and fall, convulsively; but, I saw no moving at his mouth.

'That man, Meltham,' Beckwith steadily pursued, 'was as absolutely certain that you could never elude him in this world, if he devoted himself to your destruction with his utmost fidelity and earnestness, and if he divided the sacred duty with no other duty in life, as he was certain that in achieving it he would be a poor instrument in the hands of Providence, and would do well before Heaven in striking you out from among living men. I am that man, and thank GOD that I have done my work!'

If Slinkton had been running for his life from swift-footed savages, a dozen miles, he could not have shown more emphatic signs of being oppressed at heart and labouring for breath, than he showed now, when he looked at the pursuer who had so relentlessly hunted him down.

'You never saw me under my right name, before; you see me under my right name, now. You shall see me once again, in the body, when you are tried for your life. You shall see me once again, in the spirit, when the cord is round your neck, and the crowd are crying against you!'

When Meltham had spoken these last words, that miscreant suddenly turned away his face, and seemed to strike his mouth with his open hand. At the same instant, the room was filled with a new and powerful odour, and, almost at the same instant, he broke into a crooked run, leap, start – I have no name for the spasm – and fell, with a dull weight that shook the heavy old doors and windows in their frames.

That was the fitting end of him.

When we saw that he was dead, we drew away from the room, and Meltham, giving me his hand, said with a weary air:

'I have no more work on earth, my friend. But, I shall see her again, elsewhere.'

It was in vain that I tried to rally him. He might have saved her, he said; he had not saved her, and he reproached himself; he had lost her, and he was broken-hearted.

'The purpose that sustained me, is over, Sampson, and there is nothing now to hold me to life. I am not fit for life; I am weak and spiritless; I have no hope and no object; my day is done.'

In truth, I could hardly have believed that the broken man who then spoke to me, was the man who had so strongly and so differently impressed me when his purpose was yet before him. I used such entreaties with him, as I could; but, he still said, and always said, in a patient undemonstrative way – nothing could avail him – he was broken-hearted.

He died early in the next spring. He was buried by the side of the poor young lady for whom he had cherished those tender and unhappy regrets, and he left all he had to her sister. She lived to be a happy wife and mother; she married my sister's son, who succeeded poor Meltham; she is living now; and her children ride about the garden on my walking-stick, when I go to see her.

# GEORGE SILVERMAN'S EXPLANATION

## IN NINE CHAPTERS. FIRST CHAPTER

It happened in this wise:

– But, sitting with my pen in my hand looking at those words again, without descrying any hint in them of the words that should follow, it comes into my mind that they have an abrupt appearance. They may serve, however, if I let them remain, to suggest how very difficult I find it to begin to explain my Explanation. An uncouth phrase: and yet I do not see my way to a better.

## SECOND CHAPTER

It happened in *this* wise:

– But, looking at these words, and comparing them with my former opening, I find they are the self-same words repeated. This is the more surprising to me, because I employ them in quite a new connexion. For indeed I declare that my intention was to discard the commencement I first had in my thoughts, and to give the preference to another of an entirely different nature, dating my explanation from an anterior period of my life. I will make a third trial, without erasing this second failure, protesting that it is not my design to conceal any of my infirmities, whether they be of head or heart.

## THIRD CHAPTER

Not as yet directly aiming at how it came to pass, I will come upon it by degrees. The natural manner of all, for GOD knows that is how it came upon me!

My parents were in a miserable condition of life, and my infant home was a cellar in Preston.[1] I recollect the sound of Father's Lancashire clogs on the street pavement above, as being different in my young hearing from the sound of all other clogs;[2] and I recollect that when Mother came down the cellar-steps, I used tremblingly to speculate on her feet having a good or an ill tempered look – on her knees – on her waist – until finally her face came into view and settled the question. From this it will be seen that I was timid, and that the cellar-steps were steep, and that the doorway was very low.

Mother had the gripe[3] and clutch of Poverty upon her face, upon her figure, and not least of all upon her voice. Her sharp and high-pitched words were squeezed out of her, as by the compression of bony fingers on a leathern bag, and she had a way of rolling her eyes about and about the cellar, as she scolded, that was gaunt and hungry. Father, with his shoulders rounded, would sit quiet on a three-legged stool, looking at the empty grate, until she would pluck the stool from under him, and bid him go bring some money home. Then he would dismally ascend the steps, and I, holding my ragged shirt and trousers together with a hand (my only braces), would feint and dodge from Mother's pursuing grasp at my hair.

A worldly little devil was Mother's usual name for me. Whether I cried for that I was in the dark, or for that it was cold, or for that I was hungry, or whether I squeezed myself into a warm corner when there was a fire, or ate voraciously when there was food, she would still say: 'Oh you worldly little devil!' And the sting of it was, that I quite well knew myself to be a worldly little devil. Worldly as to wanting to be housed and warmed, worldly as to wanting to be fed, worldly as to the greed with which I inwardly compared how much I got of those good things with how much Father and Mother got, when rarely, those good things were going.

Sometimes they both went away seeking work, and then I would be locked up in the cellar for a day or two at a time. I was at my worldliest then. Left alone, I yielded myself up to a worldly yearning for enough of anything (except misery), and for the death of Mother's father, who was a machine-maker at Birmingham, and on whose decease I had heard Mother say she would come into a whole court-full[4] of houses 'if she had her rights.' Worldly little devil, I would stand about, musingly fitting my cold bare feet into cracked bricks and crevices of the damp cellar-floor – walking over my grandfather's body, so to speak, into the court-full of houses, and selling them for meat and drink and clothes to wear.

At last a change came down into our cellar. The universal change came down even as low as that – so will it mount to any height on which a human creature can perch – and brought other changes with it.

We had a heap of I don't know what foul litter in the darkest corner, which we called 'the bed'. For three days Mother lay upon it without getting up, and then began at times to laugh. If I had ever heard her laugh before, it had been so seldom that the strange sound frightened me. It frightened Father, too, and we took it by turns to give her water. Then she began to move her head from side to side, and sing. After that, she getting no better, Father fell a-laughing and a-singing, and then there was only I to give them both water, and they both died.

## FOURTH CHAPTER

When I was lifted out of the cellar by two men, of whom one came peeping down alone first, and ran away and brought the other, I could hardly bear the light of the street. I was sitting in the roadway, blinking at it, and at a ring of people collected around me, but not close to me, when, true to my character of worldly little devil, I broke silence by saying, 'I am hungry and thirsty!'

'Does he know they are dead?' asked one of another.

'Do you know your father and mother are both dead of fever?' asked a third of me, severely.

'I don't know what it is to be dead. I supposed it meant that, when the cup rattled against their teeth and the water spilt over them. I am hungry and thirsty.' That was all I had to say about it.

The ring of people widened outward from the inner side as I looked around me; and I smelt vinegar, and what I now know to be camphor,[5] thrown in towards where I sat. Presently some one put a great vessel of smoking vinegar on the ground near me, and then they all looked at me in silent horror as I ate and drank of what was brought for me. I knew at the time they had a horror of me, but I couldn't help it.

I was still eating and drinking, and a murmur of discussion had begun to arise respecting what was to be done with me next, when I heard a cracked voice somewhere in the ring say: 'My name is Hawkyard, Mr Verity Hawkyard,[6] of West Bromwich.' Then the ring split in one place, and a yellow-faced peak-nosed gentleman, clad all in iron-grey to his gaiters, pressed forward with a policeman and another official of some sort. He came forward close to the vessel of smoking vinegar; from which he sprinkled himself carefully, and me copiously.

'He had a grandfather at Birmingham, this young boy: who is just dead, too,' said Mr Hawkyard.

I turned my eyes upon the speaker, and said in a ravening manner: 'Where's his houses?'

'Hah! Horrible worldliness on the edge of the grave,' said Mr Hawkyard, casting more of the vinegar over me, as if to get my devil out of me. 'I have undertaken a slight – a ve-ry slight – trust in behalf of this boy; quite a voluntary trust; a matter of mere honour, if not of mere sentiment; still I have taken it upon myself, and it shall be (O yes, it shall be!)[7] discharged.'

The bystanders seemed to form an opinion of this gentleman, much more favourable than their opinion of me.

'He shall be taught,' said Mr Hawkyard '(O yes, he shall be taught!); but what is to be done with him for the present? He may be infected. He may disseminate infection.' The ring widened considerably. 'What is to be done with him?'

He held some talk with the two officials. I could distinguish no word save, 'Farmhouse.' There was another sound several times repeated, which was wholly meaningless in my ears then, but which I knew soon afterwards to be 'Hoghton Towers.'[8]

'Yes,' said Mr Hawkyard, 'I think that sounds promising. I think that sounds hopeful. And he can be put by himself in a Ward, for a night or two, you say?'

It seemed to be the police-officer who had said so, for it was he who replied Yes. It was he, too, who finally took me by the arm and walked me before him through the streets, into a whitewashed room in a bare building, where I had a chair to sit in, a table to sit at, an iron bedstead and good mattress to lie upon, and a rug and blanket to cover me. Where I had enough to eat, too, and was shown how to clean the tin porringer[9] in which it was conveyed to me, until it was as good as a looking-glass. Here, likewise, I was put in a bath, and had new clothes brought to me, and my old rags were burnt, and I was camphored and vinegared, and disinfected in a variety of ways.

When all this was done – I don't know in how many days or how few, but it matters not – Mr Hawkyard stepped in at the door, remaining close to it, and said:

'Go and stand against the opposite wall, George Silverman. As far off as you can. That'll do. How do you feel?'

I told him that I didn't feel cold, and didn't feel hungry, and didn't feel thirsty. That was the whole round of human feelings, as far as I knew, except the pain of being beaten.

'Well,' said he, 'you are going, George, to a healthy farmhouse to be purified. Keep in the air there, as much as you can. Live an out-of-door life there, until you are fetched away. You had better not say much – in fact, you had better be very careful not to say anything – about what your parents died of, or they might not like to take you in. Behave well, and I'll put you to school (O yes, I'll put you to school!), though I am not obligated to do it. I am a servant of the Lord, George, and I have been a good servant to him (I have!) these five-and-thirty years. The Lord has had a good servant in me, and he knows it.'

What I then supposed him to mean by this, I cannot imagine. As little do I know when I began to comprehend that he was a prominent member of some obscure denomination or congregation, every member of which held forth to the rest when so inclined, and among whom he was called Brother Hawkyard. It was enough for me to know, on that day in the Ward, that the farmer's cart was waiting for me at the street corner. I was not slow to get into it, for it was the first ride I ever had in my life.

It made me sleepy, and I slept. First, I stared at Preston streets as long as they lasted and, meanwhile, I may have had some small dumb wondering within me whereabouts our cellar was. But I doubt it. Such a worldly little devil was I, that I took no thought who would bury Father and Mother, or where they would be buried, or when. The question whether the eating and drinking by day, and the covering by night, would be as good at the farmhouse as at the Ward, superseded those questions.

The jolting of the cart on a loose stony road awoke me, and I found that we were mounting a steep hill, where the road was a rutty by-road through a field. And so, by fragments of an ancient terrace, and by some rugged outbuildings that had once been fortified, and passing under a ruined gateway, we came to the old farmhouse in the thick stone wall outside the old quadrangle of Hoghton Towers. Which I looked at, like a stupid savage; seeing no speciality in; seeing no antiquity in; assuming all farmhouses to resemble it; assigning the decay I noticed, to Poverty; eyeing the pigeons in their flights, the cattle in their stalls, the ducks in the pond, and the fowls pecking about the yard, with a hungry hope that plenty of them might be killed for dinner while I stayed there; wondering whether the scrubbed dairy vessels drying in the sunlight could be the goodly porringers out of which the master ate his belly-filling food, and which he polished when he had done, according to my Ward experience; shrinkingly doubtful whether the shadows passing over that airy height on the bright spring day were not something in the nature of frowns; sordid, afraid, unadmiring, a small Brute to shudder at.

To that time I had never had the faintest impression of beauty. I had had no knowledge whatever that there was anything lovely in this life. When I had occasionally slunk up the cellar-steps into the street and glared in at shop-windows, I had done so with no higher feelings than we may suppose to animate a mangey young dog or wolf-cub. It is equally the fact that I had never been alone, in the sense of holding unselfish converse with myself. I had been solitary often enough, but nothing better.

Such was my condition when I sat down to my dinner, that day, in the kitchen of the old farmhouse. Such was my condition when I lay on my bed in the old farmhouse that night, stretched out opposite the narrow mullioned window, in the cold light of the moon, like a young Vampire.

## FIFTH CHAPTER

What do I know, now, of Hoghton Towers? Very little, for I have been gratefully unwilling to disturb my first impressions. A house centuries old, on high ground a mile or so removed from the road between Preston and Blackburn, where the first James of England[10] in his hurry to make money by making Baronets perhaps, made some of those remunerative dignitaries. A house, centuries old, deserted and falling to pieces, its woods and gardens long since grass land or ploughed up, the river Ribble and Darwen glancing below it, and a vague haze of smoke against which not even the supernatural prescience of the first Stuart could foresee a Counterblast,[11] hinting at Steam Power, powerful in two distances.

What did I know, then, of Hoghton Towers? When I first peeped in at the gate of the lifeless quadrangle, and started from the mouldering statue becoming visible to me like its Guardian Ghost; when I stole round by the back of the farmhouse and got in among the ancient rooms, many of them with their floors and ceilings falling, the beams and rafters hanging dangerously down, the plaster dropping as I trod, the oaken panels stripped away, the windows half walled up, half broken; when I discovered a gallery commanding the old kitchen, and looked down between balustrades upon a massive old table and benches, fearing to see I know not what dead-alive creatures come in and seat themselves and look up with I know not what dreadful eyes, or lack of eyes at me; when all over the house I was awed by gaps and chinks where the sky stared sorrowfully at me, where the birds passed, and the ivy rustled, and the stains of winter weather blotched the rotten floors; when down at the bottom of dark pits of staircase into which the stairs had sunk, green leaves trembled, butterflies fluttered, and bees hummed in and out through the broken doorways; when encircling the whole ruin were sweet scents and sights of fresh green growth and ever-renewing life, that I had never dreamed of; – I say, when I passed into such clouded perception of these things as my dark soul could compass, what did I know then of Hoghton Towers?

I have written that the sky stared sorrowfully at me. Therein have I anticipated the answer. I knew that all these things looked sorrowfully at me. That they seemed to sigh or whisper, not without pity for me: 'Alas! poor worldly little devil!'

There were two or three rats at the bottom of one of the smaller pits of broken staircase when I craned over and looked in. They were scuffling for some prey that was there. And when they started and hid themselves, close together in the dark, I thought of the old life (it had grown old already) in the cellar.

How not to be this worldly little devil? How not to have a repugnance towards myself as I had towards the rats? I hid in a corner of one of the smaller chambers, frightened at myself and crying (it was the first time I had ever cried for any cause not purely physical), and I tried to think about it. One of the farmploughs came into my range of view just then, and it seemed to help me as it went on with its two horses up and down the field so peacefully and quietly.

There was a girl of about my own age in the farmhouse family, and she sat opposite to me at the narrow table at mealtimes. It had come into my mind at our first dinner, that she might take the fever from me. The thought had not disquieted me then; I had only speculated how she would look under the altered circumstances, and whether she would die. But it came into my mind now, that I might try to prevent her taking the fever, by keeping away from her. I knew I should have but scrambling board,[12] if I did; so much the less worldly and less devilish the deed would be, I thought.

From that hour I withdrew myself at early morning into secret corners of the ruined house, and remained hidden there until she went to bed. At first, when meals were ready, I used to hear them calling me; and then my resolution weakened. But I strengthened it again, by going further off into the ruin and getting out of hearing. I often watched for her at the dim windows; and, when I saw that she was fresh and rosy, felt much happier.

Out of this holding her in my thoughts, to the humanising of myself, I suppose some childish love arose within me. I felt in some sort dignified by the pride of protecting her, by the pride of making the sacrifice for her. As my heart swelled with that new feeling, it insensibly softened about Mother and Father. It seemed to have been frozen before, and now to be thawed. The old ruin and all the lovely things that haunted it were not sorrowful for me only, but sorrowful for Mother and Father as well. Therefore did I cry again, and often too.

The farmhouse family conceived me to be of a morose temper, and were very short with me: though they never stinted me in such broken fare as was to be got, out of regular hours. One night when I lifted the kitchen latch at my usual time, Sylvia (that was her pretty name) had but just gone out of the room. Seeing her ascending the opposite stairs, I stood still at the door. She had heard the clink of the latch, and looked round.

'George,' she called to me, in a pleased voice: 'to-morrow is my birthday, and we are to have a fiddler, and there's a party of boys and girls coming in a cart, and we shall dance. I invite you. Be sociable for once, George.'

'I am very sorry, miss,' I answered, 'but I – but no; I can't come.'

'You are a disagreeable, ill-humoured lad,' she returned, disdainfully, 'and I ought not to have asked you. I shall never speak to you again.'

As I stood with my eyes fixed on the fire after she was gone, I felt that the farmer bent his brows upon me.

'Eh, lad,' said he, 'Sylvy's right. You're as moody and broody a lad as never I set eyes on yet!'

I tried to assure him that I meant no harm; but he only said, coldly: 'Maybe not, maybe not. There! Get thy supper, get thy supper, and then thou canst sulk to thy heart's content again.'

Ah! If they could have seen me next day in the ruin, watching for the arrival of the cart full of merry young guests; if they could have seen me at night, gliding out from behind the ghostly statue, listening to the music and the fall of dancing feet, and watching the lighted farmhouse windows from the quadrangle when all the ruin was dark; if they could have read my heart as I crept up to bed by the back way, comforting myself with the reflection, 'They will take no hurt from me;' they would not have thought mine a morose or an unsocial nature!

It was in these ways that I began to form a shy disposition; to be of a timidly silent character under misconstruction; to have an inexpressible, perhaps a morbid, dread of ever being sordid or worldly. It was in these ways that my nature came to shape itself to such a mould, even before it was affected by the influences of the studious and retired life of a poor scholar.

## SIXTH CHAPTER

Brother Hawkyard (as he insisted on my calling him) put me to school, and told me to work my way. 'You are all right, George,' he said. 'I have been the best servant the Lord has had in his service, for this five-and-thirty year (O, I have!), and he knows the value of such a servant as I have been to him (O yes he does!), and he'll prosper your schooling as a part of my reward. That's what *he'll* do, George. He'll do it for me.'

From the first I could not like this familiar knowledge of the ways of the sublime inscrutable Almighty, on Brother Hawk-yard's part. As I grew a little wiser and still a little wiser, I liked it less and less. His manner, too, of confirming himself in a parenthesis: as if, knowing himself he doubted his own word: I found distasteful. I cannot tell how much these dislikes cost me, for I had a dread that they were worldly.

As time went on, I became a Foundation Boy[13] on a good Foundation, and I cost Brother Hawkyard nothing. When I had worked my way so far, I worked yet harder, in the hope of ultimately getting a presentation to College, and a Fellowship.[14] My health has never been strong (some vapour from the Preston cellar cleaves to me I think), and what with much work and some weakness, I came again to be regarded – that is, by my fellow-students – as unsocial.

All through my time as a Foundation-Boy, I was within a few miles of Brother Hawkyard's congregation, and when ever I was what we called a Leave-Boy on a Sunday, I went over there at his desire. Before the knowledge became forced upon me that outside their place of meeting these Brothers and Sisters were no better than the rest of the human family, but on the whole were, to put the case mildly, as bad as most, in respect of giving short weight in their shops, and not speaking the truth: I say, before this knowledge became forced upon me, their prolix addresses, their inordinate conceit, their daring ignorance, their investment of the Supreme Ruler of Heaven and Earth with their own miserable meannesses and littlenesses greatly shocked me. Still, as their term for the frame of mind that could not perceive them to be in an exalted state of Grace, was the 'worldly' state, I did for a time suffer tortures under my inquiries of myself whether that young worldly-devilish spirit of mine could secretly be lingering at the bottom of my non-appreciation.

Brother Hawkyard was the popular expounder in this assembly, and generally occupied the platform (there was a little platform with a table on it, in lieu of a pulpit), first, on a Sunday afternoon. He was by trade a drysalter.[15] Brother Gimblet, an elderly man with a crabbed face, a large dog's-eared shirt collar, and a spotted blue neckerchief reaching up behind to the crown of his head, was also a drysalter, and an expounder. Brother Gimblet professed the greatest admiration for Brother Hawkyard; but (I had thought more than once) bore him a jealous grudge.

Let whosoever may peruse these lines kindly take the pains here to read twice, my solemn pledge that what I write of the language and customs of the congregation in question, I write scrupulously, literally, exactly, from the life and the truth.

On the first Sunday after I had won what I had so long tried for, and when it was certain that I was going up to College, Brother Hawkyard concluded a long exhortation thus:

'Well my friends and fellow-sinners, now I told you when I began, that I didn't know a word of what I was going to say to you (and No, I did not!) but that it was all one to me, because I knew the Lord would put into my mouth the words I wanted.'

('That's it!' From Brother Gimblet.)

'And he did put into my mouth the words I wanted.'

('So he did!' From Brother Gimblet.)

'And why?'

('Ah! Let's have that!' from Brother Gimblet.)

'Because I have been his faithful servant for five-and-thirty years, and because he knows it. For five-and-thirty years! And he knows it, mind you! I got those words that I wanted, on account of my wages. I got 'em from the Lord, my fellow-sinners. Down. I said "Here's a heap of wages due; let us have something down on account." And I got it down, and I paid it over to you, and you won't wrap it up in a napkin, nor yet in a towel, nor yet in a pockethankercher, but you'll put it out at good interest. Very well. Now my brothers and sisters and fellow-sinners, I am going to conclude with a question, and I'll make it so plain (with the help of the Lord, after five-and-thirty years, I should rather hope!) as that the Devil shall not be able to confuse it in your heads. Which he would be overjoyed to do.'

('Just his way. Crafty old blackguard!' from Brother Gimblet.)

'And the question is this. Are the Angels learned?'

('Not they. Not a bit on it.' From Brother Gimblet, with the greatest confidence.)

'Not they. And where's the proof? Sent ready-made by the hand of the Lord. Why, there's one among us here now, that has got all the Learning that can be crammed into him. *I* got him all the Learning that could be crammed into him. His grandfather' (this I had never heard before) 'was a Brother of ours. He was Brother Parksop. That's what he was. Parksop. Brother Parksop. His worldly name was Parksop, and he was a Brother of this Brotherhood. Then wasn't he Brother Parksop?'

('Must be. Couldn't help hisself.' From Brother Gimblet.)

'Well. He left that one now here present among us, to the care of a Brother-Sinner of his (and that Brother-Sinner, mind you, was a sinner of a bigger size in his time than any of you, Praise the Lord!), Brother Hawkyard. Me. *I* got him, without fee or reward – without a morsel of myrrh, or frankincense, nor yet Amber, letting alone the honeycomb[16] – all the Learning that could be crammed into him. Has it brought him into our Temple, in the spirit? No. Have we had any ignorant Brothers and Sisters that didn't know round O from crooked S, come in among us meanwhile? Many. Then the Angels are *not* learned. Then they don't so much as know their alphabet. And now, my friends and fellow-sinners, having brought it to that, perhaps some Brother present – perhaps you, Brother Gimblet – will pray a bit for us?'

Brother Gimblet undertook the sacred function, after having drawn his sleeve across his mouth, and muttered: 'Well! I don't know as I see my way to hitting any of you quite in the right place neither.' He said this with a dark smile, and then began to bellow. What we were specially to be preserved from, according to his solicitations, was despoilment of the orphan, suppression of testamentary intentions on the part of a Father or (say) Grandfather, appropriation of the orphan's house-property, feigning to give in charity to the wronged one from whom we withheld his due; and that class of sins. He ended with the petition, 'Give us peace!' Which, speaking for myself, was very much needed after twenty minutes of his bellowing.

Even though I had not seen him when he rose from his knees, steaming with perspiration, glance at Brother Hawkyard; and even though I had not heard Brother Hawkyard's tone of congratulating him on the vigour with which he had roared; I should have detected a malicious application in this prayer. Unformed suspicions to a similar effect had sometimes passed through my mind in my earlier schooldays, and had always caused me great distress, for they were worldly in their nature, and wide, very wide, of the spirit that had drawn me from Sylvia. They were sordid suspicions, without a shadow of proof. They were worthy to have originated in the unwholesome cellar. They were not only without proof, but against proof. For, was I not myself a living proof of what Brother Hawkyard had done? And without him, how should I ever have seen the sky look sorrowfully down upon that wretched boy at Hoghton Towers?

Although the dread of a relapse into a state of savage selfishness was less strong upon me as I approached manhood, and could act in an increased degree for myself, yet I was always on my guard against any tendency to such relapse. After getting these suspicions under my feet, I had been troubled by not being able to like Brother Hawkyard's manner, or his professed religion. So it came about, that as I walked back that Sunday evening, I thought it would be an act of reparation for any such injury my struggling thoughts had unwillingly done him, if I wrote, and placed in his hands before going to College, a full acknowledgment of his goodness to me, and an ample tribute of thanks. It might serve as an implied vindication of him against any dark scandal from a rival Brother, and Expounder, or from any other quarter.

Accordingly, I wrote the document with much care. I may add with much feeling, too, for it affected me as I went on. Having no set studies to pursue, in the brief interval between leaving the Foundation and going to Cambridge, I determined to walk out to his place of business and give it into his own hands.

It was a winter afternoon when I tapped at the door of his little counting-house, which was at the further end of his long low shop. As I did so (having entered by the back yard, where casks and boxes were taken in, and where there was the inscription 'Private Way to the Counting-house'), a shopman called to me from the counter that he was engaged.

'Brother Gimblet,' said the shopman (who was one of the Brotherhood), 'is with him.'

I thought this all the better for my purpose, and made bold to tap again. They were talking in a low tone, and money was passing, for I heard it being counted out.

'Who is it?' asked Brother Hawkyard, sharply.

'George Silverman,' I answered, holding the door open. 'May I come in?'

Both Brothers seemed so astounded to see me, that I felt shyer than usual. But they looked quite cadaverous in the early gaslight, and perhaps that accidental circumstance exaggerated the expression of their faces.

'What is the matter?' asked Brother Hawkyard.

'Aye! What is the matter?' asked Brother Gimblet.

'Nothing at all,' I said, diffidently producing my document. 'I am only the bearer of a letter from myself.'

'From yourself, George?' cried Brother Hawkyard.

'And to you,' said I.

'And to me, George?'

He turned paler, and opened it hurriedly; but looking over it, and seeing generally what it was, became less hurried, recovered his colour, and said: 'Praise the Lord!'

'That's it!' cried Brother Gimblet. 'Well put! Amen.'

Brother Hawkyard then said, in a livelier strain: 'You must know, George, that Brother Gimblet and I are going to make our two businesses, one. We are going into partnership. We are settling it now. Brother Gimblet is to take one clear half of the profits. (O yes! And he shall have it, he shall have it to the last farthing!)'

'D.V.!'[17] said Brother Gimblet, with his right fist firmly clenched on his right leg.

'There is no objection,' pursued Brother Hawkyard, 'to my reading this aloud, George?'

As it was what I expressly desired should be done, after yesterday's prayer, I more than readily begged him to read it aloud. He did so, and Brother Gimblet listened with a crabbed smile.

'It was in a good hour that I came here,' he said, wrinkling up his eyes. 'It was in a good hour likewise, that I was moved yesterday to depict for the terror of evil-doers, a character the direct opposite of Brother Hawkyard's. But it was the Lord that done it. I felt him at it, while I was perspiring.'

After that, it was proposed by both of them that I should attend the congregation once more, before my final departure. What my shy reserve would undergo from being expressly preached at and prayed at, I knew beforehand. But I reflected that it would be for the last time, and that it might add to the weight of my letter. It was well known to the Brothers and Sisters that there was no place taken for me in *their* Paradise, and if I showed this last token of deference to Brother Hawkyard, notoriously in despite of my own sinful inclinations, it might go some little way in aid of my statement that he had been good to me, and that I was grateful to him. Merely stipulating, therefore, that no express endeavour should be made for my conversion – which would involve the rolling of several Brothers and Sisters on the floor, declaring that they felt all their sins in a heap on their left side, weighing so many pounds avoirdupoise – as I knew from what I had seen of those repulsive mysteries – I promised.

Since the reading of my letter, Brother Gimblet had been at intervals wiping one eye with an end of his spotted blue neckerchief, and grinning to himself. It was, however, a habit that Brother had, to grin in an ugly manner even while expounding. I call to mind a delighted snarl with which he used to detail from the platform, the torments reserved for the wicked (meaning all human creation, except the Brotherhood), as being remarkably hideous.

I left the two to settle their articles of partnership, and count money; and I never saw them again but on the following Sunday. Brother Hawkyard died within two or three years, leaving all he possessed to Brother Gimblet, in virtue of a will dated (as I have been told) that very day.

Now, I was so far at rest with myself when Sunday came, knowing that I had conquered my own mistrust, and righted Brother Hawkyard in the jaundiced vision of a rival, that I went, even to that coarse chapel, in a less sensitive state than usual. How could I foresee that the delicate, perhaps the diseased, corner of my mind, where I winced and shrunk when it was touched or was even approached, would be handled as the theme of the whole proceedings?

On this occasion, it was assigned to Brother Hawkyard to pray, and to Brother Gimblet to preach. The prayer was to open the ceremonies; the discourse was to come next. Brothers

Hawkyard and Gimblet were both on the platform: Brother Hawkyard on his knees at the table, unmusically ready to pray: Brother Gimblet sitting against the wall, grinningly ready to preach.

'Let us offer up the sacrifice of prayer, my brothers and sisters and fellow-sinners.' Yes. But it was I who was the sacrifice. It was our poor sinful worldly-minded Brother here present, who was wrestled for. The now-opening career of this our unawakened Brother might lead to his becoming a minister of what was called The Church.[18] That was what *he* looked to. The Church. Not the chapel, Lord. The Church. No rectors, no vicars, no archdeacons, no bishops, no archbishops, in the chapel; but O Lord, many such in the Church! Protect our sinful Brother from his love of lucre. Cleanse from our unawakened Brother's breast, his sin of worldly-mindedness. The prayer said infinitely more in words, but nothing more to any intelligible effect.

Then Brother Gimblet came forward, and took (as I knew he would) the text, My kingdom is not of this world.[19] But whose was, my fellow-sinners? Whose? Why, our Brother's here present was. The only kingdom he had an idea of was of this world. ('That's it!' from several of the congregation.) What did the woman do, when she lost the piece of money?[20] Went and looked for it. What should our brother do when he lost his way? ('Go and look for it,' from a Sister.) Go and look for it. True. But must he look for it in the right direction, or in the wrong? ('In the right,' from a Brother.) There spake the prophets! He must look for it in the right direction, or he couldn't find it. But he had turned his back upon the right direction, and he wouldn't find it. Now, my fellow-sinners, to show you the difference betwixt worldly-mindedness and unworldly-mindedness, betwixt kingdoms not of this world and kingdoms *of* this world, here was a letter wrote by even our worldly-minded Brother unto Brother Hawkyard. Judge, from hearing of it read, whether Brother Hawkyard was the faithful steward that the Lord had in his mind only t'other day, when, in this very place, he drew you the picter of the unfaithful one. For it was him that done it, not me. Don't doubt that!

Brother Gimblet then grinned and bellowed his way through my composition, and subsequently through an hour. The service closed with a hymn, in which the Brothers unanimously roared, and the Sisters unanimously shrieked, at me, that I by wiles of worldly gain was mock'd, and they on waters of sweet love were rock'd; that I with Mammon struggled in the dark, while they were floating in a second Ark.

I went out from all this, with an aching heart and a weary spirit; not because I was quite so weak as to consider these narrow creatures, interpreters of the Divine majesty and wisdom; but because I was weak enough to feel as though it were my hard fortune to be misrepresented and misunderstood, when I most tried to subdue any risings of mere worldliness within me, and when I most hoped that, by dint of trying earnestly, I had succeeded.

## SEVENTH CHAPTER

My timidity and my obscurity occasioned me to live a secluded life at College, and to be little known. No relative ever came to visit me, for I had no relative. No intimate friends broke in upon my studies, for I made no intimate friends. I supported myself on my scholarship, and read much. My College time was otherwise not so very different from my time at Hoghton Towers.

Knowing myself to be unfit for the noisier stir of social existence, but believing myself qualified to do my duty in a moderate though earnest way if I could obtain some small preferment in the Church, I applied my mind to the clerical profession. In due sequence I took orders, was ordained, and began to look about me for employment. I must observe that I had taken a good degree, that I had succeeded in winning a good fellowship, and that my means were ample for my retired way of life. By this time I had read with several young men,[21] and the occupation increased my income, while it was highly interesting to me. I once accidentally overheard our greatest Don[22] say, to my boundless joy: 'That he heard it reported of Silverman that his gift of quiet explanation, his patience, his amiable temper, and his conscientiousness, made him the best of Coaches.' May my 'gift of quiet explanation' come more seasonably and powerfully to my aid in this present explanation than I think it will!

It may be, in a certain degree, owing to the situation of my College rooms (in a corner where the daylight was sobered), but it is in a much larger degree referable to the state of my own mind, that I seem to myself, on looking back to this time of my life, to have been always in the peaceful shade. I can see others in the sunlight; I can see our boats' crews and our athletic young men, on the glistening water, or speckled with the moving lights of sunlit leaves; but I myself am always in the shadow looking on. Not unsympathetically – GOD forbid! – but looking on, alone, much as I looked at Sylvia from the shadows of the ruined house, or looked at the red gleam shining through the farmer's windows, and listened to the fall of dancing feet, when all the ruin was dark, that night in the quadrangle.

I now come to the reason of my quoting that laudation of myself above given. Without such reason: to repeat it would have been mere boastfulness.

Among those who had read with me, was Mr Fareway, second son of Lady Fareway, widow of Sir Gaston Fareway, Baronet. This young gentleman's abilities were much above the average, but he came of a rich family, and was idle and luxurious. He presented himself to me too late, and afterwards came to me too irregularly, to admit of my being of much service to him. In the end I considered it my duty to dissuade him from going up for an examination which he could never pass, and he left College without taking a degree. After his departure, Lady Fareway wrote to me representing the justice of my returning half my fee, as I had been of so little use to her son. Within my knowledge a similar demand had not been made in any other case, and I most freely admit that the justice of it had not occurred to me until it was pointed out. But I at once perceived it, yielded to it, and returned the money.

Mr Fareway had been gone two years or more and I had forgotten him, when he one day walked into my rooms as I was sitting at my books.

Said he, after the usual salutations had passed: 'Mr Silverman, my mother is in town here, at the hotel, and wishes me to present you to her.'

I was not comfortable with strangers, and I dare say I betrayed that I was a little nervous or unwilling. For said he, without my having spoken:

'I think the interview may tend to the advancement of your prospects.'

It put me to the blush to think that I should be tempted by a worldly reason, and I rose immediately.

Said Mr Fareway, as we went along: 'Are you a good hand at business?'

'I think not,' said I.

Said Mr Fareway then: 'My mother is.'

'Truly?' said I.

'Yes. My mother is what is usually called a managing woman. Doesn't make a bad thing, for instance, even out of the spendthrift habits of my eldest brother abroad. In short, a managing woman. This is in confidence.'

He had never spoken to me in confidence, and I was surprised by his doing so. I said I should respect his confidence, of course, and said no more on the delicate subject. We had but a little way to walk, and I was soon in his mother's company. He presented me, shook hands with me, and left us two (as he said) to business.

I saw in my Lady Fareway, a handsome well-preserved lady of somewhat large stature, with a steady glare in her great round dark eyes that embarrassed me.

Said my Lady: 'I have heard from my son, Mr Silverman, that you would be glad of some preferment in the Church?'

I gave my Lady to understand that was so.

'I don't know whether you are aware,' my Lady proceeded, 'that we have a presentation of a Living?[23] I say *we* have, but in point of fact *I* have.'

I gave my Lady to understand that I had not been aware of this.

Said my Lady: 'So it is. Indeed, I have two presentations; one, to two hundred a year; one, to six. Both livings are in our county: North Devonshire, as you probably know. The first is vacant. Would you like it?'

What with my Lady's eyes, and what with the suddenness of this proposed gift, I was much confused.

'I am sorry it is not the larger presentation,' said my Lady, rather coldly, 'though I will not, Mr Silverman, pay you the bad compliment of supposing that *you* are, because that would be mercenary. And mercenary I am persuaded you are not.'

Said I, with my utmost earnestness: 'Thank you, Lady Fareway, thank you, thank you! I should be deeply hurt if I thought I bore the character.'

'Naturally,' said my Lady. 'Always detestable, but particularly in a clergyman. You have not said whether you would like the Living?'

With apologies for my remissness or indistinctness, I assured my Lady that I accepted it most readily and gratefully. I added that I hoped she would not estimate my appreciation of the generosity of her choice by my flow of words, for I was not a ready man in that respect when taken by surprise, or touched at heart.

'The affair is concluded,' said my Lady. 'Concluded. You will find the duties very light, Mr Silverman. Charming house; charming little garden, orchard, and all that. You will be able to take pupils. By the bye! – No. I will return to the word afterwards. What was I going to mention, when it put me out?'

My Lady stared at me, as if I knew. And I didn't know. And that perplexed me afresh.

Said my Lady, after some consideration: 'Oh! Of course. How very dull of me! The last incumbent – least mercenary man I ever saw – in consideration of the duties being so light and the house so delicious, couldn't rest, he said, unless I permitted him to help me with my correspondence, accounts, and various little things of that kind; nothing in themselves, but which it worries a lady to cope with. Would Mr Silverman also, like to— Or shall I—?'

I hastened to say that my poor help would be always at her ladyship's service.

'I am absolutely blessed,' said my Lady, casting up her eyes (and so taking them off of me for one moment), 'in having to do with gentlemen who cannot endure an approach to the idea of being mercenary!' She shivered at the word. 'And now as to the pupil.'

'The—?' I was quite at a loss.

'Mr Silverman, you have no idea what she is. She is,' said my Lady, laying her touch upon my coat sleeve, 'I do verily believe, the most extraordinary girl in this world. Already knows more Greek and Latin than Lady Jane Grey.[24] And taught herself! Has not yet, remember, derived a moment's advantage from Mr Silverman's classical acquirements. To say nothing of mathematics, which she is bent upon becoming versed in, and in which (as

I hear from my son and others) Mr Silverman's reputation is so deservedly high!'

Under my Lady's eyes, I must have lost the clue, I felt persuaded; and yet I did not know where I could have dropped it.

'Adelina,' said the Lady, 'is my only daughter. If I did not feel quite convinced that I am not blinded by a mother's partiality; unless I was absolutely sure that when you know her, Mr Silverman, you will esteem it a high and unusual privilege to direct her studies; I should introduce a mercenary element into this conversation, and ask you on what terms—'

I entreated my Lady to go no further. My Lady saw that I was troubled, and did me the honour to comply with my request.

## EIGHTH CHAPTER

Everything in mental acquisition that her brother might have been, if he would; and everything in all gracious charms and admirable qualities that no one but herself could be; this was Adelina.

I will not expatiate upon her beauty. I will not expatiate upon her intelligence, her quickness of perception, her powers of memory, her sweet consideration from the first moment for the slow-paced tutor who ministered to her wonderful gifts. I was thirty then; I am over sixty now; she is ever present to me in these hours as she was in those, bright and beautiful and young, wise and fanciful and good.

When I discovered that I loved her, how can I say. In the first day? In the first week? In the first month? Impossible to trace. If I be (as I am) unable to represent to myself any previous period of my life as quite separable from her attracting power, how can I answer for this one detail!

Whensoever I made the discovery, it laid a heavy burden on me. And yet, comparing it with the far heavier burden that I afterwards took up, it does not seem to me, now, to have been very hard to bear. In the knowledge that I did love her, and that I should love her while my life lasted, and that I was ever to hide my secret deep in my own breast, and she was never to find it, there was a kind of sustaining joy, or pride, or comfort, mingled with my pain.

But later on – say a year later on – when I made another discovery, then indeed my suffering and my struggle were strong. That other discovery was—?

These words will never see the light, if ever, until my heart is dust; until her bright spirit has returned to the regions of which, when imprisoned here, it surely retained some unusual glimpse of remembrance; until all the pulses that ever beat around us shall have long been quiet; until all the fruits of all the tiny victories and defeats achieved in our little breasts shall have withered away. That discovery was, that she loved me.

She may have enhanced my knowledge, and loved me for that; she may have overvalued my discharge of duty to her, and loved me for that; she may have refined upon a playful compassion which she would sometimes show for what she called my want of wisdom according to the light of the world's dark lanterns, and loved me for that; she may – she must – have confused the borrowed light of what I had only learned, with its brightness in its pure original rays; but she loved me at that time, and she made me know it.

Pride of family and pride of wealth put me as far off from her in my Lady's eyes as if I had been some domesticated creature of another kind. But they could not put me further from her than I put myself when I set my merits against hers. More than that. They could not put me, by millions of fathoms, half so low beneath her as I put myself when in imagination I took advantage of her noble trustfulness, took the fortune that I knew she must possess in her own right, and left her to find herself in the zenith of her beauty and genius, bound to poor rusty plodding Me.

No. Worldliness should not enter here, at any cost. If I had tried to keep it out of other ground, how much harder was I bound to try to keep it from this sacred place.

But there was something daring in her broad generous character that demanded at so delicate a crisis to be delicately and patiently addressed. After many and many a bitter night (O I found I could cry, for reasons not purely physical, at this pass of my life!) I took my course.

My Lady had in our first interview unconsciously over-stated the accommodation of my pretty house. There was room in it for only one pupil. He was a young gentleman near coming of age, very well connected, but what is called a poor relation. His parents were dead. The charges of his living and reading with me were defrayed by an uncle, and he and I were to do our utmost together for three years towards qualifying him to make his way. At this time he had entered into his second year with me. He was well-looking, clever, energetic, enthusiastic, bold; in the best sense of the term, a thorough young Anglo-Saxon.[25]

I resolved to bring these two together.

## NINTH CHAPTER

Said I, one night, when I had conquered myself: 'Mr Granville:' Mr Granville Wharton his name was: 'I doubt if you have ever yet so much as seen Miss Fareway.'

'Well, sir,' returned he, laughing, 'you see her so much yourself, that you hardly leave another fellow a chance of seeing her.'

'I am her tutor, you know,' said I.

And there the subject dropped for that time. But I so contrived, as that they should come together shortly afterwards. I had previously so contrived as to keep them asunder, for while I loved her – I mean before I had determined on my sacrifice – a lurking jealousy of Mr Granville lay within my unworthy breast.

It was quite an ordinary interview in the Fareway Park; but they talked easily together for some time; like takes to like, and they had many points of resemblance. Said Mr Granville to me, when he and I sat at our supper that night: 'Miss Fareway is remarkably beautiful, sir, and remarkably engaging. Don't you think so?' – 'I think so,' said I. And I stole a glance at him, and saw that he had reddened and was thoughtful. I remember it most vividly, because the mixed feeling of grave pleasure and acute pain that the slight circumstance caused me, was the first of a long, long series of such mixed impressions under which my hair turned slowly grey.

I had not much need to feign to be subdued, but I counterfeited to be older than I was, in all respects (Heaven knows, my heart being all too young the while!), and feigned to be more of a recluse and bookworm than I had really become, and gradually set up more and more of a fatherly manner towards Adelina. Likewise, I made my tuition less imaginative than before; separated myself from my poets and philosophers; was careful to present them in their own light, and me, their lowly servant, in my own shade. Moreover, in the matter of apparel I was equally mindful. Not that I had ever been dapper that way, but that I was slovenly now.

As I depressed myself with one hand, so did I labour to raise Mr Granville with the other; directing his attention to such subjects as I too well knew most interested her, and fashioning him (do not deride or misconstrue the expression, unknown reader of this writing, for I have suffered!) into a greater resemblance to myself in my solitary one strong aspect. And gradually, gradually, as I saw him take more and more to these thrown-out lures of mine, then did I come to know better and better that love was drawing him on, and was drawing Her from me.

So passed more than another year; every day a year in its number of my mixed impressions of grave pleasure and acute pain; and then, these two being of age and free to act legally for themselves, came before me, hand in hand (my hair being now quite white), and entreated me that I would unite them together. 'And indeed, dear Tutor,' said Adelina, 'it is but consistent in you that you should do this thing for us, seeing that we should never have spoken together that first time but for you, and that but for you we could never have met so often afterwards.' The whole of which was literally true, for I had availed myself of my many business attendances on, and conferences with, my Lady, to take Mr Granville to the house, and leave him in the outer room with Adelina.

I knew that my Lady would object to such a marriage for her daughter, or to any marriage that was other than an exchange of her for stipulated lands, goods, and moneys. But, looking on the two, and seeing with full eyes that they were both young and beautiful; and knowing that they were alike in the tastes and acquirements that will outlive youth and beauty; and considering that Adelina had a fortune now, in her own keeping; and considering further that Mr Granville, though for the present poor, was of a good family that had never lived in a cellar in Preston; and believing that their love would endure, neither having any great discrepancy to find out in the other; I told them of my readiness to do this thing which Adelina asked of her dear Tutor, and to send them forth, Husband and Wife, into the shining world with golden gates that awaited them.

It was on a summer morning that I rose before the sun, to compose myself for the crowning of my work with this end. And my dwelling being near to the sea, I walked down to the rocks on the shore, in order that I might behold the sun rise in his majesty.

The tranquillity upon the Deep and on the firmament, the orderly withdrawal of the stars, the calm promise of coming day, the rosy suffusion of the sky and waters, the ineffable splendour that then burst forth, attuned my mind afresh after the discords of the night. Methought that all I looked on said to me, and that all I heard in the sea and in the air said to me: 'Be comforted, mortal, that thy life is so short. Our preparation for what is to follow, has endured, and shall endure, for unimaginable ages.'

I married them. I knew that my hand was cold when I placed it on their hands clasped together; but the words with which I had to accompany the action, I could say without faltering, and I was at peace.

They being well away from my house and from the place, after our simple breakfast, the time was come when I must do what I had pledged myself to them that I would do: break the intelligence to my Lady.

I went up to the house, and found my Lady in her ordinary business-room. She happened to have an unusual amount of commissions to entrust to me that day, and she had filled my hands with papers before I could originate a word.

'My Lady' – I then began, as I stood beside her table.

'Why, what's the matter!' she said, quickly, looking up.

'Not much, I would fain hope, after you shall have prepared yourself, and considered a little.'

'Prepared myself! And considered a little! You appear to have prepared *your*self but indifferently, anyhow, Mr Silverman.' This, mighty scornfully, as I experienced my usual embarrassment under her stare.

Said I, in self-extenuation, once for all: 'Lady Fareway, I have but to say for myself that I have tried to do my duty.'

'For yourself?' repeated my Lady. 'Then there are others concerned, I see. Who are they?'

I was about to answer, when she made towards the bell with a dart that stopped me, and said: 'Why, where is Adelina!'

'Forbear. Be calm, my Lady. I married her this morning to Mr Granville Wharton.'

She set her lips, looked more intently at me than ever, raised her right hand and smote me hard upon the cheek.

'Give me back those papers, give me back those papers!' She tore them out of my hands and tossed them on her table. Then seating herself defiantly in her great chair, and folding her arms, she stabbed me to the heart with the unlooked-for reproach: 'You worldly wretch!'

'Worldly?' I cried. 'Worldly!'

'This, if you please,' she went on with supreme scorn, pointing me out as if there were some one there to see: 'this, if you please, is the disinterested scholar, with not a design beyond his books! This, if you please, is the simple creature whom any one could overreach in a bargain! This, if you please, is Mr Silverman! Not of this world, not he! He has too much simplicity for this world's cunning. He has too much singleness of purpose to be a match for this world's double-dealing. – What did he give you for it?'

'For what? And who?'

'How much,' she asked, bending forward in her great chair, and insultingly tapping the fingers of her right hand on the palm of her left: 'how much does Mr Granville Wharton pay you for getting him Adelina's money? What is the amount of your percentage upon Adelina's fortune? What were the terms of the agreement that you proposed to this boy when you, the Reverend George Silverman, licensed to marry, engaged to put him in possession of this girl? You made good terms for yourself, whatever they were. He would stand a poor chance against your keenness.'

Bewildered, horrified, stunned, by this cruel perversion, I could not speak. But I trust that I looked innocent, being so.

'Listen to me, shrewd hypocrite,' said my Lady, whose anger increased as she gave it utterance. 'Attend to my words, you cunning schemer who have carried this plot through with such a practised double face that I have never suspected you. I had my projects for my daughter; projects for family connexion;

projects for fortune. You have thwarted them, and overreached me; but I am not one to be thwarted and overreached, without retaliation. Do you mean to hold this Living, another month?'

'Do you deem it possible, Lady Fareway, that I can hold it another hour, under your injurious words?'

'Is it resigned then?'

'It was mentally resigned, my Lady, some minutes ago.'

'Don't equivocate, sir. *Is* it resigned?'

'Unconditionally and entirely. And I would that I had never, never, come near it!'

'A cordial response from me to *that* wish, Mr Silverman! But take this with you, sir. If you had not resigned it, I would have had you deprived of it. And though you have resigned it, you will not get quit of me as easily as you think for I will pursue you with this story. I will make this nefarious conspiracy of yours, for money, known. You have made money by it, but you have at the same time, made an enemy by it. *You* will take good care that the money sticks to you; *I* will take good care that the enemy sticks to you.'

Then said I, finally: 'Lady Fareway, I think my heart is broken. Until I came into this room just now, the possibility of such mean wickedness as you have imputed to me, never dawned upon my thoughts. Your suspicions—'

'Suspicions. Pah!' said she indignantly. 'Certainties.'

'Your certainties, my Lady, as you call them; your suspicions, as I call them; are cruel, unjust, wholly devoid of foundation in fact. I can declare no more, except that I have not acted for my own profit or my own pleasure. I have not in this proceeding, considered myself. Once again, I think my heart is broken. If I have unwittingly done any wrong with a righteous motive, that is some penalty to pay.'

She received this with another and a more indignant 'Pah!' and I made my way out of her room (I think I felt my way out with my hands, although my eyes were open), almost suspecting that my voice had a repulsive sound, and that I was a repulsive object.

There was a great stir made, the Bishop was appealed to, I received a severe reprimand, and narrowly escaped suspension. For years a cloud hung over me, and my name was tarnished. But my heart did not break, if a broken heart involves death; for I lived through it.

They stood by me, Adelina and her husband, through it all. Those who had known me at College, and even most of those who had only known me there by reputation, stood by me too. Little by little, the belief widened that I was not capable of what was laid to my charge. At length, I was presented to a College-Living in a sequestered place, and there I now pen my Explanation. I pen it at my open window in the summertime; before me, lying the churchyard, equal resting-place for sound hearts, wounded hearts, and broken hearts. I pen it for the relief of my own mind, not foreseeing whether or no it will ever have a reader.

# NOTES

___

### PUBLIC LIFE OF MR TULRUMBLE

1. (3) **watering-place:** fashionable spa resort.

2. (3) **Limehouse:** dockland area of east London, on the north side of the River Thames.

3. (3) **Ratcliffe Highway:** east London thoroughfare, haunt of sailors and low-life characters.

4. (4) **Doric:** the oldest and simplest form of Greek architectural design.

5. (4) **church-days:** days when divine service is held.

6. (4) **larger and better-known body of the same genus:** i.e. Parliament. Dickens expressed his contempt for the conduct of Parliament in *Sketches by Boz* and elsewhere after his experiences as a parliamentary reporter.

7. (4) **betimes:** in good time, or early.

8. (4) **strews:** spreads lightly.

9. (5) **capital:** the use of the word in relation to the original funds of a company or individual dates from the early eighteenth century. Dickens was the first English novelist to write extensively about the gap between capitalists and the poor.

10. (5) **bushels:** A bushel was a measure containing approximately 2218 cubic inches.

11. (5) **sign-board:** board or other device set up outside a shop to indicate the nature of the business.

12. (5) **truck:** hand-cart.

13. (5) **started a donkey:** commenced using a donkey to carry goods.

14. (5) **cart … waggon:** A cart is a strong vehicle with two wheels; a waggon is a four-wheeled vehicle for the transport of goods.

15. (5) **Whittington:** The story of Dick Whittington and his cat, who went to London in the belief that the streets were paved with gold and found that they were made of hard stones, was commonly told to children in Dickens's time. It was a favourite theme for pantomimes, then as now. It is a simple analogue for the story which Dickens explored in *Great Expectations*.

16. (5) **four-wheel chaise, driven by a tall postilion:** A chaise was a light, four-wheeled, open carriage. In Dickens's time, carriages were a sign of social status, like certain motor-cars today. The postilion would have ridden the horse on the near side.

17. (5) **Lighterman's Arms:** a public-house. A lighter is a large open boat or barge used for unloading larger ships and transporting goods.

18. (6) **Lord Mayor's show:** still held every November in London, organised by the newly elected Mayor for the people of London. Dickens used the giants, Gog and Magog, associated with it, in *Master Humphrey's Clock* (see p. 234, n. 24).

19. (6) **Great Mogul:** the title of the Emperor of the Mogul Empire in Hindustan, founded by Babur in 1526.

20. (7) **Lor-a-mussy!:** Lord have mercy!

21. (7) **lieges:** subjects.

22. (8) **hot-pressed, Bath post letter-paper:** a superior form of letter-paper. Hot-pressing was a method of making the surface glossy by pressing the paper between glazed boards and hot metal plates.

23. (8) **top-boot:** high riding boot.

24. (9) *sobriquet:* nickname.

25. (9) **drag:** apparatus used for recovering the bodies of those who had been drowned.

26. (9) **Captain Manby's apparatus:** Captain Manby was a prolific inventor. Born in 1765, he devoted most of his life to the saving of life, particularly from disasters at sea. The life-saving apparatus he invented consisted of a life-line sent out to stranded ships by means of a gun (see Kenneth Walthew's biography, *From Rock and Tempest* [1971]).

27. (9) **stocks:** instrument of punishment in which the offender's ankles, and sometimes also wrists, were confined in holes between two planks of wood.

28. (10) **seventy-four pounder:** gun carrying a shot of seventy-four pounds' weight.

29. (10) **eight-day clock:** long-case clock needing to be wound every eight days.

30. (11) **gauntlets:** gloves worn as part of medieval armour.

31. (11) **assizes:** sessions held periodically for the purpose of administering justice. Dickens was to return many times to the theme of the inadequacies and absurdities of the legal system, and the avarice of lawyers.

32. (12) **taken the veil:** entered a convent, thus withdrawing from the outside world.

33. (12) **court-card:** one of the coloured cards – knave, queen, king – in a pack of playing-cards.

34. (12) **might have had something to say to him:** might have been a little impressed.

35. (12) **watermen:** boatmen who plied for passenger hire on the River Thames. They were members of the Watermen's Company and wore an elaborate uniform on ceremonial occasions.

36. (12) **running-footmen:** servants employed to run before their masters' carriages.

37. (13) **sword-bearer:** municipal official who carries a sword of state before a mayor or other dignitary on ceremonial occasions.

38. (16) **Duke of Devonshire, in a little circle of his own:** seems to have been a comic phrase for extreme aristocratic exclusivity.

39. (17) **like the top of a trunk:** Trunks were most usually covered with leather, but could be covered with an animal skin instead.

40. (18) **like the anonymous vessel in the Bay of Biscay:** in the sea-song 'The Bay of Biscay' by Andrew Cherry; also quoted in *Dombey and Son*, Chapter 39.

41. (18) **deuce a cheer:** devil of a cheer; i.e. none at all.

42. (18) **recorder:** judge of a city or borough court of quarter-sessions.

43. (18) **nick:** The use of Nick as an abbreviation for Nicholas is obviously considered to be over-familiar. Old Nick was the popular name for the devil. 'Nick' as a verb means to catch or arrest.

44. (18) **statistics ... philosophical:** satirical reference to Utilitarianism, associated with followers of Jeremy Bentham and John Stuart Mill, which judges actions by their usefulness or tendency to promote the happiness of the greatest number. The political economist Mr Filer in *The Chimes* is an adherent of this philosophy.

45. (18) **tap-room:** room in a public-house in which beer is served straight from the tap or cask.

46. (19) **whereof the memory ... goeth not to the contrary:** alluding to *Blackstone's Commentaries on the Laws of England* (1765–9), 'the memory of man runneth not to the contrary', i.e. from time immemorial.

47. (20) **large book with a blue cover:** a parliamentary blue book, so-called because parliamentary reports were issued in blue paper covers.

48. (20) **Middlesex magistrates:** see Philip Collins, *Dickens and Crime*, especially on the teetotal Middlesex magistrate Benjamin Rotch.

49. (20) **yielded the palm:** granted the victory (from the palm leaf used as a symbol of triumph).

50. (20) **took heart of grace:** plucked up courage.

## MASTER HUMPHREY'S CLOCK

1. (23) **Master:** By Dickens's time the use of Master was being replaced by Mister, except in the case of young boys; but it was common usage in the seventeenth century. Here it gives Humphrey a venerable quality, in keeping with the friendly attentiveness which Dickens imagines as due to him and his circle of friends.

2. (23) **weekly numbers:** see Introduction, p. xvii.

3. (25) **Richard Swiveller:** Dickens is imagining the reactions of Master Humphrey's friends to the characters of *The Old Curiosity Shop*.

4. (25) **their occupation is gone:** alluding to Shakespeare's *Othello*, Act 3, Sc. 3: 'Othello's occupation's gone'.

5. (25) **a report that he had gone raving mad:** Forster comments: 'He refers here to a report, rather extensively circulated at the time . . . that he was suffering from loss of reason and was under treatment in an asylum' (*Life of Charles Dickens*, Book II, Ch. 8).

6. (25) **Sir Peter Teazle and Charles Surface in the School for Scan-**

**dal:** characters in R. B. Sheridan's play, *The School for Scandal* (1777); their alleged duel is reported in Act 5, Sc. 2.

**7. (25) Bedlam ... Saint Luke's ... Hanwell:** The Hospital of St Mary of Bethlehem had been used as a hospital for the insane since 1547; Saint Luke's and Hanwell were also asylums.

**8. (25) Sir Benjamin Backbite:** another character in *The School for Scandal*. It is actually 'a little bronze Pliny that stood over the chimney piece . . .'

**9. (26) double letter:** letter written on two sheets and charged double postage.

**10. (26) Vicar of Wakefield:** Oliver Goldsmith's novel, *The Vicar of Wakefield*, was published in 1766. The quotation is from Chapter 32.

**11. (29) whet:** something which sharpens or incites; now rare as a noun.

**12. (32) cricket-voice:** *The Cricket on the Hearth* was to become one of Dickens's best-known Christmas books, published in 1846. The seed of the idea for the later work may perhaps be found here.

**13. (34) alchemists:** Alchemists in the Middle Ages sought to transmute base metals into gold. Alchemical gold was also associated with the elixir of life. The crucible, made to endure great heat, was used for fusing the metals.

**14. (34) of yore:** of old.

**15. (36) alderman:** representative of a ward in the City.

**16. (36) common-councilman:** member of the Court of Common Council, which regulates the affairs of the City of London.

**17. (36) Patten-makers:** shoemakers; one of the City of London companies.

**18. (36) Sheriff:** official responsible for the administration of the law.

**19. (36) weazen:** shrivelled, shrunken.

**20. (37) Middle Temple:** one of the Inns of Court in London, where barristers have their chambers. The Middle Temple stands on the site of buildings which once belonged to the Knights of the Temple. Dickens, who once thought of being a lawyer, was a member of the Middle Temple.

**21. (37) recorder:** judge who has jurisdiction in a city or borough.

22. (37) *de facto,* if not *de jure:* in fact, if not in law.

23. (38) **Temple Bar:** the entrance to the City of London, removed in 1878. The Lord Mayor had the right to close it against the King.

24. (41) **Gog and Magog:** The statues called Gog and Magog in the Guildhall of the City of London are said to represent Gogmagog and Corineus. Gogmagog was a giant, overthrown by Corineus, the companion of Brute, who, according to legend, was the founder of the British race. The original statues were destroyed in the Great Fire of 1666, but were replaced in 1709.

25. (43) **beseem:** befit.

26. (43) **halbert:** a combination of spear and battle-axe.

27. (44) **conduits run wine:** cisterns to supply water, filled with wine at times of celebration. Wine flowed through the Cheapside conduit to welcome Henry VI after his coronation; the rebel Jack Cade in Shakespeare's *Henry VI, Part Two* commands that 'the pissing-conduit run nothing but claret wine' (Act 4, Sc. 6).

28. (44) **postern-gates:** back gates or side gates.

29. (44) **starlings:** an outwork from the lower part of the pier of a bridge to protect the pier against the force of the stream.

30. (44) **Jerkins:** close-fitting jacket, often made of leather.

31. (44) **quarter-staves:** stout poles formerly used as weapons by the English peasantry.

32. (44) **noble heads:** the heads of traitors.

33. (44) **the block, the rack:** the execution block; the rack used for torture.

34. (45) **Traitor's-gate:** the river gate of the Tower of London, by which traitors and state prisoners were usually committed to the Tower.

35. (45) **giants ... smelling out Englishmen:** alluding to the giant in the fairy-tale 'Jack and the Beanstalk' who declares, 'Fee fie fo fum, I smell the blood of an Englishman.'

36. (45) **Bowyer:** maker of bows for archery.

37. (45) **ward of Cheype:** administrative district of Cheapside, in the nineteenth century a wealthy area of London, with large and costly buildings inhabited by prosperous dealers, goldsmiths, etc.

38. (46) **buckler:** small round shield.

39. (47) **rufflers:** proud, arrogant fellows.

40. (47) **caracoling:** half-turn to right or left executed by a horseman.

41. (49) **tilting-ground:** used for jousts or tournaments.

42. (50) **mercers:** dealers in fabrics.

43. (51) **Lud Gate:** gate at the bottom of Ludgate Hill, leading to St Paul's Cathedral.

44. (52) **dirk:** dagger.

45. (52) **bookshop:** St Paul's churchyard was noted as a location for booksellers in London from the fifteenth century.

46. (52) **ordinary:** eating-house or tavern where meals were provided for the public.

47. (53) **doublets:** close-fitting garments worn by men from the four-teenth to the eighteenth centuries.

48. (56) **broken ... lamps ... carried away every bell-handle:** referring to the high jinks of young aristocratic gentlemen.

49. (61) **Simoom:** a hot dry wind, i.e. the suffocating odours from the roast and boiled food.

50. (61) **freemasonry:** The Freemasons were founded as a fraternity in the seventeenth century. New members were instructed in rituals and secret signs. The Masons remain powerful today in many parts of public life.

51. (62) **German Student:** notorious as smokers of long and fancy pipes (described by Thackeray in *Vanity Fair*, Chapters 65–6).

52. (67) **Nimeguen:** The Treaty of Nijmegen, signed in 1678, ended the war between Louis XIV and Holland.

53. (68) **look ... down:** quell or overcome with a look.

54. (75) **rubbers ... honour ... stood at eight:** terms from the card game of English whist. A team winning two games out of three is said to win a rubber. The honour cards are ace, king, queen, knave. The highest possible score is eight points.

55. (76) **wight:** person.

56. (78) **Mr Pickwick:** Dickens finished *The Pickwick Papers* in 1837, when he was twenty-five. The characters in it became national figures.

57. (79) **various libels ... which had found their way into**

**print:** alluding to Reynolds's *Pickwick in France* and other plagiarisms, piracies, etc., which had exploited the popularity of Pickwick.

**58.** (79) **Don Quixote:** The first part of Cervantes's *Don Quixote* was published in 1605; with the second in 1614, shortly after the appearance of a spurious continuation of Don Quixote's adventures. Of this other author Cervantes wrote, 'Let his sin be his punishment – with his bread let him eat it, and there let it rest.'

**59.** (82) **man behind the omnibus:** the conductor, known as a 'cad'. The fierce competition between bus companies and the strategies of drivers and cads to secure passengers are described in 'The Last Cabdriver, and the First Omnibus Cad' (*Sketches by Boz*).

**60.** (83) **trencher:** piece of wood, or plate on which food was served.

**61.** (83) **Thames . . . afire:** 'To set the Thames on fire' is an expression meaning to do something remarkable.

**62.** (83) **Witches:** Witches were a subject of intense debate in the late sixteenth and early seventeenth centuries. Reginald Scot published *The Discoverie of Witchcraft* in 1584; it was written to prevent the persecution of old, poor and simple women who were supposed to be witches. Shakespeare's *Macbeth* (1603) shows the power which witchcraft still held over the popular imagination. For a discussion of witches in the period, see Keith Thomas, *Religion and the Decline of Magic* (1973).

**63.** (84) **scraper:** appliance for removing the dirt from the soles of the shoes before entering a house.

**64.** (84) **penned a most Gracious consignment of them to everlasting wrath:** King James VI and I published a treatise on witchcraft, *Daemonologie*, in 1597.

**65.** (84) **horse shoes:** considered to be lucky; until recent times, a horse-shoe could be found in many country houses and cottages.

**66.** (84) **farriers:** A farrier shoes horses.

**67.** (87) **gibbet:** gallows.

**68.** (90) **castanets:** small concave shells, attached to the thumb, to produce rhythmical accompaniment to dancing.

**69.** (92) **mandrake:** plant with a forked root roughly resembling a human figure, supposed to have magical properties and to scream when uprooted.

70. (92) **pomatum:** scented ointment, in which apples were perhaps originally used.

71. (94) **yeoman:** countryman of respectable standing, such as a farmer.

72. (95) **Putney:** south-west London suburb, some four miles from Kingston.

73. (96) **pink:** stab.

74. (96) **church of Saint Dunstan:** St Dunstan-in-the-West in Fleet Street; the medieval church was demolished in 1830 and replaced by the present building.

75. (96) **unities:** coins first issued by James I in 1604, with a value of twenty shillings; their name (properly 'unite', not 'unity') alludes to the Union of the Crowns.

76. (96) **the plague:** Outbreaks of bubonic plague occurred regularly in sixteenth- and seventeenth-century London; the corpses of victims were carried away on carts for interment by night so as to reduce the risk of infection.

77. (97) **old London Bridge:** crossing the Thames between the City and Southwark; houses occupied the length of the bridge until the eighteenth century. The structure was replaced by a new bridge during the 1820s.

78. (98) **Bear Garden:** a place set aside for the baiting of bears, which was a popular sport.

79. (101) **Heaven-born Hopkins:** Matthew Hopkins, witchfinder-general, appointed 1644, responsible for the deaths of numerous suspected witches. He was himself hanged on suspicion of witchcraft in 1647. The phrase 'heaven-born', which implies someone specially designed by Heaven for a purpose, was often used sarcastically.

80. (103) **top-boots:** high boots which partly covered the leg, worn with riding or country dress.

81. (103) **them as wos kivered over ... blackberries:** alluding to the old ballad of 'The Children in the Wood', who lay down to sleep after being abandoned to die in the woods and were covered over with leaves by friendly robins.

82. (105) **file:** fellow.

83. (105) **speeches o' wow:** species of vow.

84. (107) **that 'ere old Carter:** the Magna Carta of 1215, traditionally seen as guaranteeing human rights against the excessive use of royal power.

85. (107) **pike:** short for turnpike, i.e. a toll-gate.

86. (107) **gas magnifier:** oxy-hydrogen gas-powered microscope, patented in 1824.

87. (107) **pumps:** light shoes.

88. (108) **gaiters:** covering for the ankle and lower leg.

89. (110) **Mr Pickwick ... unprotected female:** In *The Pickwick Papers*, Pickwick was sued for breach of promise by his landlady, Mrs Bardell, on the strength of a misunderstanding of his proposal to engage Sam Weller as a servant.

90. (112) **jocose:** playful.

91. (113) **Bamber:** aged and eccentric lawyer's clerk who entertains Mr Pickwick and the company at the Magpie and Stump with strange stories of the Inns of Court (legal societies with residential premises in central London), in *The Pickwick Papers*, Chapters 20–1.

92. (115) **a sutherly vind and a cloudy sky:** 'A Southerly Wind and a Cloudy Sky', an old hunting song of unknown authorship.

93. (116) **Doctor Commons:** Doctors' Commons, offices where wills, marriages and divorces were registered.

94. (118) **bears:** Bear's grease was used for hair-oil by men in Victorian times, and barbers would fatten up bears in order to provide the commodity.

95. (118) **gallipots:** a small glazed pot used by apothecaries.

96. (121) **fob:** small pocket in the breeches or waistcoat used for a watch.

97. (122) **a qvestion o' privileges:** one arising out of the rights of Members of Parliament, a jokey reference to parliamentary procedures.

98. (122) **be parliamentary, and call him vun:** All Members of Parliament are designated 'honourable members', regardless of their actual conduct.

99. (129) **sprig:** embroidered with little twigs.

100. (129) **knee cords:** corduroy breeches reaching just below the knee and fastened with a strap or bow.

101. (129) **the angel at Islington:** an old coaching inn and famous landmark in north London.

102. (131) **watch-box:** a kind of sentry box used by night-watchmen.

103. (131) **fetch:** double, lookalike.

104. (133) **the single gentleman:** the mysterious character in *The Old Curiosity Shop* who takes up residence at the Brasses' house and endeavours to trace Nell and her grandfather, eventually arriving too late at the village where Nell dies, by which time he has revealed himself as the grandfather's long-lost brother.

105. (134) **genius:** Sir Christopher Wren (1631–1723), architect of St Paul's Cathedral (1710).

106. (135) **the stone-gallery . . ., the whispering gallery, the geometrical staircase, the room of models, the clock:** all parts of St Paul's Cathedral. The stone gallery affords a fine view over London. The whispering gallery is famous for its acoustics. The geometrical staircase is the work of the master-mason William Kempster, and leads up to the Cathedral library. The room of models refers to a display of architectural models, including Wren's designs for the Cathedral.

107. (136) **mart:** market.

108. (137) **turn away . . . from none that bear the human shape:** The crippled Tiny Tim was to play a central role in *A Christmas Carol* (1843).

109. (138) **Barnaby Rudge:** The whole of *Barnaby Rudge* intervenes, in weekly parts (13 Feb.–27 Nov. 1841), before the clock is allowed to stop.

110. (141) **other smiles and other voices congregate around me:** The same device of imaginary children is used in 'The Poor Relation's Story' (*Christmas Stories*), and echoes Charles Lamb's 'Dream Children'.

111. (143) **up the great uniwersal spout o' natur':** dead. 'Spout' was the slang term for the chute by which articles left at a pawnbroker's were removed from the shop to a basement store-room; hence 'up the spout' meant that something had been lost to its owner, probably for ever.

112. (145) **habeas corpus:** the Act of 1679 which enforced rights under Magna Carta (1215), requiring a person who had been imprisoned to be brought before a court, so that the rightfulness of his or her imprisonment might be determined. A writ of *habeas corpus* also applied to rights of other kinds, as here in relation to property.

113. (146) **Mr Chester:** the villain in *Barnaby Rudge* who repudiates his own son.


THE LAMPLIGHTER'S STORY

1. (149) **The Lamplighter's Story:** This story is set at the time of transition from wick and whale oil to gas lamps. As with all such changes, the lamplighters feared it would lead to loss of employment. Westminster Bridge was first illuminated by gas in 1813; and gaslight became common in London and other cities soon afterwards. The lamplighter with his ladder and 'hand lanthorn' became a well-known figure in London streets. 'Gas Lighter's Poems' and 'Twelfth Night Characters', both published in 1830, suggest that the lamplighter's life was not free from danger.

But the lamplighters' fears of losing their jobs were not altogether well-founded. The last lamplighter in London retired in 1987. He travelled up from Rochester (which would have pleased Dickens) in the early morning and turned off the lamps in the Inns of Court. In the evening, he would return to turn on the lights there, and elsewhere; some had to be extinguished again at midnight. There are still 1,500 gaslights in London, including those in Buckingham Palace, which are not now manually controlled, but do have to be maintained.

2. (149) **Murphy and Francis Moore:** Patrick Murphy (1782–1847), author of 'The Weather Almanack', which predicted – or guessed – what the weather would be like on particular days. It sold 45,000 copies in 1838 and earned Murphy £3,000, a huge sum in those days. Francis Moore (1657–1715), famous for *Old Moore's Almanack*; he was an astrologer and physician.

3. (149) **vice:** vice-chairman. Mr Vice was a common abbreviation.

4. (149) **cacique:** a native chief or prince of the aborigines in the West Indies.

5. (150) **Prometheus:** the Greek God who stole fire from Heaven and taught mankind many arts. Zeus punished him for his theft by chaining him to a rock where a vulture fed every night on his liver, which was restored each succeeding night.

6. (150) **cast:** calculated.

7. (150) **whistle:** a jocular name for the mouth or throat. Sometimes the phrase is wrongly spelt 'whet'.

8. (150) **oil and cotton:** the materials used in street-lamps.

9. (151) **Gas:** see n. 1 above.

10. (151) **Pall Mall:** street in London famous for its clubs, and one of the first to be lit by gas in 1817.

11. (152) **Saint Martin's Lane:** well-known street in central London near Trafalgar Square.

12. (152) **watch-house:** guard-house, or house in which the municipal night-watchmen were stationed.

13. (152) **Father Matthew:** Theobald Matthew (1790–1856), a Roman Catholic Irish priest who campaigned for temperance.

14. (152) **Canonbury Tower:** The foundations of Canonbury Tower are pre-Roman. A priory was established there in 1253; the tower was built in the sixteenth century and embellished at the end of it.

15. (152) **bran new:** or brand new, from brand, something which has made its mark: i.e. absolutely new.

16. (152) **files:** see p. 237, n. 82.

17. (153) **Royal Society:** The Royal Society was founded in 1645 and received its charter in 1662. It has remained to the present time the academy of scientific knowledge.

18. (154) **link:** a torch made of tow and pitch.

19. (154) **small beer:** weak beer, here used as a term of deprecation.

20. (154) **game eye:** attractive and colourful, like the eye of the pheasant.

21. (154) **philosopher's stone:** a reputed solid substance believed by alchemists to be capable of turning other metals into gold or silver, which was the supreme object of alchemy.

22. (156) **Venus:** the Roman goddess of love and beauty.

23. (156) **salamander:** a lizard-like animal supposed to be able to live in fire.

24. (156) **Doctor Watts:** Isaac Watts (1674–1748) wrote a number of hymns of which 'O God, our help in ages past' is the most famous. His *Divine Songs Attempted in Easy Language for the Use of Children* was first published in 1715, and in many subsequent editions.

25. (157) **buck:** a dashing young fellow.

26. (161) **Monk Lewis:** Matthew 'Monk' Lewis (1775–1818) pub-

lished his novel, *The Monk*, in 1796. It continued to be read and enjoyed a considerable vogue in the nineteenth century. Dickens is referring to Volume II, Chapter 1.

27. (164) **banns:** banns of marriage; public notice given in a church of the intention to marry, so that anyone who wishes to object may do so.

28. (164) **Lady-day:** 25 March, the Feast of the Annunciation.

29. (165) **nankeen:** a cloth made out of cotton.

30. (165) **bill-sticker:** someone who sticks up announcements or advertisements in public places.

## TO BE READ AT DUSK

1. (167) **Great St Bernard:** highest of the Alpine passes, leading from Switzerland into Italy; the hospice of St Bernard was built on it in 962 AD and was served by Augustinian monks; its mortuary was visited by Dickens in 1846, and it is described again in *Little Dorrit*, Book 2, Chapter 1.

2. (167) **broached:** pierced or tapped, as in a cask to draw the liquor.

3. (167) **realise to me . . . our country:** Dickens is making fun of what was at the present time a characteristically American usage of the verb 'to realise', meaning 'to present to the mind of another'.

4. (168) **Chiaja:** Riviera di Chiaia was a fashionable road in Naples.

5. (168) **overlooking the service:** superintending the servants.

6. (168) **San Gennaro:** St Januarius, martyred *c.* 305 AD. His relics are held in Naples, and liquefaction of his blood is claimed to take place annually, in connection with his feasts.

7. (169) **Long's Hotel:** fashionable hotel at 16 New Bond Street in the West End of London; in 1815 Scott met Byron there for the last time.

8. (169) **rumble:** the back part of a carriage, sometimes used for luggage, sometimes for further seats.

9. (172) **all my old acquaintance many times repeated:** Dickens similarly mocks the hackneyed subjects favoured by painters in 'The Ghost of Art' (*Reprinted Pieces*).

10. (172) **coulisses:** the side scenes of a stage.

11. (172) **Duomo ... Marionetti:** Dickens describes some of these Genoese sights in *Pictures from Italy*.

12. (173) **pursued by Austria on political suspicions:** Northern Italy was at this time ruled by Austria. The Austro-Hungarian Empire ran a ruthless secret service which hunted down those who were politically suspect.

13. (173) **Altro!:** Italian for 'certainly', 'of course'; a favourite expression of Cavaletto's in *Little Dorrit*. Dickens comments on the expression in *Pictures from Italy*.

14. (174) **Carnival:** The period before Lent, devoted in Roman Catholic countries to revelry.

15. (174) **Corso:** an avenue; the name often given to the main street in Italian cities, as here in Genoa.

16. (175) **Goodman's Fields:** district in the Whitechapel area of the East End of London.

## HUNTED DOWN

1. (181) **reading for orders:** studying at university to become a clergyman.

2. (183) **actuary:** estimates insurance premiums in relation to mortality rates, etc.

3. (186) **Middle Temple:** see p. 233, n. 20.

4. (188) **Scarborough:** seaside resort on the north Yorkshire coast.

5. (189) **East India Director:** The East India Company was formed in 1600 for the purpose of trade with India. Its ever increasing power and wealth became the foundation of the British Empire in India. In 1833, it ceased to be a trading company and confined itself to administering India jointly with the Crown, which took over entirely after the Indian Mutiny in 1858.

6. (192) **draws very light:** is pulled very easily (because of his light weight).

7. (193) **chambers:** Barristers' offices are still referred to as chambers.

8. (193) **opium:** narcotic derived from the juice of the poppy. The opium trade with China became notorious for its violence in the eighteenth century; and as with the drug trade today excoriated for the lives it destroyed.

9. (194) **Julius Cæsar**: Beckwith's nickname for Slinkton refers to the ancient Roman general and dictator.

10. (194) **Boil the brandy**: Brandy glasses were warmed, as they still sometimes are, by a small spirit lamp. The warmed glass released the vapour of the spirit.

11. (196) **a sharper**: a cheat at cards.

12. (197) **cipher writing**: writing in code.

### GEORGE SILVERMAN'S EXPLANATION

1. (202) **Preston**: industrial town in Lancashire, supposed original of Coketown in *Hard Times*.

2. (202) **clogs**: wooden shoes, often used by the very poor, who could afford nothing else.

3. (202) **gripe**: something which seizes.

4. (203) **court-full**: In Victorian cities, 'courts' were obscure cul-de-sacs in densely populated, very poor areas. The implication is that her father was a rack-renter, like Casby in *Little Dorrit*.

5. (204) **vinegar ... camphor**: Vapours from heated vinegar were believed to combat infection; camphor, because of its sweet smell, was also thought to have similar properties. Nothing was known at the time about bacteria.

6. (204) **Verity Hawkyard**: The name is ironic because he is always telling lies. Hawkyard suggests his voracious greed (see *George Silverman's Explanation*, edited with an introduction by Harry Stone [California State University Press, 1984], for a discussion of the names in this story).

7. (204) **(O yes, it shall be!)**: Dickens's imitation of the rhetoric of ranting preachers.

8. (204) **Hoghton Towers**: old ruined mansion (actually called Hoghton Tower) on the road between Preston and Blackburn. Dickens visited it and wrote afterwards: 'I did not in the least see how to begin [Silverman's] state of mind until I walked into Hoghton Towers one bright April day.'

9. (205) **porringer**: a small basin.

10. (207) **first James of England**: James I reigned from 1603 to 1625. James instituted the order of Baronets of England in 1611 to raise

money for the settlement of Ulster out of the fees paid for elevation to the title.

11. (207) **Counterblast:** referring to King James's anti-smoking pamphlet *A Counter-blaste to Tobacco* (1604); the 'Steam Power, powerful in two distances' refers to the different sort of smoke from the two industrial towns of Preston and Blackburn, which would be visible, to the west and east respectively, from Hoghton Tower.

12. (208) **scrambling board:** makeshift and irregular meals.

13. (210) **Foundation Boy:** boy whose education was paid for out of the endowment of an institution.

14. (210) **presentation to College, and a Fellowship:** admission to university, and a stipendiary position there.

15. (211) **drysalter:** a dealer in chemical products, used for a variety of purposes.

16. (212) **myrrh, or frankincense, or yet Amber, letting alone the honeycomb:** costly gifts. The comb which is full of honey suggests the sweetener of material reward.

17. (214) **D.V.:** *Deo volente,* God willing.

18. (216) **The Church:** i.e. the Church of England.

19. (216) **My kingdom is not of this world:** John 18: 36.

20. (216) **What did the woman do, when she lost the piece of money?:** Luke 15: 8.

21. (217) **read with several young men:** acted as tutor to several students.

22. (217) **Don:** fellow of a college.

23. (219) **Living:** ecclesiastical benefice, which used to be in the gift of wealthy landowners.

24. (220) **Lady Jane Grey:** Queen of England for ten days in 1553; executed 1554. She was noted for her learning and especially her proficiency at languages.

25. (223) **a thorough young Anglo-Saxon:** referring to Victorian worship of Saxonness as *true* Englishness, exemplified in Charles Kingsley's *Hereward the Wake,* etc.

# DICKENS AND HIS CRITICS

The shorter fiction, reprinted in this volume, appears together for the first time. It has not therefore been the subject of sustained critical debate. The selected bibliography contains references to all the major works on Dickens's shorter fiction, which concentrate on the Christmas Books and stories. 'George Silverman's Explanation', the last of Dickens's completed works, remains the exception in that it has continued to be the subject of varied critical interpretations and judgements, ranging from the dismissive to the deeply appreciative.

John Forster in his *Life of Charles Dickens* (1874) comments only on the enormous sum of £1,000 which Dickens was paid for the story. George Gissing in *Charles Dickens: A Critical Study* (1898) recognised the power and skill of the story, but thought its tone to be that of 'uncompromising bitterness'. Among more recent critics, John Carey in *The Violent Effigy: A Study of Dickens's Imagination* (1981) discusses the young George in relation to other children in Dickens's work, seeing him, like Pip, as reflecting Dickens's own humiliation in the 'blacking factory'. Other critics – for example, Edgar Johnson in *Charles Dickens: His Tragedy and Triumph* (New York, 1952), K. J. Fielding in *Charles Dickens: A Critical Introduction* (1965) and Michael Slater in *Dickens and Women* (1983) – have discussed various autobiographical resonances in the story. Q. D. Leavis in *Dickens the Novelist* (1970), who also develops the comparison between Pip and George Silverman, finds the story to be significant and representative, illustrating Dickens's continuing power as a creative artist. Other commentators over the last sixty years have concentrated on readings and interpretations based on the writings of Freud: notably, K. B. Bradby in *The Dickensian* 36 (1940), U. Pope-Hennessy in *Charles Dickens* (1945) and Deborah A. Thomas in *Dickens and the Short Story* (1982). The most balanced and thorough discussions of Dickens's artistry in 'George Silverman's Explanation' remain

Harry Stone's in *Studies in Philology* 55 (1958) and in his introduction to his edition (California State University Press, 1984). He also makes numerous and interesting references to it in *The Night Side of Dickens: Cannibalism, Passion, Necessity* (Ohio, 1994).

# SUGGESTIONS FOR FURTHER READING

John Forster's *Life of Charles Dickens* (3 vols, 1872–4) remains the classic, indispensable biography; the most recent edition is the two-volume Everyman Edition, ed. A. H. Hoppé (1969). The standard modern biography is Edgar Johnson's *Charles Dickens: His Tragedy and Triumph* (2 vols, 1952), but two more recent ones are also valuable: Fred Kaplan's *Dickens: A Biography* (1988) and Peter Ackroyd's remarkable *Dickens* (1990). Dickens's letters were first collected in three volumes of the limited Nonesuch Edition of Dickens's works (ed. Walter Dexter, 1938). These are being superseded by the magnificent Clarendon Press *The Pilgrim Edition of the Letters of Charles Dickens*, ed. M. House, G. Storey, K. Tillotson *et al* (1965 – in progress). The latest volume to appear, vol. 9 (1997), covers the years 1859–61.

*General:*
Slater, Michael, *Dickens and Women* (1983).
Wilson, Angus, *The World of Charles Dickens* (1970).

*Shorter Fiction:*
Andrews, Malcolm, 'Introducing Master Humphrey', *The Dickensian* 67, January 1971, pp. 70–86.
Carey, John, *The Violent Effigy: A Study of Dickens's Imagination* (Oxford, 1981).
Chesterton, G. K., *Criticisms and Appreciations of the Works of Charles Dickens*, ed. Michael Slater (1992).
Collins, Philip, *Dickens and Crime* (1962).
Fielding, K. J., *Charles Dickens: A Critical Introduction* (1965).
Glancy, Ruth F., *Dickens's Christmas Books, Christmas Stories, and other Short Fiction, An Annotated Bibliography* (Garland Bibliographies, New York, and London, 1985).
Glancy, Ruth F., 'Charles Dickens', *Dictionary of Literary Biography* (British Short-Fiction Writers 1800–80), Vol. 159, pp. 84–105.
Glancy, Ruth F., 'To be read at dusk', *The Dickensian*, Spring 1987, pp. 40–7.

Stone, Harry, *George Silverman's Explanation*, edited with an introduction and notes (California State University Press, 1984).
Stone, Harry, *The Night Side of Dickens: Cannibalism, Passion, Necessity* (Ohio, 1994).
Thomas, Deborah A., *Dickens and the Short Story* (1982).

# ACKNOWLEDGEMENTS

———————

I would like to thank Dr David Atkinson and Professor Michael Slater for their help in compiling the notes for this edition.

# CHARLES DICKENS
## IN EVERYMAN

*The Everyman Dickens is the most comprehensive paperback
edition available, with all the original illustrations*

**Bleak House**
*edited by* Andrew Sanders
*A great mystery unravelled*
£5.99

**Great Expectations**
*edited by* Robin Gilmour
*From Newgate prison to society
drawing rooms – Pip's hopes and
dreams of becoming a gentleman*
£3.99

**Hard Times**
*edited by* Grahame Smith
*Dickens's bleak vision of
mid-Victorian England*
£3.99

**Oliver Twist**
*edited by* Steven Connor
*An innocent's journey through
London's underworld*
£4.99

**Martin Chuzzlewit**
*edited by* Michael Slater
*Classic examination of greed
and hypocrisy, by turns disturbing
and hilarious*
£4.99

**Nicholas Nickleby**
*edited by* David Parker
*An exciting tale of the young
Nicholas making his way in
the world*
£5.99

**The Old Curiosity Shop**
*edited by* Paul Schlicke
*A story that has provoked more
extreme responses than anything
else Dickens wrote*
£5.99

**A Tale of Two Cities**
*edited by* Norman Page
*The classic English evocation
of the French Revolution*
£3.99

**Holiday Romance and Other
Writings for Children**
*edited by* Gillian Avery
'Holiday Romance', The Life of
Our Lord', 'A Child's History
of England', *available only in
Everyman*
£5.99

All books are available from your local bookshop or direct from:
Littlehampton Book Services Cash Sales, 14 Eldon Way, Lineside Estate,
Littlehampton, West Sussex BN17 7HE *(prices are subject to change)*

To order any of the books, please enclose a cheque (in sterling) made payable to
*Littlehampton Book Services,* or phone your order through with credit card details (Access,
Visa or Mastercard) on 01903 721596 (24 hour answering service) stating card number
and expiry date. *(Please add £1.25 for package and postage to the total of your order.)*

In the USA, for further information and a complete catalogue call 1-800-526-2778

# CLASSIC FICTION
## IN EVERYMAN

**The Impressions of
Theophrastus Such**
GEORGE ELIOT
*An amusing collection of character
sketches, and the only paperback
edition available*
£5.99

**Frankenstein**
MARY SHELLEY
*A masterpiece of Gothic terror in
its original 1818 version*
£3.99

**East Lynne**
MRS HENRY WOOD
*A classic tale of melodrama,
murder and mystery*
£7.99

**Holiday Romance and
Other Writings for Children**
CHARLES DICKENS
*Dickens's works for children,
including 'The Life of Our Lord'
and 'A Child's History of England',
with original illustrations*
£5.99

**The Ebb-Tide**
R. L. STEVENSON
*A compelling study of ordinary
people in extreme circumstances*
£4.99

**The Three Impostors**
ARTHUR MACHEN
*The only edition available
of this cult thriller*
£4.99

**Mister Johnson**
JOYCE CARY
*The only edition available of this
amusing but disturbing twentieth-
century tale*
£5.99

**The Jungle Book**
RUDYARD KIPLING
*The classic adventures of Mowgli
and his friends*
£3.99

**Glenarvon**
LADY CAROLINE LAMB
*The only edition available of the
novel which throws light on the
greatest scandal of the early nineteenth century – the infatuation of
Caroline Lamb with Lord Byron*
£6.99

**Twenty Thousand Leagues
Under the Sea**
JULES VERNE
*Scientific fact combines with
fantasy in this prophetic tale
of underwater adventure*
£4.99

---

All books are available from your local bookshop or direct from:
Littlehampton Book Services Cash Sales, 14 Eldon Way, Lineside Estate,
Littlehampton, West Sussex BN17 7HE *(prices are subject to change)*

To order any of the books, please enclose a cheque (in sterling) made payable to
*Littlehampton Book Services*, or phone your order through with credit card details (Access,
Visa or Mastercard) on 01903 721596 (24 hour answering service) stating card number
and expiry date. *(Please add £1.25 for package and postage to the total of your order.)*

In the USA, for further information and a complete catalogue call 1-800-526-2778

# CLASSIC NOVELS
# IN EVERYMAN

---

**The Time Machine**
H. G. WELLS
*One of the books which defined*
*'science fiction' – a compelling*
*and tragic story of a brilliant*
*and driven scientist*
£3.99

**Oliver Twist**
CHARLES DICKENS
*Arguably the best-loved of*
*Dickens's novels. With all the*
*original illustrations*
£4.99

**Barchester Towers**
ANTHONY TROLLOPE
*The second of Trollope's*
*Chronicles of Barsetshire,*
*and one of the funniest of all*
*Victorian novels*
£4.99

**The Heart of Darkness**
JOSEPH CONRAD
*Conrad's most intense, subtle,*
*compressed, profound and*
*proleptic work*
£3.99

**Tess of the d'Urbervilles**
THOMAS HARDY
*The powerful, poetic classic*
*of wronged innocence*
£3.99

**Wuthering Heights and Poems**
EMILY BRONTË
*A powerful work of genius – one of*
*the great masterpieces of literature*
£3.99

**Pride and Prejudice**
JANE AUSTEN
*Proposals, rejections, infidelities,*
*elopements, happy marriages –*
*Jane Austen's most popular novel*
£2.99

**North and South**
ELIZABETH GASKELL
*A novel of hardship, passion*
*and hard-won wisdom amidst the*
*conflicts of the industrial revolution*
£4.99

**The Newcomes**
W. M. THACKERAY
*An exposé of Victorian polite*
*society by one of the nineteenth-*
*century's finest novelists*
£6.99

**Adam Bede**
GEORGE ELIOT
*A passionate rural drama enacted*
*at the turn of the eighteenth*
*century*
£5.99

---

All books are available from your local bookshop or direct from:
Littlehampton Book Services Cash Sales, 14 Eldon Way, Lineside Estate,
Littlehampton, West Sussex BN17 7HE (*prices are subject to change*)

To order any of the books, please enclose a cheque (in sterling) made payable to
*Littlehampton Book Services*, or phone your order through with credit card details (Access,
Visa or Mastercard) on 01903 721596 (24 hour answering service) stating card number
and expiry date. (*Please add £1.25 for package and postage to the total of your order.*)

In the USA, for further information and a complete catalogue call 1-800-526-2778

# SHORT STORY COLLECTIONS
## IN EVERYMAN

**The Strange Case of Dr Jekyll and Mr Hyde and Other Stories**
R. L. STEVENSON
*An exciting selection of gripping tales from a master of suspense*
£1.99

**Nineteenth-Century American Short Stories**
*edited by* Christopher Bigsby
*A selection of the works of Henry James, Edith Wharton, Mark Twain and many other great American writers*
£6.99

**The Best of Saki**
*edited by* MARTIN STEPHEN
Includes Tobermory, Gabriel Ernest, Svedni Vashtar, The Interlopers, Birds on the Western Front
£4.99

**Souls Belated and Other Stories**
EDITH WHARTON
*Brief, neatly crafted tales exploring a range of themes from big taboo subjects to the subtlest little ironies of social life*
£6.99

**The Night of the Iguana and Other Stories**
TENNESSEE WILLIAMS
*Twelve remarkable short stories, each a compelling drama in miniature*
£4.99

**Selected Short Stories and Poems**
THOMAS HARDY
*Hardy's most memorable stories and poetry in one volume*
£4.99

**Selected Tales**
HENRY JAMES
*Stories portraying the tensions between private life and the outside world*
£5.99

**The Best of Sherlock Homes**
ARTHUR CONAN DOYLE
*All the favourite adventures in one volume*
£4.99

**The Secret Self 1: *Short Stories by Women***
*edited by* Hermione Lee
'A superb collection' The Guardian
£4.99

---

# AMERICAN LITERATURE
## IN EVERYMAN

**The Marble Faun**
NATHANIEL HAWTHORNE
*The product of Hawthorne's two
years in Italy, the thrilling story
of young Americans in Europe*
£5.99

**The Portrait of a Lady**
HENRY JAMES
*A masterpiece of psychological
and social examination, which
established James as a major
novelist*
£5.99

**Billy Budd and Other Stories**
HERMAN MELVILLE
*The compelling parable of
innocence destroyed by a fallen
world*
£4.99

**The Red Badge of Courage**
STEPHEN CRANE
*A vivid portrayal of a young
soldier's experience of the
American Civil War*
£3.99

**Leaves of Grass and
Selected Prose**
WALT WHITMAN
*The best of Whitman in
one volume*
£6.99

**The Age of Innocence**
EDITH WHARTON
*A tale of the conflict between love
and tradition by one of America's
finest women novelists*
£4.99

**Nineteenth-Century American
Short Stories**
*edited by* Christopher Bigsby
*A selection of the works of
Henry James, Edith Wharton,
Mark Twain and many other
great American writers*
£6.99

**Selected Poems**
HENRY LONGFELLOW
*A selection spanning the whole
of Longfellow's literary career*
£7.99

**The Last of the Mohicans**
JAMES FENIMORE COOPER
*The tale that shaped American
frontier myth*
£5.99

**The Great Gatsby**
F. SCOTT FITZGERALD
*Much loved story of passion
and betrayal, glamour and
the powerful allure of the
American dream*
£4.99

All books are available from your local bookshop or direct from:
Littlehampton Book Services Cash Sales, 14 Eldon Way, Lineside Estate,
Littlehampton, West Sussex BN17 7HE (*prices are subject to change*)

To order any of the books, please enclose a cheque (in sterling) made payable to
*Littlehampton Book Services*, or phone your order through with credit card details (Access,
Visa or Mastercard) on 01903 721596 (24 hour answering service) stating card number
and expiry date. (*Please add £1.25 for package and postage to the total of your order.*)

In the USA, for further information and a complete catalogue call 1-800-526-2778

# WOMEN'S WRITING
## IN EVERYMAN

### Poems and Prose
CHRISTINA ROSSETTI
*A collection of her writings, poetry
and prose, published to mark the
centenary of her death*
£5.99

### Women Philosophers
*edited by* Mary Warnock
*The great subjects of philosophy
handled by women spanning four
centuries, including Simone de
Beauvoir and Iris Murdoch*
£6.99

### Glenarvon
LADY CAROLINE LAMB
*A novel which throws light on the
greatest scandal of the early nineteenth century – the infatuation of
Caroline Lamb with Lord Byron*
£6.99

### Women Romantic Poets
1780 – 1830: An Anthology
*edited by* Jennifer Breen
*Hidden talent from the Romantic
era rediscovered*
£5.99

### Memoirs of the Life of Colonel Hutchinson
LUCY HUTCHINSON
*One of the earliest pieces of
women's biographical writing, of
great historic and feminist interest*
£6.99

### The Secret Self 1: Short Stories by Women
*edited by* Hermione Lee
*'A superb collection'* The Guardian
£4.99

### The Age of Innocence
EDITH WHARTON
*A tale of the conflict between love
and tradition by one of America's
finest women novelists*
£4.99

### Frankenstein
MARY SHELLEY
*A masterpiece of Gothic terror
in its original 1818 version*
£3.99

### The Life of Charlotte Brontë
ELIZABETH GASKELL
*A moving and perceptive tribute
by one writer to another*
£4.99

### Victorian Women Poets
1830 – 1900
*edited by* Jennifer Breen
*A superb anthology of the era's
finest female poets*
£5.99

### Female Playwrights of the Restoration: Five Comedies
*edited by* Paddy Lyons
*Rediscovered literary treasure
in a unique selection*
£5.99

All books are available from your local bookshop or direct from:
Littlehampton Book Services Cash Sales, 14 Eldon Way, Lineside Estate,
Littlehampton, West Sussex BN17 7HE (*prices are subject to change*)

To order any of the books, please enclose a cheque (in sterling) made payable to
*Littlehampton Book Services*, or phone your order through with credit card details (Access,
Visa or Mastercard) on 01903 721596 (24 hour answering service) stating card number
and expiry date. (*Please add £1.25 for package and postage to the total of your order.*)

In the USA, for further information and a complete catalogue call 1-800-526-2778